Sally Krykant is a writer originating from Leicestershire.

She has lived in Suffolk for 33 years and works as a psychodynamic counsellor. She has also worked as a jazz singer here and abroad. She has a son and a daughter. Now she spends her time writing, reading avidly, spending time with her grandchildren, gardening, walking, cycling, playing tennis and serving her local church.

This is her first novel. She is currently writing her second entitled, The Corset and is working on an anthology of short stories.

Seeds of Doubt

by

Sally Krykant

Sally Krykant

Seeds of Doubt is dedicated to Mary Voakes,
my mum whose anecdotal stories inspired it to be written.

ROSE, RUTH AND CHARLOTTE

1919 – 1936

Chapter 1

Rose hated the midday sun. Directly overhead, it burnt her neck and arms leaving her hot and sticky. Unaware of plant lice living on the hops she scratched at her neck and back. She was thirsty but could find nothing to quench her thirst, only a handful of blackberries which tasted sour. It was the hottest part of the day and she deduced from this that a break was imminent. Hodgkiss, foreman of the gang, would call it but if he was drunk it would be forgotten. Then they would all labour on. Rose hated him. His overbearing physique, bellowing voice and bovine eyes made her nervous and twitchy. Eyes that were set so far apart she could never be sure if he was telling her off or the person standing next to her. This fuelled her contempt. Much more than the sweltering heat and Hodgkiss, Rose detested hop picking.

Her mother, Gert had promised them all a nice time in the countryside away from the dirt and grime of London. They had caught the train from London Bridge and unwittingly laughed and joked all the way to Kent. Gert had made it sound like a holiday. No chores for a long time. Fresh air, fun and a few bob at the end of each week to show for it. It did feel like that to begin with. Rose and her five brothers had never seen cows and sheep roaming freely before. Plenty of stiffs hanging outside the local butchers and chunks of bloodied meat wrapped in paper ready for the pot. Unlike her brothers, the novelty soon wore off and she began to feel isolated.

Tom, the eldest of her brothers, was the keenest picker in the whole gang and seemed to idolise Hodgkiss. At fifteen, he ducked and dived around the East End, earning enough money for his keep with a little left over to help his mum pay her way. When September came he couldn't wait to get back to the hop fields. He loved the fresh air and the heady smell of the bitter beer scent wafting out onto the lanes and across the countryside. He took home the most pay each week for which he earned his mother's respect.

Arthur at fourteen and Fred at twelve were clever enough to go unnoticed by their foreman, by working hard and keeping a low profile. The crafty pair made sure that they picked the vines with the largest bunches of hops, sometimes the size of small pears. Their baskets filled up quicker than most for which they were all paid a penny a bushel.

Johnny, who was ten, hated it as much as Rose and was having a hard time of it. The avid reader in the family was nowhere near as physical as his brothers and came in for a lot of bullying from the older lads. Jack, the baby, was eight and missed his mother, although he would never have dared to admit it. Jack hated his nick name. Silly Boy Lemon. When Hodgkiss cuffed his ear or bawled at him, the tears in his eyes were sufficient proof to everyone that he was.

Rose flopped down on the edge of the hop field. The rest of the gang were working hard, hidden deep within the heavily laden bushes. She inspected her hands. Sore, grimy and blistered from handling too many spiny stems. Hands that were made to play the piano. Nan Bella said so. Tearing down the vines made her back ache, so when Arthur and Fred did the work for her she agreed to pick the lower vines. After a while she realised that she had been given the hardest work. These hops were more tangled and took longer to strip. She lagged behind the rest every day and disappointed her mother with her measly take home pay of a few shillings. Tom laboured away from dawn until dusk and earned a regular ten shillings except on a wet week when he struggled.

Rose yearned to be at home and to be treated like her twin sister, Ruth. Life was so much simpler for her back in Weymouth Terrace. Rose pictured Ruth in her mind's eye. She sat at the kitchen table, with her good leg swinging back and forth, while her gammy leg rested across the long bench which her brothers crowded each meal time. Her mother would be sitting opposite. Ruth and Mother. Always together. They might be shelling peas, sifting flour, kneading dough. It was Wednesday. Oxtail soup day. They would be dipping warm bread into it, in silence. A natural silence, born out of spending so much time in each other's company. Ivor, the lodger would have picked up the oxtail, on his way home from the docks where he worked. Rose raised her nose and sniffed the warm air. She imagined the rich, meaty odour of the soup, kept warm on the range. She yearned to see her mother. Small with generous hips and always a stray wisp of hair stuck to her forehead. A permanent look of menace at sons who gave her back-chat and got themselves into mischief.

As she dehydrated in the midday heat, a sick feeling in the pit of her stomach overpowered her and she vomited into her lap. A rich, red and purple stain soaked her skirt. In a panic, she snatched off her cotton bonnet and dabbed at it, making it much worse. Sweat sizzled on her forehead and her long auburn hair stuck to her face and neck. She had to get to the water butt. It stood in front of the hut, where they all crowded in at night. Like fowls in a coop, only a filthy, grey sheet divided the men and boys from the women and girls. It made her itch to even think of it. Most of the hop farms had huts for the men and huts for the women and she wished she was working on one of those. Although the wooden hut was large enough to be divided she could not get used to sleeping on a palliasse. The straw filled mattress was uncomfortable and she yearned to get into bed each evening with Ruth at home.

She got to her feet and surveyed the field in search of Hodgkiss. When there was no sign of him she scrambled toward the water butt. Within yards of reaching it, she heard a familiar voice yelling at her.

"Hey sis, you lazy cow. You'll be for the high jump if the boss catches you scivin'."

"I ain't. So just mind your own business, our Tom. I don't feel well."

"Heard it all before Rosie. You gotta pick your quota just like everyone else."

With that said, Tom flashed his handsome, brown eyes at his sister. Rose watched his curly hair disappear, inside the rows of hop bushes again. She felt small and inadequate but was determined not to cry. She limped to the water butt and tossed the lid to one side. Next, she scooped handfuls of water, up and over her face and neck. Its coolness gave her some relief. Hastily, she stepped out of her skirt and plunged it into the water. The heat of the day would soon have it dry again.

With this in mind, she was oblivious to the sound of the bushes, rustling behind her. A rough hand took hold of her bony shoulders and swivelled her around. It was Hodgkiss. Rose let go of the skirt. It slopped to the ground.

7

Her heart pounded in her young chest.

"What the 'ell do you think you're up to? Rose ain't it?"

"I was hot and I've been ill, so I thought I'd try and clean it up," she stammered. At the same time she tried to cover up her drawers.

"You got your monthlies, gel?"

Rose blushed and looked down. For the first time, she noticed that the purple, red stain had seeped through to her under wear. She had never heard periods spoken about like that before. Sometimes, in bed at night, she would wonder aloud with Ruth what it would be like to bleed from between your legs. They would continue to comfort each other with the false hope, that as they were twins, their periods would start together. Then, just before the hop season began, Rose had had her first one without her sister. It made her feel grown up. As her mother cut up some rags for her to use, she felt closer to her. Closer than Ruth for a change.

"Well, don't stand there gawping like a stray alley cat. Get yourself dressed and back out there on the field. I tell you when you have breaks and it ain't yet. Go on gel, in the hut or else."

Rose held onto her skirt which was dripping all over the place but she was grateful that the confrontation was over. It hadn't been all that bad. Another chance to tidy herself up and prove she could work as hard as the others. Another chance to prove to her mother that she wasn't a lazy cow or a dozy mare. For a split second she felt warm toward Hodgkiss, for taking her in hand and bringing her to her senses. The foreman sensed how nervous she was. The sight of her, so young and vulnerable, half dressed, brought out the worst in him. Any conscience that might have prevented him from doing what he did next, was overpowered by the blood coloured stain on her drawers. It was as if she was damaged goods already. In an instant, he loosened his trouser belt. Rose felt a thwack against her backside. "Or else" had come, sooner than expected. With a hefty nudge, he shoved her into the hut and down onto the floor.

Rose was too shocked to cry out or struggle. Hodgkiss straddled himself across her. The weight of his bulging frame, forced out the breath from her tiny body. With one hand clamped over her mouth, he tugged at the buttons on his flies and brought out the thing she dreaded most. When his words came, they were spoken as if he had just run a marathon.

8

"Lie still and it'll be over in a few minutes. Just lie still."

Rose bit down hard and tasted blood as the thing which she had giggled about with Ruth, tore at her soft insides. His hairy hands kept her pinned to the floor of the hut, one on each pubescent breast. Rose took her punishment. Five or six explosive thrusts up into the core of her and then he shivered and slumped forward. It was all over. She could have cried out for help but she chose not to. The beast he had become licked its lips. He had feasted well. Now he fell asleep on top of the scraps. A solitary tear rolled from her eye as she caught sight of her hand that was made to play piano. Rose smelt his beer and woodbine breath. Hot bile stung her throat. From a deep, dark place inside, she knew she would never be the same again.

Above her head, the cobwebs looked denser than before and the blanket which divided them at night seemed more soiled. Suddenly, a new strength came to her aid and she tore at his shirt and hair.

"Tell anyone about this and you'll live to regret it," he threatened.

The door of the hut creaked and banged behind him. Rose lay still for a few minutes, feeling imprisoned. A light breeze was rattling the window panes, through which golden rays from the afternoon sun were spreading their warmth all around her. It was as if they had only now dared to come out of hiding to comfort her.

In the distance, she heard voices calling one to another. She felt suddenly fearful. What if Tom found out about this? He might take the law into his own hands. The thought made her shudder. She rolled onto her side and curled up into a ball. A cold and slimy wetness trickled from the wounded place. She wiped it away with her drawers which had been ripped off her and tossed to one side. She sat up and rocked back and forth, staring at the skirt which had been the cause of all her problems. Slowly, she crawled to her makeshift bed, at the foot of which she kept a carrier bag containing all her belongings. She pulled out a spare skirt and, with difficulty, pulled it on. Every movement felt like agony. The wet one, she quickly rolled up and concealed in the bag.

Timidly, stepping outside she felt like immersing herself in the clear, cool rainwater inside the butt. Would she ever feel clean again? What to do now? Go back to the field or run away? Run and never stop, until the wind had whipped him from her. Where would she run to? All the way back to

London was out of the question. Field after field might carry her there but the country was a maze to her, made up of hedges and ditches and farmland in between. Its labyrinthine proportions might swallow her up. Rose feared she would never be seen again.

She made her decision. In order to survive, she would have to go back to the fields and pick hops like she had never picked them before. Beyond that, she had no idea. There was safety in numbers and if she kept quiet, Saturday would eventually come around again. Then, she could return to her mother and sister. With these thoughts forming in her mind, she limped back to work.

Chapter 2

Ruth felt bored and let down. Her mother was late getting back from a visit to Billingsgate fish market. She had promised to stay only five minutes at nan Bella's house, nearby. Meanwhile, Ruth was to sit still and wait for her return but how was she expected to sit still, hour after hour? It made her feel pathetic, stuck behind with the others who had not been allowed to go hop picking.

Ruth kicked the fallen leaves that had collected outside her home, on Weymouth Terrace. Although she and Rose were identical twins, she appeared smaller than her sister due to her handicap. Both girls had a tendency to frown and look serious which belied their prettiness. When their tempers were raised which was often in a house governed by the male sex, they turned a deep scarlet. Ruth flashed her deep blue eyes across the road. Sadie, the doll was in her usual position, sitting in the bay window opposite. She was staring out the window. Nicknamed 'the doll' by adults and children alike, she was the saddest, palest, most disliked little girl on the terrace. For all her pink frills and ringlets, she had no friends. Her mother made all her dresses. Always pink and frothy with layers of fancy, starched material, bought from market stalls, rummage sales or end of lines from haberdashery shops. Sadie sat day after day in the window, like a museum piece collecting dust. It did not occur to Ruth to go and call for Sadie. No one did anymore.

Freddie Spencer was no better with a hole in the heart. Some days he looked luminous which made his veins stand out even bluer than usual. Whenever he saw Ruth hanging around on the terrace, he would try and befriend her.

"Go away Freddie Spencer, your breath stinks," Ruth would tell him and stop chalking patterns on the pavement.

"Only wanted to play marbles but I don't suppose you can with a gammy leg."

"Wouldn't play with you anyway, balloon heart."

Ruth could be as cruel as the other cockney urchins at times. She hated the thought of a hole in the heart. Once, she had been playing with a red balloon, and one of her brothers had pricked it out of spite. Ruth had watched it crinkle and wither as the life inside it ebbed away. She imagined Freddie's heart to be red and blistered like the balloon. What if she were to play with him and his heart burst in the same way. One minute he would be there and the next gone. Vanished beneath a pile of crumpled clothes.

Ruth missed her sister. They had never been separated before. Always in the same class at school, in the same double bed at night. They shared all of life's ups and downs. She had resented her handicap before but never as much. This time, instead of trying to keep up with the rest of her family, she had been excluded completely.

The sun was shining rich and golden all the way down the terrace. Ruth was on the lookout for her mother again. The only sign of life, apart from a couple of stray dogs, was the organ grinder way off in the distance outside the Feathers. He had stopped grinding and was drinking ale from a pewter mug. Every now and then Ruth was dazzled by the sun which was catching the metal whenever he lifted it to his lips. His work was finished for the day. Ruth wished he would wander up her end of the terrace. He had a pet monkey always dressed from head to toe in a lime green satin suit. Her leg felt too heavy to walk the distance to the Feathers to pet it.

She shivered and went back inside. It was cold in the kitchen. The stove had gone out. The sun never seemed to find its way to the back of the house. Ruth cut herself a large slice of bread and spread it with dripping. Then she slouched out to the back yard where the hens were taking dust baths. She swallowed the last piece and wiped her hands on her coarse, brown skirt. The washing was drying on a clothes horse. Apart from this, there was only enough room for a couple of chairs outside the back door. The rest of the space was taken up by the masterpiece which her father had built for his treasured hens. Ruth limped to the egg box and looked up. With her mother out of the way she made a momentous decision. She would climb on top and sing her heart out. First, she managed to clamber up onto the egg box. That morning, the elastic had gone in her drawers. Gert had given her a belt to keep them up. Ruth spotted a rusty nail. It had been half hammered into the roof, beneath which the fowls perched every night. She lifted up her skirt and untied the belt. After many attempts, she lassoed the nail with the belt. All of Ruth's strength was in her upper body. Holding onto the ends of the belt, as if they were reins, she took a deep breath and tested the strength of the nail. It felt safe.

Next, she hoisted herself up to the roof, like a steeplejack by swinging her good and bad leg alternately, up the side. Then she flung her whole body forwards and landed on a bed of moss, cobwebs and crackly leaves, dispersed there over many seasons. It cushioned her landing. Ruth felt a mixture of excitement and guilt, for doing the most dangerous thing she had ever done in her life.

After a while, she stood up shakily and looked down. The hens appeared decidedly smaller from up top. She kicked off her drawers which had fallen down around her ankles in the struggle. They landed outside the back door. When she had tested the strength of her father's carpentry, by walking about a bit, she proceeded to march to the tune running through her head.

"It's a long way to Tipperary, it's a long way to go", had been all the rage during the war, a few years before. Then, as she grew in confidence, her sweet, soprano voice soared over the walls into next door neighbours' gardens. The only bit of greenery she could see was in Martha Webb's yard, two doors down. It consisted of some mint growing through the slabs and a holly bush. People grew vegetables elsewhere on allotments.

Ruth let rip. Her voice seemed to act like a catalyst for community spirit. After only a few bars had been sung, windows were flung open and neighbours began to comment. Her audience was made up of dockers, factory workers, fish porters, craftsmen, dustmen, waiters, cleaners and those always out of work.

"Cor blimey, Gert's girl should be on up West."

"Yea, she's bloody grand."

"If I had a daughter that could sing like that, I'd have her up on stage, as quick as you can say, Jack Robinson."

The cacophony of street wise voices shouted one to the other. In their own way, they were making music. Not as tuneful as Ruth's singing, but rhythmical and the lyrics rang true. As her marching song reached a crescendo, she heard a scream from down below. Her mother was back.

"How the 'ell did you get up there?" Gert Drew was getting ready to catch her wayward daughter. In her scramble to get down, Ruth mistimed her footing and half slipped, half plummeted to the ground. Before she blacked out, she saw a figure standing behind her mother. It was Ivor Zalenski with a look of admiration in his eyes.

Ivor had been lodging with the Drew family for the past year. When Alfred, Gert's husband died, she took in washing and mending which just about put food on the table for her and her seven children. When Ivor answered her advert, strategically placed in the local pub, she felt blessed.

He got on well with all of her children, teasing the girls and making toys for the younger boys. They missed their father and so it felt good to have a man about the house again. Ivor was a good role model for her sons. He had not fought in the Great War but had seen plenty of the world as a sailor in the Polish Merchant Navy. The muddy odour of the Thames had brought with it the welcoming smell of fish, pie and mash, pea's pudding and jellied eels as his ship docked in the port. On his daily strolls about the streets he laughed at the costermongers finding them cheeky and comical. He would never pass a fish monger without taking home a pint of whelks, cockles or mussels. Gert was so grateful to him and smiled as her children crowded round him for equal shares.

He soon forgot his mother's borsch soup, pork cutlets and honey cakes and bought instead thick slabs of bread pudding oozing butter and smothered in sugar and cinnamon which he also shared with his new found family.

He quit the navy as soon as he could and got a job as a waiter but his English let him down. Soon he resorted to manual work at the East India Docks where he unloaded goods all day coming in from overseas. Tall and willowy with a love of poetry and music, he stood out amongst the muscle and brawn of the other men. His wit and charm won him friends and his faith in human goodness seemed to ward off any enemies he might have made in a foreign country. He had always been a saver and soon acquired the nick name of "Ivor Fiver". He lent money to those having to rear large families on a pittance. He laughed and joked charging only a miniscule amount of interest. Foreigner or not the Cockneys not only befriended him but had the utmost respect for his gumption.

Ruth adored him for his comical and caring personality. She loved how he teased her and Rose and how his wavy, black hair fell onto his forehead. When he ran his fingers through it, immediately, it would flop back again. He was different to all the other men who cussed and blinded on the terrace. He even smelled different. While they reeked of hair oil and sweat he washed in carbolic soap and smelled of wood shavings from his carvings. His lemon aftershave freshened up the whole house when he was about.

Ivor worked hard, met a girl called Amy for a drink now and again and helped the family out whenever he could. For now, he could not imagine being anywhere else. Being an insightful man, he soon realised that Gert protected Ruth more than the others. She kept her too close at times which made him feel sorry for the girl. Occasionally, he tried to make conversation with Ruth when she appeared to be lonely or sad. She seemed happy to be taken into her mother's confidence on matters that the others knew little or nothing about. Ruth derived a sense of power from this but her greatest saving grace was her spectacular singing voice. Everyone admired it, including him.

Down at the Feathers Public House, he overheard snatches of conversation about the family. Alfred had been a conscientious objector. He had refused to go to the trenches. When he became ill, it had been too late anyway. White feathers floated silently through the letterbox down onto the doormat. Even his neighbours, whom he had known for years, gave him stick for being a pacifist. Fred, the barman seemed more sympathetic.

"Poor bugger had to sit it out at home. Dr White said he wouldn't have made it as far as the boats taking them across. Consumption's a killer. He didn't last long."

Ivor did not know how confused Ruth felt about her father. She idolised him but knew instinctively that Rose was his favourite. One of her earliest memories was sitting on the back door step watching her in the hen run with him, digging over the soil pounded day in, day out by the chickens. She was not allowed to venture inside because of her leg. Sobbing and wailing made not a scrap of difference. It was Rose who ended up having all the fun, getting dirty and feeding her feathered friends with juicy worms. Worse still was the way he bounced her up and down on his lap, all the while crooning his favourite tune. "Goodbye Rose" had been all the rage before the war. As soon as Ruth discovered she could sing, she learnt all the words and tune by heart and joined in with him. The fact that she shared his love of singing did not go unnoticed by him and she felt proud when he harmonised with her.

Ruth was intelligent and soon began to ask questions. Couldn't she have an operation like the boy at school who had had a hump removed from his back, she begged. Alfred explained that she had one leg shorter than the other. The doctors suggested she wear a calliper and then a built up shoe later on. Ivor was usually around on Saturday afternoons. In between polishing his shoes for a night out with Amy and chain smoking woodbines, he would watch the elfin girl sing her heart out from his bedroom window overlooking the terrace. Whenever she got the chance, Ruth lined up her friends and neighbours in a row along the gutter and entertained them. With favourite songs she knew from school or from musicals she had seen down at the two penny rush. The snotty nosed urchins sat spellbound.

"Roll up, roll up, 'ere Danny Davis don't push in. Sit dead still or I won't sing a note."

Ivor laughed at her affectation.

"Right you are. This one is dedicated to my mum and dad. He used to serenade her with it. It's called 'When Love is Young'."

"When love is young in springtime
And boys are youthful too,
And girls are so alluring,
What can a fellow do?
A look, a smile, a dimple,
You're caught, you're captured, stung,
There's danger in the very air,
When love is young"

Whenever Gert was in the crowd that gathered, she would mouth the words and feel proud that the song she had taught her daughter was remembered so perfectly. She led the applause and made sure everyone paid attention. Then, with peekaboo actions, Ruth delighted them all with a famous Dolly Hackett song. The sweetness of her young soprano voice made "Pretty Baby" sound much more refined than the original version.

16

Sometimes Rose would shadow her sister and join in. Although she wasn't tone deaf she could not hold a tune. As if at a pantomime, the audience would hiss and boo and tell her to sit down which she did good humoredly. For her encore, Ruth trilled like Dame Nellie Melba her own rendition of 'Home Sweet Home'.

It did not matter to her at these moments that she had a crippled leg. Ivor noticed her grow significantly taller when they put their hands together and clapped. Her brothers shared the job of taking the hat round. Sometimes, amongst the farthings a whole penny was to be found. Whenever Ivor could afford it he would toss in a three penny bit. Ruth always handed it over to her mum.

Ivor stretched out on his bed and pictured these scenes in his mind's eye. So different to the Ruth only a few hours before who had to be carried inside to her bed with Gert frantically leading the way. The moment he had her in his arms she had come to and blushed as he lowered her onto her bed. He dared not admit to himself how attractive he found her. Now, with only Gert and Ruth downstairs, he enjoyed the tranquil atmosphere in the house. Tomorrow, the boys and Rose would be back from Kent. He wouldn't get a moments peace. Until then, he felt the luckiest man alive as he watched his smoke rings ascend to the ceiling.

Chapter 3

The cart laden with the last of the hop pickers, sped along Weymouth
Terrace. It had dropped off everyone except Rose and her brothers and
Martha from two doors down. Hodgkiss tugged at the hacks reins. Dust flew
up, off the road, into their faces. The old mare slowed down to a canter.
Rose squinted, watery eyed. She had felt numb travelling along on the train
back to London. A journey that she usually loved and had fun on. Swept
along by her brothers from platform to bustling streets and out to where
Hodgkiss had his mare tethered at the Bird in the Hand beer garden,
belonging to a distant cousin. Those last few bumpy miles had seemed like
an eternity. Squashed between Tom and Martha she kept her eyes fixed on
the muddied floor of the cart. They all seemed to be talking at once, vying
for the most attention with their jokes and laughter, while she felt invisible.

Tom, Arthur, Fred, Johnny and Jack jumped down and raced each other
toward their house. Rose climbed down last. She took one final look at the
man who had scarred her for life. He sat, round shouldered, his eyes fixed on
the road ahead. Sensing the cart empty, he lashed the mare and set off again.
Rose stood stupefied at the side of the road, gazing after the cart until it
disappeared from sight.

For the past two days, she had kept her head down. Mostly while they
picked, Hodgkiss had sprawled under a tree, slept, picked his nose or sipped
from a hip flask. At night, she had slept fitfully and dreamt of him forcing
himself on top of her, only this time, in full view of the whole gang. Martha,
Tom's girlfriend, informed her the next morning that she had been going

raving mad in her sleep, saying all sorts of weird stuff. Rose, panic stricken, urged her to tell her more. Freckle faced Martha giggled and tormented her with "That's for me to know and for you to find out."

Rose hated her. What Tom saw in her she would never know. Tall, fat and ugly, she came from a family of charlatans according to her Nan Bella. The thought of gobby Martha knowing anything about what had happened filled her with dread. To confide in Martha would be a mistake. She could never be trusted to keep a secret.

Hodgkiss ignored her as if nothing had happened. Rose wanted to scream, holler, rage, claw his eyes out, take a knife to his thing. She needed to vent her feelings about the monster who was their foreman. Instead, she kept her feelings locked up like caged animals, until their ferocity began to gnaw at her insides. For the first time in her short life, she suffered headaches and the pit of her stomach felt heavy. Rose limped slightly from the injury. She spoke slower than usual, in a morose voice, as if she might be overheard.

An anaemic sunlight did its best to welcome her home. It was lunch time on the terrace and so not a soul was about. Rose walked toward the front door, left ajar by the last of her brothers. Inside, she could hear her mother's voice greeting them warmly. The smell of fish boiling on the stove, made her feel queasy. She ducked into the first room off the hall which she shared with Ruth. She had always resented it. Just because her twin was handicapped, she had to sleep downstairs instead of having one of the larger bedrooms, upstairs. However, she could not have been more grateful for the position of her bedroom in the three storey house as she was at that moment.

Rose removed the soiled skirt and drawers from the carrier bag and hid them under the brass bed she shared with Ruth. A wash stand stood behind the door with a chipped, metal bowl on it. In an alcove opposite the bed hung a rail with the few dresses and skirts they possessed and a battered pine chest of drawers which contained their underwear and hand knitted cardigans and jumpers. It had belonged to Nan Bella and had seen better days, before being transported across Europe, strapped to a cart.

The wash bowl still contained some tepid water left over from Ruth's wash earlier. With a tiny piece of carbolic soap, she strip washed herself, as fast as she could and noticed her face in the mirror above the wash stand. It looked weather beaten. Her eyes seemed smaller, shrunken by upset and fear. Rose clawed at her skin, her neck, arms, stomach, until she arrived at the wounded place. She flinched as she dabbed it, gently and then changed into another dress which was hanging on the back of the door, placed there earlier by Gert. She felt camouflaged for now. A knock came on the door. It was her mother.

"Come on Rosie, hurry up, your bloater's going cold. It's your favourite. There'll be no mash left if you don't come now." Gert tried turning the door knob.

"What you doin' in there anyway? Don't usually take you as long as this?" Rose held her breath until her mother went away.

"Don't say I didn't warn you. Too slow to catch a cold, that one." She heard her mutter under her breath. These last words stabbed at her heart. It was Ruth who was slow, not her. It was as if their mother always had to blame her for everything, to make herself feel better about Ruth. Tears welled into her eyes. After all she had been through. Well, she would never tell her mother what had happened to her only to be told she was too slow to catch a cold. Before she left the room, Rose raised the sash window and threw out the bloodied water. She heard it slap the steps down to the airy and forced the window tight shut again.

The kitchen was crowded with her brothers all the way down one side of the table. Ruth was beside their mother, opposite. Her chair stood empty. It felt warm and stuffier than usual.

"About time and all. Here you are then." Gert handed her a plate of bloater and mash. Her hand trembled as she picked up her fork. All eyes were on her, especially Ruth's. Gert looked from one to the other and smiled. Just like peas in a pod. Same turned up noses, same long auburn hair, same expressions. Only now, Rose looked brown like a country bumpkin. She was beginning to look more grown up than Ruth. There was something else, too, that she couldn't quite put her finger on. She looked more worldly.

"Tom tells me you've picked like a good 'un this week, our Rosie."
Rose placed four shillings and six pennies on the table in front of her mother.

"Good girl. Have a penny for some sweets."
Rose would normally have been happy at her mother's generosity but instead just picked at the fish. Everyone exchanged bemused glances. Ruth knew,

20

that there was something wrong with her sister. She hadn't even made a single comment about the bandage round her head. She broke the silence.

"What you gonna buy Rose, cocoanut mushrooms or fizz bombers?" Rose shrugged her shoulders and felt a lump in her throat. It was a piece of potato that had not been mashed properly. The urge to cough, uncontrollably, was doused by a gulp of water from a cup, quickly handed to her by her mother. Gert felt sure the girl was in trouble. She hadn't once made her sister laugh since walking in. Rose's antics and stories never stopped usually. Like the one about Mrs Shaw, a fat, jolly lady who rolled over onto her false teeth one night and then walked around the next day with them stuck to her backside, saying she couldn't find them anywhere. Tom had nicknamed her the arse chewer and they had laughed about it ever since. Another night when Rose couldn't sleep, she had counted, by the light of a lantern, how many times Martha had slapped her own face. Flies flew in through the window, left ajar, to keep them from suffocating. Once inside, their mission was to dive bomb as many humans as possible. It had been hilarious, to look back on it, with her family in the warmth of the kitchen.

Outside, a short walk away from the hut was a ditch for excrement which the flies feasted on. This had been dug in haste by the farmer, since his dedicated hop pickers' closet had been turned into a hen coop. Every member of the gang was supposed to take their turn digging it over or shovelling it away. Most of them were too done in to bother. The flies were a real nuisance and the slapping of hands on flesh was he night time lullaby which got you to sleep or kept you awake. A couple of times they had a sing song round the camp fire. She especially liked singing the hop pickers song.

"When he comes to measure,
He never knows where to stop,
Ay, ay, get in the bin and take the bloody lot."

All the hop pickers were aware of being swindled. The measurer would compress the hops, making a bushel into a quart, thereby getting more hops for less money to each picker. Being powerless to change it, all they could do was to make up ditties and songs to get it off their chests.

Although she enjoyed this, she made light of it. Ruth would have felt like she was missing out even more.

"Anyway, Rose, I hate to have to disappoint you when you're doing so well, but I won't be sending you again. Nan Drew ain't feeling too well and needs some 'elp, so as you're her favourite…"

Gert poured herself another cup of tea and noticed an instant change come over her daughter. The seriousness seemed to disappear. She sat more upright in her chair.

"I expect you'd rather keep on with your brothers."

"No!"

Rose found her voice at last. It cut through the atmosphere in the kitchen, as sharply as the knife Gert had used to top and tail the bloaters. Rose was smiling now and shovelling her meal into her mouth. Everyone laughed with relief. For the moment Rose felt delighted. All she wanted to do was hang onto her mother's neck and kiss her flushed cheeks. Instead, she put the coin in her pocket and left the table.

"All right if I go and buy some sweets now, Mum. I'll wash up when I get back."

"Course you can. The rest of you, out you go. I've got a lot of work to do."

"Come on then, Ruth."

The kitchen emptied out and Gert was left alone. She pumped water into the sink, heating it up with a kettle full of boiling water from the stove. Soon, she forgot her misgivings about Rose. She became lost in amongst the domestic drudgery which had become her life. Gert had always been a daddy's girl while her brothers were spoiled by Bella. When her father died she had felt lost and in their shadow. Then Alfred had taken an interest in her from next door but one and they had courted from childhood much to Bella's disapproval. When they begged her to get married she had said yes believing her daughter to be in the family way. Gert smiled at the memory. Little had her mother known that she had been a virgin on her wedding night but with a mother like Bella she had learned how to connive to get her own way. Then the babies had come along one after the other. Once again Bella disapproved while Gert loved every minute of being a mother even though it got harder each year and was a constant struggle to feed and clothe them all. She and Alfred were inseparable whether her mother judged him a good catch or not. He was a good provider when he had the work but when he was on short time, she used every skill she had to make ends meet including charring, taking in laundry, and sometimes pulling pints at the Feathers when they needed a bar maid. Even when he became ill, she soldiered on denying to herself that she might lose him. Then when the war came and he stayed at home, she counted her blessings that he was still with them.

Just now and then, in between tidying beds, washing, ironing, sweeping, cooking, darning, and countless other chores, she would remember Alfred. He had left her with seven children and no money put by for a rainy day. God bless Ivor, she thought, looking at the bundle of chopped wood he had collected on his way home. Without him, they'd all be in the workhouse or worse. She turned her mind to more comfortable thoughts.

Rose seemed happy to be staying with her nan, for the foreseeable future, down in Spitalfields. With that thought in mind, the warning voice that had unsettled her earlier, subsided.

The sisters linked arms and walked the length of Weymouth Terrace to the sweet shop. Rose usually felt impatient at how long it took them, with Ruth always dragging them down. That day, she could not have cared less if it had taken them until closing time. She was back in the bosom of her family, safe again. Saturday afternoons were always a hive of activity on the terrace. It seemed wherever the girls looked, one of their brothers was to be spotted among the crowds. The Drew boys were well known for being in on everything. All except Johnny who usually went down to the cut to read. There he would cast out a float to make himself appear more credible to the other anglers. Then settle himself down to read his latest book, borrowed from the school library. He hardly ever checked his line to see if he had caught anything.

As Rose and Ruth drew level with the first of two pawn shops on the terrace, they came face to face with Tom and Martha kissing in a doorway. Tom ever mindful of how his mother felt about Martha, pushed her away but she stuck fast to him, like a limpet. She knew perfectly well how much the twins disliked her and so decided to try something outrageous on their brother. Her eldest sister, June had taught her all about French kissing and she was dying to try it out on Tom. At fifteen, Martha had not done it yet, much to June's surprise. She had done that and much more and was known as the terrace bike. Now she was encouraging her sister not to be so prudish.

23

Tom opened his mouth to acknowledge his sisters. At the same time, Martha stuck her tongue into it and closed her eyes. Rose and Ruth stared as they French kissed. Then she sucked on his neck like a parasite. The girls, as if joined at the hip, strode off again in disgust.

"What did you do that for? You saw Rose and Ruth gawping at us."

"Why, didn't you like it?"

"Course I bloody well did but save it for later. Not in public."

"There's more where that came from, Tom Drew."

The twins passed a second hand furniture shop, where most of their own house furniture had come from, a butchers, greengrocers and an ironmongery, where Arthur helped out. His boss was having a liquid lunch in the Feathers and the drowsy boy was left in charge. He lay stretched out in front of the shop in a tin bath. He was worn out from hop picking. The girls giggled and left him to it. If he got the sack it was his own fault.

They crossed the road, dodging a tram as it rattled by and stood on tiptoe to see through the window of the Feathers. If they could spot their uncles, they might be given an additional sixpence between them but today they were not in luck. Just past the pub was Wormleightons, where children from the surrounding neighbourhood bought their sweets. Row upon row of glass jars stood to attention in the window display. The girls had tried every sweet in those jars, at some time or another. There was never much money left over for luxuries but Ed Wormleighton was a kind hearted man. If a child could afford a farthing for some sweets, he would allow them to taste others, to buy the next time. He delighted in watching the expressions of some of the poorest children in the East End.

Ed was a widower. Originally, he ran the shop with his beloved wife. They had been childless but she constantly reminded him that they were fortunate to have so many children to nurture, each and every day. This they had done. Generations of them. Mrs Wormleighton radiated a light from within which more than compensated for the inside of the dingy shop. With her gone, it was more obvious that a single gas mantle struggled to illuminate the delicacies which lay beneath the counter and on the shelves. The twins made their selections. Barley twists for Rose and gobstoppers for Ruth. Ed served them. His apron gave away that he had been working on sherbet out the back. He had layered up all the colours of the rainbow in a huge glass jar. All except indigo. He had not quite arrived at the correct combination for that but he continued to work on it, in his spare time.

As he placed their purchases inside a brown paper bag, he asked after their mother. He liked to keep up with local news and gossip.

"So you're going to keep your Nan company then, Rose? That's a good girl."

Rose noticed that he was only paying half his attention to what she was saying. He was busy eyeballing Ruth who was looking, longingly at a dish of blackberry and custard boiled sweets. With the tips of his fingers, he pushed them towards her. His encouraging smile and reassuring nod gave her permission to take one. She did so and Rose followed suit. He stood back with his arms folded, looking from one to the other, awaiting their approval. They made all the correct sounds and he chuckled.

"Another winner, take one more each and if that's all, I had better get back to my sherbet. Take care girls and remember me to that pretty mother of yours."

He disappeared into the back room. The twins left the shop and headed back home. What they would have given to see inside the heart of Wormleighton's emporium. It never occurred to Ed to invite any of them to do so. Whilst it thrilled him to know that he brought joy and excitement to so many, he was wise enough to understand that to show them where it took place would be to destroy the very magic that he wished to procure.

Rose sucked on a scarlet gobstopper that she had swapped for one of her barley twists. The sisters didn't make any conversation. If it didn't come naturally to them then they didn't bother. The house was silent when they got back. Ruth poked her barley twist through the wire netting and dared the chickens to peck the end off. Rose lay down on their bed. Overhead, she could make out the muffled footsteps of Gert and outside the screams, laughter and tantrums of her neighbours'. It was dusk by the time she stopped staring into space. The gobstopper was no longer huge inside her mouth. It had reduced to the size of a pea. She stuck out her tongue in the mirror. It was bright red. She felt thirsty and in need of some food. The ache had returned to the pit of her stomach.

Chapter 4

It was nearly Christmas and had been snowing heavily all day. For the first time Rose felt bored. Thinking about the fun they would be having at school unsettled her. So far, helping her nan had been satisfying, safe and comfortable. It had been an escape from Kent and the hop fields. A chance to get out from beneath her mother's critical judgements. It was simple and straightforward with its daily routines. Like a time of convalescence, Rose had grown stronger and pushed what had happened to her to the furthest corner of her mind.

Life at school would be so different, especially now they were nearing the end of the Christmas term. Everyone was always excited and busy. The year before she had been chosen to play a wise man in the nativity play. The new music teacher, Mrs Duthie, had even paid her a compliment, telling her that she had offered the frankincense, beautifully, with very expressive hands. Then, because her class had filed out of assembly in the most orderly fashion, they had been chosen to decorate a huge fir tree brought into the hall.

For a whole afternoon, Rose and the others made snowflakes out of white paper and cut out gold and silver stars. Then she had been selected to place glass baubles onto the tree, while Geoffrey Harris, the tallest boy in the school, crowned the tree with a gorgeous fairy covered in sequins used year in, year out.

She had missed out on the Christmas dinner too, and wondered if her mother would be reimbursed, after paying all year round, into the school Christmas club. Ruth, by now, would have learnt the most difficult carol and have been chosen to solo in the concert. The traditional opening of the post box was one of the biggest losses. Usually, she and Ruth ended up with the most Christmas cards between them. Then the bell would clang for the last time, until they started back in the New Year. Rose always felt a mixture of sadness at leaving her school behind and gladness to be starting the festivities at home.

She watched the snowflakes falling and sighed sadly. It would have been her final year at school. Soon she would be fourteen. Old enough to go to work. She glanced at the clock on the mantelpiece. It would be chiming four o'clock in five minutes. At four, her nan would wake up with a start, after taking a long afternoon nap. Then they would have their tea. Rose was allowed to prepare it. Jam, bread and butter and whatever cake her nan had managed to make. Today they had made scones together. The daily routine never varied. Up at six, they spent almost every minute together, apart from when Rose ran errands along the High Street. Nan Drew had varicose veins and high blood pressure. Rose was told to help her as much as possible. She learnt a lot.

How to black lead the grate, make dumplings, light the boiler and dolly tub their clothes. Jobs which her mother insisted on doing herself. Nan Drew supervised everything she gave Rose to do. "That's it girl, that's the way" or "now you weren't listening." She might sigh or tut, but Rose always went to bed with a sense of achievement.

She sat down on an embroidered foot stool by the open fire and surveyed the room. It was small and cosy. Her nan sat by the fire in a rocking chair. Brightly coloured embroidered cushions, stitched painstakingly over the years, covered the horse hair sofa. Solitary years, spent husbandless. He had been killed down at the East India Docks. Crushed by a load, mistimed by his gaffer. She would never forgive that man, as long as she lived. On a highly polished sideboard were pictures of her dear George, in uniform, taken before he went away to the Boer war. Over and over it would go in the old girls mind. How he had survived shrapnel and bullets all those miles away in Africa only to be brought down on his own soil by the man who paid his wages. Rose's favourite photograph was of her nan and granddad together, taken up West, by a posh photographer.

Rose placed a fresh log on the fire. The room had grown chilly. Four o'clock and her nan sat bolt upright, as if a red hot poker had been shoved up her back. Her birdlike eyes opened and an arthritic hand smoothed away a stray curl, escaping from her top knot. She rolled back the sleeves to her frilly white blouse, as if to say she meant business and cleared the back of her throat. Croakily, she asked the same question which she asked every afternoon at four.

"Well Rose, its tea time. What we got?"

"Beef dripping on bread, Nan. You said we'd have it for a change."

"Go on then girlie and let the tea stand, like I told you, in the pot, before you pour it."

She stretched her short, bony arms and panted, appearing to be hot.

"Hurry up. I'm so parched, I couldn't spit a feather."

Outside in the scullery, Rose got everything ready. First, she cut the bread as finely as she could. Her nan only had a few teeth left. She could not be expected to chew on a doorstep which was her name for Rose's first attempt. Two china cups and saucers, milk jug and sugar bowl, apostle spoons, plate of bread and dripping. Buttered scones with a dollop of jam, scooped into a small, glass bowl. When she had checked and rechecked, she carried the tray back into the parlour. The old woman inspected everything and smiled.

"Lovely, but you've forgotten one thing." Rose felt disappointed and frowned.

"Doilies remember? I like the food covered while it's being carried from the kitchen. Don't want any dust settling on it."

"Oh yes Nan, sorry."

"All right Rose. Just this once, we'll take a chance. Go on, tuck in."
They sat and ate, both staring at the fire. Rose ate a good deal more than her nan, who broke off small morsels and placed them in her mouth. She sucked everything like a baby. They always ate in silence, because talking at meal times, according to her nan, caused heartburn. Rose certainly did not want her heart to burn. While she ate, she studied the ornaments above her head for the umpteenth time. A fat, brass Buddha presided in the midst of an assortment of bric-a-brac.

"You like that, don't you?" her nan broke their vow of silence. She took a sip of tea.

"Mm...it's nice."

"Your granddad bought that off a sailor down the docks. It's worth a few bob. You can get it down and have a look when you're finished."

Rose gulped her tea down and wiped her greasy hands onto her smock. She stood on tip toe and removed the oriental creature from the shelf and sat down again.

"What's a Buddha nan?"

"God, don't ask me. All I know is, it's something them Asian people worship, far away."

Rose polished it with her sleeve and gazed at its fat belly and bald head. She was entranced. The snow continued to fall. It grew dark. Soon they would have to light the gas mantels but, for now, the shiny object seemed to light up the space around the fire with a yellow glow which Rose was absorbed by. She had only travelled as far as Kent. This strange looking object had come from another continent, far away. So far, that you would have to set sail on a ship to travel there. It might take months, maybe even longer than that. All thoughts of school vanished from her mind as she played with these fantastic ideas inside the confines of her nan's parlour.

While her favourite grandchild imagined all sorts of weird looking lands and fabulous foreign faces, her nan inspected her. Rose was putting weight on. Her face had changed since September. It had filled out and lost its healthy glow. She looked run down. Yet, she ate well and opened her bowels regularly. The syrup of figs saw to that. She slept like a log. Most mornings she had to wake her. That was her only criticism of the younger generation. They would lie in till seven if you allowed them to. She was a hard worker once she was up. Maybe, she was working her too hard.

Rose stood up and placed the Buddha back on the shelf. It was then that the shrewd, old woman noticed the swelling in her granddaughter's belly. The smock wasn't hanging at all loosely as it used to. Rose squatted on the floor with her back to her nan's chair and warmed her hands.

"Rose, have you started your periods yet?" Rose was shocked at her nan's sudden frankness.

"Yes, Nan. But Ruth hasn't."

"When?"

"Couple of months ago now. We always thought we would have them together."

"Just because your twins, doesn't mean that would happen. Have you had one since you've been living with me?"

"No nan."

"Have you been sick at all, child?"

"Yes, a couple of times, first thing and sometimes I feel it in the day. I think it's when I eat too much."

"Well, I think you might be eating for two."

"What Nan?"

"I think you're carrying, Rose."

"Carrying what?"

"Oh good God, hasn't your mother taught you anything? You are nearly fourteen."

Rose stared, open mouthed. She dare not imagine what she was being accused of.

"A baby Rose...who's your boyfriend?"

"I ain't got one, Nan." Rose felt panic rising in her throat and began to cry.

"Honest to God?"

"I swear on my mum's life."

"There's no need for that." Her nan raised herself from the rocking chair, for the first time that afternoon. Rose heard her brittle bones creak. The old woman took the poker and viciously prodded the logs to give a blaze. When the flames licked the back of the chimney, she asked her another question in a very even voice.

"Has anyone touched you...down there?"

Rose hesitated. Then the floodgates opened. For the first time in three months the memory of what Hodgkiss had done came back to haunt her. Rose knelt at her feet. Nan Drew was so tiny, it was difficult for her to comfort the girl but she managed to rub her back, soothingly.

"Now, I want you to tell me from the beginning what happened, darling. Don't be scared. Your old Nan ain't about to tell you off."

After Rose had finished, she felt some relief. Her nan had not said a word but held her hand and listened intently. Then she grew angry.

"I knew no good would come of your mother sending you hop picking. I've heard of this sort of thing happening before. You say his name's

Hodgkiss. I think I know the bloke... lives over Hackney way."

In between sobbing, Rose asked her nan what would happen to her when her mum found out.

"Cor blimey, finds out! She's had seven of her own. You'd think she would have spotted it by now. Now calm down. You are going to have a baby Rose. It's not the end of the world but I tell you, that swine ain't going get away with it. Not if I have my way." Rose had never seen her nan so angry.

Nan Drew hated the monster for putting her favourite grandchild in the family way but it went much deeper than that. She had lost six children. Alfred had been her only surviving baby. She had even lost him. First to Gert and then to consumption. Here was his daughter, telling her she was carrying, at the tender age of thirteen. To have been forced was a terrible thing but a baby was precious. There would be no question of getting rid of it, or giving it away. As long as she had a breath in her body, she would see to that.

The next day, Rose returned from running an errand and found Nan Bella sitting in Nan Drew's rocking chair, flagged on either side by her uncles, Jack and Bill. They were drinking tea. Nan Drew rested on the horse hair sofa.

They all gave her a warm welcome. Nan Bella was much taller than Nan Drew. She was a magnificent looking woman, with an olive complexion and hair swept back into a huge, thick bun. It was the colour of salt and pepper and had been a glorious, shiny ebony in her heyday. She and Nan Drew were the same age but Bella looked ten years younger. Her handsome uncles resembled their mother, with the same olive complexion and deep brown eyes. Rolled up shirt sleeves revealed powerful biceps. These had been built up over years of heavy lifting. Together they ran a furniture removal business.

Rose knew that Nan Bella came from Romany gypsies and had been married to Bernard Baldini, her grandfather. They had worked in a circus across Europe, before deciding to settle down in England. Gert, Jack and Bill were first generation Baldinis not to live the Romany way of life.

"Hallo Rosie. You're getting a big girl. Pretty as your name," Bill said, flirtatiously, while Jack offered her his knee. Rose declined and forced a smile.

"Good to see you Rose. We'll arrange your piano lessons, someday soon."

"Yes, Nan," Rose answered shyly, taking off her coat and warming her hands by the fire. She loved her nan's voice with its foreign accent. It sounded exotic and gave her a special presence, like royalty. She too was from a faraway place, like the Buddha.

"Well, you must come and pay me a visit soon. Bill, Jack. We had better be making our way home. Thank you for the tea, Ida."

"Here you are, Rose. See you soon." Jack reached into his waistcoat pocket and brought out a half crown. Bill followed suit. So much money. She was delighted. She would be able to buy presents for Christmas, for the first time ever.

Rose washed the tea cups. She did not question the presence of Nan Bella, in the home of Nan Drew. They had been neighbours for years, until Bella moved into a bigger house. They still called in from time to time. Rose hummed a carol she had heard carolers singing at the front door the previous evening. It was one of her favourites.

"We will rock you, rock you rock you..." The tune helped her to overcome the nausea she kept experiencing. So she was going to have a baby. The Lord Jesus had been a baby, lying innocently in a manger. That's what all the carols were about but there was nothing good and innocent about the one she was carrying.

She wiped her hands on the tea towel and went upstairs to her nan's bedroom. Quietly, she stripped off all her clothes and stood naked before the full length mirror. Her breasts had become fleshier. They were no longer the size of cherries but had blossomed to the size of a good windfall apple. She cupped them in her hands. They felt womanly with weight. She traced her stomach lightly. From the side, she could see what her nan had spotted the day before. She had not attached any importance to the swelling. Too much food equaled getting fat. Every day, for three months, she had eaten the lion's share.

Rose began to shiver. It was freezing cold in the bedroom with icicles stuck fast to the window ledges outside. No thaw was expected yet but it was out of fear that she trembled. Rose pulled on all her clothes again and returned to the kitchen. Every now and then, she stopped to place her hands on her swollen belly and to whisper a prayer to God, to send the baby away.

Meanwhile, her nan dozed in the parlour and dreamt about the meeting which she had called. She knew she could trust the Baldinis. They would not let her down. They had integrity and looked after their own. Hodgkiss would get the hiding of his life. One that he would not forget in a hurry. No more sniffing around young, innocent girls. She sucked on her teeth and slept like a baby.

Not many miles away, George Hodgkiss was preparing for his usual, solitary Christmas. A rag and bone man by trade, he had taken over the business after his father died. He never knew his mother. She had been a young girl when she married his father and was made old before her time. Henry Hodgkiss had been a cruel tyrant of a husband who had knocked her about from morning till night. None of his neighbours dare interfere but it was much to their distaste. East end women expected to receive a back hander from time to time. When money was tight or their men came home with a skin full but Henry Hodgkiss had been a sadist who kept her on the go, covering her with bruises even when she was pregnant with George. She grew paler and thinner until one day, shortly after giving birth, she took to her bed and died. A wet nurse had been brought in to give the scrawny baby a start in life. George had not been expected to live but with the woman's breast milk and what had been described as a miracle by Henry's neighbours, the boy had survived. From early infancy, Henry wrapped him in a blanket and took him with him on the horse and cart.

It had always been him and his old man for as long as he could remember. He wasn't interested in any juicy gossip about his father's past and lived his life according to his father's philosophy. Ask no questions and you'll be told no lies. Feather your own nest whenever possible. Rag and boning came easily to him. It was a simple life. He bought and sold everything from bric-a-brac to horse saddles. The cottage he lived in was tumbling down around him. It was difficult for visitors to distinguish where the yard ended and the living quarters began. He had not taken the time to thin his stock out since his old man had died over ten years before.

Furniture spilled out from his front door onto a lean to porch. Coat stands, trunks, boxes of every make and design, were thrown onto various piles according to their importance and size. A suit of armour he had once been asked to dispose of by a gentleman down on his luck stood to one side of the doorway like a sentinel on duty. Harnesses and saddles hung from dilapidated fences and broken down hand carts and wagons stood rotting beneath them. Prams, dolly tubs, couches spewing horsehair, beds, mattresses, tin baths and a huge brass bed blocked the entrance to his outside privy. He no longer bothered with it, choosing to use whichever chamber pot was handy at the time. There were dozens of them placed strategically around the yard. It was one of his more childish games to see how far he could shoot his pee and this amused him greatly. To excrete, he dug a hole at the back of his property and filled it in.

In spring and summer, he would have the horse hitched to the cart and be out and about by seven around Hackney, Bethnal Green, Shoreditch, Stepney, Whitechapel and Bow. Sometimes he ventured up West. He bought and sold and was paid to cart belongings away. Here, he made a killing. Widows and spinsters who had no one to do their heavy lifting for them were taken to the cleaners. He charged them whatever he liked. He had no scruples. During the autumn, he was taken on as a foreman for the hop picking season. The winter found him either in his local or sleeping it off in bed. Sometimes, he paid a visit to the local brothel but this was becoming rarer. He was usually too drunk to perform.

On Christmas Eve, he was to be found sitting in his kitchen surrounded by old mangles, buckets, coal scuttles and jars of pickles that he had bought as a job lot. His sink was full to the brim with encrusted pots and pans. On the mantelshelf above his head, a candle burned. The only sound that could be heard was the tearing of feathers as he plucked a pheasant for his Christmas dinner. They fell silently around his feet like colourful snowflakes. Red, orange, gold, tan, black and yellow. When he was finished, he spread a knob of butter over the bird and placed it on a tray, inside the range. Next he stoked the fire to cook it and to keep him warm. With a roll up in one hand and a jug of ale in the other, he settled down on an old chaise longue and inhaled deeply. Many nights he spent in the same way with only his Alsatian bitch Bessie to keep him warm.

At forty, he was set in his ways like his father before him and looked ten years older. Night began to fall, when he heard someone moving about outside in the yard. He was used to kids climbing over his fence and nicking stuff, so he had trained Bessie well. If she didn't take care of them then he would give them a good slapping. He was looking forward to the day when one of his mantraps came into its own. Bessie hadn't barked, so he stubbed his cigarette out. It was time to take action. From an assortment of pokers, he grabbed the heaviest looking one and ventured outside.

He need not have worried, for he recognised the two men walking towards him. The Baldini brothers, obviously wanting to discuss some business with him. Sometimes the two businesses worked hand in glove. As they drew nearer, Hodgkiss extended his right hand to shake Bill's, as was the custom. Instead of a firm, respectful handshake, he felt a blow to the side of his head. The poker flew out of his hand clattering onto the flagstones, demolishing a heaped up pile of tins in its wake. It had taken him by surprise but he was still standing. Mustering up all of his strength, he flung his arms and fists around, hoping to land a couple of worthwhile punches. They would have to talk later about what had pissed them off. Perhaps he owed them money. Something had riled them enough to use brute force on him. Usually the brothers were gentlemen.

Hodgkiss was aware of the painful blows to his chest and back. Jack and Bill had won medals for boxing in their youth and were using all their skill. The older man remained on his feet, right up until a punch to his groin sent him coughing and spluttering into a pile of horse dung. Once they had their man on the ground, they let rip with their hob nail boots. Hodgkiss did not have time to cry out for help. None of his neighbours would have come to his defence had he done so. After a while, his hands flopped by his sides. He was no longer protecting his head. The Baldini brothers were out of breath by the time they had finished. Jack puffed and panted.

"That'll teach you, you bastard."

"Come on, he's had enough."

They left him moaning behind them and went out the way they had come in. He had forgotten to bolt the gates. Bessie was oblivious. She was dining out on a huge ham bone, placed strategically at the back of the cottage earlier.

Chapter 5

Rose returned to a bustling house on Weymouth Terrace. Jack and Johnny met her at the front door with their new wooden cars. Ivor had been busy, chiseling them to perfection. The snow had fallen for weeks and so the older lads were already out on a sledge he had made for them. The deep snow reminded Ivor of his native country, where sledging took up most of the winter. She noticed how her mother had decorated the hallway, with sprigs of holly and ivy and paper snowflakes which the others had brought home from school. They were stuck all over the walls. It felt as though her mother had made a special effort for her homecoming.

"Don't dawdle Rose. Let's get in the warm," Nan Drew pushed past her and made her way to the kitchen. She heard her mother greet her warmly. The smell of a Christmas feast wafted down the hallway to her. Food which her mum had paid all year round for, to cook for them and fill their bellies. The turkey sizzled and spat in the oven, alongside roast potatoes and parsnips and a huge pudding steamed on the top. It felt different to Rose to come home as a visitor. Usually, she would be the one to open the front door to her nan. She wondered if Nan Bella and her uncles would be coming as well.

She snapped out of her daydream and hung her coat on the stand, suddenly remembering that she had presents to give everyone. Rose found Ruth in their bedroom, going through her gifts.

"Happy Christmas, Sis."

"Hallo Rose. Happy Christmas. Come and open your presents."

The girls grinned at each other and Rose made a face at the yellow jumper her sister was wearing.

"Where did you get that monstrosity from, our Ruth?"

"Mum knitted it in her spare time. Don't worry, you've got one an' all."

They giggled. Rose sat on the edge of the bed and unwrapped her presents, tearing away brown paper and string. The first was a green jumper that looked three sizes too big. Rose was grateful for that and slipped it on over her head. It concealed her belly well. Then out of an old knitted stocking dropped an orange, some monkey nuts and a small bar of chocolate, from Wormleightons. Gert gave them all the same year in, year out. Rose ate the chocolate ravenously. They had not had time to have any breakfast that morning, as the taxi cab had come for them early. Ida Drew moaned about the expense of it compared to the horse drawn hansom cab of her day but as it was Christmas, she supposed she should push the boat out a bit. She ignored the driver when he doffed his cap and held his hand out for a tip. Rose kept all this from Ruth. It had been her first ride in a taxi cab and it had been thrilling and had made her feel important. She did not wish to make Ruth envious or feel left out. The next gift was from Nan Bella. A lovely orange pair of warm, fluffy slippers. Rose slipped off her shoes. They were squelching melted snow. After wringing out her socks and dumping them in the wash bowl, she tried them on. The slippers fitted a treat. She looked down at Ruth's feet. Hers were bright blue. They had never had slippers before. The last present she opened was from Ivor. It was a small wooden box with the lid carved into the shape of a flower. Rose had never seen anything so beautiful.

"What did he make you?"

"My broach. Look it's a bird. He says it's a lark because I'm always singing."

"It's lovely."

Rose opened her carpet bag and rummaged through her clothes until she found the presents she had been able to buy. She handed one to Ruth.

"Eh? Oh Rose, I ain't got you nothing."

"That don't matter...hope you like it."

Ruth ripped off the paper and brought out a snow shaker. She stared at the scene within it. A mountain covered in snow and a lake beneath and blue birds flying by.

37

"It's lovely Rose. Thank you."

"And if you shake it Ruthie, look." Both girls watched as the glass came alive, with snow tumbling down over the mountain. Neither had seen anything so magical.

"Oh yea. This an'all from Nan." She brought out a cushion which her nan had embroidered. The woolen threads depicted a cat. Ruth took it and threw it on the bed. It landed on top of several others, given as presents over the years.

"Not another ruddy cushion." The twins laughed.

"Right well, I'd better go and give the others theirs." Ruth followed her down the hall and into the kitchen. It was warm and cosy. Her mother was busy tasting the gravy. Nan Drew was almost asleep, perched on a chair next to the boiler. Johnny was under the table with Jack, playing cars. Ivor was outside building a snowman.

"Hallo love. Happy Christmas. Would you like a cup of tea?"

Once more, Rose had a feeling of being a guest in her own home. She wasn't sure whether she liked it or not. It felt strange.

"Yes please, Mum. Happy Christmas."

Gert poured her a cup of tea. Rose brought out another gift which she had carefully wrapped in some tissue paper.

"This is for you, Mum."

"Eh?" Gert looked surprised and flustered. For the first time that day, she sat down and wiped her hands on her apron. Rose sipped her tea and watched her mother, opening her first Christmas present ever, from one of her children.

The ripped paper revealed a small bottle of lavender toilet water and some fulnarna powder for her face. Gert felt very touched. She reached across the table and patted Rose's hand.

"They're lovely, Rose. How could you afford...?"

"I saved up. Put some on."

"Later love, when I have a wash down."

"All right, Mum. Thanks for my jumper. It's lovely." The twins smirked at one another. "Here you are, Jack." A hand popped out from beneath the table. It snatched at the small parcel. He was used to getting all the hand me downs from his brothers, and so was delighted to receive two, nearly new, lead toy soldiers to add to his collection. Rose had had a lot of fun searching the pawn and second hand shops, for presents, around Spitalfields.

"What about me?" Johnny asked

"Here you are, you an' all." Gert watched her son tear off the paper, to reveal a book. 'A Tale of Two Cities' by Charles Dickens. He whooped with delight and kissed Rose swiftly on the cheek. The wooden car was forgotten as he went to find a quiet place to read.

"I've got gloves for Tom and sweets for the others. Where are they all?"

"You've done us all proud, our Rose." Gert felt fit to burst with pride, at what her girl had done for them.

"I bought some snuff for Nan."

"I thought as much. She had a sneezing fit just now." Gert laughed with her girls as the old woman sucked on her teeth, fast asleep.

"I don't suppose your money ran to anything for Ivor, did it?"

"Yes. Don't worry. I ain't left anyone out. Got him some tobacco for his pipe."

Gert beamed at her and then announced that dinner would be ready very soon after she had tested the vegetables and basted the turkey.

When they were all seated round the table, Ivor asked Gert if he could say grace. He could see how hungry they all were and so cut it short. He carved the turkey, standing at the head of the table instead of their father and the vegetables were handed around. Gert poured the steaming gravy. The meal just stretched to ten plates. When it was time for Christmas pudding, Gert took a key and unlocked a small cabinet over the sink. She brought out a bottle of brandy usually kept for medicinal purposes. Pouring two huge spoonfuls over it, she asked Ivor to stand by to light it. Everyone was amazed at the sight of the pudding on fire but the gentle blue and yellow flames soon went out. Then dollops of thick cream were ladled over each portion. Rose felt warm and happy, in amongst her family again. For now, she could forget about the conversation she was going to have with her mother when Christmas was over. Nan Drew had made her promise to tell Gert what had happened.

After the table was cleared away, everyone went back to their gifts and pursuits. The girls joined Ivor in the yard, putting finishing touches to the snowman. They made a nose with a tiny piece of coal and a smile with peelings from the sprouts. Gert washed up and then went for a lie down.

Later, the fire in the parlour was lit and they were joined by the Baldini side of the family. A huge plate of turkey sandwiches was brought in. Nan Bella bought a Christmas cake and two flagons of ale. Soon the house filled up, with cousins and aunts and uncles. Ruth looked forward to this part of Christmas day, more than the others. She sang the loudest and kept the sing song going, when everyone else had tired of it and were wanting to play cards. Ivor was the first to leave the party, after a slice of cake and a glass of ale. Even though they all insisted he stay, and Ruth hung on his arm, he did not want to outstay his welcome.

Rose sipped her tea and ate Christmas cake. She remembered other Christmases, when her father was still alive. Year in, year out, they said the same things and made toasts to the best Christmas ever but this year had felt so different. When she thought of the baby she was going to have, it filled her with dread and she wondered what it would be like next Christmas.

Then one by one, the guests left and wished her good luck with her job interview on their way out. Rose snapped out of her reverie. She had completely forgotten about it and once more she was filled with dread.

Greens was only two blocks away from Weymouth Terrace. Rose had had to pass it every day on her way to school but had never really noticed it before. On the day of her interview, it was raining heavily and her shoes were letting in water again. She comforted herself with the thought that her mother might hand back some of her first weekly wage for her to buy herself a new pair.

A sign outside told her to report at the desk on the first floor. Rose climbed a winding flight of stairs to a pokey office at the top. Here, she was told to wait for Mr. Stephens who would be interviewing her. The woman looked her up and down as if she were not to be trusted and ushered her to a chair. Rose looked about her while she waited and concluded that Greens was the dingiest place she had ever set foot in. Even Wormleightons sweet shop was lit up by its treasures inside but there was nothing here to make it sparkle. Least of all the old woman typing, furiously, behind her desk. Greens was a horrid shade of brown. Bannisters, stairs, window frames and walls were drab and worn out. A hooter sounded. The woman got up from her chair and descended the stairs.

A few minutes later, a young man came running up the same flight. He placed the typist's chair a yard or so away from Rose and sat down.

"I'm Mr. Stephens. We may as well do the interview here, as its break time. Marjorie won't mind."

Rose shuffled around on her seat and looked him over. He was about the same age as Tom and wore a suit a couple of sizes too big for him. Greasy blonde hair framed his pimply forehead and he looked as though he had a foul smell under his nose. Rose thought his voice sounded high falutin'. In his hand he clutched a sheet of paper with some questions written down. They had been handed to him earlier by the busy manager of Greens. He had tried to memorize them but had felt too nervous to make a good enough job, and so carried them with him, just in case. He seemed serious and trussed up to Rose.

"You are here about filling. Is that right?"

Rose looked blank.

"Yes, well, there is a vacancy for stuffing mattresses. Mostly wool, cotton, horsehair. Some feathers. When we think you are proficient in that department, (here he broke off to read his script), you might be able to progress to tufting."

Rose continued to stare. "Buttoning department, to keep the filling in, you see."

He glanced at her vacant face out of the corner of his eye. To cheer her up and to lighten the atmosphere, he said, "Oh yes, you will learn the art of mattress making here.

"Do you like stitching?"

Rose nodded even though her mother did all the stitching and mending in her house. Gert was always stabbing her sore fingers with the needles. Thimbles didn't seem to help. She looked down at her hands in her lap, made to play the piano and sighed heavily.

"When can you start?"

"Tomorrow?"

"You would have to be here for eight o'clock every day and work till six. Half a day on Saturday and Sunday off. Pays five shillings a week which will go up if you are a quick learner and make progress and we can put you on piece work if you are fast enough and then you earn even more...er...Miss Roberts, the forelady will explain as you go along...all will become clear... we can...er (he read from his script again) only allow you to be sick three times and ....well...I'm sorry, but you're out on your...er...understand?" She nodded again.

"Right, well we will provide you with an overall and tools. I think that's all."

He checked his list again and realised he still had something important to say. He stood up and so did Rose. He was tall and thin and towered above her.

"Right, we will give you a trial. Be on time. That is all we ask. We are a very busy firm with lots of orders to get out each week...er...understood?"

"Yes, Sir."

The lad smirked at the respectful reply and felt suddenly very senior. His closing statement came out with much more confidence.

"Right you are. See you in the morning."

Rose left the premises. It was still raining. After walking the first block her feet were so heavy with water that they squelched bubbles up through to her insteps. She ran for cover and sheltered in the doorway of a tea shop and emptied out her shoes. Inside it looked lovely and cosy. Girls dressed in black with white aprons and caps were rushing about, serving well groomed ladies. Tea, piping hot and cake stands full of cream sponges and dainty sandwiches made her mouth water. She had never had tea in such a place. The waitresses looked like silent movie actresses in their uniforms and makeup. Rose imagined how wonderful it would be to work in a place like that but did not, for a moment, consider herself good enough to. You had to be tall, pretty and a cut above to do a job like that, she decided.

On the other side of the street, a newspaper boy was dragging his papers in out of the downpour. Once he had them in the dry, he pulled his jacket around him and dug his hands deep into his pockets for a bit of warmth. After a while, he began to shout, "Read all about it. Local murder. Rag and bone man beaten to death, read all about it." Rose shuddered and made a run for it. Such horrible news to start the New Year with. Well, at least she had some good news for a change which would, hopefully, soften her other news. She reached the front door drenched to the skin and out of breath. Once inside her bedroom, she stripped off her wet clothes and towel dried her hair, taking time to conceal her condition with a baggy jumper. Full of trepidation she made her way to the kitchen. Her mind was made up. It was now or never. She would tell her mother.

Gert greeted her in the kitchen. She seemed pleased that she had found a job but at the same time was preoccupied. Gert poured Rose a cup of tea who sipped at it grateful to be in out of the wet weather.

"I've just been talking to Martha's mother and guess what? That foreman...what was his name...Hodgkiss, that's it...he's been found murdered."

For a moment, it did not register with Rose, who was intent on getting warm.

"You know Rose, that foreman...when you went hop picking." As if she had been struck by lightning, the full force of what her mother was talking about, caused every nerve in her body to stand up on end. In the fraction of a second it took for that to happen, Rose slumped onto the range. Gert strode to her side and pulled her off. The kitchen smelled of singeing hair. Rose had completely passed out. Gert lay her down onto the kitchen floor and snatched one of the cushions, always to hand, placing it beneath her head. From out of the sink, she grabbed a dish cloth and made it into a cold compress for her daughter's forehead. Whatever had made her swoon like that, she wondered? Gert ran to the front door and hollered for someone to fetch the doctor.

"I'm on me way, Gert," a neighbour shouted back and did an about turn. She ran back to the kitchen and found Rose trying to sit up. All the colour had drained from her face. Gert knelt down and cradled her to her bosom.

"There, there, it'll be all right."

Rose tried to speak but her mother could not decipher what she was trying to tell her.

"Lie still sweetheart. Don't try to talk. I've sent for the doctor."

Somewhere above her, Rose could hear her mother's reassuring words. She needed to tell her mother everything. Nan Drew had told her to and now she knew she must but all the blood had rushed from her head and the words were stuck fast inside her mind. Round and round they went, like a Ferris wheel with her stuck at the top with no way down.

"He did it to me...mum...a baby. I'm having a dead man's...a murdered man's...baby...it hurt mum...I bled..."

When Rose came to, the doctor was standing by her side with her limp hand in his. She was lying on her bed. Trauma was the first word she heard spoken.

"Follow my finger, Rose," he was saying.

Her eyes moved slowly, concentrating on his nicotine stained finger. Her father's had been the same. The doctor brought out his stethoscope and warmed it up.

"Can you sit up, Rose?"

With the help of her mother, Rose rested against her pillows. He asked her to take deep breaths and held it against her chest and back. Rose trusted Dr. White and his craggy face. He was one of the kindest people she had ever met. He had always been the family doctor and had brought them all into the world.

"Good, strong heartbeat."

Then he asked her to pull up her jumper so that he could examine her abdomen. Pressing firmly all around it, he gave nothing away by his expression. He pulled her top down again and patted her head. She could have been one of his own grandchildren.

"Rest Rose. I'm just going to have a word with your mother."

They left the bedroom and walked down to the kitchen. Over a cup of stewed tea, he informed Gert that Rose was almost four months pregnant. She had probably passed out due to over exertion and not enough to eat. Gert buried her face in her hands and sobbed. She felt so guilty and ashamed. All the signs had been there for ages now. She had chosen to ignore them, hoping that she might be wrong. There were so many other things to worry about

"Just give her some tender loving care and I'll call back at the end of the week."

Gert decided to keep this to herself. There would be too many questions from her inquisitive children. After a while, she got unsteadily to her feet and prepared a soup from all the vegetables she could find with plenty of salt and pepper for taste. She prayed Ivor would bring something home to add extra nourishment. After a while, Gert felt faint and reached into her brandy cupboard for a bottle of smelling salts. They helped to clear her head. Gert steeled herself for the task in hand. Rose and the baby would need her undivided attention.

Why hadn't she warned her daughters about the wicked ways of young men? How they said the right things to get into your knickers, until they put you in the family way. She had been fortunate to meet Alfred. He had been her one and only boyfriend and the love of her life. Always respectful and caring before and after they were married. She cut up some onions and her eyes watered, mixing with her tears. She could not bring herself to walk the short distance to the bedroom where Rose was sleeping.

When Tom raced down the hallway, with Ruth in the hand cart, she was still stirring the vegetable soup. He ran upstairs to get changed. He was meeting Martha, behind the park huts for a snog. With a bit of luck, she might give him a quick feel as well. Ruth stared at her mother. One look told her that all was not well.

"What's up, Mum?"

"It's Rose. She's lying down. Dr. White says she's suffered a trauma."

"Is she all right?"

"Yes, don't worry, she'll be fine. Just needs our love and care, he said."

"Well, what's a trauma, anyway?"

"I'm not all that sure. Go and keep an eye on her Ruth while I get the dinner ready."

Gert heard her leg iron grate down the hall. She usually confided everything in Ruth. All her money worries, aches and pains and even the truth about Alfred when the others knew nothing but this felt worse than all of that put together. Her girls were so close, it would cause Ruth such heartache. She would keep it to herself for as long as she could. They would all know soon enough.

Chapter 6

Ruth was so excited on her return from a wonderful day at school. She felt fit to burst with her news. They had been learning a new song called, 'The Vagabond'. When Mrs. Duthie played the opening bars, Ruth knew she was in for a treat. The melody appealed to her and she soon sang it, note perfect, while most of her class mates struggled. Jane Duthie knew a good voice when she heard one having been a concert singer herself. She clapped her hands energetically and waited for the class to settle down. She pushed her horn rimmed spectacles to the bridge of her nose and ran a hand through her blonde wiry hair. Her lip twitched as it was apt to do when she was excited. She may have been petite in size but her presence in the classroom made the children want to sit up and take notice.

"Now boys and girls, listen to Ruth, please. Take your time. Don't rush it Ruth. Stand at the back, over there."

Ruth felt as if she were being punished until the music teacher winked at her. She explained to the class that Ruth was overpowering them with her superb soprano voice. How could they begin to sing the correct notes, if they could not hear what she was playing? Ruth had never been teacher's pet before. Feeling different, for as long as she could remember, she hated being singled out except when it came to singing. She knew beyond a shadow of a doubt that she was talented. Therefore, on this occasion, it felt reassuring to be in the spotlight. When the bell rang for playtime Ruth hung about collecting in the sheet music. She handed them to Mrs. Duthie who was looking at her with admiration.

"So where did you learn to sing like that, Ruth?"

"My mum says it's natural, Miss. She sings, too. It runs in the family.

"Indeed? Well, I think you should have your voice trained. Don't look so worried. You would be taught how to breathe properly and how to get the most out of your voice. You are in your last term at school. What are you going to do when you leave?"

"Me, Miss...oh, I don't know. Help me mum at home, I expect."

"Not work at all then?"

"Not with me leg. My mum wouldn't like me to."

"That is a shame. I wonder if I could call round and speak to your mother. It would be a crime to let such a lovely voice go to waste."

"I suppose so but she's always busy. I don't know when..."

"Just let me worry about that. Weymouth Terrace is where you live. Am I right?"

"Yes Miss. Number ninety two."

"Right, well thank you for your help, Ruth. See you next week."

As Ruth left the classroom to join her friends in the playground, she felt enough courage to tell her teacher, "I love the way you speak. You're not from round here, are you?"

"Indeed, I'm not. How observant of you. I'm from Aberdeen in Scotland."

"I love your accent, Miss."

"And I love your voice - so we have something in common."

Now, face to face with Rose, her hopes and dreams were crushed. The sight of her sister confirmed the fear that she had been trying to ignore for months. Rose had begun to change, even before she had gone to keep their nan company. It wasn't just the way she spoke or interacted with her that had changed. Ruth had found the soiled dress and drawers. When she saw the dried blood, she feared the worst. Her sister must be dying of consumption like their father. While Gert was busy pegging out the washing, she had made sure the dress was plunged beneath all the other clothes steeping in the boiler. Ruth felt guilty for not telling her mother. They had no secrets but on this occasion she did not want to upset her. Female intuition told her that her mother might not be able to take many more knocks. On the other hand, she felt sorry for Rose who was at the mercy of her mother's critical remarks. She wanted to protect her sister.

That evening Ruth and her mother washed Rose and put her into a clean, flannelette, night gown. They did not speak to her or each other. Ruth plaited her hair. Gert encouraged Rose to get into bed. She had been sitting for hours in the armchair by the window, staring out at the terrace. They could not get her to drink any of the soup. Gert said that was all they could do until Dr. White's next visit. Traumas had to be handled with kid gloves, she said.

As the weeks passed, Rose felt more and more locked inside herself, as if she had gone to sleep with her eyes still open. She felt nauseous after every meal and wondered if she was going to die. Only now and then did she sense someone, out of the corner of her eye, visiting her sick room. The words they spoke to her evaporated into thin air. When Gert broke down and sobbed, Rose made every attempt to comfort her but as much as she tried, the will to do so abandoned her. At one point, she was shaken like a rag doll. At another, someone slapped her across the face. It did no good.

Way off in the distance, Rose could protect herself from the monster taking over her body. In her mind's eye it featured Hodgkiss in every detail, even down to his bovine eyes. Day by day her mind erected a wall between her and the outside world behind which the Ferris wheel whizzed her round and round to greater heights. At times she felt that she would never find her way back down to earth.

During the fourth month Rose felt the baby move inside her. It was the quickening. To Rose, it was the hand of Hodgkiss groping, making certain that his offspring was safe. She flung herself out of her chair and cut her head open. The force with which she made contact with the window pane was so great that it shattered, creating a jagged hole for her to try and push through. Her hands went first. Someone came running and found her in a pool of blood. At the same time a passerby heard what sounded like a dog whining. He hurried by thinking if he had a pet, he would not treat it so unkindly. Rose heard the sound of her own pitiful voice before she blacked out. When she came to her wrists had been bandaged and voices swam over her head.

"I'd never send her away Doctor. She might be better when it's born."

"Of course, Gert but she might get worse."

"Time is a great healer. I do believe that. We'll get her right again, between us."

"Do you know who the father is, yet?"

"No, and I'm not going to let that worry me. Just so long as our Rose is safe and looked after."

"I hear Tom took the job at Greens, instead of Rose?"

"Yea, he hates it but it's more money coming in, which helps 'an all."

"Well that's good news. Good. I shall come again in a couple of days. Keep an eye open round the clock. She may try to hurt herself again."

"Oh my God, I hope not. It's been so hard, keeping it from the young 'uns."

They left the room and Rose wet herself.

Rose had always led the way in everything the twins did together. This time it felt like not only had she gone on ahead of Ruth but that she was never coming back. At the end of January it was their birthday. They were fourteen.

They had planned so many dreams together in bed at night. From the looks of things Rose would never be able to take piano lessons. As for her singing ambitions, she might as well kiss her voice goodbye. Mrs. Duthie had been true to her word. She had called at the house but it had been on a day when her mother was exceptionally busy.

"Perhaps I can call back when you have more time?"

"I'm always busy with seven mouths to feed." The death knell had sounded when she overheard the next bit of conversation.

"As a matter of fact, I think Ruth had better leave school, sooner rather than later. I'm beginning to need some more help with Rose. If you could pass that on to the headmaster, I would be grateful." Gert had shut the door on the only hope Ruth had of escaping a life of drudgery. She wept bitter tears and hardly dared look her mother in the eye for fear of giving herself away. She felt contempt for her.

The weather outside was cold and bleak, as was usually the case on their birthday. Gert could see how despondent Ruth was and so allowed her to bake a cake. She spent all morning doing it. A sponge with jam and butter cream in the middle. Two sisters, Ruth sighed, with no futures. There were no candles to blow out, no presents to open. Even Nan Bella had forgotten them. She cut two large wedges of cake. Gert gave them each a kiss and went back upstairs to do some mending.

"Happy birthday Rosie," she said, holding out the cake for her sister to take.

"Aren't you going to eat it? I baked it special for us." Rose simply stared. Ruth felt like crying but swallowed her emotion. She placed the plates side by side on the chest of drawers. The cake looked light and was still warm, fresh from the oven. Ruth sat on the bed and inspected her deranged sister. How could she get through to her? Up to this point, she and her mother had only fed, washed and dressed her and then got on with the business of the day. No one had tried talking to her to see if they could get through the barrier she had erected. The fact was that she had gone for a job interview one morning as the Rose she knew and come back, fainted and turned into a complete stranger.

"Rose, do you remember last year, how we spent our birthday, with Nan Bella? We had a big tea and then she took us to the doll museum. We loved it. Do you remember the tiny pieces of furniture inside the dolls' houses and that gorgeous, massive one? It was Georgian and our favourite."

Rose stared at the rain pelting down outside, vacant as ever. Ruth persevered.

"What about the year mum and dad took us all to the fair? We got caught up top, on the big wheel for ages. Scared to death weren't we?" Ruth caught her sister's eye with a puzzled expression in it. Ruth noticed a glimmer of some memory or recognition and so she continued.

"We had some candy floss and Johnny won two goldfish. Arthur beat Fred, at showing off his strength and Tom tasted beer out of dad's glass, for the first time. It nearly made him sick and we all laughed."

Rose turned away again. Ruth felt disappointed and angry. No birthday treat, no singing, no sister, or life worth living. She took hold of Rose by her shoulders and shook her. Then, when Rose did nothing, she slapped her across the face. When she saw the red marks erupt on her sister's cheek, she immediately felt guilty and kissed her better.

"Sorry Rose. I didn't mean to hurt you. It's your birthday. I love you. I'm so sorry." She hugged her demented twin and left the room in tears. No one was there to comfort her. Gert was having a cat nap.

Tom returned from Greens and went out again to call for Martha. The others came in and handed Ruth a couple of cards they had made at school. The house, on her birthday, hung with a despondency which no one could explain. Even the younger ones seemed tired and out of spirits. Their mother said they must be coming down with something, they were all so quiet at supper.

Ruth felt too depressed to talk and the day past into oblivion. That night she cried herself to sleep on a mattress which had been placed alongside the bed she had shared since infancy. It wasn't right for her to share a bed any longer with Rose who wet herself most nights. She had no one to talk to and wanted to curl up and die. In the distance, she could hear the sound of music coming from Ivor's bedroom. It lulled her to sleep.

Ruth truly believed that life could not get any worse. Mind numbing chores, day in day out. Nursing of the sister she had always revered was so difficult to come to terms with that she felt as though, she too, had joined the ranks of the living dead. Then her mother called a family meeting to explain that Rose was expecting a baby and that was why she had become so poorly. They all listened with mouths agape. No one, more so than Ruth who could not take it in. Tom swallowed hard and crossed his fingers, hoping that what he and Martha got up to would not result in the same thing. Johnny was the only one who seemed delighted with the news. His eyes shone behind his spectacles and he said how much he liked babies.

"We've all got to help. It's not easy for her, as you can see but she will get better."

"What shall we do then, mum?" Arthur, ever practical, piped up.

"For the moment we just have to keep an around the clock vigil."

"What's a vigil?" Jack inquired.

"It just means that we have to keep our eyes on her, so that we know she's safe."

They all nodded in agreement, feeling an importance and camaraderie they had not felt since their father died.

"Right, well, as you love babies so much, our Johnny, you can be first to sit with her. Arthur, you're next."

Johnny walked toward the bedroom with some trepidation as his mother called the rota. Once inside, he noticed a peculiar smell, a bit like the fowl house when it was his turn to clear it out. Gert was finding it increasingly hard to keep up with all the soiled sheets. Rose sat in her usual place but this time he noticed her wrists had been bandaged. He could not understand why.

He had not been told about her suicide attempt.

"Hallo Rosie. Would you like me to read to you?"

He sat on the edge of the double bed. Rose still resembled his sister which gave him some relief. However, on closer inspection, he noticed that she was wearing some sort of harness, like reins. These were keeping her strapped to the chair.

He felt confused at the sight. On his way to fetch his copy of Black Beauty which he had won in a composition competition at school, he convinced himself that his mum knew best.

Ruth's opinion of her sister altered over night when she heard the news. Every bit of compassion she felt was replaced by anger, bordering on a murderous rage toward her. For Rose to keep something as momentous as this from her felt like a betrayal. Over and over in her mind she discounted all the boys in the street. It must have happened with someone over at their nan's. At Christmas she had seemed so grown up giving out her presents. All the while she had kept her dirty secret to herself. The bare faced liar. She decided that the purgatory that was now inflicted upon her had been brought about by the wrong doings of her twin. If she suffered, then, she would make sure that Rose's life would be a complete misery too. Now, whenever Rose was set free from her chair to go to the toilet, she made it her business to be the one to tie her to it again. She secured the restraints around her sister's bulging midriff and gave an extra tug to the rags which bound her wrists.

She had never felt malicious before. The feeling scared her. Since school had been terminated on her behalf, she found no outlet for these overwhelming feelings. The only light at the end of the tunnel was the smell of Ivor's pipe smoke and his music which pervaded the upstairs rooms whenever he was in.

One night when she felt so murderous toward her sister that it frightened her, she found her way up to his bedroom and stood outside on the landing. Inside she could hear some lovely music playing which she had never heard him play before. He must have bought a new recording. Spicy aromas seeped at the same time through the cracks of the door. He was cooking his evening meal over the fire. He did this most evenings when he was at home. He realised the struggle Gert had to feed her family. Nine out of ten times he would decline the offer to join them for supper.

Ruth felt compelled to knock on the door and join him. She yearned to be made a fuss of but try as she might to knock, she felt the threatening presence of her mother, as if she was standing behind her. In reality it was Gert's mending night and she was busily stitching down below in the kitchen. After hesitating for another few minutes, she attempted to creep away but the sheer weight of her caliper on the creaking floorboards brought Ivor to the door.

"Ah...Ruth, it is you. How can I help you?" Immediately, she burst into tears at the sound of his friendly voice. He responded by placing an arm tenderly around her shoulders and led her inside. He pulled out a handkerchief from his shirt pocket.

"Sit down, sit down, warm yourself," he said plumping up a cushion on a chair next to the fire.

"S..sorry, I shouldn't have bothered you." Ruth blew her nose.

"It's no bother at all. A damsel in distress is always welcome to my humble abode." He said this with such theatricality that she smiled.

"I was just preparing my supper of sausage and mash. Would you care for some?"

She had picked at her stew and dumpling hours before and so felt hunger pangs in her stomach. What would her mother say? Well, for the moment, she would forget what she might say.

"Oh, yes please. I mean if you have enough."

"I have plenty." He beamed as he added further garlic and herbs to the meat.

Ruth relaxed a little and took a look around the bedroom. She could not believe that she was still inside her own home. It was the most splendid room she had ever seen. His furniture was unusual. The chair on which she sat was spun with a gold colour thread and was hexagonal in shape. It complimented a similarly upholstered seat beneath the window which intertwined. The love seat made her think of all the romantic heroines she saw down at the pictures and felt a growing awareness of what it might be like to have a boyfriend. These mature fantasies caused her to blush. As Ivor dished up their supper, her eyes rested on the four poster bed which hung with velvet drapes. They were drawn together like curtains at the end of a stage performance. The fireplace had been polished by her father and Ivor took great care not to neglect it. This made the rest of the house seem positively shabby and unkempt. Her uncles had helped Ivor to furnish it having been given an instruction to keep an eye open for anything romantic and well made. They liked their sister's foreign lodger even if he was a bit eccentric and had done him proud. He handed her a plate of food and sat down on a stool next to her.

"Now Ruth, why were you crying?" He tried to eat slowly, like a gentleman, but was so hungry after working a twelve hour shift that he wolfed it down and leapt up to refill his plate a second and a third time.

"I feel so awful, most of the time, shut up in this house with mum and Rose. I feel like a prisoner." She tried a mouthful of mash and liked the taste of garlic, something her mother never used. Then she continued to eat while he did the talking.

"Yes, it must be difficult for you. Rose is so unwell these days, hardly knowing who you are anymore. She's going to have a baby soon, isn't she?" Ruth blushed again. She suddenly felt disloyal.

"No one was supposed to know that, outside the family."

"I apologize for being so blunt but I couldn't help noticing the other day when I passed her in the hall on her way to the lavatory. My sisters all have children back in Poland. You do have the baby to look forward to, you know." She had not considered this before.

"What would you like it to be, boy or girl?"

"Oh, a girl. We're outnumbered by the boys, as it is."

"A girl it is then. I too have nephews and nieces. It is very nice to be an uncle. I am sure you will like being an auntie."

He drew out of his shirt pocket a leather wallet, from which he took a faded photograph. He pointed out his brothers and sisters and a row of boys and girls, sitting cross legged on the ground in front of them. They were all captured smiling broadly and had the same black hair as Ivor. Ruth liked the look of them. She wondered if they always knew what to say, like he did. She was warming to the idea of being an aunt.

"That's better. You have a lovely smile. Much better than crying."

Ruth felt more confident in his company and asked about the music he was playing.

"Mozart. Did you like it?" She nodded. "Then we shall listen again."

He took her plate and passed her an apple and some cheese. As she bit into the delicious apple he wound up the record on the turntable again and conducted the violins with his free hand. They whiled away the rest of the time, in silence, listening to Mozart.

Whenever she got the chance Ruth would escape to his room where she was introduced to Chopin, Bach and Beethoven and other classical composers. Ivor did not hold back. He complimented her voice all the time watering the seed that Jane Duthie had sown many months before.

"You have a lovely voice which should not go to waste." He introduced her to light and grand opera. In return she played the few recordings she possessed of romantic music written for shows and films. Nan Bella had bought them for her. Ruth watched his expressive face and hoped he would approve. Ivor found the sight of her clutching them to her chest very touching. Music was a vital part of her life and he felt he would have to help her if he could.

He began to change. He no longer spent so many evenings in the company of Amy, his Cockney girlfriend. He found her too common for his taste and preferred the company of Ruth. She was young and naive but full to the brim with enthusiasm for life and possessed rich ideas and talent. During the day he whistled the tunes from her records and looked forward to seeing her again. Ruth felt flattered by his attention. The school girl crush she felt for him was developing into something unfamiliar to her.

One evening, Ivor produced some roughly typed copies of poems he had written for her to read. Ruth supposed that the lyrics to the songs she sang were all the poetry she knew. That night, while Rose snored erratically, she lit the gas mantle and turned the light down as low as possible to read by. Through his poems she learned his views of the world and especially his beliefs about love. How tenderly a man should love a woman almost brought her to tears. She felt certain that her father had loved her mother in the same way. Would someone, could someone ever love her in this way? Would her deformity make it an impossibility?

Twice a year for as long as she could remember she had visited the Shoreditch Infirmary to be checked over and given the next size caliper. On her last visit she had been informed that her leg was stronger and straighter and it was time to do without an artificial aid. Part of her was excited about throwing away the ugly contraption. It had been the cause of so much sympathy from friends and neighbours all her life. "Poor little mite," she had heard too many times. It still galled her. The other part of her feared stepping out from behind the crutch which she had clung to. She wondered what it might feel like to be like all the girls down the terrace. After all, the doctor had reassured her that her legs were now fully grown and the difference in their length had become less over the years. She might always walk with a limp but that was up to her. If she persevered she might reduce it by half. Any day now she was to be fitted with a built up shoe at the hospital.

When she turned off the gas and settled down on the mattress, she wondered how it might feel to be touched by Ivor, to lie next to him on his magnificent bed. To draw the heavy curtains around them shutting out the rest of the world. It did not matter that he was twice her age. She loved him with a passion and he returned her love. The poems were a testament to that. Ruth longed to go to him but instead turned over and watched her sister sleeping in the gloomy light. She wondered if Rose had loved the father of her baby. Suddenly, she felt ashamed of herself for hating her so much.

"Sorry, Rosie", she whispered. Regret slowly eroded the anger and she wished she could share her secret with her.

Chapter 7

Jack and Bill Baldini carried on with their lives as normal. When they heard the news that George Hodgkiss was dead, they could not believe it. They left him on Christmas Eve, as far as they knew, beaten but alive. He had been groaning with pain but, they believed, far from death's door. The newspaper revealed that he had died from blows, repeatedly, to his head and from internal bleeding. Later, the coroner would report that he had choked on his own vomit and exposure to ice cold conditions had caused him to freeze to death.

They could not begin to admit to killing him. They agreed on an alibi. They were to say, if linked to the scene of the crime and questioned, that they had spent Christmas Eve sorting out paper work at their mother's. She kept their books for them and agreed to back their story. After that, they had returned to Shoreditch and from nine o'clock until closing time, had downed pints of ale at the Feathers. This last bit was true.

When Bella Baldini found out about the death, she called them to her house for a meeting. It was a large, Victorian house on a leafy street, not far from the fish market. Everything was highly polished throughout the rooms. She lived downstairs, choosing to spend most of her time playing piano in the parlour. The back room was only used when the priest called round from the Roman Catholic church, where she worshipped or when members of her music circle called to see her. It housed all of her fine bone china in a huge, walnut cabinet. The fire would be lit, dainty sandwiches consumed and copious amounts of tea drunk. Off this room was a tiny study which she used as her bedroom.

Bella had been a shrewd business woman all her life. She ran the circus' finances as well as performing acrobatics on the backs of ponies as they cantered round the ring, while Bernard flew overhead on the trapeze. Now, she let out the upstairs rooms to lodgers. The latest was a Jewish lady of means who had run away from her overbearing family. She taught at a Hebrew school for young ladies in Golders Green. She was quiet, tidied up after herself and handed over a handsome rent each week.

Bernard Baldini had died of a massive heart attack when Gert was five years old. The money from the sale of the circus made sure that Bella and their three children were well provided for. Bella became a money lender. She had neither the time nor the inclination to feel sorry for herself. Any love she may have felt for her dead husband, she now poured into her two handsome sons. She felt a deep sense of pride to live in the first house ever owned by the Baldini family.

When Jack and Bill arrived, she was more than ready for them. She had specified three o'clock which was when she drank tea and ate cakes prepared by her daughter's in law, Florrie and Maggie. A custom she had acquired on acquaintance with Ida Drew. They entered and doffed their caps. They suspected they were in for a hard time from the matriarch of the family and had been dreading it. Bella smiled. She loved her boys with a passion but today her smile was false. They were special to her, unlike Gert, who had been a daddy's girl. A daughter who had disappointed her mother. With Gert's looks and figure, she had hoped for a better marriage but she had been stubborn and insisted on Alfred Drew, the boy next door but one whom she had known since childhood. He had matured into a good enough young man but was a simple soul with no ambition. With an apprenticeship in French polishing he had been constantly in and out of work. Then, much to her disappointment, he had been a conscientious objector for which she had lost any respect she might have had for him. Her boys had gone to war and come back heroes, to tell the tale. She had been so proud of them.

Poor Gert had been left with seven children and no money. It was a disgrace. She helped out whenever she could and did her best not to forget her grandchildren's birthdays but there were too many of them. Christmas was a different matter and she enjoyed spoiling each and every one of them. However, in between, she expected her daughter to use her wits as she had had to do.

Jack and Bill smiled back at her and followed her into the parlour, kissing her in turn on the cheek. Bella raised her right hand as if to embrace them but slapped their faces instead, as hard as she could. There was no doubt in her mind that they were responsible for the death of Hodgkiss.

"Whatever possessed you to kill a man? Killers, that's what you are. My family name is disgraced. We take care of our own - yes - but we have never been involved in murder – never."

"But mother..." Jack tried to explain

"Silence - do not try to defend your actions. You and your brother have done a terrible thing and I am ashamed of both of you. You two are my life. If the police catch you..."

"They won't mother..."

"Do not speak again, until I ask you to. You do not deserve free speech, after what you have done. You may have been spotted leaving the premises. You may have dropped something that you were carrying in the fight. Any clue could lead the police straight to you." They hung their heads, like two school boys. Bella sat down and sighed.

"Some might say that he got what he deserved. I might say that myself, if it had been done properly, through a court of law. I cannot believe you took the law into your own hands and now a man's blood is on those hands."

She took a deep breath and looked from one to the other, gesturing for them to sit down.

"Now, you may speak."

"No one saw us leave, Mother. We're certain. Not a soul was about that night and as for dropping something. The only thing we dropped was a bone, to keep the dog under control."

"I don't think they'd link a gnawed old dog bone to us, Mother, do you?"

"How dare you make fun of me. You think this is a laughing matter? Well do you?"

Bill turned bright red and rubbed his head with his knuckles. He had not come up against his mother's wrath since he was a boy. She could see how uncomfortable her sons were but felt no inclination to let them off the hook.

"Do Florrie or Maggie suspect anything?"

"No, why should they? They don't know about Hodgkiss or what he did to Rosie. They don't even know Rose is pregnant. They don't see Gert or the family much these days."

"There's bound to be questions about who the father is, when she has had the baby."

Bella poured three cups of tea and handed them each a piece of cake on a plate. She was getting a headache. At her age, she should not have to think about such unpleasant matters. They sipped their tea in silence for a while.

"You two could go over to France of course, get right away and on down to Italy. We still have some family left down there. Until it all blows over."

"That would look too suspicious right now. But we've been considering emigrating to America for a while now."

"Whatever do you mean?"

"Just that we've heard they are welcoming people like us with open arms and it would be a good life out there in New York. Plenty of work for everyone."

"Have you told Maggie and Florrie about your plans?" she spat out.

"No Mother, not yet. Now this has happened, it's all had to go on the back burner."

"Well, I for one know that Florrie and Maggie wouldn't want to leave their homes. Their roots are well and truly here in London. You and your pipe dreams."

Jack and Bill glanced at each other and kept their thoughts to themselves. It did not do to rile their mother especially now after all that had happened. Bella dismissed the idea immediately from her mind as fanciful. Even though she had travelled herself and had many wonderful adventures, she could not imagine life without her sons They did so much for her. Heavy lifting and chopping wood for her fires. Their wives were like daughters to her. More so than Gert. They managed all her housework between them, for which she gave them a small wage. All she had to do was cook, shop and entertain herself.

Just then, they heard the stairs creak. It was the Jewish young lady, home early from work. All three held their breath, as they heard her footsteps on the landing. Then the bedroom door slammed shut. They wondered if she had overheard the conversation and continued in whispers.

"You see how nervous all this is making me. I cannot relax even here in my own home. Your father would turn in his grave..."

Jack and Bill felt ashamed and sat in silence.

"I will continue to pray for you. That is all I can do for now and hope that the Almighty will forgive you. Only the Lord knows what is in your hearts and if you are truly sorry."

After a long period of silence the two grown men squirmed in their seats. Bella decided to let them go back to their lives for the moment. That night while she tossed and turned in her bed, they drowned their sorrows in the Feathers.

Chapter 8

Rose gave birth on the first day of June, nineteen hundred and twenty. A girl weighing seven and a half pounds, with a mass of black hair and a heartbroken wail. She was normal with all her fingers and toes. Gert got down on her knees and thanked the Lord. She had feared the worst after such an abnormal confinement.

The day was hot and stuffy. Ivor found an off cut of wood to prop open the bedroom window. Rose had been her usual catatonic self. Doctor White was duly summoned as soon as Gert noticed some blood in her daughter's drawers. Her own births had begun the same way. First a show, followed by a flood of water and then a need to promptly push away the pain. None of her own had taken as long as this one, however, to come into the world. They had all seemed eager to get out and join their siblings.

Gert cleared away the bloodied sheets, towels and bowl of water and came in to study Rose, slumped against her pillows. She had grown to gigantic proportions toward the end of her pregnancy. Sitting, day in, day out had done her no favours. Her appetite had gone from one extreme to the other. Gert hoped that an increased interest in food meant a growing interest in life and she was coming back to them.

Doctor White rolled his shirt sleeves down and checked her pulse. It was still racing. He felt very strained. The birth had been an ordeal for all of them. Thank God it was over with the child safely delivered. At one time, he feared he might lose both of them. He glanced across at Ruth, who was rocking the baby, gently, in her arms. She had dressed her in a long, cotton nighty and wrapped her in a crocheted shawl which they had all worn before her.

Ruth had seen too much for a girl of her age but she had been tirelessly helpful. As competent as a trainee nurse, she had administered water to her sister and kept her cool. She had even sung lullabies to try and calm her down. Now, she thrived on taking care of her niece. Gert had been busy too fetching and carrying hot water and towels and uttering words of encouragement to her daughter throughout. When the doctor groped around inside for the afterbirth, Rose refused to oblige him with one final push.

A silence hung over the room. The contrast between what they had all just witnessed and now felt overwhelming. They were all in shock. For almost six months Rose had not uttered a single word nor shed a solitary tear. As she became bigger Gert trusted her more and became lenient with the restraints. Rose took to wandering the house as if in search of something. Once Gert found her listening outside the kitchen to their conversations within. Gert would glare at the boys if they laughed too long or loud. She hated Rose to think she was a figure of fun so spontaneous laughter had all but been banished from the house. Rose had become a cuckoo in the nest which they all resented. Just before the birth her walkabouts had stopped.

As her labour pains intensified, Rose grew more and more agitated. It was coming. It was splitting her in two as it reared its ugly head. At first, she thrashed around on the bed, whipping her head from side to side. Then as everyone tried to reassure her, the dormant volcano finally erupted, spewing forth a lava flow of abuse, hatred, fear and hostility. Rose believed she was about to die.

Gert could not believe how many oaths her daughter knew. She sounded like the Irish navvies who were digging the new roads out of London.

"I'm dying. The bastard's killing me. It's tearing me apart. You, you bitch, help me."

Doctor White took out a wooden instrument from his bag and offered it to her to bite down on. This she did from time to time, for which they were all grateful. When the contractions became unbearable, she spat it aside and began again.

"It's all your fault, you old mare. You shouldn't have sent me. She let him do it to me. You old whore."

Gert felt shocked and embarrassed and could not make any sense of her daughter's ranting. All of the doctor's instructions went unheeded and when she hollered at Rose to stop pushing and pant while they turned the baby's head, Rose pushed even harder. Gert witnessed her daughter tear, horribly.

She had never seen so much blood. Rose continued to strain. Ruth cried hysterically while their mother held out a towel at the foot of the bed, ready to catch the new born. After a final, horrifying push, when it seemed that Rose might pass out with all the debilitating effort, the baby girl slid onto the towel.

Gert handed her granddaughter to the doctor who took her with trembling hands and slapped her on her crumpled bottom. She let out a whooping cry which sounded like a minor imitation of her mother. Ruth instantly asked to hold her. Only out of the corner of her eye, did she dare look at the creature in the bed, slumped and semi- conscious. With the baby cradled in her arms, she walked away from her sister, to the furthest corner of the bedroom. The new life seemed to represent a fresh start for her. Ruth felt more than willing to turn her back on the old one.

Rose refused to have anything to do with her baby. The first time Gert offered the child to her, she screamed and blacked her mother's eye. After that Gert and Ruth took total responsibility. When Rose's breasts became engorged with milk, she seemed oblivious. It leaked out and seeped through all her clothes. As much as Gert hoped to help her daughter, she dare not approach her. The milk went to waste. Rose no longer trusted the two people she loved most in the world and the feeling was mutual. The baby stayed with Ruth all day and at night slept in a cradle beside her grandmother. Ruth felt complete. A man to love and a baby to take care of was an antidote to the sadness she felt over the abrupt end to her school life. She took on the role of mother, willingly and was grateful to Rose for making it so easy for her. She did not feel guilty. Instead, she held onto the only part of her sister that she could nurture. She enjoyed the constant round of nappy changes, nursing, bathing, dressing and playing with her niece.

During the summer evenings, when all her maternal duties had been carried out and the baby was sound asleep, Ruth sat outside in the yard with Ivor. They chatted until dark. It amused them to hear Jack or Johnny complaining about being sent to bed, too early.

"It's still light mum, can't sleep."

"I'm sweating mum, can't sleep."

"Turn over and get to sleep or I'll come in there and box both your ruddy ears."

"But mum..."

"But nothing...if you wake the baby up. I'm warning you."

Eventually, after much grumbling and thrashing around, they would settle down.

A month passed and still no name had been chosen for her. Ivor thought it to be in poor taste. Where he came from, babies were christened immediately with two or three Christian names. He decided to broach the subject with Ruth.

"Me and Mum have had some chats about names but we feel rotten. It's Rose's choice, after all. We just keep hoping she'll get better and then she can pick a name herself."

"But it may take a long time and the baby can't wait forever. You are more like a mother to her, Ruth. What names do you like?"

"There is one. We were learning about George III at school, before I left and he was married to Queen Charlotte. I think it's a lovely name and we could shorten it to Lottie."

"Lottie. Little Lottie. That sounds very nice."

They sat in silence. Ruth wondered what Tom and Martha were up to, while Ivor was thinking if only he was the right age for Ruth. How wonderful it would be. Before she realized what she was saying, the words were out of her mouth.

"Ivor, do you think Tom loves Martha?"

"I don't know but they do spend a lot of time together. I expect that must mean something."

Like us, she thought. "Tell me about your life, in Poland."

"Again?"

"Yes, I love the sound of it."

"Well, I am from a large family and I am the second eldest. My papa was a farmer and my mother helped out on the farm. They worked very hard, from morning until night but were never too tired to spend time with us in the evenings. He played the piano and she played the violin and we would sing. In winter we had deep falls of snow and we would ski over the fields, to the bibliotheque and to school and back. We liked to ice skate on the lakes.

My eldest brother saved my life once when I disappeared through a sudden crack in the ice."

"You've never told me that before," she said horrified. Ruth immediately felt fond of this older brother.

"We had straw fights in the huge old barn. Our mother allowed us to sleep out there. It was a great life for a boy."

"What brought you to foggy, old London?"

"I always loved the thought of seeing the world and having adventures, so I ran away to sea. I've seen many countries and many dirty ports but when we docked here, I knew I had to stay and find out what all the fuss was about. The atmosphere was fantastic and the people were so friendly. I felt at home."

"You've never wanted to go back?"

"Oh yes, one day I shall return but only for a visit."

"Do you write to your parents, to let them know you are safe?"

"Often. They know all about the Drew family."

Ruth felt proud but dare not ask him how much they knew about her friendship with their son.

"Who taught you how to write poetry, so well?"

"Oh, I'm not sure it is good but on long, dark nights at sea, I would find my thoughts easy to put down on paper and so I scribbled away." He laughed modestly.

"I hope you will be published, one day."

"When, and if I am, I shall look you up. I hope you will accept my humble offering of a book of poetry." Ruth smiled. She couldn't see into the future but for now, she was content with her lot. Even though her leg felt lighter without the caliper she hated the ugly black shoes she had to wear. Ivor never let her down always being on hand to give her words of encouragement by telling her how well she was doing.

"Don't look down Ruth. Hold your head high. That's it. Forget. Like when you sing."

Gert watched Ruth and Ivor together. Theirs was a true friendship. She felt so grateful to him for giving up his spare time to help her. Every night for weeks he had held onto her hands and led her round the small garden, instilling a new strength in her. Ruth trusted him completely and with her growing confidence was learning to balance her body in order to walk properly for the first time in her life.

Chapter 9

When August came, it was scorching hot. Nineteen twenty, they said, had produced one of the hottest summers in living memory. The houses on the terrace were swarming with flies. They had never had to contend with so many. Nothing escaped them. Meat that usually stayed fresh in the pantry, was soon over run with maggots and stinking the place out. If someone died, they had to be nailed down sooner than usual in the front parlour. All the toddlers and babies down the terrace screamed at the tickling sensation as the flies landed on them throughout the day. Lottie was no exception. In her cotton dresses and bonnets she looked the bonniest baby Gert had ever seen but her incessant wailing wore her out. The heat was getting them all down. As soon as this infestation died away the emergence of wasps became the new nuisance. Every garden had its own array of jars, with jam or honey inside, to lure them to their sticky deaths. The worst was yet to come.

Bugs. The annual outing of the East Ends arch enemy was just around the corner. They were anticipated with dread. Bugs that fed on wall paper paste were soon to be unleashed. Gert tried to prepare for their arrival, in advance, by washing all the walls down with buckets of Lysol water, recommended to kill the creatures stone dead.

On one exceptionally hot day, she and Ruth were to be found wearing overalls and turbans. Buckets containing the lethal mixture were painstakingly heaved from room to room. Ruth was just as determined to exterminate them as her mother but Gert was carrying out most of the work. She soldiered on, carrying Ruth's bucket whenever it became too much for her. By lunch time, they were so overcome with the heat that a strip wash was necessary in the kitchen. Gert tried to ignore the pain in her arm and chest. When they were back in their clothes, she unlocked the back door and enjoyed the breeze, blowing fresh air throughout the house.

Rose seemed to behave herself more since Lottie had been born. She sat without restraints, ate all her food, without making too much mess, even feeding herself at times. When Johnny read to her, Rose seemed to enjoy it. Gert felt certain that she was making a recovery.

Rose felt lighter after giving birth. The monster was gone from her insides. She was not so high up on the Ferris wheel. The wall was slowly being dismantled between herself and the world. Some days, she tried to make sense of what had happened to her by talking to herself, aloud. Everything from hop picking to giving birth was being worked into a kind of surreal pattern and fitted together like a jigsaw.

On these days, her family felt uncomfortable around her and left her to it, in the confines of her bedroom. As she mulled it over, Hodgkiss took more and more of a back seat somewhere in the recesses of her mind.

After a cup of tea with Ruth in the kitchen, Gert felt optimistic.

"Tell you what, now we've finished, what say we take our Rosie out for a walk round the block?"

"Do you mean it, Mum?"

"Course I do. She's been good lately. I feel so sorry for her, cooped up, day in day out. Shall we try?"

"Oh yes, Mum. That would be marvellous."

When they started out, Gert warned them that she was tired, so they would venture no further than once round the block. Rose seemed to understand and held onto her mother's arm, willingly. The terrace was fairly quiet with most children down at the cut, swimming to cool themselves off. A few women were out on the front, cleaning windows, washing steps or beating carpets. Others were still battling inside with the bugs. Some smiled or waved, sweat dripping from their flushed faces.

Gert held her head high. Judge her all they might, she would not allow her shame to get the better of her. It felt a miracle to be out with her two daughters, after what they had all suffered for months. The breeze kept them cool and they squinted against the sunlight. She felt proud of herself and her family. They had pulled Rose through. As they walked, Gert patted Rose's hand for reassurance while Ruth pushed the pram.

After a while, places and things began to look familiar to Rose and she recognized where she was. They were going in the direction of Spitalfields and Nan Drew's house.

"Nan Drew."

They stopped. Gert exchanged glances with Ruth. They could not believe it. She had spoken for the first time, in the voice they remembered, neither mumbling nor menacing.

"Yes, Lovie. This is the way to your Nan's."

"Can we go?"

"Well Ruthie, what do you reckon? Will your leg hold out?" Gert could not stop herself from mollycoddling her daughter, even though there had been a vast improvement in her mobility. " 'Course Mum."

Half an hour later they arrived at the home of Ida Drew. As usual she was asleep with her mouth wide open. They had not seen her since the birth. This surprised Gert. She knew how much the old girl loved babies. She lifted Lottie out of the pram. The sisters watched their nan stir and glance up, bemused. Her routine had been disturbed but she called to them to come round, through the back gate.

After the twins had been sent to make tea, she inspected her great granddaughter and liked what she saw. She was pretty and growing well.

"So how is Rose now, Gert?"

"I can't believe it, Ida. I really think she's going to be all right."

"Well that's good news" and she placed the baby on her foot and bounced her up and down, singing 'Ride a Cock Horse' in a rasping voice. Gert felt light hearted for the first time in many months. Rose and Ruth brought the tea things in and they all sipped their tea. Each one took it in turn to hold the baby except Rose who watched her from a safe distance.

"Well girls, there's a tanner - go and treat yourselves." They checked their mother's face to see if that was all right. Gert nodded her approval. She had to give Rose her freedom back sometime. The weather was fine and she was with Ruth.

While they were gone, Ida poured more tea and asked after her daughter in law's health. She noticed how worn out the younger woman looked. Gert said she couldn't complain and kept her ailments to herself.

After a few moments of silence, Ida found her mind wandering back to the year before, when Rose had stayed with her. Even now, she didn't know if Gert knew who the father was. She believed that Gert neglected important details. She would have made more time for her children had she been given the chance. There was more to being a good mother than merely feeding and watering them.

"So, did you ever find out who the father was?"

"No, Ida and it don't matter. If he's worth his salt he would have come forward but he ain't. Anyway, we don't need him."

Ida Drew was tired and irritable, and was still seething over Gert's decision to send Rose hop picking, in the first place. It was out before she knew it.

"It was that foreman, Hodgkiss. He forced himself on her."

Gert's tea spilled into her lap.

"You what? No...he couldn't be...how do you know anyway. What makes you so sure?"

There was a malicious streak in the old girl. She had always been jealous of her daughter in laws fertility. Now she felt, for once, she had the upper hand.

"Rose broke down here one day last year when she was staying with me. She confided in me."

She looked triumphant. This last statement pierced at the very heart of Gert. Her children could always confide in her, right down to Jack, her baby. Surely they knew that. Guilt gripped her insides and she blamed herself for always being too busy.

"He interfered with her. The baby's his."

They both looked at Lottie, so small, so perfect, asleep and innocent. To think she had been born of a rape. It felt unbearable and Gert began to cry.

Now Ida had the upper hand, she went for the jugular, twisting the knife as she pushed it all the way in.

"And he a murdered man," she tutted.

Gert looked at the wicked old woman through her tears and noticed a guilty expression sweep over her wrinkled face. In an instant, she began to feel dread. She knew how her family operated.

"Ida, tell me the truth, do you know anything about that? Rose told me my mum and brothers visited you one day."

"You may as well know, you've every right. It was Jack and Bill that did it. They didn't mean to but they got carried away."

Gert felt the life ebb away from her legs as she took a step backwards and landed on the horsehair sofa, with a thump.

"Just got carried away…they killed a man for God's sake."

"Yes they did. It's unfortunate but he had it coming. He was scum."

She could not stay and listen to anymore cold and calculated reasoning. She quickly placed Lottie back into her pram in the hall.

"I need some air. I'll let myself out."

When she got outside, she found Ruth down on one knee, trying to console her sister. Rose had flopped down onto the path and burst into tears. She was rocking herself backwards and forwards.

"What happened?"

"I was chasing her and you know she's always faster than me. By the time I got to Nan's gate, Rose had gone inside. Then she ran back out and had hysterics. It must be the heat, Mum."

Gert knew exactly what it was. Rose had overheard the conversation indoors. The pain in her chest was getting much worse. Now, she had to get Rose all the way back to the terrace. Ruth couldn't understand her sister's sudden collapse. It had been a lovely afternoon. Just like old times.

Chapter 10

Gert decided not to tell the doctor about the increasing pain in her chest. She guessed, correctly, that he would insist on sending her to the hospital for some tests, which would mean spending time away from her family. She also decided not to send any of her children hop picking again. Their lives had changed too dramatically since the previous year and she would not let them out of her sight.

Rose had been on a steady decline since the outing to her nan's house. Her hands were never still and she had taken to slapping her head. Something seemed to be brewing in Rose. As she punished herself, she tried to make sense of what she had overheard that afternoon. Hodgkiss had been murdered by her uncles for molesting her. Her thoughts became wilder and took on a life of their own. She neither ate nor slept. It was as if Hodgkiss hounded her day and night for revenge. Her uncles were every bit as bad as him. At least he hadn't killed anybody. They were worse than him. Murderers. An eye for an eye and a tooth for a tooth. He hounded her for revenge, day and night. Her warped reasoning came up with a plan. Perhaps, if she did this one last thing for him, he would give her peace.

Almost a year to the day of the rape, Rose was listening for sounds in the house. All her brothers had left for school, Tom for work. Ruth and her mother were in the kitchen, making bread, up to their elbows in flour. Rose got up from her chair. Her fingers worked deftly, sliding a hair grip out from its secret place, in the lining of her carpet slippers. She had become adept at unpicking the lock on the bedroom door and soon heard it click. In the hall, she grabbed the nearest coat and hat off a peg and pulled them on, over her nighty. They belonged to her mother and were several sizes too big. Rose left the house, alone, for the first time since she had become ill.

The police station was not far away. A ten minute walk in the opposite direction to the Feathers. The sergeant behind the desk had just settled down to read the paper when Rose pushed through the doors. He batted the smoke away from his pipe to take a closer look at the young woman, seemingly done up for some cold weather. The thermometer behind him read seventy degrees. John Smith was a kind man who took his job seriously but with an air of friendly humour. He knew what it was like to grow up the hard, tough way but had always wanted to be on the side of law and order. He was content after walking the beat for many years to spend his time, up to retirement, behind the desk. After promotion to sergeant came a transfer from his beat in Limehouse to Shoreditch. He was still getting used to the local faces.

As Rose approached the counter, he began to see she was no more than a girl. When she glanced up at him, he saw how hot and sweaty she looked beneath the coat. Rose was pale and out of breath. She cleared her throat. The words she had been practicing on her way began to take shape inside her mouth.

"I know who murdered Hodgkiss. It was Jack and Bill Baldini, my uncles," she mumbled to herself.

He stood up and placed his paper, gently, on the desk. With one stride, he faced her on the other side of the counter. He beamed down at her.

"Yes, Miss and what can I do for you?" His voice boomed, filling the entire space. Rose took a couple of steps backwards and began to feel intimidated. He sensed her nervousness and said in a softer, more caring tone of voice:

"What brings you here today, my dear?"

Her heart rate slowed down, gradually, as she glanced from side to side and behind her. There was no one else about. He ran his eye over her. She looked as though she might suffocate in the hat and coat. They, obviously, did not belong to her.

"Would you like to sit down a minute?" he asked as he lifted a section of the counter which had divided them and stepped through.

Rose looked down at her slippers and began ringing her hands. It was wrong to have come here. John Smith seemed like a black giant, looming over her head.

"My uncles murdered him."

"Who my dear?"

Rose felt a slapping fit coming on but rubbed her hands together instead. He felt very sorry for her.

"Would you like to take your coat and hat off a minute? It's very warm today. I could get you a glass of water."

She glanced over her shoulder at the doors. She needed to escape. The sergeant walked back through the counter. He poured her a glass of water. It sounded refreshing. Rose felt thirsty and took the glass from the counter, where he had placed it. John Smith watched at a distance. She drank every drop and put it back again.

"I think I'll join you," he said and he poured himself a glass and also downed it in one, wiping the drops from around his mouth with the back of his hand.

"Another for you?"

Rose shook her head. "Your uncles murdered someone you say?"

"Hodgkiss", she hissed.

The sergeant glanced at the poster on the wall, above her head which was offering a £100 reward for information which might lead to this man's killer. No one had come up with a single clue and now this young girl was grassing on her own kin.

"What did you say their names were?"

Rose repeated them.

"How do you know?"

"Heard Nan tell Mum."

"And who is your mum?"

"Gert."

"Gert who?"

Rose became confused. Suddenly, she wondered if her mother would be pleased or angry with her over this. Her mind raced as quickly as her pulse. Rose felt desperate to be at home, safe in her chair by the window. At that moment a rowdy drunk was manhandled through the doors by a bobby on the beat. John Smith intercepted and helped lead him away which was just enough time for her to make her escape. By the time the drunk had been placed in a cell to sober up, Rose had disappeared. She half ran, half stumbled back to Weymouth Terrace. Like a fox gone to earth she made it safely back to her bolt hole.

Fortunately, Gert and Ruth had been too preoccupied to notice her gone. She slipped the hat and coat back on the stand and seated herself in the window again. Not long after, she heard the familiar sound of her sister singing as she came to inspect her.

"Hallo, hallo, must have forgotten to lock the door," she said, light heartedly. "Anyway, no harm done. You look a bit hot and bothered, our Rosie. Perhaps you're coming down with something," she muttered, absentmindedly, as she propped open the window to let some air in. With Lottie dangling from her hip, Ruth left the room singing a nursery rhyme. Rose heard the key turn in the lock and Ruth's footsteps on the stairs. She felt exhausted. Soon she fell asleep.

The unholy racket outside on the terrace woke up half the neighbours. Curtains twitched and gas mantles glimmered as curiosity got the better of Gert's so called friends. Whatever was happening to her and her family, they wondered? Half pitying, half suspecting that she brought it on herself, they stared out at the free entertainment.

Florrie Baldini was the cause of the commotion. The small, buxom woman was terrier like in her insistence and was not about to release her prey. She kicked, punched and slapped the door, rattling the knocker loose, as she screamed to be let in. Gert opened it, fearfully.

"Right, where is she, the mad little bitch? I'll kill her when I lay my hands on her."

"Who do you mean, Florrie? Whatever's happened?"

"Whatever's happened?" Her voice rose to fever pitch. She pushed past Gert to the room where her nieces slept but her way was barred.

"You'd better get out of my way."

"I'm not going anywhere until I know what you are going on about."

"It's your Rosie, the little traitor. The cow bag's only gone and told the police that my Bill's a murderer. That rag and bone man who was found on Christmas Eve. I know she's gone barmy but this is the last straw. She needs locking up."

"Florrie, try and calm down. I'll put the kettle on."

"Calm down. How can I? The police came round to arrest him and they've got Jack an' all. Maggie's in a right old state. She's got the kids at hers. It's a pack of lies, Gert. How can I calm down?"

The more Gert talked to Florrie, the more her temper was subsiding. She could hear the girls stirring on the other side of the door and the boys were spying on them from up on the landing. She gently nudged her toward the kitchen and whispered in a threatening tone of voice, for them to all go back to bed.

"She'll go to hell for this. What a wicked little liar."

Gert lit a match underneath the kettle and installed her sister in law on a chair, nearest the stove. With a deep breath, she placed two cups on the table and sat down opposite.

"Florrie, I hate to have to tell you this...but it's true. Jack and Bill did do it."

Quickly she added, to soften the blow that they had not meant to. Florrie stared, open mouthed, speechless and then turned away, bringing her arms and head down with a thud onto the table.

"'Ere stop that. You'll give yourself a growth."

Gert comforted Florrie as best she could. Her nightdress became sodden with the smaller woman's hysterical tears.

"What am I gonna do Gert, with him in gaol and me with three mouths to feed?"

The same as me with seven mouths to feed, she thought but kept it to herself.

"There, there, love. It might not come to that."

"But it will. They'll hang for it as sure as God made little apples and it's down to your Rose." Her temper was mounting again.

"Rose isn't in her right mind these days, Flo, you're right but I can't imagine when she would have told the police. We keep a watch on her and we've started locking her in again. She hardly utters a word."

"Well, she got out and now my life's in tatters. As soon as they said it was Bill's niece who had come forward acting strangely, giving them names and then disappearing, I knew it had to be her. I can't believe it. My Bill couldn't do a thing like that. Why, what for?"

"Well it couldn't have been Ruth, she's always with me."

"Oh, I'm not daft - I asked whether she had a limp or not and they said no. So there's no mistake - it was Rose."

"Drink your tea, Florrie and stay the rest of the night. You say Maggie's got the kids?"

"Yea," she whimpered.

"You can kip in with me till light and then get back to them."

The hurricane had blown itself out, just as Gert knew that it would. She helped Florrie upstairs to her bedroom.

The next morning, Gert took her a cup of tea and comforted her again.

"You mustn't be angry Flo with Bill. He and Jack only did what they thought was right."

"I just don't get it." The buxom woman gazed into her tea as if it was poison.

"Florrie. Hodgkiss forced himself on our Rose. He's the baby's father."

"Oh my God."

"I know. How do think I feel? All I know, is that my brothers did what they thought was right and it backfired on them."

"But why did she tell on them? You'd think she'd be grateful for what they did."

Gert shrugged her shoulders. That she could not answer. One of life's mysteries. Perhaps it always would be. She left Florrie sipping her tea and went downstairs to the kitchen. It felt as cold as a mortuary. The boys sat in silence. Tom took the lead.

"Mum, why would Rosie make up a story like that?"

Gert could not put off explanations any longer. Her children deserved her honesty. She sighed deeply and took her place at the head of the table.

"Now, you're all old enough to know the truth but I don't want this to go any further. Do you understand? No one, outside the family must know from us. They'll know soon enough. First of all, when you went hop picking, did you see Hodgkiss with Rose?"

They all shook their head, surprised at the question.

"Well he hurt her so much she suffered a trauma. What you don't know is, he was the father of the baby. Your uncles were so angry that they gave him a good thrashing which was no more than he deserved. No doubt about that."

All the boys nodded in agreement.

"Trouble is they went too far. That's what you heard Aunt Florrie raving about last night. Fact is, Rose shopped them to the police and now they're behind bars."

Tom let out a long, low whistle. Jack stared horrified. Arthur and Fred, ever practical, wondered if they would be able to work for their uncles now. It had always been their ambition to do so. Johnny could not help himself. His imagination was working overtime. Sworn to secrecy, they each left the house. Ruth was yet to discover the truth about her sister. Gert thanked God that Ivor had stayed out the night. She would keep it from him for as long as possible. She felt so ashamed.

Florrie left the house in a stupefied state and Gert made Lottie's first bottle of the day. As she did, a searing pain rushed along the length of her left arm. Try as she might to reach her medicine cupboard for the smelling salts she was unable. Gert collapsed onto the kitchen floor.

Rose and Ruth woke up to a silent house. Ruth got dressed and went to open the bedroom door. It was still locked. After yelling to be released and getting no response, she decided to climb out of the bedroom window. Rose, meanwhile, appeared at her side with a grip. Ruth could not believe it. She witnessed her deranged sister unpicking the lock. So that was how she had escaped time after time. She smiled at her and gave her a hug. Rose yawned and got back into bed.

Ruth heard Lottie upstairs in her cot, crying for her bottle. Something was wrong. She found her mother on the floor of the kitchen. Doctor White was there almost immediately. Through her tears, she heard him explain that she hadn't suffered. The massive heart attack had taken her quickly. She must be a brave girl. He would send word to her grandmothers. They would come soon. Tom was fetched from Greens. They were a family and must all stick together.

Gert was laid out in an open coffin in the parlour, until the day of the funeral. The children visited her each afternoon after school. Tom after work.

Some cried while others were too shocked to feel anything. They held hands. Sometimes, Ivor would say a prayer over the body to comfort them. Rose was kept away. Doctor White advised that it was too much of a risk to allow her to see their mother. She would not be able to grasp the situation.

Ruth went about doing the chores and minding Lottie, until Ivor came home from work. Stoically, she carried on, as she knew her mother would want her to. In the day, when the house was quiet, she entered the candlelit parlour and spent time alone with her mother. It neither frightened her nor made her cry. The time felt precious. It felt natural to be with her, even in death. They had spent so much time in each other's company. The parlour had been kept for high days and holidays. Events which the Drew household could hardly ever afford. Every Monday since leaving school, she had followed Gert around the house. The parlour furniture received the most elbow grease from her mother's ample arms while Ruth flicked away cobwebs from the corners of the room with a feather duster.

"This would fetch a few bob, you know, Ruthie", she would inform her.

"I ought to flog the lot and put the money by for a rainy day."

Ruth knew that Nan Bella had given the walnut dresser, table and chairs to her mother as a wedding gift. She knew how much her mother treasured it. There were always rainy days in their house but the furniture remained where it was. No one ever came to the house to buy it.

The night before the funeral, Ruth took her mother's small, cold hand in her own.

"Don't worry anymore, Mum. I'll look after them all. The boys are nearly big enough to fend for themselves, anyway. Rose and Lottie won't come to any harm, with me and Ivor looking out for them. You just rest and soon you'll be in heaven with Dad. Give him our love."

The next morning, Nan Bella arrived at six o'clock in a taxicab to sort out the children for their mother's funeral. She, like Nan Drew, wore black from head to toe. Edwardian skirts and jackets with heavily veiled hats which concealed their red rimmed eyes. Soon, all the boys were dressed in their Sunday best. She had bought only one black dress for Ruth, as Rose was not allowed to attend the funeral. She was going to be minded by Martha's mother for the duration along with Lottie.

The procession was led by the two grandmothers. Behind them walked

Ivor and Florrie and last of all the children. They followed the coffin, placed inside a glass hearse, pulled by a horse wearing a black plume. Everyone came out onto the terrace to wave her off. It was early October and warm. Gert had predicted an Indian summer. A gentleman from over the way was crying. He blew his nose into a big, white handkerchief, muttering that she was one in a million and the sun always shines on the righteous. Others doffed their caps and women removed their overalls and aprons. One of their own, taken from them for no reason and so young. Many wept, holding onto their nearest and dearest. The woman who assisted in Wormleightons sweet shop prayed devoutly, using a rosary. Her boss had shut his shop for the day, while the Feathers was going to close earlier that night, out of respect. The pawn shops would remain open for business. The people needed them for survival. Gert would have understood.

By the time they reached All Saint's Church, they were hot and sticky. Tom wiped his tears away when he saw Martha in the crowd. Bella swallowed hard. She knew her daughter had been made old before her time and wondered how she had managed to survive at all. With only money made from washing, mending and a single lodger, would have seen them all in the workhouse, sooner or later. She chose to feel angry with her for not inheriting her business acumen. It was easier than feeling the guilt, she would, otherwise, have been riddled with. After the short service, the reverend laid Gert to rest. All the boys sobbed at the side of the grave. Ruth comforted her brothers feeling too numb to cry. The sun shone brilliantly on their way back and the boys loosened their ties. Their faces were grimy from crying so much.

The adults stayed indoors while the children sat outside on the steps. Each had a sandwich in one hand and a fairy cake in the other, baked the previous day by Nan Drew. Martha's mum said that Rose behaved herself while Lottie slept in her arms, the whole time they were gone. She hurried back to her own brood.

After several cups of tea, Florrie had a suggestion to make.

"Now, I know it's early days but...well..I'm trying to think of a solution. I'm prepared to take Johnny and the other two, Fred and Arthur. That means I'll be up to six mouths to feed."

"Of course, Tom has his own plans," Ivor spoke up. Tom had always found Ivor a willing friend and confidante.

"What's that, then?"

"He is going to marry Martha and move in there."

"Well, that's one less to have to worry about," Bella sighed. "What about the girls and Jack?"

"Maggie said she'd take Ruth and Jack. She's no bother. Anyway, she was a lovely little helper to her mum. God rest her soul." Florrie blew hard into a lace handkerchief and dabbed her eyes.

"What about Rose and her baby?" Ivor was not a man to beat about the bush.

Florrie grew tight lipped and quiet. They all read her mind. She wanted nothing to do with Rose or her bastard.

"Well, you know I love Rose the best of the bunch but since she's gone off her rocker, I think she ought to go away." Ida Drew piped up. Ivor felt very sorry for the girl and spoke up in her defense.

"Couldn't someone take them? What about you Mrs. Baldini?"

"Absolutely not. It's going to be bad enough attending the court when the trial starts. How can I be expected to nurse a sick mother and a baby day in day out. I agree with Ida. She should go away for her own good."

"Let's face it," Florrie summed up. "She should have had proper treatment, right from the word go but Gert was stubborn. God rest her soul. I don't like to talk ill of the dead but she kept her at home until terrible things happened."

"Do sing another tune, Florrie," Bella sniped, tired of her whining and feeling protective of her daughter's memory.

"Right, that's settled then, apart from the baby," Ida reminded them.

"Perhaps Maggie will take her if Ruth looks after her," Ivor suggested.

A silence hung over the parlour. Few tears were shed. It grew dusky. Florrie was the first to hurry away to break the news to Maggie. The others dispersed, glad to leave. Without Gert's warm, hospitable presence the family home had deteriorated to a shell of its former self.

One by one, the fate of those sitting out on the steps had been decided.

A week later Ruth took Ivor to one side as he waited outside on the pavement for Arthur and Fred. They were going to help him carry his furniture and possessions to the Feathers where Ivor was going to live for the foreseeable future.

"I know we haven't had much time lately to talk but before we say goodbye, Ivor…"

"What is it Ruth…?"

"Well, I feel so ashamed of my family after all that's happened. I'd hate for you to think badly of us…" Ruth began to cry and he embraced her not wanting to let her go.

He felt confused about their relationship. She would be living with Jack and Lottie at her Aunt Maggie's. Perhaps it was time for him to forget about her. She was far too young for him and a man of his age should know better than to string a young girl along. At the same time, a glint of hope remained in his heart. He battled with his conflicted feelings and said.

"Your uncles made a mistake and now they will have to pay for it."

Ruth cried harder. "I'll never understand why Rose did what she did. Perhaps it's right that she's going away. Perhaps they'll cure her in the hospital."

"I sincerely hope so." Ivor kissed her on the forehead and then lugged a chest of drawers onto his shoulder. He was soon joined by her brothers. Ruth gazed after him till he turned the corner by the Feathers and disappeared from her sight.

Chapter 11

Ruth woke up with her worst headache to date. She felt for lumps and counted three. All at the back of her head, where Maggie had swung her punches. It was pitch black inside the coal shed. The smell and taste of soot made her cough. She was too upset and weary to call out for help. There was hardly any air and she was scared of choking. Then she remembered Lottie and Jack and began to panic. Where were they? What had she done to them? She understood perfectly why Maggie hated her. The resemblance to Rose caused her loathing. She told her so, repeatedly.

She could just make out it was dawn, as a watery sunlight filtered underneath the door. She had lost count of the beatings she had been victim of in the two weeks since her uncles were convicted of murder at the Old Bailey.

Two or three times a week, while the case was being tried, they had attended the court. Nan Bella had laid on transport for them all but had not attended herself. They met up with Florrie and their young cousins outside and sat in the public gallery. Sometimes, Arthur, Fred and Johnny were allowed to miss work and school to attend. Ruth was always glad to be reunited with them, even under the circumstances. With Lottie on her knee, she listened to the prosecution strategically dismantle any defense offered to the judge and jury.

In cold blood, they heard, the rag and bone man had been beaten to death. The fact that he had been guilty of molesting the defendants' niece seemed to carry no weight and were insufficient mitigating circumstances. The fact that Rose Drew could not be called as a witness made their side of the story almost irrelevant. Even if she had been of sound mind, there was no evidence to suggest that she had not given her consent to fornicate. At this,

Ruth felt outraged. Her poor sister's name was being trampled into the mire. At one point, had it not been for Tom's intervention, she would have been held in contempt of court for speaking her mind. Ruth was still trying to come to terms with her sister being sent away.

On sentencing day, Jack and Bill faced a judge wearing a black cap. The sight of which caused Florrie to faint. Maggie sobbed. The Baldini brothers, their husbands, were to hang by the neck until dead and may God have mercy on their souls.

Maggie was a tall woman, built much like a man, with a flat chest and broad shoulders. She was plain, unlike her sister in law. Florrie always wore makeup and had her hair frizzed. Despite this, she had a round, dependable face and appeared to be of solid character. The things she prized above appearance, were good, hearty meals on the table and a laugh and a joke with her children. At first Ruth had seen this side of her aunt, as she willingly did all the chores she was given to do. Jack went to school as normal. Ruth missed Ivor but tried to put girlish desires out of her mind. She missed her mother and still cried herself to sleep but was grateful for a roof over her head.

Then, Maggie changed profoundly. It began with feeding her own children and allowing Ruth, Jack and Lottie to go hungry, as if she no longer noticed them. As if she were trying to block them out. Ruth was so hungry at times that she would steal leftovers and share them with her brother. While Maggie dozed, she stole milk and cake from the pantry for Lottie, who howled much of the day with hunger pains.

As well as the neglect, Maggie became physically cruel. She pinched and slapped Lottie. Her nappies were never aired properly. Her clothes were always the last to be washed in the dolly tub. Ruth was not allowed to look after, play with or cuddle her.

On one of her nightly pilgrimages to the pantry, she was met at the foot of the stairs by her aunt who had been asleep in the kitchen.

"Been at my pantry, have you, you thieving little cow. I say what you eat and when. Scum like you don't deserve to live, let alone eat." With every word, she prodded Ruth's chest who felt trapped, with a cup of milk in one hand and some cheese in the other. Maggie pushed her to the floor and kicked her. The milk spilled all over the floorboards.

"As for that brother of yours. He won't be going to school for the time being. Not now I've rearranged his face." Ruth begged her to leave Jack and Lottie alone.

"It's my fault. I took the food, not him."

"Don't tell me what to do, missy. Sister of a mad, lying little bitch who turned her own in." Maggie punched her and Ruth felt her front tooth crack.

That night, Maggie paid her another visit when she was in bed. Ruth lay, petrified, beneath her unwashed sheets. This time her aunt was different. The bed creaked and groaned beneath her weight, as she sat down beside her. Oblivious to what she had done earlier, she rocked slowly backwards and forwards.

"My Jack's going to hang, Ruth. What am I going to do? Oh my God." After wailing and agonizing, she left the room as if in a trance.

Then Ruth had been beaten, regularly, and locked in the coal shed. Now she waited in the dark to be let out. After dozing on and off for hours she heard a voice coming from the other side of the coal house door.

"Are you all right, Sis?"

"Yes, Jack, are you?"

"Yes."

Jack had been made to stand about for hours in the rain without a coat. His teeth chattered as he answered her questions.

"Do you know where they all are?"

"No, but I overheard Aunt Maggie telling Aunt Florrie that she couldn't stomach Lottie around anymore."

"Are you sure?"

"They were getting the washing in. I heard her clearly."

Ruth feared for Lottie's life. They needed to get some help.

"How's your face, Jack?"

"All right, I think. The swellings gone down. It's not so painful."

"She might let you go to school again. Listen Jack, we have to get word to Miss Duthie, to come and help us."

After some time, Maggie came outside and released Ruth.

"Go on in, before I change my mind. There's bread and dripping and water on the table." Ruth stumbled inside, followed by Jack. Unkempt and bruised, they scoffed the food and drank the water. Ruth had dehydrated from over exposure to the coal dust and gulped several cups down.

Maggie's children sat round the kitchen table eating bowls of mutton stew. Ruth and Jack perched on the end of the bench. Maggie stared at them. Ruth instinctively knew her aunt was up to more evil. This was the calm before the storm. Suddenly, with a huge grin on her face, she dropped her trump card onto the table. Papers. Ruth read the writing at the top of the page.

"Copy of Adoption Papers for Charlotte Drew."

She did not understand. Then Maggie began to giggle. She was enjoying their bewilderment.

"She's gone. The little bastard is gone. Adopted, and there's nothing you can do about it. As her legal guardian, I can do what I like with her. So I have. So you can stare till your eyes pop out. She ain't coming back."

Jack broke down and sobbed. Ruth felt violently sick and regurgitated the only meal she had eaten in days, all over the kitchen floor. It wiped the leer from her aunt's face. She leapt forward and pushed Ruth's face down into it.

"You dirty mare. That's all the gratitude I get for feeding you. Go on, get upstairs the both of you, out of my sight," she hollered after them.

Jack took hold of his sister's hand. At that moment, Ruth reminded him of Rose. It scared him. He did not want to lose both his sisters. When they got upstairs, he gently wiped the vomit out of her hair with a wet rag, he found in a bowl. Then he encouraged her to sleep. Perhaps she would feel better after a good rest. Before he left the room he heard her whisper, "Miss Duthie, she's our only hope, Jack."

The next morning, he was up early before his aunt. Jack decided to ingratiate himself with her as much as he could. He lit the fire and put the kettle on the hob. He had watched his mother do it a thousand times. By the time Maggie stirred he had the tea made and poured. She did not hate him as much as Ruth or Lottie and accepted the tea with a grunt. Whilst she sipped her tea, Jack, cleverly dusted himself with flour from the pantry to conceal his bruises. He was dressed and ready for school. Maggie had no objection to him going. As soon as he got there, he ran to find Mrs. Duthie who told him to calm down and get his breath back. When she had the gist of what he was saying, she spoke to the headmaster who telephoned the police.

Maggie was sleeping by the fire when three, official looking people turned up on her doorstep. Jane Duthie was accompanied by a police officer and a representative from the NSPCC.

"We have reason to believe that you have been mistreating your niece and nephew who now reside here with you and also a baby."

"Ooh the lyin' little sods. I've taken them in, given them shelter. I ain't done nothin' wrong."

"We are entitled to search your premises for evidence of how the children are being treated."

Maggie hurled further abuse at them as they wandered from the kitchen to the parlour. Upstairs, they found Ruth almost unconscious on her bed. Maggie had given her another beating. Her jaw was swollen and there was still evidence of vomit in her hair. Jack had not been able to do a thorough job the evening before.

It was decided to bring charges against Maggie. Her own children were taken away from her. It was noted how healthy they looked in comparison to Ruth and Jack. Until a home could be provided for them Jane Duthie agreed to take them in.

The same day that Ivor moved his furniture to the Feathers, he escorted Rose to an asylum for the mentally afflicted on the outskirts of Putney. They travelled by taxicab. Rose gazed out the window in silence. He was grateful to her for not having a slapping fit or worse. Since leaving Ruth that morning he had felt so sad and now she was gone to her aunt Maggie's. He would have stayed to see Rose settled in but was advised to leave quickly to prevent worsening the ordeal. As soon as he left, Rose repeatedly slapped her head and refused to eat. It was then decided to put her on the ward for those suffering with the most severe mental afflictions. These patients were kept downstairs. They were not allowed to venture upstairs where family members visited the paying sick. They were considered too dangerous, too far gone, or totally absorbed in themselves to think about visitors from the outside world.

A bed was allocated to her. Someone had died in it the previous evening. There had been no time to change the sheets. Her suitcase was searched for anything which she could harm herself or others with. When satisfied, the helper pushed it out of the way beneath the bed. Someone else stripped her off and pushed her under a cold shower. Another ran a nit comb through her hair searching for unwanted lice. Then she was led back to her bed where she slept, fitfully, for three days. She had been injected with a solution which made her feel like she was floating. In this state Rose moulded herself into her filthy sheets.

Bedlam went on around her. Inmates fought or cried hysterically. Others sat in corners quietly rocking backwards and forwards. One man attempted to get up the stairs. Whenever helpers were distracted, he would make a run for it. Getting upstairs was the only light at the end of his tunnel. Many talked gibberish. One young woman fluttered around like a fairy. She told everyone that she was Marie Lloyd's daughter and that she was going to follow in her mother's footsteps on the music halls.

Paying patients were taken care of upstairs in light, airy wards. Each patient was allotted a bed, a side cabinet and a tall boy for their clothes and belongings. Many had a room to themselves. The reasons for their admittance varied. Melancholia was the asylum's bread and butter. Women who had suffered miscarriages or those who could not have children and were now suffering with severe depression were put together with pregnant girls left in the asylum by their ashamed parents who did not know what to do with their socially outcast daughters. Soldiers suffering with panic attacks and flashbacks from serving in the Great War sometimes shared a room with those merely suffering with their nerves.

All were attended by nurses who had knowledge of wounded, gassed or dying men, brought back from the trenches. Now they adapted to nursing wounded minds. They rose to the challenge and were bright, cheerful and efficient. Their wards were sterile with crisp cotton sheets. Doctors examined, diagnosed and prescribed. It was all very civilized.

When Rose woke up she remembered her suitcase and reached under her bed for it. Days before, a group of her fellow inmates had shared its contents and then used it as a latrine. She grew anxious and searched around for it. The entire basement was made up of rooms completely devoid of boundaries. To walk about wherever they chose was their only freedom below stairs. It taught them nothing about respect for human life nor gave them any dignity. Privacy became a thing of the past.

As Rose roamed the rooms and corridors, hands reached out for her. She soon became wise to others of her world. She gave off a threatening, wild impression of her true self. As wary of others as she was, so they were frightened of her too. She soon forgot all about her suitcase. On her travels she came across a room which had been emptied out many years before. It was darker than the rest. Apart from human excrement and the stench of urine, there was no sign of life. It had been used, at one time, for recreational purposes by one of the more imaginative helpers but this idea had soon petered out, along with any innovation which were few and far between.

The bars on the windows shut out most of the light leaving eerie shadows to form shapes along the walls which disappeared and then reshaped. The room reminded her of the basement at home where she had played with her siblings, during and after the coal was delivered. It had been fun to black up and have dust fights. Suddenly the room fell into blackness and her mood changed instantly. She imagined a gigantic sack of coal being hurled down on top of her and a delusional cloud of dust billowed and chased her from the room. Eventually, with a pounding heart, she found her bed and hid beneath a dirty, grey blanket.

Once a day, excrement was cleared away by two fierce looking women who hollered for them to stay out of their way. Twice a week, hot, soapy water was swept over the floor boards. They were fed meals twice, sometimes three times a day, according to who was working on the rota. Some were more humane than others. Several times a day inmates were restrained, some were slapped and many abused. An assortment of medicines came round on a trolley and were administered from glass stoppered bottles, mostly for the purposes of sedation or keeping their bowels regular.

Personality disorders, schizophrenia, traumatic anxiety, psychosis were little understood by any of the doctors, nurses or helpers at the asylum. Those below stairs were clubbed together under one banner and were commonly referred to as 'the lunatics.'

Rose spent her days eating porridge for breakfast, coagulated soups and stews for dinner and, if she was lucky, bread and lard or jam for her tea. Beverages consisted of weak tea or water. It was not until a patient scratched themselves or smelled foul, that a carer brought water for them to wash in. Hair was cut into short back and sides, for both sexes, to avoid hair lice.

There were no past times to stimulate the mind. Therefore patients abused each other verbally, physically and sexually instead. In this environment, apart from roaming the rooms, keeping perpetrators at bay, making up stories and fantasies in her mind, Rose slept almost ten years of her life away.

Chapter 12

Ruth sat at the side of the stage, with dozens of other girls of her age. Her mood changed from minute to minute. What was she doing there amongst so many pretty girls to compete against? When will it be my turn to show them what I can really do? The auditions were underway and her number was still to be called. She had chosen a favourite song and had followed Jane's instructions to the letter, applying makeup and twisting her hair into a fashionable roll, at the nape of her neck. Jane had lent her a smart, fitted tweed jacket and a long, flowing, red skirt. Ruth could not believe how grown up she felt.

Unfortunately, time spent waiting to perform had resulted in her usual self doubt. She hid her feet beneath the skirt and wondered why she had bothered to attend. Well, she would just have to make the best of a bad job. Something she had managed to do all her life, so far. Ruth sighed and smiled at the skinny, blonde girl sitting next to her. She held her number close to her chest with trembling hands. For a moment, Ruth did not recognize her.

"Hallo Ruth. Is this your first time?" Sadie the doll asked.

"Yes...cor blimey, it's you. I didn't know you without all the frills and lace."

Ruth felt awful as soon as the words were uttered.

"Sorry, Sadie."

"It's all right."

"Is it yours?"

"No....my mum's been dragging me to these flaming auditions, ever since I can remember. I never get anywhere. I can't sing or dance. I'm hopeless."

Ruth felt really sorry for Sadie and saw her in a completely new light. So that was why her mother made her look so fancy all these years. To impress judges.

"I'm next after the dying canary and then it's you." They giggled together at the stout girl's quivering voice out on the stage.

"Good luck this time, Sadie. That's a lovely outfit. Satin, ain't it?"

"Yes. Thanks. I won't bother to wish you luck, Ruth. As I said, I've been all over London auditioning and I've never heard anyone who can sing like you. You'll walk it."

"Thanks Sadie but if it does depend on walking it, I don't think so, do you?"

Ruth raised her eyebrows in mockery of her leg and they laughed again. She was beginning to warm to Sadie just as number fifteen was called by a voice up in the gods. It was the celebrated Albert Howard. Sadie took her place, out on the stage and Ruth's stomach knotted up again. Sadie was right about her voice. It was breathy and all the top notes were flat. Poor thing. To be forced to sing in front of people against your will must be a terrible experience. It was bad enough for her and she felt passionate about showing off her talent.

The deep voice interrupted Sadie and kindly thanked her for coming. As she left stage right, she smiled over at Ruth and winked. She did not look upset. She was used to rejection.

"Right, number sixteen, please."

Ruth took a deep breath and walked out into the spotlight. She handed her sheet music to a handsome, young pianist and received an encouraging smile.

Albert Howard stubbed out his cigar as soon as she began to sing. He leaned forward in his seat. "I Ain't Got Nobody" was being sung as if it had been written for her. It sounded fresh and the maturity of her voice made him believe the lyrics. At the end, he applauded and told her to report for rehearsals the following week.

Ruth glided off the stage and out into the foyer where Jane was waiting for her.

"I couldn't see anyone. The spotlight was blinding. All I could hear was his voice way up in the gods and when he said yes...blimey."

"And what do you think to the Hackney Empire?"

"Marvellous, so big and the stage with me in the middle. The pianist smiled at me. Oh Miss, I mean Jane, I can't wait." Ruth still could not believe that she was on first name terms with her new legal guardian.

"Thank you...thank you." Ruth clutched Jane's arm and they went in search of a cab.

"Whatever for? You're the one who's done all the hard work. Come on, I've got some bubbly on ice ready back at home. Let's go and celebrate."

The taxicab took them to a magnificent Georgian house in Camden where Jane had lived with her husband, Michael. They had met when she was singing soprano in her youth on concert platforms in Scotland. Michael had inherited his uncle's antique business and his lovely home in London. Before they left Scotland to take up residence they had donated an annual scholarship to her old music college in Edinburgh. Now a widow she found herself teaching some of the poorest children she had ever known. They seemed like the very heart and soul of the East End and helped her to get over her grief and gave her a great sense of achievement. Fate had dealt Ruth a cruel blow. Losing her mother, sister and her niece all at once gave Jane no choice but to nurture the girl's God given talent. Now living under her roof in the heart of London, she was determined to promote it. Whilst she felt very sorry for Ruth's twin sister she was determined not to let it interfere with Ruth's chance of happiness.

Albert Howard considered Ruth to be the strongest singer in the chorus and chose her to understudy the lead role. During the last week of the run, the girl playing Jack caught influenza and Ruth stepped in. Tradition called for the female to wear tights in the role of Jack. This was out of the question. It would draw attention to the built up shoe. To all his disclaimers, he said that Ruth was the only one ready to play the part which she knew by heart. As Jack, she did not have to be graceful but boyish. He ordered the wardrobe department to make her some new clothes with trousers instead. Ruth was nervous but knew she could pull it off. "Look up and forget. Like when you sing," had become her mantra, thanks to Ivor.

For her debut, as the star of the show, all her brothers were in the audience with their girlfriends, including Tom and Martha, newly married. Afterwards, they all went back stage to congratulate her and to share a glass of champagne. Martha chose not to drink. Instead, she turned her back on

Ruth. Tom drank two glasses and burped loudly.

"Waste not, want not, Martha."

Martha loved Tom even more, now she was carrying his child. He was a good husband; always buying her gifts with his overtime money from Greens. She adored the mother of pearl earrings she was wearing and doused herself in lavender toilet water that he had bought for her birthday. A scent which reminded him of his mother.

On the day of the back stage party she asked him to keep his jacket on. She had done a rush job, turning the collar of his shirt and darning a couple of holes where the cotton had frayed with age. Martha felt self conscious in Ruth's company these days. She was becoming glamorous and popular, while she was losing her figure and could barely read or write. Martha had always been jealous of Ruth's voice since childhood. While everyone clapped and cheered on the terrace after her performances, she had hidden at the back of the crowd. To give her confidence a boost, she reminded herself that Ruth might have talent, good looks and live in a posh house these days but she was the one with a handsome husband and would soon have a beautiful baby. She knew how good it felt between her and Tom in bed at night. Poor old Ruth would never know what that felt like. As soon as a bloke got down to the nitty gritty, her leg would put the poor blighter off. With this in mind, she was soon laughing at the antics of her brothers-in-law, trying to chat up the pretty girls from the chorus.

The theatre emptied out. Johnny and Jack sat on the stage with their legs dangling over the edge into the orchestra pit. Johnny loved the smell of the greasepaint and the newly created wooden scenery. His sister had entered a different world and he was falling in love with it. He and Jack had a lot of news to catch up on.

Johnny now lived with Nan Bella who had relented and taken in one of her grandchildren. Johnny, the book worm, was quiet which suited her. Every time she went to the library, he accompanied her and withdrew as many books as he could. It was the only good thing about living with her. He told his attentive brother how hard a taskmaster she was. He had chores to do and she had also got him a spare time job at the fish market which he detested. Johnny hated stinking of fish but his nan was unsympathetic to his bathroom requirements.

"Your uncles worked hard all day long. A man's sweat is a thing to be proud of."

"But I stink of fish Nan, not sweat," he insisted.

"Nonsense."

It was as if the old girl had lost her sense of smell along with her marbles he said since the hanging. Jack could not believe how his brother could just say the word outright. He never talked about it to anyone and still felt ashamed. For many nights afterwards he had not only cried himself to sleep for his mother but had suffered belly aches whenever he imagined their execution. Ruth just got on with life and seemed happy now she was singing in the theatre. Tom was busy working to make ends meet before the baby came along and he hardly saw Arthur and Fred. It was as if nothing had ever happened. He wondered if he might be able to talk about it to Johnny but the moment was lost as Johnny told him the most wonderful story which he said was true. It sounded far-fetched to Jack but he listened spellbound all the same.

It had begun the day Nan Bella was dozing in the parlour which she liked to do after supper. Johnny went to explore the bedrooms upstairs. There was a second flight of stairs to an attic room which he was forbidden to venture up. On that day he broke the rules. Outside the room he could hear snoring coming from within. His imagination soon ran riot. A monster from another planet was asleep in there. All the books he read just then were science fiction and he believed extra-terrestrial beings invaded from time to time. He tried peering through the keyhole but it was too dark to make anything out. When he heard his nan coughing downstairs, he tiptoed away to his own bedroom.

Two weeks ago, he had found out exactly what the attic bedroom contained. A huge coffin was brought to the house by an undertaker and his assistant. It had been snowing. Johnny opened the front door to the two men on his way out to school. After school he ran all the way home. He had some important questions to ask his nan. When he arrived, she was out so he ran upstairs to the attic to find the room empty. Only a bed stood pushed up against the wall. It had been stripped bare. There was no monster although the room had a fusty, stale odour which instantly reminded him of his home on Weymouth Terrace after Rose became ill.

In a corner, on a table there was a Bible and an out of date newspaper, turned to the racing page. Jutting out from beneath the bed were two worn out hobnail boots. At the foot of the bed was a soiled nightshirt and a pair of stained long johns. Behind the door, hanging on a nail was a huge army coat. In the pockets of which were two empty whisky bottles.

That night, after supper, Johnny broached the subject of the coffin with his nan.

"You may as well know. It was for Frankie Baldini. He was your grandfather's wayward brother. A lecher and a drunk who tried it on with all the ladies, including me. That is, until your grandfather kicked him out of the circus. Someone told me your uncle was in the workhouse. Well, that was his just deserts but I knew your grandfather would not want me to leave him there. So I took him in but only on the condition that he kept to his room. He certainly did that, the old drunk. Hardly touched the food I took up to him every day. Well, now he's gone and good riddance."

Jack listened and felt sorry for the uncle he would never know. He had been kept out of the way like a prisoner. There had been no lying in the parlour for Frankie Baldini. One concession she did make for the old man, was a Roman Catholic service with full mass. The service had gone on and on. Johnny was only one of the two mourners there. The burning incense had caused a tickle in his throat and he had coughed throughout. He could not keep still at the side of the grave. His feet were killing him. Nan Bella made a lot of promises she did not keep, including a pair of new shoes. He had long since outgrown the pair he was wearing.

Later on that day, she asked him to help her sort out the few belongings Frankie had left up in the attic room. As soon as that was done she would have the fumigators in. Then she would advertise for a new paying tenant.

"You're never going to guess what happened next!" Johnny stood up for theatrical effect in the middle of the stage and acted out the last and most exciting part of the story. Jack was entranced.

As Johnny heaved the old army coat off the back of the door and down the two flights of stairs, the lining came away spilling its guts. Nan Bella was ahead of him, when suddenly, hundreds of large, white fivers came fluttering past her over the banister rail, all the way down onto the parquet floor where it settled as silently as snow. Awestruck, they stood side by side in the hall, surrounded by the most wonderful sight Johnny had ever seen.

After a while spent gawping, Nan Bella whispered rather breathlessly that she felt faint but when he returned with her smelling salts she was on all fours energetically gathering in her windfall. Johnny helped her to pick up every last note and together they counted on the kitchen table a small fortune. Well over a thousand pounds.

He had hung around expecting to be given some kind of reward which he would have spent on books. However, his nan had other ideas. She banked every last penny the next day.

"And do you know Jack. Turns out, he'd been carrying the fortune around with him for over twenty years stitched into the lining of his great coat. Yet all that time he lived like a pauper."

That night, when Jack was snuggled up in his bed, he felt envious of his brother's adventure but before he fell asleep, he said his prayers and thanked God that he was living with Jane Duthie and not Nan Bella.

Ruth was fifteen at the end of January nineteen twenty one. A celebration was held for her birthday with all of her brothers and Martha gathered together for the first time in Ruth's new home. They laughed and danced and sang and played charades and drank sherry and champagne and ate posh nosh as described by Tom, Arthur and Fred afterwards to their friends. The boys had made a collection and bought her a wind up gramophone to play all her old records on that she had only been able to listen to with Ivor. Now she could play them to her heart's content. She felt thrilled and very touched by their solidarity in making her feel so special.

Two things caused her sadness. The first was not sharing the day with Rose and the second was the absence of Ivor. Tom described to them all how he had visited Rose in the asylum and watched her from behind a screen. He had seen for himself how ill she still was, slapping her head all the time.

"Two big women, just like gaolers they were, held her down on a chair. It wasn't a pretty sight. Sorry to upset you, Sis, on your birthday but you've got to forget about her and get on with your own life now."

"Do any of you see Ivor these days?" she asked them after this latest news about Rose had sunk in.

"Sometimes, sis but he's either working or seeing his girlfriend. We normally have a pint in the Feathers on a Friday night. Now and again we bump into him. He wishes to be remembered to you." Ruth felt herself blush a little and changed the subject.

"Time for a song. Come on Jane, do the honours." Together they belted out,' My Old Man Says Follow the Van', with Ruth doing all the actions that had them all in stitches. The last present she received was in an envelope from Jane with the name and address of a music teacher. It stated that she was to have a dozen lessons with him in London.

Jane had arranged them with an old friend of hers. Edward Toule had retired from the stage many years before. His main claim to fame had been teaching Ivor Novello before the war for a few weeks until the great star moved onto pastures new. They began in spring when the weather was fine for her to travel backwards and forwards. After the first three lessons Ruth was always late. Still situated on New Bond Street, Edward glanced out of an upstairs window onto the street below and rapped his knuckles on the window sill irritably.

She had the most sensational gift. That was not in doubt but there were still a few rough edges to work on before he was willing to put his label on her. Resistant or not, she would have to put her mind to it, if they were to continue.

He glanced over at an ornately decorated, French clock which stood on the mantelpiece. It struck quarter past the hour. She was wasting his time and Jane's money. Their two hours together were slipping by. He hated wasting time, having never missed a cue or curtain call in his life.

Now at fifty five, he was a full time drama and singing teacher. He worked because he needed the money, having spent much of his small fortune on his young man of the moment. Nowadays, he had no energy for that sort of thing and lived, quite happily, with two tortoise shell cats. They were all the companionship he needed.

The doorbell chimed and he made his way downstairs to let her in. With a flamboyant gesture, he greeted her. There the usual excuse about missing her tube connection which made him see red and count to ten. He decided to punish her by putting her through her paces, without first offering her a cup of tea or a cold lemonade, which was his custom.

On her way to see Edward, Ruth had been ruminating on her situation. She had loved starring in the pantomime, even if it had only been for a week. It had helped her enormously with her confidence and had felt like a dream come true. There had been some offers from agents to manage her and talk of her playing this part or that. Jane had managed things cautiously. Ruth was only fifteen. She could not run the risk of her being taken advantage of. When the time was right for her to take on a more serious engagement, she would help Ruth to find the best person to represent her. For the moment, she must continue to learn her art.

There was also talk of Ruth changing her name from Drew to Duthie. This would be her stage name if and when she had real success in the theatre. The Baldini case had been covered in the newspapers and Rose Drew had been mentioned as the victim of the murdered man. Someone, somewhere would no doubt remember this name and connect it to Ruth and try to ruin her career. For now she was safe but as her guardian Jane had to protect her future.

Ruth was upset to begin with but trusted Jane to have her best interests at heart. Besides, she was still so ashamed of her uncles that she did her utmost to block out the murder. Changing her name helped her to do that. Ruth Duthie had a certain ring to it anyway and so she agreed.

Ruth really resented having to have singing lessons. She just wanted to get on with it but at the same time, she felt a bit of a fraud. It had been a throwaway comment from her brother, Tom, at the after the show party which caused her to question herself.

"So, what you doin' next Sis?"

"Jane thinks I should take singing lessons with some ponsy bloke up West."

She spoke the words in a conspiratorial way which made her eldest brother grin from ear to ear.

"It's good to hear you talk like one us still, Ruthie. You sounded like you'd got a bloody plum in your mouth in that pantomime."

This last quip of her thoughtless brother had stayed with her. Part of her

100

still worried and wondered what she was doing, mixing with toffs. Edward Toule fitted this description. To top it off, he was effeminate or as her brothers might say, a brown hatter. Although a big part of her respected him, the cockney urchin in Ruth wanted to run a mile. Therefore, she was to be found dawdling or window shopping to while away some of the time on the day of her lessons.

After being shown up to the practice room, she sat down on the chair, opposite the piano and realized he was in a mood with her. There was no drink on offer and he was warming up at the piano as if his life depended on it. She had annoyed him. Edward stopped playing and cracked his knuckles, one at a time. Ruth found his idiosyncrasies off putting, especially when it came to feeding his cats. He would share his meal with them using a tiny silver fork. They were his babies and he spoke to them in a high pitched, girlish voice, in between shouting encouraging remarks to her as she practiced her scales.

Nothing was as eccentric, though, as the way he dressed. When they were to work on impassioned speeches, he would greet her at the door wearing a dramatic red or purple smoking jacket. If they were working on a lighter song, from musical theatre, he would don his baggy trousers, with a colourful dress over the top. Ruth had to suppress her shock and horror, the first time she had witnessed this. The caftans were finished off with a knotted scarf at the neck. Today, he certainly meant business.

He was wearing a black pin stripe suit with spats and a purple, velvet velour. He sat, waiting for her to slip off her coat and ran his fingers through his dyed, black hair. He cracked his knuckles again and played the opening bars of, 'Keep the home fires burning'.

"I haven't done any warm ups, yet." Ruth reminded him.

"No, you haven't, have you, dear. Well, that's because we haven't time, now you're almost half an hour late. So come on, straight in."

Ruth blushed but rose to the challenge, thinking she had done pretty well.

"Come on Ruthie love, you can do better than that. Remember the breathing and feel it from here." He placed his womanly hands firmly around her midriff. Ruth loathed the sensation she felt at his touch. Today, he pinched her slightly before pulling them away. They began again. He was singing it with her. His high pitched tenor sounded like a castrato and Ruth giggled. He stopped playing and sprang up onto the balls of his feet. Even at full stretch, he was only an inch or two taller than her.

"Are you making fun of me?"

Ruth respected his strict regime but could not help finding him funny.

"Course I ain't," she giggled.

"Right, back to elocution lessons." Edward knew that she hated them the most. Her face fell.

"I thought we'd finished execution lessons, ages ago."

"Duckie, they are the main reason for you being here. To learn how to pronounce correctly using the King's English, as well as sing powerfully. Do not be tiresome or I shall have to go and lie down and then you will have wasted all of Jane's money."

"I only want to sing, not ruddy act. When I sing, I do pronounce properly."

"Learning how to act will give you more scope and broaden the parts on offer to you, Sweetie."

"Don't Sweetie me. I've had singing and acting lessons until they're coming out my ruddy ears."

"Well if you are going to make the grade, I suggest you have a bit more patience."

"Do me a favour. I've been bloody patient since I was knee high to a grass hopper."

Although he had been annoyed with Ruth, he did not want to upset her too much. He could see that she was becoming angry herself. Work was in short supply these days. He did not want another client quitting on him.

"Calm down, Ruth. Try not to resort to coarse language."

"Calm down. Don't you ever switch off, you old poof."

"Now, there's no need for that sort of talk. We'll do a song of your choice."

"No, let's don't eh? I've had enough of your hands pinching me in like a bloody girdle, every time I don't hit the right note. If I didn't know you was an old queer, I'd think you was an old lecher."

With that said she grabbed her coat and raced down the stairs and out onto the street. All the way home on the tube, she broke out into uncontrollable giggles. She knew her brothers would have been proud of her. The way she had handled old Edward Toule. He was probably dusting himself off with some face powder. He had gone a funny purple colour and looked all of a sweat. She laughed out loud and hoped that Jane would not be too angry with her.

Chapter 13

Salvation came for Rose in the form of a takeover bid of the asylum. Headed by a new breed of doctor, a humanitarian committee was formed and profound changes introduced. Frederick Munro had trained for many years in psychoanalysis, studying under Forenczi, one of Sigmund Freud's supporters in Switzerland.

As a young boy, growing up in the ghettos of Glasgow, life had not been easy but he had always felt better off than many, coming from poverty stricken backgrounds. From an early age, he had ambitions to become a doctor. Unfortunately for him, but fortuitously for those he now came to heal, he could not stand the sight of blood. He, therefore, studied sciences of the mind. Frederick resembled the old King, Edward VII but had a physique twice as large with a mass of red hair and a beard to match.

From childhood he had always attracted the worst sort of attention because of his size. Children made fun of him while adults thought he should act more grown up, mistaking him for a much older boy. For a while he became withdrawn until his father had taken him to his first football match, Celtic versus Rangers, from which he never looked back.

Frederick joined his local team as goal keeper and was worth his weight in gold. Very few goals got past him into the net. He would have loved to continue playing well into adulthood but there was no money to be made and he was bright as well as athletic. His father saved his pay as an unskilled worker on the new tramway system around Glasgow to send his son to Edinburgh University to study medicine. This was not for him and so he worked his way around Europe on his own grand tour until by chance he attended a lecture on psychoanalysis by Sigmund Freud in Paris.

He immediately identified with its subject matter and worked by day and studied at night until his professional training began. He was a lover of women but had never married. His work was his life and helping men and women to recover from neuroses and other disorders of the mind made him happy. Where ever he went success followed him. His was a truly lovable personality because of his love for others. He could always see the funny side to any situation and filled the hospital with resounding belly laughs.

However, on his first inspection of the lunatic wards the smile was wiped off his face. He was violently sick and immediately ordered the rooms to be fumigated. The thirty surviving inmates were showered and fitted out with new clothes and shoes. A ward was prepared for them above stairs. For the first time, since being brought to the asylum, they experienced daylight streaming through the windows. Many were startled or blinded by it. Curtains were drawn for some of the patients, until they grew accustomed to it again.

Frederick Munro, so fascinated by the human condition himself, could not understand why no records had been kept of these patients. All he had to go on was a book containing a name, age, and date of admittance. What they seemed to be suffering from or what treatment they had received, was a mystery.

He surmised, correctly, that the thirty malnourished human beings, now in his care had been locked away from the outside world and were a lot worse off than when they were first admitted. Like neglected plants, they had been starved of light, food and space to develop and grow. They had all but withered and died.

One of the first patients he felt encouraged by was Sophie who still fluttered around like a fairy. She seemed reachable, even though she was immersed in her own, deluded world. By dancing and hopping, she was expressing herself. In a pink sequin bag, she carried a birth certificate. Frederick could not believe that the emaciated girl, with a developmental age of eight, was fifty years old. He wondered what had retarded her.

Another woman of indeterminate age interested him. She had scrubbed up well and after being dressed and groomed, was rather handsome. One of the helpers said he remembered the exact day she had been brought in. She had taken his cousin's bed who had died the night before. She had only been

105

a young girl.

Although she appeared much older, the doctor estimated she must be in her late twenties. He decided to work with Sophie and Rose, immediately, to see if he could solve their mysteries and release them from their prisons. The couch and free association would be out of the question. First, he needed them to trust him and so attempted to engage them in a variety of activities.

He believed in a balanced diet and fresh air which all the inmates were now receiving. Exercise and games were introduced to stimulate their bodies, as well as their minds. He also hoped to alter their patterns of behaviour. Running about, jumping over obstacles, ball games, helped to release tensions built up to fever pitch, over many years. Sophie took to this enthusiastically. Like a ballerina, she gladly mirrored all his movements. Rose could not understand what she was supposed to be doing but trusted Sophie enough, to step over a hoop or too.

The asylum stood in acres of grounds. A team of gardeners were kept on to tend it. Now, all the inmates were allowed outside, to enjoy the beauty of the flower beds and wildlife. They were encouraged to walk in pairs, always having sufficient carers to accompany them.

On one of their constitutionals, Reg made a run for it, towards the greenhouses. He was a tall, stick of a man with a bald head and bulging eyes. The doctor, working in another part of the garden, witnessed his bid for freedom and signalled to his helper to back off. Reg ran inside the first greenhouse he came to.

Frederick approached the doorway. Reg was standing, transfixed. The gardener was not frightened of him. He continued to prick out seedlings, transferring them to bigger pots. After a while, as if something fell into place for Reg, he armed himself with a stack of pots and joined the gardener at his work station. Reg knew what he was doing. His fingers worked deftly and a tranquil expression came over his face. Doctor Munro felt sure that this patient had led him to the answer.

He began to observe his patients, closely, for clues which might lead him to who they were in their past lives. He already knew Sophie loved to dance. That had been handed to him on a plate. Patients like Rose remained a mystery. A piano was brought into the recreational room. Easels, paints, paintings, clay, books, a dressing up box and other instruments were also brought in.

For the first time in months, Rose stopped slapping her head and made a bee line for the piano. She sat on the stool and looked from her hands to the keys and back to her hands. He wondered if she had played and whether she would play again. Clara, one of the other patients stepped forward and pushed Rose to the ground. She sat at the piano and flexed her fingers as if she owned it. Beethoven's Moonlight Sonata echoed around the room. Most patients listened, open mouthed. Music had become a thing of the past. Such beauty left them dumbstruck. A few sobbed. Clara got to her feet and curtseyed. She had obviously been a performer.

To the doctor's delight, many who had sat in catatonic states for years, now picked up a trumpet, blew into a mouth organ or banged a drum. Others chose to hide behind their mental barricades. Rose was one of these.

After many months of trying to engage Rose in an activity, Doctor Munro almost gave up hope. However, on one autumn day, something happened to fire his imagination again. Outside, in a yard, fenced off from the main gardens, two cleaners were methodically working their way through the asylum's carpets. This was in readiness for the cold winter months ahead when chores such as these would be forgotten until spring.

One by one, they heaved them onto lines suspended above the yard. The two char ladies wiped the sweat from their brows and with great strength, beat out every bit of grime and dust. Both were in their late thirties, with many mouths to feed and were grateful to the newly established, mental hospital for their work. They felt little fear as they went about their daily tasks, while patients roamed free. Frederick Munro and his team had instilled a new feeling of trust in everyone who worked or attempted to recover at the hospital.

On the same day, Rose was feeling especially withdrawn. Ever since being pushed off the piano stool by Clara, she had displayed no interest in her surroundings at all. Doctor Munro studied her, as she slapped her head and repeated a word which sounded like kiss. After a while, Rose decided to take a walk outside which took him by surprise. He followed her through the open French windows of the recreation room, toward the same yard where the women were taking a tea break. As soon as she spotted the women, she became agitated and tried to retrace her footsteps, only to find the doctor behind her. Immediately, her hand began slapping her forehead again. The women stared at her utterly bewildered. He smiled in their direction. An inspired guess urged him toward the discarded carpet beaters. He picked one up for himself and held out the other to Rose and waited for her to take it. She continued to slap her head. The doctor began to imitate her. With one hand he beat the carpets whilst with the other he slapped his forehead. This caught her attention.

After a while she walked toward his outstretched hand and grabbed the beater. He continued to slap and beat. To his delight Rose copied him. After a time, he forced her hand away from her forehead onto the carpet beater. Rose carried on beating the carpet with two hands. She seemed to be getting something out of this new experience. It was as if she were beating a person instead of a lifeless carpet. He stared in astonishment as she released a life time of pent up rage. The exertion left her feeling worn out but exhilarated. After a while she stopped. Her arms dangled at her sides. She panted and sweated.

The doctor, meanwhile, instructed the bemused women to leave some carpets out on the line in the yard at all times. They would certainly be used again.

When, finally, he held out his hand for the beater, Rose swiped the air with it. This new object had become important to her like a child with a treasured toy. From that moment, whenever she attempted to slap herself, she was led outside to the yard by a carer.

Not long after this series of events, a real breakthrough occurred. Rose took to cleaning. From a discarded sock, to a pair of knickers, she used anything she could lay her hands on and cleaned all day long. Floors, walls, doors. She polished sinks, taps, tiles and furniture. She had found something that she liked to do, albeit obsessively. Soon, she was given dusters, floor cloths, soaps, buckets, brooms, mops and her own cupboard to lock them away in. Overnight, she stopped slapping herself. Rose began to feel at home and trusted Frederick Munro implicitly. Her most favourite place in the hospital and she would have admitted in the whole world, was inside the office of the doctor.

It smelled of tobacco and leather. She cleaned it religiously. First, she polished his huge oak desk, then his tall book shelves, removing each volume one by one, lovingly caressing them to her breast. On the mantelshelf were photographs of the doctor with a pretty, young lady with a bobbed hair do and a skirt up to her knees. Deep down inside, Rose felt a pang of jealousy which always made her turn the photograph face down. The other one she loved. It was of the doctor alone, in plus fours, cap and jacket. He was holding a walking stick somewhere mountainous. He looked happy and handsome with his stylish moustache and beard. After lingering for a few moments, she would pick up her usual speed and finish of the sink and taps.

All these jobs were carried out in the same order, every day. Rose never swapped them about. It felt safe and comforting to keep to her routine. The huge black couch, she left until last and always wondered what it might feel like to sleep on. The impulse to try it out was getting stronger every time she cleaned it.

One wintry day when the wind was whipping the leaves outside across the lawn, Rose approached the couch and buffed it up. She felt lifeless, having cleaned without a break for almost eight hours. No longer could she resist the temptation to climb aboard and rest. Soon she was asleep.

When Doctor Munro returned from his ward rounds, he found her there and went about his business as quietly as possible. He wrote his notes, drained a cup of coffee, placed the upended photograph the right way up as usual and then sat on a comfortable chair which he placed behind the couch. As the fire burned itself out he waited patiently. Rose was dreaming about faceless men and women. A child was crying as usual in her dream. Then she began to stir as the room grew chillier. She woke up wondering where she was. The couch whispered and breathed accommodating her every movement. She heard the doctor's voice coming from behind her.

"It's all right Rose. You can lie there as long as you like."

She felt startled and glanced at him over her shoulder and dug her fingernails into the leather.

"I wanted to talk to you anyway. So it's good that you are here. Just relax and feel at home. Thank you, for looking after this room for me, Rose. I am very pleased with it."

109

His voice sounded soothing. He was saying nice things to her. It felt scary but she knew she could trust him.

"Yes, I notice all the wards, refectory and kitchen are looking better than ever. I am very grateful for all your hard work."

Rose released her grip on the leather and relaxed her shoulders. She loved the way he said her name.

"Now, why don't you lay back. Look, I'll place this cushion behind your head."

As he did so, it reminded her of someone, somewhere years before.

"That's the way. Have a good rest."

She could make out the shape of someone from the past. It was small and withered and was instructing her from behind, just like he was now.

"Nan Drew." The words came out clearly. He was amazed but remained calm.

"Did she, Rose? What did she draw?"

This confused her. Rose held her breath and closed her eyes, shutting him out.

"Take your time. Can you see her drawing, in your mind's eye?"

A mountain of cushions appeared. The shape sat on the top of them, peering down at her.

"Cushions."

"She drew cushions?"

"Made cushions and..."

"Yes?"

"Everywhere."

"Did she give any to you?"

"Me and..." Rose bit her lip. She could not remember who else. There were others, she felt sure but their names were lost somewhere deep inside her.

"She made cushions for you and others?"

Rose had opened a drawer and found it lacking in contents. She felt disappointed and then angry. She grabbed the cushion from behind her head and threw it across the room where it landed on top of the grey, dying embers. Doctor Munro quickly retrieved it and took hold of her hand, poised ready to slap her head. He guided it to the cushion and encouraged her to punish it instead.

"That's it, better out than in."

After a while her anger subsided and she swung her legs over the side and looked down at her feet. She felt very small and childlike.

"Good girl. Well done. Perhaps we can have another chat in a day or two."

Rose could not understand the praise that she was receiving but it made her feel better inside. The drawer was shut again, for the moment, but not as tightly as before. Some of its contents were spilling out over the sides. She climbed down from the couch and picked up her dusters and polish.

After she left the room, Doctor Munro got out her file and hurriedly committed to paper what had come to pass. Not only had Rose free associated with him in his room, using the couch but he knew that this was the first real conversation she had had in years. He felt like celebrating and lit a cigar.

The next time she was called to his office, she felt nervous. Something had upset her before but she felt the need to try again.

"Right then Rose. I see you're ready. That's it. Make yourself comfortable."

For the past few days her mind had raced along as swiftly as her hands at her work. At times, it felt as though it would trip her up, she felt so dizzy. For years, she had not been able to think clearly. The images in her mind had been trapped in a foggy haze. Gradually, the sketchy outlines were taking shape and, instinctively, she knew that Frederick Munro was the only person who could help her to colour them in. She lay back and closed her eyes.

"I wonder how you feel today, Rose?"

There was no answer. They sat together in silence. Rose enjoyed the peace and quiet in the room, with just the beating of her heart and the ticking of the clock. Then a memory of a similar day, holding something shiny in her hands. Then butterflies in her stomach as terrible questions were being asked. Rose felt pressure on her chest and stomach. She raised her fists to something above her as if trying to force it away. Doctor Munro scribbled everything down, wondering what it might mean. Rose breathed more rapidly and lashed out with her feet this time as well as her hands.

"What is it, Rose?"

"Kiss, kiss."

"Someone's trying to kiss you, Rose?"

"He's come for me." She let out a pathetic scream.

If ever she was going to stand a chance of making progress, he was going to have to risk more with her. Obviously, she was in touch with a repressed memory that was terrifying her.

"That's it Rose. Shake it off. Get rid of him once and for all."

After several more moments of deep, emotional and physical distress, Rose seemed to faint. The doctor felt her pulse. It was steady. He held smelling salts under her nose and she came round coughing and spluttering.

"It's all right, Rose. You are safe. Nobody is trying to kiss you against your will."

Her eyes grew wild and she flung herself off the couch, landing on her knees at the doctor's feet. She could no longer see that it was the kind, caring doctor who was trying to help her to her feet. Hodgkiss seemed to be towering over her again as he had all those years before when she had been a girl. Panic was causing her to hyperventilate and momentarily she blacked out. Doctor Munro called for a carer to see her back to her ward and to bed. That night he gave instructions for Rose to be watched. Completely exhausted, she slept all the next day. It was a long time before she dared to enter the doctor's office again.

Chapter 14

As Ruth's career took off, in variety shows and musicals, her aunt Florrie grew more and more depressed. All of her children had left home. Two daughters, Beth and Lily, worked in service. Eddie joined the merchant navy, as soon as he was old enough. Arthur and Fred now shared a room in Bethnal Green. They had tried salvaging their uncles' furniture removal business but had failed miserably. Neither had a head for business and besides no one wanted to hire the nephews of murderers. Arthur kept his job on at the hardware shop which just about paid his rent and Fred turned his hand to whatever came his way, from labouring on building sites to sweeping the roads. Sometimes he was taken on down the docks when extra pairs of hands were called for. On these occasions he would bump into Ivor and after work meet up with him and Arthur for a pint at the Feathers. They had stopped visiting Florrie who had been kind enough to them for a while.

Now grown men, they were too busy earning a crust and chasing girls to bother about her. Little did either realize that Florrie had become obsessed with Ruth's success. There was one question, she had still not come to terms with. How could Rose have shopped her own uncles? Even if she was mad, blood ran thicker than water. At first it had satisfied her, knowing that Rose was locked away in a lunatic asylum. That was a fair punishment to fit her crime. Every night, she prayed for her cruel niece never to return to the outside world.

As her thoughts became more distorted, she turned her attention to Ruth. The other she devil. Same looks, same build, same genes. She too must be evil but instead of being condemned to life inside a mad house, Ruth was living it up in the West End. Risen from the ranks of the chorus line to starlet and now starring in Ivor Novello musicals. Money, fame and fortune were all hers and she had even changed her name from Drew to Duthie.

For the past ten years she had watched with interest as her niece became the toast of London. She collected clippings from every newspaper, she could lay her hands on and stuck them in a book. At night, she brooded in bed and stared with a burning hatred at her collection and wondered why she suffered with indigestion and palpitations. No longer did she pine for her husband Bill. Instead, she engorged herself with cakes, suet puddings and meat pies, while she plotted and schemed. Many times she was tempted to go to the newspapers and divulge who Ruth Duthie really was but it would only mean dragging Bill's memory through the dirt. God rest his soul. No, she had to think of something much worse to knock her high and mighty niece off her pedestal.

When Eddie returned on shore leave, the house seemed deserted. The back door was unlocked which led into the scullery. It was dark inside. His feet made contact with all kinds of scattered debris. Not until he managed to find his torch, at the bottom of his rucksack, did he finally understand the extent of the damage. The place was a tip. The flashing light picked out his size nines, indented in what could only be a white film of flour. In between, were his mother's tiny footprints. Egg shells, cake mixture, boxes, packets, scraps of food and breadcrumbs, seemed to be stuck to every surface, including the walls.

Eddie felt hesitant to check the upstairs. He had seen many atrocities on his voyages around the world. None had been worse than the sight of a leper, without his legs and a disfigured face, moving a rotting carcass around on crutches. He reminded himself that he was a grown man. Whatever he came across, he would be strong enough to deal with. Before he reached the landing, the smell of rancid body odour pervaded his nostrils. Was it his mother's corpse, decomposing inside her bedroom, he wondered?

He kicked open the bedroom door and came face to face with two dark, staring eyes. Florrie had been tucking into a rice pudding. As soon as she heard the door bang against the wall she aimed her dirty spoon at him, as if it were a dagger. Eddie felt some relief at seeing her alive. She had almost doubled in size, since his last visit a year before.

"Mum, it's me."

"Who?"

"Eddie, Mum. I'm home on leave."

She screwed up her eyes in the dim candlelit room and a flicker of recognition turned into a smile.

"Come to see your old mum, then?"

"You ain't old yet, Mum." He picked up some dishes on his way to the bed. The stench in the room was making him feel sick.

"What's up? You ill?"

"Me ill? Never had a day's sickness in my life." He ignored her and continued to clean up the mess. Florrie seemed oblivious. She let out a ripping belch and pushed the pudding basin down to the bottom of the bed.

"Look Mum. We'll get you cleaned up and then I've got to get back to the ship. I've got forty eight hours."

True to his word, Eddie not only swept, scrubbed and dusted the house, he helped his morbidly obese mother into a tin bath which he had placed in front of a log fire. She was far too big to sit in it so he helped her to kneel, as far down into the water as she could go, so as not to get stuck. Florrie seemed unconcerned about her boy seeing her naked. Eddie had always respected his mother and so averted his gaze as she undressed and climbed in. She splashed about in the water like a baby, new to the experience.

As he sat waiting for her to clamber out, his mind wandered back to the night his father had been taken. Arrested, handcuffed and led away to a black Maria. He and his sisters had been woken up to say their goodbyes. He could still feel the fond ruffle of his hair from his father's familiar hand. He had never spoken to him again after that night. Fishing expeditions together had come to an abrupt end.

It had been all right for his sisters. They still had their mum but he had always been the apple of his dad's eye. Then after, his two cousins came to live with them. It had been all about fighting for his rights in the new pecking order. He sensed he was still his mother's favourite. She dished up the most food onto his plate and sometimes gave him an affectionate squeeze but, by the time he was sixteen he could not wait to get away.

As he patted her dry, he wished he could stay a bit longer. She needed someone to take care of her. For now, he could only do his best. When he

115

left on Sunday evening, she was sitting on the rocking chair dressed in clean clothes. He had even braided her long, silver hair.

"Sorry, Mum, I've got to go, or else I'll be for the high jump. Now, you've got all the grub you need and I've chopped some wood. There's stacks outside the back door. I've sent word to Beth and Lily. They're going to keep an eye on you."

He gave her a peck on her cheek, slung his rucksack onto his broad back and with a last lingering look, headed off out the back door, down the alley. He wondered if that was the last time he would ever see her alive.

"You look nice in your uniform," she hollered after him. "Thanks, Son."

Eddie did not hear her. The memory of his mother soon receded, as thoughts of girls waiting for him in the next port cheered him up.

That night, as Florrie rocked herself to sleep, she made up her mind to pay her high and mighty niece a visit and put her straight about a few things.

Ruth Duthie took her final curtain call and accepted a bouquet of pink, star gazing lilies from her leading man. She was starring in a musical revue, at Drury Lane. All her favourite songs had been written into the show, including Sally, About the Boy and We'll Gather Lilacs. She stepped back into line with the rest of the cast.

At last the curtain came down and an atmosphere of love and congratulations swept her along to her dressing room. She closed the door on the bustling activity which made up the back bone of theatrical life and took a few minutes to compose herself.

With a deep sigh, she poured her customary glass of champagne which had been uncorked for her. It tasted divine. She closed her eyes and relaxed. Reporters hanging around outside could wait as well as photographers and adoring fans. Ruth stretched out on her chaise longue for a few more stolen minutes and drained the glass. When she reached for the bottle again, she caught sight of a note pinned to her illumined mirror. Admiring her pretty self, she decided that stage makeup brought out the best in her features. The note read: "Your aunt is waiting to see you at the stage door. Urgent."

"Must be Florrie," she spoke the words aloud, beginning to feel a fluttering in her chest. "How odd. Haven't seen or heard from her in years." She had heard about Maggie's demise in the workhouse and had made a conscious decision to stay away from anything or anyone connected to her past life. She rang through to Charlie.

"Is my aunt still there?"

"Certainly is. Shall I send her round, Miss Drew?"

"Yes. Oh and Charlie, hold off everyone else until we've finished. There's a love."

"Certainly."

Normally it would have taken a woman of Florrie's age only a couple of minutes to make her way from the stage door to Ruth's dressing room but in her obese state, it took nearer to ten. During which time, Ruth had suffered a whole range of emotions. A mixture of loathing, gratitude and compassion. Grateful to her for taking in two of her brothers after the death of her mother, compassion for her having to fend for herself and the children after the hanging but deep down, Ruth still loathed the woman for instigating the banishment of her beloved sister from everyday life, her home and family. A knot tightened in her stomach when a knock came on the door.

"Come in."

Florrie revealed herself in all her morbid glory. Ruth did not recognize her.

"Sorry, you'll have to wait to clean the room, I'm expecting someone." The woman was all out of proportion. Such a large body on such a small frame. She looked red and blotchy and was finding it difficult to breathe. The woman looked ill. It was a warm July evening. The long cotton dress she was wearing looked more like a night gown. Her shoes had the toes cut out to give her cramped feet room to manoeuvre.

"I'm Florrie, Ruth. Can I sit down? I've come a long way."

Ruth's eyes opened wide in horror at the woman who was now glancing round the room, taking in every detail with a sneer on her face. Feeling suddenly intimidated she had to remind herself who she was.

"Are you going to offer me a seat then?"

"Of course." Ruth waved her aunt to a settee in front of her changing screen. Florrie fell onto it with a thud.

"How about a swig of that...looks like champagne?"

Ruth quickly poured her a glassful, spilling most of it in her haste. The older woman swigged it back and wiped her mouth on the hem of her dress.

117

"God, you're a toff now and no mistake. God it's hot in 'ere."

"Is it? I hadn't noticed." Her dressing room always felt cool to Ruth, after being under the spotlights during performances.

"Did you see the show?"

"Did I what...? No, I can't afford to see ruddy shows not on what I have to live on." Florrie did not wish to lose her temper and after a few moments, attempted a smile and a more cordial approach to the conversation.

"Well then...'ere we are. It's been years since we've seen each other, ain't it Ruth?"

"Ten."

"Ten years since Jack was hanged and poor Bill. Yes, you're right." Florrie screwed up her eyes as if to stop the tears from flowing and then became agitated.

"But I ain 't come to celebrate that now, have I? Cor blimey, no..."

Ruth was becoming impatient with her grotesque aunt. All she wanted to do was change and join her company and go out.

"Aunt Florrie, could you tell me why you have come, then?"

"Of course gel. I'm getting to it, but first," and she pointed to the bottle of half full champagne. Ruth poured another glass for her. This time with a steadier hand and held it out for Florrie to take. She downed it in one and belched loudly.

"I've come to tell you a story, so I hope you're paying attention."

Ruth noticed a wicked expression come into Florrie's piggy eyes and sensed she was not going to like what she was about to hear.

"Before the war, there was a girl. A young woman really, I suppose you'd call her. About fifteen. The age you were, the last time we set eyes on each other. Well, cut a long story short, she was a singer on the music halls. A good singer, a bit like you. She was doing all right too. Going places. On the same bill as Noel Coward who was just starting out himself. One night, after the show, her leading man invited her into his dressing room for a glass of bubbly. Just like we've been enjoying, Ruthie."

Her name spoken so familiarly, made Ruth squirm in her seat.

"Well now, this young girl was as innocent as the day is long. She didn't know the man she was falling in love with was famous for seduction. He was a lecher, loved young girls. Younger the better. She was a virgin. Didn't know the first thing about the facts of life. After two glasses, she felt one hand on her breast and the other unlacing her dress. He assured her everything was fine. He loved her. Poor thing believed every word. Well, after he had his wicked way, he didn't want to know her. That night he put a bun in her oven. She didn't know what to do. Too scared to tell her mother or to get rid of it. She just hoped for the best. Carried on in the show. No one suspected to begin with but the third and fourth months passed by quickly. By her fifth month she began to show and pulled her corsets in tighter and tighter. If the theatre manager had caught wind of it, she'd have been slung out on her ear. Well, she stopped eating and the baby was born early. It had mortified inside her. Needless to say, the poor slip of a thing died giving birth to it."

"What on earth has all that got to do with me?"

"The girl was your auntie. Gert's sister."

Ruth gasped. "You're lying. My mother had no sister, only brothers."

"That's where you are wrong. She had a sister, like you had Rose and she lost her sister just like you lost yours. Your mother would turn in her grave if she knew what you did now. It's the last thing she would ever want you to do. I can hear her say it, as if she was here, now in this room. "She's wicked, Florrie. Only thinks of herself.""

Ruth jumped to her feet. In a voice she did not recognize, she shrieked.

"Get out. I don't believe you. Not for one moment. You...you...evil old bag. Get...out!"

"With pleasure. I'll leave you to your conscience, dearie." Florrie staggered out the door.

Ruth burst into tears. It could not be true. An aunt who was on the stage and died in childbirth. Never. Her mother had confided everything to her. It was just a warped figment of a bitter, old woman's imagination. Or was it? Her mother had kept Rose's pregnancy a secret to begin with and then they hadn't known about Hodgkiss until she felt it necessary to tell them. Perhaps she could be secretive when it came to such delicate matters. She felt confused and rang through to Charlie asking him to send anyone away who might be congregating around the stage door. She had a migraine. That night over supper with Jane she put on a brave face but a seed of doubt had begun to germinate in her mind.

The only person Ruth could think of to turn to for an explanation was her Nan Bella. Nan Drew had died five years before. The following weekend, before the matinee performance, she hailed a taxi outside the theatre and directed the driver to her nan's house at the back of Billingsgate fish market. Johnny greeted her at the door. He now stood six foot three inches in his socks and was still bespectacled. With a new found confidence he ushered her in over the threshold and into the parlour. Senior librarian at the local library, Johnny stood, proudly in front of a roaring fire, rubbing the warmth into his back and thighs. Master of the house.

Bella looked fragile, asleep in an armchair. She had been propped up to receive her visitor half an hour before. Ruth knew she had suffered a stroke but was shocked to see how thin and frail her favourite nan had become. Her mouth seemed crooked and she was dribbling in her sleep. Ruth bent over to kiss her clammy forehead.

"It's taken her down her right side. She can hardly move and her speech sounds like gibberish," Johnny whispered. Nan Bella had won his affection and respect over the years but he was still a little afraid of her.

"How do you manage?"

"That's where Daisy comes in. She's been a brick, sis. Washes and dresses her. She lives with us now." He blushed, as he informed his older sister of this new development. Johnny had taken over the running of the house since his nan had become ill.

"So, is it serious with you and Daisy?" She followed him into the kitchen where they could talk without disturbing their nan.

"You can be the first to know. We're getting hitched as soon as I've saved enough money for a decent ring."

"Congratulations, Johnny." She felt genuinely pleased for her sensitive brother and knew they would be happy. She had only met Daisy, briefly, at the theatre and at parties but she seemed always to be hanging on his every word.

"So where is she?"

"She's round at the market buying some nice conger eel for my tea."

"I thought you hated fish."

"No...it was only when I worked there as a nipper. I couldn't face it but

120

now I love it. She cooks it just like Mum used to for all of us."

Ruth sat down heavy hearted at the kitchen table. The mention of their mother reminded her of why she had come.

"You all right Sis?"

"Never better. I've everything I want. It's just that...I haven't seen Nan for ages, or you for that matter."

Johnny blushed again as he put the kettle on the stove and tried to conceal a huge poster pinned to the kitchen door. It was almost hidden from view as he stood in front of it.

"Oh, I see, I've got a fan," Ruth laughed at the sight of herself, splashed full length with Flannigan and Alan in a variety show, entitled Underneath the Arches.

"Yes, Daisy's always on about you to everyone. I suppose you'd call yourself a star now?" He felt too embarrassed to admit how proud he was of her himself.

"It's hard work but I love every minute of it."

"And you speak posh."

He poured the tea and grinned at her. "What about your love life. You're not getting any younger."

"Cheeky sod." She sipped her tea. "I've had a few dates in my time but I'm not ready to settle down yet. Mister Right hasn't come along. I'm not so lucky as Daisy."

"Yes. She's a grand girl. Takes great care of me and Nan."

"Well good for you, Johnny. You deserve it." Neither of them mentioned Rose. No one did anymore. It was taken for granted. It was as if she was dead.

Ruth drained her cup and Johnny poured her another. It wasn't every day that his posh sister came visiting. He wanted to impress her with good manners he had learnt from his nan. She sipped it while he lit a woodbine and smoked.

Drops of rain spit at the window. They watched the coal burn in the kitchen grate. It took her back to Weymouth Terrace and times spent with her mother. It felt warm and cosy and without complication. For a split second, she forgot where she had to be and what she had to do that afternoon. The moment passed. She stood up and pulled on her kid gloves.

"Remember me to Nan when she wakes up. Poor old thing."

"I can't promise that she will remember you. She may but some days she isn't with it at all. The doctor says he can't do much more for her."

They parted company with a brief hug and a promise to see each other soon. Ruth returned to the theatre. Outside, she paid the cab fare. On her way inside she signed several autographs for her fans and got on with what she did best.

However, she could not forget the visitation from her deranged aunt. Most of the time she was able to convince herself that the story had been a figment of an embittered woman's imagination but try as hard as she might to ignore the butterflies in her stomach and palpitations in her chest on making her entrances, she could no longer pretend that she was not bothered by it. Ruth began having nightmares. In them, her mother was sitting on the front row of the audience, waving an accusatory finger at her.

Sometimes, she dreamt about the phantom aunt performing on the stage. Always with the face of Rose as the two became merged together, both with unwanted pregnancies. After a while, she became so tired she was told to take a rest on doctor's orders.

One night, when the dreams were at their worst, Jane heard Ruth call out and went to her bed side.

"Another one of your bad dreams, Ruth?"

"Not my old nightmares. This is something different."

"Can I fetch you anything?"

"No, but I think it's time I told you what happened..." Ruth confided in Jane about Florrie.

"The wicked woman. Your mother would have been so proud of you. I have a friend who works at Somerset House. She will be able to trace this so called sister of your mother's but we both know it's a malicious lie."

True to her word, Jane confirmed that there was no truth to Florrie's tale. Ruth was relieved but at the same time deeply distressed to realize how much her aunt hated her to make up such an elaborate story to hurt her. The past had reared its ugly head and with it, all the sorrow and self doubt she had felt years before. Ruth needed a complete rest and Jane knew that the best tonic she could think of, would be for the two of them to take a holiday far away from London.

Chapter 15

After six months, Rose was confident enough to clean inside the doctor's office again, although therapeutic sessions were out of the question. She was still in a fragile state of mind. In a file dedicated to her, the doctor had compiled a set of notes. Christian name, gender, a family including a nan who drew and made cushions and a possible molestation. Traumatic anxiety afterwards had led to a catatonic state, paranoia and self harm with some psychotic episodes.

Since nineteen thirty, under Frederick Munro's leadership, the mental hospital had opened its doors to so many patients in need of treatment, that some of those who had made progress, were encouraged to seek life on the outside. Now almost thirty years of age, Rose had spent half her life sick or institutionalised. Frederick Munro did not give up on her. As soon as he considered her to be strong enough to resume therapy, he was able to add a mother, a sister and many brothers to her history, as well as a father who was a French polisher and kept chickens. He deduced that he had died of consumption and that Rose had been heartbroken. Rose did not engage with him about the rape. He knew nothing about an unwanted child. Along with Lottie, Rose had buried her uncles and their crime deep within her. As time went by, he began to consider her one of his successes. She no longer self harmed, related to those around her, speaking, usually when she was spoken to and, although she remained guarded, was able to take responsibility. Rose had become one of the most motivated people in the hospital.

When Clara and Sophie were secured placements elsewhere, Rose began to feel lonely. Sophie, who had had a mild stroke, could no longer flutter around like a fairy. By using her precious birth certificate, they managed to trace a distant cousin who graciously agreed to give her a home. Clara had made great strides in handling her behaviour. Doctor Munro had an aunt who lived in London. She needed someone to read to her and play the piano, as she was partially sighted. Clara couldn't wait to do the two things which she loved most in the world. She was to live in, have her own quarters and be paid as well. Her faith in humanity was restored.

Rose joined in with their farewell party and enjoyed the sing song around the piano. When it had been time to say goodbye, Rose shed the least tears and comforted the older women. For a week afterwards, her appetite for cleaning was insatiable. Clara and Sophie had felt like the only true siblings she had ever had.

Rose now took responsibility for teaching others how to keep the hospital spotless and sanitary. This impressed Doctor Munro so much that he approached hotels, restaurants, large country houses, schools and colleges. He felt sure that she could earn enough money to support herself on the outside. After much rejection, the London Borough Council was the first to show an interest in her. They agreed to give her a trial period as a lavatory attendant in the heart of Piccadilly Circus.

On a crisp, cold spring day in nineteen thirty six Rose left the asylum. A carpet of aconites and crocuses taken for granted, year in year out, heralded a new beginning for her. After breakfast, she stripped her bedroom walls of the cuttings she had collected over the years. Most were of the royal family, George V and Queen Mary, the Duke and Duchess of York with their lovely daughters, Elizabeth and Margaret. She placed them affectionately inside a folder and packed them in a suitcase, bought especially for her departure. She buttoned up her new double breasted, flared coat and placed a brown velour hat, shaped like a flower pot, on top of her head. Frederick Munro held onto her ice cold hand and they left the room together. Once in reception, Rose said goodbye to all the patients and staff. Everyone had come to see her off.

Frederick reassured her that he wanted to see her for regular visits. Her life line gave her one, last bear hug and walked away. With fear and trepidation, she walked through the front door and out across the lawn. With only one backward glance, she pushed through the wrought iron gates and heard them clang shut behind her.

While Rose took her first baby steps back into the civilized world, Ruth left London behind for the first time in her life. Aberdeen in Scotland was her destination with Jane. Although she felt outside her comfort zone, she laughed and joked nearly all the way there on the train. It was only when she fell asleep, exhausted from covering up her worries and fears that Jane noticed her troubled expression. They travelled all day and through the night.

When they arrived the next morning, they were greeted with broad Scots accents which Ruth could not understand. While Jane went away to find out the times of public transport Ruth holed up in the station waiting room and fell asleep again. They had an hour to wait for the bus which would drop them on the outskirts of the village where they would be staying. There was no food to be had and Ruth's stomach rumbled. Jane could see how tired and disappointed Ruth looked but reassured her it would all be worth it. The bus dropped them at the bottom of a lane. It had started to drizzle with rain.

"Just another five minutes dear and we'll be there."

Just when Ruth thought things could not get any worse the cottage came into view. It was the prettiest house she had ever seen. Jane's father had been a tenant farmer for thirty years on the estate and had never owned it but as soon as it came up for sale Michael Duthie had bought it. Jane reached up into the porch and found the key. She felt relieved to see Ruth smiling.

"Come on, I'll show you round."

Ruth couldn't believe how warm and cosy the cottage felt with floral armchairs and a Welsh dresser in the kitchen and lace curtains at the windows in the snug living room. The fire had been lit and logs stacked at the side. On a table in the kitchen was a packet of tea, some milk and sugar, bread and cheese to start them off.

"Oh good, my neighbour's been round. I only have to send a telegram and they do all this." Ruth smiled. Jane explained how some of its primitive features had been replaced with up to date trappings but the black leaded range still stood proud in the kitchen. Gas mantles now lit the beamed rooms replacing oil lamps of Jane's childhood. There was no electricity in these parts yet but there was running water from a tap even though the pump still worked in the yard. Ruth made cheese sandwiches while Jane poured the tea.

Ruth fell in love with the quaintness of the place and couldn't wait to get her hands dirty. Her city clothes were soon replaced with dungarees and wellington boots that she found hanging in an outhouse. She could not wait to get up each morning and collect the eggs for their breakfast. For the first time in years she made bread again. Aberdeen Angus with their long, rust red coats were the most beautiful animals she had ever seen. The city girl soon forgot her troubles as she relaxed away from the spotlight. Fresh air, simple chores and many walks in the braes and by the beck to the village shop for provisions soon put colour back into her cheeks.

Ruth and Jane got to know each other better as they played cards and drank homemade wine in the evenings, supplied by their nearest neighbour, a mile away.

Each day was a replica of the day before and for that she was grateful. On days when it did not stop raining, she stayed indoors willingly, curled up with a book in front of the log fire. One day , Jane explained how difficult it had been to break away from such a loving home. Her parents had hated to see her go as she was an only child but they realized singing was her passion and helped her all they could.

"I can't believe you grew up here. You're so lucky."

"Aye, but I didn't think so when I was a teenager. I felt cut off from the world and needed to branch out."

"Your parents sound lovely."

"There's an album here somewhere." Jane rummaged through dozens of books along the shelves and sat back down with Ruth.

"This is my mother and father in their Sunday best, ready for the kirk. A rare photograph of them taken together. They were always so busy."

Ruth saw a resemblance between Jane and her mother. Their clothes were plain and probably they had had to make do and mend just like her own parents. She stifled a giggle at the kilt her father was wearing in the photograph.

"Oh aye, he always wore the kilt on high days and holidays. Not that there were many of those."

After a month, Ruth felt strong enough to return to London and her work. She hoped to return to Aberdeenshire again someday. The cottage, she decided, would make a very nice honeymoon retreat should she ever find the right man. They had made a conscious decision not to listen to the wireless nor read a single newspaper while they were away. Theirs had been a complete break from the world.

Back in London, they caught up with all the news. Winston Churchill was still trying to make Parliament see sense, pushing for rearmament in the event of another war with Germany. Throughout the nineteen thirties he had been making himself unpopular with his belief that Hitler and his bullies were posing a dangerous threat to the rest of Europe. Everywhere, there were arguments for and against another world war. Pacifists preached peace in our time. They argued that another war would be more catastrophic than the Great War. Anyone on the side of Churchill was considered a war mongerer.

Jane was a pacifist. Ruth sided with her and protested that Winston Churchill was a fine man, politician and orator but he was spreading fear throughout the nation. She did not really understand the details of the debates going on around her. At home, in the streets of London demonstrations for both sides were taking place. Even in the theatre, she could not escape from having a point of view. All she knew for certain was that her dear father had been a conscientious objector. If that was good enough for him then it was good enough for her. She really did not wish to be brought down by such bad news when she felt so much better. Every day she said a prayer of thanks for the love and support she had received since the death of her mother. Jane had made her singing career possible. She had mastered the built up shoe over the years and lessons in deportment and flowing fashions had all but eradicated the problem.

As Ruth approached her thirtieth birthday she could not help wishing that she had a man in her life and children of her own. She could spoil her nephews and nieces whenever she chose but it did not fill the aching void deep down. Lottie was always in her thoughts. Had her adoptive parents given her a good life? What was she like now she was growing up? She wondered what Rose might be like at thirty and could not allow herself to think the worst. Over the years she had finally accepted how ill her sister had become but when Tom brought news that Rose had left the hospital and was working somewhere in London, Ruth was determined to see her again. She was obviously better and she would no longer be fobbed off.

"The first thing I did, Sis, was to ask for her address but they told me it was confidential. I saw this big, tall doctor who told me she was doing well and going back for regular check' ups with him but he said it was up to Rose. When she was ready to meet us again, she would be the one to find us". Once again Ruth felt thwarted.

On her actual birthday itself, she found herself alone in the house. In need of a stiff drink she wandered down to the kitchen. She took a highly polished glass flute and a bottle of champagne back to the drawing room. With every sip she felt discomfort turn to anger. Where was Jane? Why had she left her all alone on her birthday? Then she began to cry. The empty bottle lay at her feet.

"Still a virgin at my age. Even Rose had a baby..." she slurred her words.

"No man will ever want a baby with me..."

Upset and tipsy, she sprawled across the sofa, her head in a cushion. She had many admirers whom she permitted to kiss and cuddle her but something always stopped her from taking things further. Soon she was asleep, dreaming a familiar dream. They were girls, she and Rose, laughing together. A cushion being snatched from beneath a jumper and tossed way up in the air. Rose turning and running off with her in pursuit, crying after her to come back.

"It's all right, Ruthie. Another of your bad dreams?"

Ruth's head ached. When she sat up, the room had been transformed. Now it was decked out with flowers. Chandeliers and candelabra lit up every nook and cranny. Some furniture had been stacked in the summer house to make room for dancing. They had worked around her.

"Well you are the birthday girl and you did need to sleep it off. I've hung your dress up and run you a bath. You've an hour dear, so do hurry."

Ruth nodded and tried not to stagger to her feet. She passed a quartet of musicians setting up to play. The hallway had been festooned with balloons and streamers. Ruth craned her neck and could see caterers putting finishing touches to the buffet. Quails eggs coated in aspic, caviar, a smoked salmon, surrounded by tiger prawns. A leg of pork next to a rack of lamb wearing miniature white chef's hats. Salads, hams, cheeses and exotic fruits adorned the table. A huge basket of plaited warm rolls sat next to a dish of softened butter. On a table opposite, syllabubs, fruit flans, gateaux, sorbets and a large jug of cream. This spectacle of extravagance especially for her cheered her up. She had only had a liquid lunch and felt ravenous.

At eight sharp, the guests began to arrive with Johnny and Daisy first. They looked more like brother and sister with gold rimmed spectacles and curly blonde hair. Then the rest of her brothers came in with their embarrassed wives who had done their very best to look the part, borrowing or stealing from each other to put an outfit together. They made short shrift of several glasses of champagne offered to them by waiters in penguin suits, to give them Dutch courage. Jack was the only unmarried brother but had brought his girlfriend, Lilian whom he had met backstage in the theatre. While she was in charge of props and costumes, he had trained to become a spark. The only other member of her family to work in the theatre. She felt very proud of all her brothers.

Actors and actresses chatted loudly to one another, each trying hard to upstage the next with their banter and in jokes. Socialite friends and acquaintances of Jane picked their way through the rooms to find one another. Ruth still soaked in a bubble bath when Jane knocked the door.

"Do hurry up, Ruth. They're nearly all here. I've never seen so many presents. You lucky thing."

Ruth dried herself off and looked across at the dress, lying on the bed. After all these years, she still could not get used to another human being laying out her clothes. It went against the grain and seemed a crime against her fellow man. A cut above, her mother would have said. It felt more like being spoilt or pampered. She climbed into her cami knickers and brassiere and pulled on the sequin gown. Immediately, she felt like a fraud. It should be worn by a beauty, not Ruth Drew. The weight of the dress made her back ache instantly. Beautiful costumes were acceptable. It was for the sake of her art that she put up with those but this was pure vanity.

"A load of old foldyrolls," her mother would have said. Since her holiday she had been able to knock her mother off her pedestal more frequently but her judgmental expressions would always be invasive at times.

"Are you ready in there?" Jane rushed in looking flustered. "Come on, let me help you with that."

"No. I can do it." Ruth snapped and tried to temper her voice at once.

"Sorry, nerves that's all."

"No need. Just the usual crowd. I'll leave you to it then. Oh, by the way. I bumped into an old friend of yours on Oxford Street, this afternoon. That's why I was so late getting back." Jane's head ducked out of the bedroom door before Ruth could ask for more details.

Chapter 16

Jane Duthie never forgot a face, especially when it was such a distinguished one. The first time she had bumped into Ivor Zalenski had been memorable. Years before, when she had made it her business to speak to Ruth's mother, he had collided with her out on the pavement. She had never known a man to apologize so profusely nor bow so low. The last time had been at the school gates, when he had been volunteered by the family, to meet Ruth out with the hand cart. It had appalled Jane to see how the young girl was shipped about, like so much meat. Ivor had looked embarrassed and been stuck for words. She had wondered if, he too, felt the same.

The afternoon of Ruth's party, she had been rushing along Oxford Street trying to find a suitable present for Ruth to cheer her up when she had spotted him looking in a jewellers shop window. She slowed to a halt and studied him. He had aged well. Tall and still slim with a mop of black wavy hair, greying slightly. She guessed he must be in his forties by now. She touched his arm. He turned and looking surprised lifted his hat. He did not recognize her at all which amused her.

"Sorry, I never forget a face. I'm Jane Duthie. I used to teach Ruth at Shoreditch Elementary School."

"Ah yes. I remember, now. How is Ruth getting on after all these years. I mean...well, I know she is successful... but what I mean is...," he hesitated to ask if there was a man in her life.

"Fine. Absolutely grand. It's her birthday today, as a matter of fact."

"Let me see now. She must be in her twenties. The last time I saw her, she was in pantomime and no more than a girl."

"Between you and me, she's celebrating her thirtieth birthday. Quite the

132

mature woman these days."

"She's become a true artiste. I always told her she would, you know."

"I see you're looking at rings. For anyone special?"

"An engagement ring for my girlfriend. After many years of courting, I am determined to pop the question."

"That's wonderful, Ivor. I'm sure you will make her a very good husband." Jane found herself warming to this charismatic man.

Although Ivor felt slightly embarrassed, he also felt he could trust Jane and so confided, almost in a whisper.

"Well really, it is an ultimatum. Either she agrees to become my wife or I shall simply call it a day. We have both been avoiding commitment, I fear, for far too long."

"Well, I'm sure she will accept. I wish you both all the luck in the world. Anyway, I must love and leave you. There's still so much to organize for the party tonight and I still have to buy her a present. Lovely to see you."

As she began to disappear into the crowd, she hesitated, and looking back at Ivor, who seemed so unsure of what he was looking for, shouted, "Ivor, if you'd like to come tonight with your intended, we're at Victoria House, Camden Lane. I'm sure Ruth would love to see you again."

"I shall, I shall," he beamed and gave up looking for a needle in a haystack. They were all far too expensive anyway. He would offer the ring his mother had recently posted to him. She wanted him to have it in case he ever met the right girl. It had been an eternity ring, given to her by his father when she was sixteen. As he made his way back to the tube station, he felt a fluttering of excitement. He had no intention of missing Ruth's party, with or without Amy.

The party at Camden Lane was in full swing. Songs taken from the American songbook were being played with vigour by the band and the guests had begun to eat, drink and circulate, coming out of their respective comfort zones to embrace people they might normally have run a mile from. When the doorbell rang for the umpteenth time Jane smoothed her dress down over her hips and putting a hand to her hair, studied herself in the mirror. She might be getting decidedly greyer with each passing year, but she still had boundless energy. Humming Night and Day by Cole Porter, she pinched colour into her cheeks and decided she would have to do. As she swung the front door wide a blast of freezing cold night air took her breath away. Ivor in all his cream linen suited glory stood on the threshold. An evening suit might have been more appropriate but this added to his air of dashing eccentricity.

"I found you easily. Came by taxi."

"Welcome Ivor. I'm so pleased you could come. Where's Amy?"

"I'm afraid it's off." he explained stepping in from the cold. He had no overcoat or hat to hand her so she scooped a glass of champagne from a passing waiter's tray and placed it in his hand to make him feel at home.

"Not that it was ever on, really. When I asked her to marry me she doubled up with laughter. When I asked her what was so amusing, she told me someone else had beaten me to it. I believe she has been two timing me all these years with a Cockney fellow."

"Oh you poor thing." Jane felt genuinely sorry for him but the way he delivered his news was comical. She knew Ruth would be delighted to see him and that would make him feel better. She led the way to the most magnificent room he had ever seen. A log fire was throwing out a welcome. On such a bitterly cold night as this, he was grateful for the warmth. He had fished out his one and only suit for the occasion, knowing full well that it was meant for sunnier climes. Ivor stood with his back to the fire and enjoyed the splendid room before him. His face lit up.

"I must say you're taking the news well, Ivor."

"Not at first but I feel sure that everything has a reason. We just weren't meant to be together. It is fate. I feel it in my bones."

"Well, good for you. So glad you came anyway."

Ivor took out a small package tied with string from his inside jacket pocket.

"I have a present for Ruth. Where is she?"

"Oh, she'll be down in a minute. Ruth Duthie always likes to make her grand entrance. I'll put it with the others. By the way, you know the family. All her brothers are here somewhere. Don't hide away in here all night."

She left him alone again taking his gift to sit with numerous others of varying shapes and sizes on an oak sideboard in the study.

Meanwhile, he had time to take in his surroundings. Two gigantic, incandescent chandeliers lit up the room furnished with comfortable settees and an exquisite red velvet chaise longue. In the furthest corner from where he stood a magnificent grandfather clock chimed eight o'clock. A baby grand piano caught his attention and he wondered if they had musical evenings in this room with Ruth entertaining. A variety of antique furniture and ornaments added to its opulence. Such an aristocratic room reminded him of his own furniture which he had had to sell when the Drew family went its separate ways. Since then, he had lived above the Feathers, in a furnished room.

Through the open doorway he watched as waiters offered champagne to new arrivals. He was beginning to relax and ventured outside the room to take another glass. Ruth had done well for herself, there was no doubt about that. Then he felt butterflies in his stomach. She had been no more than a slip of a girl back then. Now, she was a mature woman. A star of the stage and used to finery. What if she did not give him the time of day?

Ruth was dressed and sober. Although she felt nervous, she was ready to carry off this occasion. It was in her honour and she felt grateful to Jane. She owed her so much. By the time she left her bedroom, a conviction was growing inside her. Her mind was made up. No more feeling sorry for herself. No more deadening the pain with champagne. She was a woman now. A child no longer. Ruth Duthie of independent means. She was going to take control of her destiny and the first thing on her agenda was to find her sister. With these thoughts in mind, she descended the stairs which were garlanded with flowers and streamers.

Candelabra flickered, lighting her way. One by one, the guests caught sight of her and a ripple of applause went up which was the signal for the band to play "For She's A Jolly Good Fellow".

Ivor stepped into the hallway again and was in time to see the beautiful woman Ruth had become. Everything about her sparkled. From the sequin dress she was wearing to her hair piled up on high with loose, curls cascading to her chin. The most lovely sight of all was the light in her eyes. He watched as she exchanged kisses with men and women alike. The way she received gifts, some nonchalantly, others with great appreciation, did not go unnoticed. He witnessed her unguarded expressions as she accepted a witticism from one, a piece of sarcasm from another. She had grace and a lovely sense of humour. Ivor felt suddenly quite insignificant and out of place. In his panic, he wished he could leave the house but the flames stood behind him and Ruth in front. He turned back to the fire.

"Ivor?"

He turned around expecting to see Jane but it was the lovely woman instead. Ruth blushed deeply. She marvelled at how handsome he still was. Her shyness gave him more courage and he smiled back at her.

"Welcome."

She held out her hand to him which he kissed gently and held onto. So much was going through his mind in that instant that he could not contain the words.

"Princess. Yes. You are as radiant as a princess."

"Oh Ivor. I've never been called that before. You're still the flatterer."

"Me?...no...not flattery. I mean it. I like the flowers in your hair but it should be...how do you say... a coronet."

Ruth laughed. He could hear the young girl again. She took a glass of champagne.

"Excuse me for a while, will you? I'll be back."

"Go ahead. It's your party. Happy birthday, Ruth," and he kissed her lightly on her cheek. She moved away from him as sedately as she could. Normally, she would have felt self conscious with a man staring after her, inspecting her every move but this was Ivor. He was back in her life and he had made her feel beautiful.

Ivor made his way into the room where the band was playing and spotted Tom in a corner surrounded by his brothers and a couple of show girls. As usual, he was telling filthy jokes which every now and then provoked uproarious laughter.

"Salt of the earth," Ruth said aloud, smothering a prawn with mayonnaise. She had quickly circulated and then found her way back to Ivor.

"Who, my dear, is the salt of the earth?"

"Oh, I was thinking of my family, past and present. All East Enders."

"Well, I have not come here to reminisce. You must be happy on your birthday Ruth. Let's dance."

"I don't."

"Don't what?"

"Don't dance. Can't you remember?" She raised her dress slightly to remind him.

"Nonsense, come." Ivor led her onto the dance floor. A tango was playing. He gripped her waist with his strong hands, before she could object and lifted her into the air, placing her gently back down. Ruth wished she had consumed more champagne. Ivor sat back on his haunches and demonstrated a Cossack dance, which soon cleared the floor. She giggled and threw her head back girlishly. Springing back up to his full height, he took a bow. Once the applause died down he spread wide his arms and masterfully caught a hold of her furthest shoulder. The music was sultry and sensual, and he encouraged her to sway in time. Ruth found herself being furled and unfurled, away and then back toward his chest, until she felt giddy. Some were shocked at the eroticism of their movements.

"Like intimate foreplay before coupling." one suggested.

"Good old Ruth. It's about time she had a man in her life."

"Yes, and such a handsome one."

Tom pushed to the front. "Bloody 'ell, it's old Ivor causing the sensation."

"Didn't realize we had Casanova lodging with us, all those years ago" Johnny quipped and they all laughed again. Ruth didn't care. It felt good to have a partner for a change and Ivor had made her feel different...alive.

Later, when Ruth was seeing her guests out, everyone asked her the same question. Who was he and where had he come from? How long had she known him? "All my life," she thought. Ivor was the last to leave. "I will call a taxi but first I would like it if you would open the present I bought for you."

"Oh yes, please." She led him into the study.

"Goodness me. What a lot of pressies and all for little old me." He slipped his arm around her waist, this time to prevent her from tripping. She was very drunk.

"Where's yours?"

Ivor spotted the brown paper parcel sitting right on the top and handed it to her.

"Thank you so much." Ruth squatted down onto the carpet, pulling him down beside her. She tore away the paper and string like an animated school girl to reveal its contents.

"Ivor...it's your poetry and it's published."

"It's nothing. I hope you like it." Now it was his turn to blush.

"I'm certain I will...love it. Oh Ivor". Without a moment's hesitation, Ruth flung her arms around his neck and kissed him, full on the lips. He pulled away for a second and looked into her eyes. In them, he saw the same expression he had always enjoyed years before. He knew all he needed to and returned her kiss.

"Come on." Ruth led the way to her bedroom. "Don't forget the book. You can read your poems to me when we wake up, in the morning."

Sally Krykant

CHARLOTTE

1930 - 1939

Chapter 17

Charlotte felt the flow of warm pee seep through her flannel knickers and trickle down her legs. Skinny legs which propelled her forward to her place of safety. The lookout bridge was in her sights. She had no time to notice the earth, swallowing up each droplet, plopping onto a scorched pathway.

"Come on, Lennie, run for your life," she screeched.

She and Leonard Bloom were being chased by Shopley's bullies and she felt aroused. Aroused enough to wet herself with every stride. Leonard's arms flailed the air, his plimsolls socked the ground as he frantically tried to catch up with her. At the bridge, Charlotte glanced backwards over her shoulder. They must have dispersed. Nobody there. Danger must be imminent. She could smell it, taste it even, as they lurked down in Cropper's Wood, like partisans, ready to ambush them on their return. Her flat, bony chest heaved and fell and she half whispered a reassurance.

"We're safe now, Lennie, they've disbanded." Her lie did no good.

"Speak for yourself, Lottie. I'm never safe." He gasped the last bit. He was no runner. He loved reading and arithmetic. Charlotte tugged at his home knitted pullover.

"Of course you are. Safe as houses. You're with me, aren't you?"

Leonard doubled up, trying to catch his breath, while his playmate heaved her featherweight body up onto the bridge. She spat a gob full down into the water below. Leonard scrambled up beside her and spat one down himself. His brown eyes scrutinized the bubbles of spittle, as they smacked the water.

"Mine went the furthest." Charlotte yelled.

"No it didn't. It never does."

"Yes it did, you rotten Jew boy," she hollered and leapt backwards, off the wall of the bridge. She screwed up her eyes and jutted out her chin, pulling the most wicked face she could think of. She felt like the Snow Queen, all powerful and magnificent"

"Not you as well. I thought you were my friend."

"Might be, might not be, yid face." She stuck out her tongue. Leonard began to cry and grazed his shin, sliding to the ground. Now, he felt physical as well as emotional pain. He soon recovered and wiped the snotty tears away.

Charlotte at ten was two years younger than Leonard and had befriended him at a time when no one else wanted to know him. In nineteen thirty people of Shopley had not yet come to empathise with the Jewish plight. All the villagers knew was that the Blooms were rank outsiders, from an ethnic culture which had nothing to do with their own. If bad things went on in Europe, it was nothing to do with them. They had enough to contend with, with the Depression.

Being the only Jew at Shopley Primary School meant he had to bear the brunt of incessant jibes and bullying. Charlotte usually found his company fun but if he crossed her, in the simplest of ways, she would always pull out the same trump card that everyone else used.

"You know I don't mean it. It's just that you never let me win." She snatched a windfall apple from her satchel and flopped onto the warm earth. Keeping one eye on Leonard and the other on the woods, she sucked the juice out of the fruit and enjoyed the smell of her own pee, steaming out into the sunlight. After a while, she tossed the core away and extended her upturned palms towards her pal.

Charlotte's best feature was her hands. Long white fingers performed, meticulously, on the cello for Miss Winterbottom, her teacher in the town and at the piano on family occasions. They grew impatient, tapping her knees.

"I'm waiting."

Leonard blinked, straightened his spectacles and obediently took out a cardboard box from his satchel. Placing it carefully onto Charlotte's outstretched hands, he clasped his bleeding shin and awaited her approval. She flicked off the lid and inspected the contents. Just as she had specified.

Liquorice all sorts, gums, sherbets, fizz bombers, plenty of barley twists and six red gob stoppers. She ran her eye over the sweets once more and replaced the lid. After what seemed like an age of silence to Leonard, she smiled sweetly.

"You've done well, Lennie. I'll always be your best friend," she gushed, in her most, sickly, baby voice. Leonard felt pleased with himself even though his insides ached with the guilt. If ever his father or mother found out about the weekly, thinning down of their stocks, he would be in disgrace. Worse still, he would have to give up Charlotte's friendship.

She scrambled to her feet, tossed two waist length, rats' tails down her back and picked her nose, thoughtfully. The boys were stirring the bushes down in the woods, or was it the wind? Leonard shivered, hoping that the lookout bridge would save them. Charlotte had told him all about her lucky land spot, where the ruins of a Viking stronghold still stood. It had protected Shopley from invasion and would protect them too. She pretended to be a damsel in distress, crying out from the top of the bailey. A handsome knight was coming to save her from those monsters across the North Sea. Today, however, she cut her fantasy short.

"Come on, Lennie Penny, I'll race you home, the long way round."

"Oh, Lottie, can't we cross the fields just for once. It's much quicker."

"Don't be silly, Leonard. You know we can't be seen together.

The spring sunshine was still warm and bright when Charlotte raced through the large, iron gates which presided in front of Shopley Vicarage. Shoots of sweet smelling honeysuckle and wisteria were making their debut on the walls of the Victorian establishment and daffodils and hyacinths gave off a heady perfume in their symmetrical borders either side of a flagstone pathway.

On numerous occasions, Charlotte had been ordered to remove her shoes in the outhouse before entering the adjoining kitchen but she refused to be treated like one of the many tradesmen who came to the house. She insisted on entering by the front door, as did her father's parishioners and ladies from her mother's circle. She rang the bell feverishly, poking her fingers through a large brass letter box.

"Hurry up Mabel, it's me," she announced, in a loud, commanding voice. A stout, young woman, in a black and white uniform scurried over the parquet flooring to answer.

"Stop that chuntering, Mabel, or I shall tell mother. You know she loathes chuntering."

Mabel sighed, tutted and turned on her heel toward the kitchen, knocking a tall aspidistra stand a shade off balance. Charlotte made her nervous. Her very presence caused Mabel to make mistakes. She loathed the child. Charlotte grimaced and ran upstairs. If only the plant had smashed to smithereens. She and Mabel might have come to some sort of an arrangement.

Once inside her bedroom, she plonked herself down onto her four poster bed which took up most of the room and placed the incriminating evidence squarely in front of her. Throwing off the lid she took out a barley twist.

Downstairs, a long carriage clock struck four thirty. Cedric, the cat stretched and yawned in front of the fire in her father's study. All the fires were lit throughout the year since her mother felt the cold. Too many, ancient trees shaded the house which caused damp, cool air to seep into her bones giving her rheumatics. Rachel Kemp constantly reminded her husband who promised to have some of them cut down but he never got round to it.

Rachel was a fastidious woman who kept her eye on everything which went on in the vicarage. Mabel, single-handedly, performed all the domestic chores, from making the beds from scratch each day to black leading the grates and polishing the little silver that they had. The Kemps expected a hard day's slog in exchange for her keep and Sundays off. She never complained, even though her sister earned an extra five pounds a year, for doing far less down in the village for the vet and his family.

The only drawback was Charlotte. Never, in all her dealings with her own sisters, brothers, nephews and nieces, had she come across such a spiteful nature. Charlotte felt contempt for Mabel but no more so than she felt for most human beings. Even her mother and father were subject to her indifference at best. Most people she came in contact with seemed a necessary evil to her in order to get what she wanted.

She lay on her back, in the middle of the huge bed and twizzled the twist round and round until it reduced to a sharp point. This, she proceeded to prod her tongue with, enjoying the painful sensation until she tasted blood in her mouth. Charlotte enjoyed times like this, alone in her bedroom.

Everything about the room satisfied her. Lace at the window complimented the lace trim of her patchwork quilt and cushions. Four pot dolls sat in a row on a shelf, while a dozen pretty dresses hung up in a carved, oak wardrobe.

A fire was lit, made safe by a metal guard. China jug, bowl and drinking cup stood next to the window on an ornately tiled wash stand. Her favourite books and sheet music were tidily filed away on a bookcase. The only object which seemed out of place in this altogether comfortable room, was a battered teddy bear, dressed in a cotton dress and placed strategically in isolation on a stool in a corner. Charlotte despised it for looking so scruffy and yet on nights when she could not sleep, it was the first thing she reached for. The familiar smell of her own spittle and breath on its, almost, non-existent fur, kept her from throwing it away. Her mother told her she had had it since a baby.

Charlotte pictured her father, Reverend Ernest Kemp, downstairs in his study. He might be chatting with one of his parishioners or labouring away at his next sermon. Her mother would be supervising the evening meal, having just arrived home from one of her many charitable works. At six she would join them for supper in the dining room. Usually, she would wander down to the kitchen for a glass of milk and a cake, provided by Betty the cook but today she had more than enough to satisfy her appetite.

After a while, her feeling of complete satisfaction was disturbed by a noise coming from outside her bedroom. She stopped sucking on a gobstopper and rolled onto her belly with one ear cocked like a gun dog. A low moaning was coming from along the landing. It sounded inhuman. Charlotte decided someone must have broken in and hurt themselves in the process. She slid hesitantly to the ground and tiptoed out of her room to investigate.

The noise was coming from her mother's bedroom along the landing from her own. Someone was in there, rummaging through her things, possibly stealing her jewellery which had belonged to her grandmother and would one day be hers. This she had to put a stop to she decided. She bent slightly to look through the keyhole. At first, she found focusing difficult but after a while what she witnessed made her gasp. On the bed, her mother was sitting astride her father. Her day dress which she wore to meetings for the sick and needy was unbuttoned to the waist and her father's hands were groping around inside. The whining noise was emanating from her mother's throat. Her father seemed to be muttering under his breath, intermittently, with his eyes tightly shut.

Charlotte backed away, returning to the sanctuary of her room. She climbed onto the bed and curled into a ball. They hardly spoke to each other. Never had she seen them as much as smile at each other or hold hands. Yet there, inside her mother's sacred bedroom, they had been in close contact performing some kind of ritual. It left her feeling shocked and confused. Soon she fell asleep. While she slept her parents descended the stairs and returned to the business of the day. When the dinner gong jarred her senses, Charlotte sat bolt upright and wondered in her clammy semi- conscious state whether what she had seen had been a dream.

Chapter 18

Leonard passed by the warren on the outskirts of Shopley and counted fifteen rabbits. Charlotte had introduced him to the place, the summer before, when he had arrived from London with his parents. Lying on their bellies in the dust, beneath an elderberry bush, she had fascinated him with her knowledge.

"They breed like flies, Lennie. Always at it."

"At what?"

"Mating, baby. You don't know anything." Neither did she but many of the boys went rabbit hunting with their fathers and were a mine of information.

"You know, to make their babies."

They had parted company about a mile away from the vicarage, so that no one would suspect them of carrying on a friendship. Not that Charlotte's parents minded. She was encouraged to be friendly with all the village children. It was *her* decision to try to keep it a secret. Most of the children disliked her, so to be openly friendly with Leonard would alienate them even further. On the outer rim of Leggatt's wheat field they shook hands, formally and headed off in different directions.

Leonard soon found himself at the brow of the hill which led down into the village. He felt tired and dirty and was longing to swill his face and hands with cool water. Then he would read until his mother called him down for supper. His stomach rumbled at the thought. He passed by Ong's, the post office stores. It was Wednesday. While others closed in the afternoon, Ong's remained open all day. Leonard thought it a strange name for the shopkeeper to have since she wasn't Chinese and neither had her husband been but then who was he to question anything, a stranger to Suffolk.

It was inside Ong's that most pieces of gossip were created, enlarged upon and distributed. Agnes Ong spotted Leonard through the latticed frontage and dragged herself up to a standing position. She stepped out from behind the counter and forced one leg in front of the other, until she got to the open doorway. Sciatica was the bane of her life and made her appear much older than her fifty years. Her grey hair was gripped back into place either side of her ears and fell in waves to her neck. She had always had fine hair ever since a child so much so that her mother had never let it grow beyond this point when all the other village girls had had long manes of thick hair. Even now when some of them came in for provisions she still envied them. Her face wore a startled, sometimes harsh expression but no one would say she was unkind. She wore a long, brown, woollen skirt and a blouse with sleeves always rolled up to the elbow, which gave her an air of being ready for anything.

"Leonard Bloom," her voice rasped, like finger nails drawn down a blackboard.

"You're to come in with me until your mother gets back from town. She's with your father at the hospital. It's something and nothing, so don't look so worried child."

"What's...what's the matter?"

"Put them big brown eyes away boy and come in. You can 'elp me bag up some flour."

Leonard followed her inside like an obedient pet. A mixture of smells and aromas which usually delighted him, went unnoticed. Herbs and spices, coffee and tea, fruit and vegetables, jams and chutneys, cheeses and hams. Agnes turned around, awkwardly, to hand him some brown paper bags and found him in tears.

"Now as I said, there's no need for that. He'll be all right. It was just a nasty black out, when he was reaching for a fresh lot of gob stoppers from the top shelf. It might even be that he needs a pair of spectacles and nothing more, so you stop it, will you. Here, have an orange and shut up."

Agnes Ong had no children and did not really care for them but there was something about Leonard which appealed to her. This child was different as were his parents. They were from a culture she knew nothing about. They had risked everything to make a safe life for their son. She admired the Blooms and stuck up for them, in defiance of her neighbours' tittle tattle. It was the first time she had been called upon to help out and she did so, willingly.

"No thank you." Leonard blamed himself for being an evil brat. If he had left well alone, there would have been no necessity for his dear papa to reach up to the top shelf and black out.

She left the boy to his own devices and served two customers. The first was Jonathon Leggatt. As soon as he had returned home from Cropper's Wood, his mother had sent him on an errand, to keep him out of her way. He spotted Leonard, sitting on top of a huge sack of potatoes. He was feeling groggy after so many adventures with Charlotte and all the crying he had done. He could hardly keep his eyes open. Jonathon was determined not to miss his chance. The tall, well built farmer's son raised his voice"

"Ma Ong, was that your phone?"

She was the owner of one of only four telephones in the district and was proud to be on the same footing, as the doctor, the vicar and the vet.

"Eh...I didn't hear anything, boy. Hang on, while I check it out the back."

She moved so slowly, that he had more than enough time to do his dirty deed. Taking a catapult from the back pocket of his shorts, he aimed a conker between Leonard's eyes. "Ready, steady, aim...fire", he whispered and was just about to render Leonard unconscious or worse, when a flash of genius rushed to his dull brain. His attention was drawn to the cash box sitting on top of the counter. With great speed, he snatched at one of the few notes in a small wad at the back and hid it in Leonard's satchel.

"False alarm, no one there. Now you just run along, as it's going to take me at least half an hour to get all this lot together. Come back afore closing."

"Right oh, Ma Ong."

"And don't you call me that again, do you hear. I'm Mrs Ong and don't you forget it." The bell jangled over the door and he breezed out with a snigger on his lips. "I'll fix you, Jew boy."

The second customer was Betty Rushbrook, Rachel Kemp's cook.

"Afternoon and a lovely one it is, too. Now, I'd like a bag of mixed spices, as it's my baking morning tomorrow up at the vicarage and I've almost ran out."

"Yea." The shop keeper disliked the woman, intensely, so full of airs and graces had she become, since working for the vicar. She remembered their fathers labouring on Huffey's Farm and the two of them stone picking, first thing, before school.

"What the..." Betty noticed Leonard.

"Poor lad's father had to go to hospital, after a blackout."

"Oh well, I'm sure it'll be nothing." As soon as the cook realized who they were talking about, she dismissed it from her mind.

"Well, I'm not so sure. For a young man he looks double his age. Must be all that carry on they've had to go through, in them far off countries."

"Well, I'm sure I don't know about that. Would you hurry as I have to start the evening meal in a quarter of an hour?"

"Right you are." She weighed and bagged up the spices, making sure she did not utter another word.

"I'm sorry, but I only have a pound note."

"Quite all right. I've got lots of change."

Mrs. Ong opened the cash box and rummaged through her takings.

"That's funny. I know I took two ten shilling notes from Farmer George's man this morning. Came in to pay for their supplies."

"Please hurry."

"Oh wait a minute though. That boy, Jonathon was just in here. He said he heard the phone ringing. Young scoundrel must have stolen one, while I was out the back."

"Well, if I were you I'd check every lad who's been in here today." She ran a suspicious eye over toward Leonard. He was slumped over, sound asleep.

"No, weren't him. He's been fast asleep."

"How slothful - could have been pretending. I'd check."

Betty Rushbrook now seemed to forget the time and stood with her feet riveted to the oak floorboards. She was resolved to see justice done. Mrs. Ong disliked her in that moment, even more than usual but felt compelled to do as the cook suggested.

"Leonard, wake up."

Leonard jumped up immediately and pushed his spectacles up to the bridge of his nose. He remembered where he was. Then he sighed and

149

shivered.

"Is my father home, yet?"

"Leonard, what have you got in your satchel?"

"Um...my school books and pencils; packed lunch tin. Nothing else." He had handed over the incriminating evidence earlier to Charlotte.

"Can I have a look?"

"Of course," and Leonard smiled his most charming smile. For the first time that day he felt confident.

Betty Rushbrook stepped forward, snatched his satchel off him and handed it to Mrs. Ong. At length, her hand emerged holding the errant ten shilling note. Leonard's eyes grew larger and he gulped.

"There you are. You have your thief. I believe that's my change."

Agnes Ong was, for once in her life, lost for words. With trembling hands she sorted out the triumphant cook's change and sat down with a thud. The bell jangled behind her. The cook made her way back to the vicarage, feeling elated. It wasn't every day that a criminal was caught red handed. Especially one who encroached on your community, when he had no right to be there in the first place.

The next day, Leonard followed two droplets of soapy water racing each other down the window pane. It was as if the shop was crying too. His father was bed ridden for the foreseeable future, they said. It was all his fault. He should never have befriended Charlotte Kemp. Just because he was desperate, he had allowed her to lead him down the wrong path. The righteous path which his mother was always talking about was no longer his to travel. He was going straight to hell.

He took a clean rag and buffed up the wet glass until it shone with a brilliance in which he could see his own sad reflection. It was eight o'clock in the morning. He had already laid a fire in the parlour, scrubbed the floorboards free from muddy footprints, polished the window displays and glass cabinets and replenished the stocks. His father would never black out again. He was in charge now. Leonard slopped the contents of the bucket through to the scullery and wiped his hands.

He yawned, stretched and took a biscuit from the pantry. He found his mother weeping in the parlour. She was dressed in a dishevelled way having been up all night. Her black, glossy hair hung loosely like a cape around her shoulders. He was used to seeing it plaited neatly and swept up into a bun at the back of her head. A bowl of cold porridge stood on a tray in her lap.

"How's father?" he asked, reluctantly, fearing the answer.

Esther Bloom had not heard him come through from the scullery and quickly wiped away her tears.

"He's sleeping, Lennie. I'll try and give him his breakfast again when he wakes."

As if Leonard's presence had given her a new source of strength, she laid the tray aside and patted the couch for him to sit beside her.

"You are a good boy. Your father and I appreciate all your hard work. Later, take an assortment as a treat." She enfolded him in her arms and hugged him tightly. Leonard felt a mixture of warmth and contentment but the overwhelming feeling was guilt. Nevertheless, he stayed put until she released him.

Next, she brushed her hair and braided it with efficient fingers. Pins, in a mother of pearl dish, she worked into it until she resembled the mother he took for granted. He loved to watch her serving customers in the shop. She always displayed patience and kindness and knew how to handle the rough and tumble children who made the shop seem untidy, with their outbursts and silliness.

He left her and wandered upstairs to visit the sick room. It had been almost dark when the horse and cart brought his father back from the hospital. Everything had seemed a blur. Now, with the curtains thrown back the cold light of day exposed the cruel reality. Joseph Bloom had taken the stroke down his right side. His face appeared crooked and his body slumped against his pillows. Spittle dribbled down his chin. Although he did not make a sound, his knitted eyebrows gave him a look of great anguish.

Leonard backed away from the stranger in the bed. He ran downstairs, through the parlour, into the shop and out the door. Esther had begun to prepare a broth when she heard the bell jangle. First customer of the day, she surmised, drying her hands. When she saw the shop empty, she thought she was hearing things. Shock could do that to you she supposed and returned to the kitchen.

Leonard ran past Ong's, the vets, the Angel inn, the school and out of the village by way of Huffey's Fields. Not stopping to catch his breath, he ran by the dilapidated row of labourers' cottages which began the ascent out of the village. He was soon past the menacing vicarage and heading toward Cropper's Wood. His legs felt weak but they kept on pounding the earth until he found himself inside the woods.

He jumped over brambles and undergrowth, alerting his mind to the prospect of traps. The last thing he registered, before colliding with Jonathon Leggatt was Sam Miller's goofy teeth. The dappled light picked out the glistening saliva. Sam looked both wicked and shocked in that last second. They tumbled onto the ivy clad carpet. At first, the bigger boy was shocked and dazed but when he realized who had disturbed his tranquil truanting, his strength flowed back into his arms and legs. He threw Leonard to one side.

"It's the Jew boy. Can't keep his big, fat nose out. Like a cuckoo in the nest!"

He scrambled to his feet. He had been blowing an egg which was now in slimy splinters, in the palm of his hand. He wiped its contents onto his backside. Leonard lay on the ground while they discussed what to do with him. Sam shook with adrenalin and stepped forward.

"We could murder him and bury him here, Johnny. No one would ever know."

"Or care much. Hear that Bloomy - we could kill you, if we wanted."

Leonard lay as still as possible, trying hard to get his breath back. His spectacles had shot off in the collision and were buried beneath a tangle of ivy. The faces gawping down at him were blurred. Suddenly, Jonathon grew angry about the egg that had been crushed. For a clumsy, oversized boy, he was always careful when it came to handling eggs. The intruder had interfered with his precision. He was going to have to pay for it, even more than usual. He kicked Leonard twice and flopped down onto him, punching his face and head.

At the same time, he encouraged Sam to follow suit. The skinny boy was no longer angry and managed to slap Leonard's face and pull his hair a bit. Although the beating was painful, his state of mind helped him to take it. After what he had done to his father, he deserved a good hiding. Jonathon finally dragged him to his feet and kicked his shins. He was enjoying himself but not nearly as much as if Leonard had fought back. He was taking his medicine too quietly. He was weird.

Jonathon's aggravation soon blew itself out. He pushed the smaller boy down onto the ground in disgust.

"Come on, Sam. We've got eggs to collect. Watch it next time, Bloom bag."

Leonard heard the bracken and leaves rustle as they left him to it. When they were out of earshot, he attempted to stand up. So that's what it's like to be ambushed in Cropper's Wood, he thought. He ached all over and found it difficult to breathe. His eyes were swollen and he had lost his glasses but he felt a sense of pride at having survived the attack. He had taken it like a man.

On the edge of the wood he could just make out the light shining and so he headed in that direction. Still mindful of traps, he staggered out into the daylight. It had begun to rain. Just another spring shower. Leonard clutched his chest as a dull pain caused him to cough and catch his breath. In front of the lookout bridge, he collapsed. Not until midday did one of farmer George's labourers find him and carry him home.

"Whoever, did this to my son will pay for it," Esther Bloom muttered, under her breath while the doctor dressed Leonard's cuts and bruises.

"Try not to get yourself too upset. You've enough to contend with at the moment with Joseph."

She wiped away an angry tear and held onto Leonard while the doctor bandaged his chest. He suspected the boy had a broken rib or two.

"The swollen eyes should start to go down in a day or two but he'll have a couple of shiners, that's for sure."

He tried to pacify her. It was a bad fight the boy had been in but he had seen much worse. He had been a scrapper himself in his time and had a broken nose to prove it. Never set right he had worn it like a trophy.

"The ribs should knit together nicely. He's certainly breathing better. Any problems and we'll get him to the hospital but I don't foresee that. I'll leave a couple of powders for his aches and pains. Keep him off school for a week. I'll call again after that."

The doctor admired the lad for not snitching on the perpetrators. They had always had a code of honour when he was a boy and it was good to see that times had not changed that much.

After he had gone, Esther made herself a strong cup of tea and sat down in the parlour. She studied the photographs of her mother and father. On one, they seemed very happy on a charabanc outing to Southend with her and her sister as children. Next to this cherished photograph was an assortment of Joseph's family. The Blooms looked decidedly more anglicised in some photographs than in others. In a tailored suit which he had made himself, Joseph's father squared up to the camera with his wife seated beneath him. Her feet placed neatly together with her hands resting in her lap. She looked both prim and proper and submissive. They had not risked their lives fleeing pogroms with Joseph in Russia to have their beloved grandson brutalised in this way. She vowed to them that she would keep him safe. Her mind was made up. He would no longer attend the village school, where so many times, he had been bullied and beaten. She would educate him herself. Leonard was a bright boy. He would learn the business. Joseph would recover and be grateful for his son's help. He would have no objection. With these thoughts in mind she began to relax while her husband and son slept soundly upstairs.

Chapter 19

In the autumn of nineteen thirty Charlotte began her life at the Badington Private School for Young Ladies. The Kemps had decided that she should leave Shopley Primary and attend an altogether, more cultured environment. There she would meet well bred girls, from middle class families and broaden her mind. The curriculum included all the subjects they believed would be helpful to a vicar's daughter. English, arithmetic, geography, history, scripture and music. Badington excelled in music. It boasted a first rate orchestra which Charlotte would join straight away. The couple had saved ever since their daughter was an infant for a formal education. Although the fees were expensive, they were not impossible to meet.

On the afternoon of her departure, Betty and Mabel came into the hall to say goodbye. Betty gave her a swift peck on the cheek, while Mabel held her hand, limply for a second, then let it go. Both women were glad to see the back of her. Earnest Kemp heaved the trunk, which contained all his daughter's worldly possessions, onto the roof of his car and strapped it down. Rachel Kemp struggled with the cello. This, she placed next to Charlotte on the back seat. As she watched the little girl clutch the instrument, she felt a mixture of emotions. Some sadness at seeing her go but a greater feeling of relief. She prayed that she would not be disagreeable at her new school. She sighed deeply giving her daughter a hurried kiss on the cheek.

The car door slammed shut. Charlotte felt sorry for herself. She hated her new uniform. It looked frightful. A navy blazer and matching velour hat. She glanced up at her bedroom window and felt butterflies in her tummy. To think she was having to leave her dolls and pretty dresses behind. Nothing

155

would ever be the same again. With a deep sense of foreboding, she heard the car engine start up.

Her mother was busy with a diary full of appointments which meant that her father was going to see her off at the station, alone. Appointments which could have been cancelled or postponed. Rachel hated goodbyes. It would have felt positively cruel to wave off her ten year old daughter. She took out a handkerchief and dabbed at her eyes, while the car crawled down the drive and through the gates. On entering the house, she realized that they were perfectly dry. She had not shed a single tear.

Charlotte remained outwardly stoical, even when her father asked her if he would be all right, she kept her misgivings to herself. He reassured her that Miss Lindsey would be there to meet her at her destination and waved her off with a guilty smile. Charlotte glanced out of the open window as the train pulled out of the station. White, billowing clouds of steam engulfed him. Then he was gone.

The train journey took forty five minutes. Betty had wrapped up some freshly baked biscuits in grease proof paper. She also had a bottle of milk to drink. She removed them from her brand new satchel and enjoyed her meal, as the sight of familiar corn fields raced past her. Croppers Wood came into view and then the lookout bridge. Then it all went black as the train flew through a tunnel and out the other side. Soon everything familiar was being replaced by a flatter landscape which made her realize that she was completely alone.

She settled back on her seat refusing to cry. Instead, she thought about Leonard. How she despised him for not returning to school. He had also rejected her. She promised to make him pay for it and crunched on the last of her biscuits.

By the time the train reached Badington, Charlotte was covered in crumbs and milk stains. She felt hot inside the warm compartment. Her velour lay crumpled on the floor. With trepidation, she slid back the door and stepped out into the passage way. She joined the back of a queue. As she stepped down from the train, a porter met her carrying her trunk.

"Hallo there, Missy. Your father told me to look after you." She followed him through the crowds of passengers. Some, just arriving like herself while others pushed by her, eager not to miss the train. On the other side of a white picket fence stood a woman, dressed entirely in black, waving a piece of cardboard, on which she recognized her name chalked in capital letters.

The sight of the woman made Charlotte yearn to be in the warmth of her bedroom or the vicarage kitchen, dipping her fingers into cake mixture while Betty's back was turned. Even Mabel was preferable to the old crow now before her. Seated side by side, in a trap pulled by a horse no bigger than a pony, Miss Lindsey read her the riot act.

"Badington runs like clockwork, from eight in the morning until eight at night, when it's lights out. Always has and always will."

It was hate at first sight. The woman smelled of moth balls which made Charlotte feel sick.

"Yes, Miss Kemp, you will enjoy Badington, if you are zealous, well mannered and try to fit in. We have very little trouble at the school."

Miss Lindsey sniffed and sat back, bolt upright, having delivered her speech. Out of the corner of her eye, Charlotte checked her companion over. Miss Lindsey was a thin, bird like creature, with a long chin which jutted out from beneath a skull tight hat. The peak of which hid her eyes. She was all chin and cheek bones, Charlotte decided, as she grappled with her blazer buttons. It was a hot day.

"No, don't do that. It would not do to arrive at the school looking slovenly, now, would it?"

Charlotte could not be bothered to protest. She had plenty of time to think of something to ruffle the old crone's feathers. Her attention wandered to the young lad who had been steering the trap through the countryside and down a winding lane, towards a red brick building now in view. As they approached he jumped down and doffed his cap in her direction, before opening wide the gates to let the vehicle pass through.

Charlotte had never been acknowledged by an older boy before. It made her feel special. Springing back up onto the trap, he grinned, knowingly, at her. He disliked Miss Lindsey, too. Charlotte noticed a gap, between the bottom of his jacket and the top of his corduroy trousers. She could not take her eyes off this stray piece of flesh. It did not repulse her. On the contrary, she derived a delicious sense of voyeuristic naughtiness. The discovery caused her to squirm around in her seat.

"Do sit still Miss Kemp, we are almost there."

Just outside the main school building, the driver jumped down again and unloaded her trunk. So strong, Charlotte ruminated. Not at all like her father who had looked old and short of breath, earlier in the day. He then supported Miss Lindsey by the arm as she descended, via a small stool he placed at her feet. Then he raced round to Charlotte's side. She was waiting, precociously. Before he could take her by the elbow, she placed her hands onto his broad shoulders and smiled her most seductive smile. He responded by gripping her waist with his powerful hands and swinging her to the ground. This girl is different, he thought. None of the others had ever been so forward.

"Well, I never." Miss Lindsey was too shocked to utter a word of reprimand. Instead, she fixed her eyes on the lad and said, "That will be all Henry," and led the way. Charlotte followed, turning back to grin at Henry who was disappearing with the pony and trap round to the stable block. She loved the way he smiled back at her. It was satisfying to make a young man take an interest.

"Don't dawdle girl and remember to stand up straight, at all times. Deportment is of the essence. When you meet Miss Coulthard, our Head Mistress, only speak when spoken to. Then you can join the rest of the girls in the refectory for supper."

The same night, sprawled out beneath her new bed covers, Charlotte dozed. The girls were extremely well behaved. As soon as lights out was called by one of the prefects, a deathly silence fell inside the dormitory. She felt a little homesick but decided not to dwell on that. Instead, she turned her mind to Henry. Ever since she had stumbled across her parents' intimacy through the keyhole of her mother's bedroom, she had not stopped wondering about mating and the human body.

Every human body she knew was always completely covered up, from toe to chin. Henry's flesh fired her imagination. She fantasized about the rest of his body. What he might look like naked. She had only seen herself in the nude. Just a skinny little girl but she was beginning to sprout some sort of down on her matilda. All the girls at Shopley called their vagina by this name. She felt her tiny breasts and decided that they were becoming more rounded and fleshy.

In amongst her musings, she remembered her meeting, earlier, with Miss Coulthard. The Headmistress had protruding teeth which made her bottom lip forever wet. She said "um" a lot which irritated Charlotte. All the girls at Badington won points for their respective houses and enjoyed their time there. She was to join Beaver House, the oldest in the school with a wonderful reputation. Then, when the interview was over, Miss Lindsey led her up to the dormitory which she was to share with seven other girls. A winding staircase took them to the upper floor of the building. Charlotte decided that it must have been an attic bedroom for servants at one time. It reminded her of Mabel's bedroom in the vicarage. The beds were immaculately made and she wondered who carried out this task, little realizing that everyone was responsible for their own. After dumping her satchel on one of the beds, she was allowed to wash her face and hands.

Miss Lindsey waited patiently, perched on the nearest bed. Charlotte noticed her yawning. Sniggering behind the hand towel she pretended to accidentally step on Miss Lindsey's foot. The foot which was home to a bunion the size of a shallot and which caused her to limp at the best of times.

"Oh, I'm sorry, Miss Lindsey. I didn't see your foot. It's so dark in here."

That bit was true. Only two gas mantles had been left on. The pain had taken her breath away. She rose up and fluttered from foot to foot like an injured black bird. Charlotte tried hard not to giggle. Miss Lindsey stopped and grabbed her by the arm, dragging her out of the room and down the steep stairs to the refectory for her supper.

Row upon row of young ladies, dressed exactly like herself, stopped eating to take a look at the new arrival. On a platform, a woman in a black gown and mortar board clapped her hands and told them that it was rude to stare. Miss Lindsey, now thoroughly worn out and seething from the carelessness of her latest charge, pushed Charlotte onto the end of a long bench and left her to it.

The server, at the top of the table, scooped some stew into a bowl. One by one, it was passed down to her. Someone poured her a glass of water. Everyone ate in silence. Conversation was not permitted at meal times and for that she was grateful. What could she possibly have to say to a complete bunch of strangers? During the pudding, she noticed one girl trying to catch her eye. She had huge brown eyes and wore her black hair tied back in a ponytail. Her permanent smile irritated Charlotte.

Once they were finished, all the dirty crockery and cutlery was systematically passed along the row. The servers stacked them and carried them through to the kitchen. It all looked horrible to Charlotte. Once more, she was reminded of Mabel and Betty at home. Last of all, they stood up to recite the compline prayer. After which, the eldest of the black crows came to inspect the tables, before choosing the most impressive one to lead the way out. As the lesser mortals waited, Charlotte felt a tinge of pride at being chosen to leave in third place. On reaching the playground, the single file broke up into special cliques and once more she found herself on her own. She made her way back to the dormitory where the girl with the big, brown eyes was already getting herself ready for bed.

Charlotte was not used to being liked and so ignored Eva, suspiciously. Once inside the dormitory, she noticed that her new found friend was in the bed next to hers. Charlotte got out of her uniform and into her night dress without making any eye contact. Eva did the same. Soon, the attic room was full and 'lights out' had been called.

She fell asleep with a devilish smirk on her face. She couldn't wait to see Henry again.

Charlotte settled into the Badington way of life by keeping herself to herself and adhering to all the rules and regulations. All her teachers described her as a model pupil. However, to her peers she was an enigma. When they caringly asked her if she missed her parents, she answered them in a nonchalant way, tossing her former rats tails, now neatly plaited, over her shoulder. It was as if their friendly enquiries were of no real importance to her. They were shocked to find Miss Charlotte Kemp so unaffected by being sent away from home. When for many weeks, some for months, had spent every night crying themselves to sleep.

It was the custom to sit on the end of a new girl's bed and talk of homesickness. Of course, she would be expected to shed a tear. One by one, they fell away. The new girl was not capable of a tremble in her voice, let alone bawling for her mother. Charlotte heard their whining voices whispering about her and enjoyed their disappointment. They were ordinary little girls, babyish in their devotion to their mothers while she was magnificent. She grew bored listening to them each night as she combed her plaits into long, luscious waves.

Eva Rosenthal held back at first. She was an avid observer of those around her. At home, she watched her parents dote on one another, while her brothers were rowdy and playful. At Badington, she noticed girls gel with one another or spitefully fall out over little or nothing. Eva went about her business quietly.

Coming from a united family, she was secure in herself, confident and content. She chose her friends carefully and related well. Never before had she been so drawn to anyone like Charlotte.

Eva was a shrewd girl for her age. It did not escape her notice how Charlotte seemed always the outsider who did not particularly warm to anyone or anything. Always talking with a superior air and becoming bored easily with conversations. The yawn if someone took an interest in her, the eyes which looked toward heaven if someone tried to befriend her. Charlotte Kemp was the most secretive, unfriendly, uncaring person she had ever met. All of which, only seemed to make her more appealing and wonderful. As much as she tried to ignore her and get on with her other friends, she knew, deep down, that she and Charlotte would become inextricably linked, possibly soul mates and this she had no resistance to.

It was during orchestra practice that they began to bond. Both girls were gifted. Charlotte on cello and Eva on violin. So much so that their music teacher was soon running out of pieces for them to show off their duet skills. To begin with, this was all the communication they seemed to need but as they exchanged musical banter, they grew to respect one another.

Gradually, the other girls in the orchestra grew disheartened or drifted away. For those who stayed, it soon became apparent that Charlotte and Eva were the stars of the show and they played second fiddle. Be that as it may, the two promising proteges were immensely respected by their peers. Eva, sweet and caring, the harmonious one. Charlotte, wild and dramatic who caused the most tension and discord between them.

Soon it became apparent to their music teacher that they needed more than she could give. Therefore, just before their fifteenth birthdays, a meeting was held between both sets of parents and Miss Meakin, presided over by Miss Coulthard.

"I have been exploring several avenues for them but I think this conservatory of music is the best place for them to develop their skills further to prepare them perhaps for the Royal Academy of Music later on." Miss Meakin placed in the hands of both fathers some information.

"Are they... I mean is Charlotte really that good?" Earnest Kemp felt agitated at the thought of even higher fees while his wife, proud of what their daughter had achieved, was in agreement. She should be allowed to progress. Especially if that meant Charlotte going even further away than Cambridgeshire. Miss Meakin pointed out that they could receive music tuition at home with advanced peripatetic teachers as an alternative. Rachel knew that would never do.

During the past four years, Charlotte had caused mayhem on her return in the holidays. Rachel could not understand why such a talented child should wish to go out of her way to make things so unpleasant and cause so much embarrassment for her parents. Sipping her tea, she listened with a growing conviction that she should continue her studies as far away from Shopley as possible. As she recalled her first half term holiday she studied Miss Meakin's face. She was a mousy coloured creature with red rimmed eyes. Rachel suspected that the soreness had been caused from years of trying to keep her wayward daughter under control and failing miserably.

Charlotte had laid low in her bedroom for the first two days, refusing to eat anything. She had put the whole house under a cloud. Then Mabel had declared that her eternity ring had gone missing. The vicarage was in an uproar as cupboards and drawers were gone through. Every mattress was turned over in the bitter search. Everyone suspected Charlotte of taking and hiding it. Incidents like this had stopped happening in her absence. It was too much of a coincidence now she was back. It was as if everyone had taken a vow of silence. No one gave vent to their feelings nor confronted the child. On the last day of the holiday, the ring had, mysteriously, turned up on Mabel's whatnot stand. Reverend Kemp said it was a miracle. Mabel, Betty and Rachel knew, full well, it was no miracle and prayed hard to Jesus to punish the wicked little madam before she did something she might live to regret. Last Christmas when she was home had been much worse. Rachel had been in high spirits, organizing the village pantomime. It had been a splendid turn out. Farmer George and Farmer Huffey had played the ugly sisters with Mrs. Ong agreeing to take part for the first time, appearing as the fairy god mother. Directing the Christmas pantomime kept her busy for weeks and she enjoyed every minute of it. To witness Mrs. Ong decked out in a white, lacy gown with cardboard wings and a Shirley Temple wig, made life worth living. Even the Blooms had come with Joseph pushed in a wheelchair. Jonathon Leggatt played Buttons and his dopey sister Mary played Cinderella. When she forgot her lines, Charlotte sniggered but had then offered to prompt. The evening had been a triumph.

Rachel had sighed with relief and turned her attention to the annual parishioners Christmas party, always held at the vicarage. There was the tree to be dressed, poultry still to be collected and cooked as well as all the vegetable trimmings and puddings to be steamed. She, Mabel and Betty worked in harmony and it was the only time of the year when the house felt truly warm and inviting. Throughout the vicarage the smell of pine gave a lovely fragrance. The hall, stairs and dining room were decorated from top to bottom with holly and ivy and sprigs of mistletoe in between. Mulled wine was always prepared by Reverend Kemp who considered it a man's job. With all the hubbub of preparing for numerous guests, it wasn't noticed until two hours before sitting down to eat, that Charlotte had gone missing.

After searching every corner of the house from cellar to attic rooms, it was decided to send out a search party with flaming torches, around the surrounding countryside. Ditches, barns, sheds, hedgerows, stables, fields, forests and woods were combed, until everyone was exhausted.

Rachel had been more angry than worried. Why did the girl always have to be the centre of attention? She had managed to snatch the spotlight away from her, even on that occasion.

On the night of the pantomime, Charlotte had been so jealous of Mary in her starring role, that she had picked a fight with the scrawny, snotty nosed girl. Jonathon had walked in on them and threatened to tell her parents how spiteful she had been to the star of the show, if she didn't give him a feel. At the same time, he warned his sister not to breathe a word of it or else she would receive a Chinese burn.

He and Charlotte agreed to meet in Croppers Wood where he could not believe his luck. Her enthusiasm for the male anatomy had grown tenfold, since entering Badington. She prodded and poked, manhandled and massaged, following the sluggish instructions to the letter. The boy had never known such excitement and neither had she. She seemed to welcome his rough hands touching her in all her sensitive places.

"Let me lie on top of you and give you a good seeing to."

Charlotte drew the line at this. In her immature mind, she had promised herself to Henry, back at Badington. She rose to her feet and pulled her knickers up.

As they left the wood, dishevelled and damp, they saw gleaming in the distance, the sight of burning torches like glow worms in the dark.

"Christ, they're after us. What the 'ell we gonna do?"

He was almost crying. She could not believe he was such a coward.

"Just say you found me in the wood all alone. Upset and by myself. It's simple. You'll be a hero."

At that, the brainless boy brightened up and dragged her, by the arm, towards the throng.

Rachel remembered the gossip that had continued to spread for months after. She snatched the document as if her life depended on it and was the first to sign, hesitantly followed by her husband.

Eva could not stop giggling in the dormitory that night. They were going to study at a conservatory of music in Sussex. The news, delivered by Miss Meakin, after their parents had departed for home, made her feel grown up and special.

"It's been my dream, since I was seven, to become a professional musician, Charlotte. If we study hard, there's no reason why we won't be able to play in one of the top orchestras in London, one day."

Eva lay back on her bed and tried to contain her excitement. Charlotte combed her hair and yawned. It felt good to be moving on to more adventures but she secretly wished her friend would calm down a bit and listen to her latest news. In some ways, she took her talent for granted. She felt passionate when she played one of her favourite pieces and excelled in conveying this to her audience. At times like this she felt in command and her desire to be noticed aroused her. Just like she had felt with Jonathon in the wood and how she felt every time she imagined Henry doing things to her in the stable block at Badington.

So far, she had not confided in her friend who seemed much younger. She wasn't sure how she would take it.

"Eva, do you like boys?"

"Mm?" Eva was deep in thought, thinking about her future.

"Boys. Has anyone ever kissed you?"

"Absolutely not." Eva felt indignant. She swung her legs over the edge of her bed. Now her friend had got her attention. "Have you ever been kissed?"

"More than kissed, if you must know."

"What do you mean?"

"I've been touched all over and done the same to a boy who lives in Shopley. His, you know, his thing was like putty in my hand to begin with but then it grew to a gigantic size." Now it was her turn to giggle as she indicated with her hands about a foot in length much like a fisherman exaggerating the length of his catch.

Eva shuddered and did not understand how or why her best friend could indulge in such nasty, evil practices. She would slap a boy if he were to make any sort of advance. Her brothers had begun to date girls of their own age around King's Lynn. Now she wondered if they got up to such awful things with their bodies which Charlotte was vividly describing.

As if she could read her mind, Charlotte enquired, "You must have seen willies before Eva, with two handsome brothers."

Eva blushed and did not know what to say. Now the flood gates were open, Charlotte could not resist letting her in on her deepest, darkest thoughts.

"I bet Henry's got a big one."

Eva wondered if there was something wrong with her friend. On the most important day of their young lives, all she could think or talk about was boys and what they got up to. She got herself a drink of water and sat back on her pillows. Or maybe there was something wrong with her. One or two of the other girls had bragged about kissing and cuddling boys, on their return to school but no one had been as explicit as Charlotte. It had all seemed innocent fun. In answer to her friend's probing questions, she had never wanted to see her brothers' private parts. I'm a respectable, God fearing Jewish girl. I love my family, my pets and my music. One day, she hoped to meet someone and marry them but until then she would study hard and remain chaste.

She kept these thoughts to herself and looked forward to getting away from Charlotte for a while in the holidays. Eva felt homesick for the nurture of her mother and playfulness of her dear father. They were quiet all through supper and after compline kept out of each other's way.

On the last day of term, the school emptied out. Some pupils were fetched by chauffeurs, while others had trains to catch. Eva and Charlotte were in this latter category. While Eva waited with a handful of girls and Miss Lindsey for the pony and trap with the cart hitched onto the back of it for carrying excess passengers and their luggage, she wondered where Charlotte had got to. The heat from the morning sun was fierce.

"At last," she murmured as Henry made an appearance. He looked exceptionally hot and bothered.

"Where is Charlotte Kemp? I have ticked off everyone else's name on my list. They have trains to catch." Eva sensed something was wrong and quickly covered up for her friend.

"Oh, she had to run back for something she had forgotten, Miss."

Henry helped Miss Lindsey climb up into the trap. She was grateful for the assistance but even happier that Charlotte Kemp was moving onto pastures new. She had been a trouble maker and no mistake. The passengers, with their luggage, now waited expectantly. All heads turned to see Charlotte running towards them. With both hands, she was frantically trying to button her blazer so that her satchel was dragged and battered along the ground. They were all shocked to see how unkempt her hair looked, hanging down round her shoulders.

When Henry lifted her to join them in the back, Eva spotted mud and straw on her friend's shoes.

"Do your hair up, young lady. You look a fright," Miss Lindsey spoke, sharply, over her shoulder.

"Yes, Miss."

Charlotte took out a ribbon from her satchel. After plaiting her hair, she held out the end for Eva to tie in a neat bow. After which, she turned around in her seat and caught her friend's eye. With a gesture which was all too familiar to Eva, she demonstrated with her hands a certain length. Eva trembled. No one else in the back understood her hand signal. The pony sprang into action at the gentle encouragement of Henry and they moved, slowly, toward the train station, leaving Badington behind them.

Chapter 20

The sun was sinking behind Cropper's Wood and Leonard lost all track of time. He was marking trees for felling. Work which would keep Sam Miller and his brother busy for at least another fortnight. Unusually, he had left them in charge of the yard. Now, he hoped everything would be ship shape on his return.

He blinked hard and scribbled on the bottom of his work pad. He wished he had brought his spectacles. He needed them in the twilight. It was getting cooler and he shivered. A monk jack deer grazed a short way off, indifferent to his presence. A pheasant croaked his warning to another male to keep away from his harem. Leonard was at home with the wildlife which stirred and hid away with each passing hour.

"My Leonard, how you've changed." The familiar voice cut the air, just like a pistol shot at dawn. His clipboard slipped from his hand and he lost his balance for a moment. He could not make out who it was without his spectacles.

"Don't you recognize me? It's Charlotte." She stepped over the bracken and undergrowth towards him.

"Charlotte?" He heard his own heart beating in his chest.

"Your one and only friend, from years ago?"

Leonard could hardly believe it. He stooped to pick up his afternoon's work, feeling as vulnerable as when he was a boy and she was in command.

"Don't look so surprised. I am still the vicar's daughter. I do come home from time to time."

"It's just that...I'm sorry to stare. You caught me by surprise. How did you know where I was?"

"I didn't. Don't you remember, how I used to love roaming about all over the place?" she lied. Sam Miller had told her where to find him when she had called by the yard earlier.

"I can't believe it, after all these years. I can hardly believe it's you."

"Well it is Lenny Penny. I'm here in the flesh. Can I still call you that?"

"Of course you can. I always liked the way you said it."

She stepped closer toward him. The evening air was beginning to feel damp. She reached out and touched his arm, reassuringly. Leonard remembered the torch in his back pocket and switched it on. The beam picked her out. At sixteen, she was a buxom young woman with a mane of shoulder length, blonde hair. She smiled, warmly, at him. The skinny playmate had turned into a voluptuous beauty.

"I'll have to be getting back. Have to lock up."

"Oh, I wish you'd stay for a while, Lenny. It's like old times. I have a jacket. We could catch up."

The years slipped away when she spoke his name. Just as though they were being chased again by Shopley's bullies.

"It's so cosy in here." Charlotte laid her jacket on the ground and flopped down onto it. The torchlight picked out her expectant face and just like before, he found her hard to resist.

She explained how upset she had been when she had been sent away to school. How before that she had missed him when his mother taught him at home. She asked after his parents and told him how she had made a special friend who attended the conservatory of music with her. Leonard was impressed and hung on her every word.

"Why did you leave so suddenly? I heard you had been caught stealing, red handed."

"I'd almost forgotten about that." It was of no importance now. He felt relaxed.

"Well, I'm sorry to have got you into so much trouble, Lenny."

"What do you mean? Trouble?"

"Sweets. Remember?"

"Oh no, I was never caught taking sweets for you. It was in Ma Ong's shop. Some money turned up in my lunch box. God knows where from. Ma Ong never said a word. She's a kind old biddy."

"All these years, I thought it was my fault."

"It was nothing to do with any of that. My mum got sick of me being

169

bullied that's all."

"Thank heavens for that. So I hear you're quite the business man now and still so young. How did you manage it?"

"Uncle David came over from America and inspired me, I suppose. He has a much bigger business over there and could see the potential for development here, so..." Leonard liked the respect in her voice. She looked radiant. He wanted to kiss her. Instead he would walk her home. He was no longer a second class citizen. Reverend Kemp gave him many jobs to do around the vicarage and at last most of the overbearing trees had been felled. As these thoughts passed through his mind, he felt Charlotte's long fingers trace the length of his manly arm and fondle the nape of his neck. Slowly, she pulled his face down to hers. He groaned with pleasure, as her fingers unbuttoned his shirt and groped inside.

"Are you cold?" she whispered, "because I feel very warm and safe here with you."

He replied by kissing her mouth, gently. That was all the encouragement she needed. Charlotte shifted onto her haunches. Her breasts were level with his lips. She ran her hands through his dark, wavy hair and he sought out the mounds of flesh, which escaped, easily, from inside her dress. She didn't wear any underwear. Leonard was shocked and felt a tinge of guilt. Charlotte pushed him back and got astride him.

"Is this your first time?" she whispered again

"Yes."

"Mine too. It was meant to happen here, Lenny. In our old haunt. Us. Together."

She lied again and writhed about on top of him, enjoying how he was pleasuring her. For a beginner, he was doing everything right. Taking his time. Waiting for her to respond and holding back, until she was satisfied. Even when she laid down and he took his turn, he was gentle and loving.

She could not believe he was a virgin. She had suffered at the hands of Jonathon Leggatt and after waiting for five years, Henry had been a complete waste of time. Built like a wrestler, large and powerful, he had no self control and took his pleasure selfishly.

They lay in each others arms, until very late. Leonard could not believe what he had just done. They had taken a huge risk and he hoped that nothing bad would come of it. He would not worry about that for now. It had been amazing and he could not wait to see her again.

Leonard had developed into a tall, muscular young man. Everyone in Shopley said so, especially the young ladies. They drooled over him, every time they entered Blooms shop. Over the years, they tried hard to engage him in some sort of conversation. Did he miss school and company? Did he not get bored with the company of his mother all day, every day? Was his father ever going to get better, so that he might be free? More than this though, they were interested in courting him. Hint all they might, Leonard smiled placidly and changed the subject.

He was doing extremely well on his own having started up a timber yard, at the back of the shop. Part of the orchard had been felled to make room for his premises. He kept himself to himself and worked every hour he could to pay back to his parents the wrong he had done them. Deep down, he still blamed himself for his father's demise.

Local girls were of no consequence to him. He heard rumours all the time about them. Jonathon Leggatt and his cronies had put paid to their innocence. Even Sam Miller had deflowered one or two of the less desirables.

"He stepped into his father's shoes, from day one," Mrs. Ong sang his praises to a newcomer in the village. "Hated school, he did, so his mother taught him herself at home."

"Well, I never did."

"She's a remarkable woman. Done a fine job. He's such a gift for business. Supplies wood to all the builders round and about, from here to Waybridge and up to Norwich. Got two working for him, too. Only eighteen and done all that."

"Well, I never..."

"Never thought he'd make such a handsome, young man. Scrawny little devil he was but there you are. Another of life's mysteries."

"Well..."

"Right, that'll be two and three pence." She cut the woman short, realizing that she was about as exciting as a hot cross bun with all the currants sucked out.

The woman paid and Agnes Ong watched her cross the road, to the vets where she cleaned. She noticed Leonard give her a friendly wave, before unloading the truck parked outside the newly erected gates to his yard.

Many of the local woods and forests, belonging to the farmers were managed by him. Instead of payment, he was allowed to help himself to timber. He had, that morning, collected a load. It still had to be planed, sawn to length, loaded and delivered before the end of the day. Sam Miller had come to work for him and then his brother, as the business took off. They were reliable and hardworking, simple lads. Leonard oversaw everything and delivered himself, maintaining good relations with his customers. He and Sam often laughed over a pint of ale about their fight in Croppers Wood when they were lads. Jonathon joined them for a drink now and then in between courting his latest conquest.

Esther thanked God, every day, for her son. Such a fine, young man was a gift from heaven. Joseph was bed ridden after suffering more strokes. Each morning, after feeding him his breakfast, they talked to each other, using pen and paper. Joseph found it difficult to speak but he still had his senses. He knew Esther was agitated about something.

"What's wrong my love?" The spidery handwriting asked.

"Nothing. What do you mean?"

"Tell me."

"You will think me foolish."

"So there is something you're not saying."

"I want our son to meet a nice, Jewish girl. He has so much to offer. Yet all he does is work and never meets any nice girls. He refuses to ever go to the synagogue with me. He does not follow any of the traditions. He has no real faith."

"He is only eighteen...," he paused to get his second wind. "He has many years ahead of him to meet a nice girl and settle down." After such a colossal effort, he collapsed back onto his pillows.

Esther could not take her eyes off her son, labouring as usual, outside in the heat of the day. Work and making more money than he knew what to do with, was his god. It caused her restless nights. Guilt loomed large in his motives. She sensed this in her son but could never work out why.

"I know him better than he knows himself. I know, oh yes...how he

172

holds a candle for the vicar's daughter and she is no saint. The rumours I hear are terrible. What does she want with our son?" She turned her attention toward her husband who had fallen asleep.

When it had first begun, Esther could not say but she had soon become suspicious. Leonard only ever delegated to the Miller brothers when she was home in the holidays. Suddenly, he would appear behind the counter, willing to help out in the shop whenever she came in. How he blushed when she flirted with him. It was inappropriate for her to be so tactile with him, especially in front of his mother. She had no shame. When she left the shop he would strut around like a proud peacock with a knowing smile on his face. She prayed for him to see what a temptress she was and to lose interest.

Little did Esther realize why Leonard kept so busy. He relied on his work more than ever, to forget what he had started with Charlotte the year before. He had cooled to her and wanted his uncomplicated life back. Most of all, he wanted back his self respect. Her demands on him were becoming outrageous. The last time they had met had been the final straw.

"Take me here, Lenny." She raised her skirt and leaned so far back against the lookout bridge that he feared she might fall in.

" Don't be ridiculous, Charlotte. What if someone sees us?"

"Oh. So, I'm ridiculous now, am I? You didn't say that last night in the orchard. No, I suppose because we did it in the dark."

She let her skirt fall to her calves and lit a cigarette. She was angry with him.

"I didn't know you smoked."

"Well I have, for ages. There's a lot you don't know about me."

"I'm beginning to realize that."

He suddenly felt awkward and drained of any energy. At first, he could not get enough of her but recently she had not been content to make love in secret places. He could no longer be irresponsible. This time, she had gone too far. Thank God he wouldn't be seeing her again until Christmas.

"You've spoilt my last day here. How could you be so cruel?"

He hated to see her cry and attempted to comfort her.

"Go away. Don't touch me. You rotten Jew boy."

Leonard could not believe it. She had not changed a bit since she was a child. Everything had to be her way, even if it compromised them both or she would resort to calling him names. He wished it didn't still hurt him but it did. Worse than ever. For the first time in his life, he felt an overpowering urge to strike someone. He grabbed her violently and pushed her against the bridge. Charlotte went limp in his arms and laughed in his face. He could smell alcohol on her breath. This stopped him in his tracks. He let go of her and ran his fingers through his hair, at his wits end.

"You've been drinking. It must be the drink that makes you like this."

He remembered how she had drunk him under the table one night at the Angel and couldn't take her hands off him.

"I don't need a drink to make me crave you. I love you, Lenny Penny."

She gushed the words in her usual babyish voice but this time it had no effect on him. He couldn't wait to see the back of her.

"Come on. I'll walk you home. I've got work to do."

"Work, work, work. Go to hell. I can find my own way back."

"Fine. Just you do that." Leonard felt so angry that he took off in the direction of the village and didn't look back once. She could stew in her own juice, he thought.

"I'll fix you, you rotten Jew boy," she muttered under her breath.

After three months, Leonard's temper had burnt itself out. He missed her and longed to be with her again. She had written to him to invite him to the end of term concert. Her parents could not go. They would be away, on their first missionary trip to Africa and she would be spending Christmas alone at the vicarage. They could have it all to themselves, she tempted him. Leonard would have felt excited at the prospect had it not been for a dread of what might be expected of him. If only her appetites were normal. He sent word back that he would be attending. He felt sorry for her. To have parents who sent you away in the first place and then to leave you in the Christmas holidays to work overseas. He considered them selfish.

When Charlotte received his reply, she ran to the practice rooms where Eva was playing and bragged about their escapades. Eva tried hard to ignore her wayward friend and concentrated harder on the notes.

"You're a shameless hussy. You know that, don't you?" She began again from the top of the sheet music.

Charlotte giggled and ignored her friend. She was used to her disapproval by now. Eva was beginning to feel inadequate since she had nothing to confide about.

Later, the same day, as the two young women got undressed for bed, Charlotte was still full of news about Leonard Bloom.

"He made every inch of me tingle. Shock waves went through my body, again and again. We did it everywhere, the woods, the orchard...everywhere."

The half-hearted smile vanished from Eva's face. Charlotte could be so perverse. It frightened her.

"Tell me more about Leonard. What's he like as a person?"

"Oh yes". Her face softened as she climbed into bed. "He's wonderful. It was ecstasy. He is so tender but I like it when he's rough. He knows how to please me."

She yawned and pulled the covers up. When she fell asleep, Eva pondered on Leonard Bloom. It sounded like a good, old fashioned, Jewish name to her. She couldn't wait to meet him.

As the end of term approached, Charlotte and Eva chose their musical pieces for the Christmas concert. They were to play with the full orchestra but would be showing off their individual virtuosity by soloing. Eva felt nervous. Her whole family was coming, including her grandparents from London. She reminded herself that she was also going to meet the fascinating Leonard Bloom. She prayed hard not to let her contempt show for this young man who had been so disrespectful of her friend. She prayed to be polite and not to blush every time the sordid scenes played in her mind which her friend had described in the most lurid of detail.

Charlotte was nervous for a different reason. Anticipation at seeing him and what would happen when they were alone together kept her adrenalin pumping. So much pent up sexual frustration to release, hopefully, after the concert party.

The whole place was buzzing with excitement. Every young woman taking part could not wait for the performance to begin. They had all worked so hard to be note perfect and now the day had arrived to put everything they had been taught into action. They had been forewarned that there might be talent scouts in the audience to offer professional engagements as well as family and friends.

Eva looked innocent in a lilac silk. Charlotte appeared worldly in an off the shoulder red lace. She had removed a white flower, strategically placed to cover the cleavage to expose her bosom. As they applied rouge and lipstick, both girls felt butterflies in their stomachs.

It was time for the orchestra to take their place on stage. They were tuning up by the time Leonard arrived. He had given himself the whole day to drive from Suffolk, stopping at a pub for a ploughman's lunch. He caught sight of Charlotte completely focused on her instrument. She looked magnificent. After a while she seemed satisfied and caught his eye and licked her lips. He smiled back and waved his programme. Then when the audience had stopped shuffling about all was quiet and they began to play their first piece.

Charlotte had told him about Eva and so he looked closely at the violinists and wondered which one she was. A young lady in a lilac dress caught his eye and he rather hoped that it was her. She was so pretty. While Charlotte played with a stern almost manic expression on her face, the other one appeared calm with a warm smile as if she was really enjoying herself. After a while she stood up and played her solo. He glanced down the list of performers and arrived at her name. Eva Rosenthal. Yes, it was Charlotte's friend. She had been given the most difficult piece of the day for which she was given the longest applause. Leonard felt deeply moved by the sweetest sound he had ever heard. He couldn't wait to meet her. She was obviously Jewish. His mother would dance for joy if he made the acquaintance of a Jewish girl. He would do anything to please her and it would prove no hardship to make friends with the lovely young woman on the stage.

Each soloist took another bow at the end of the concert encouraged by the conductor and then the audience filed out into the huge refectory. Charlotte dragged Eva to the nearest lavatory. They were both hot and bothered and ran their wrists under the cold water tap. Charlotte reapplied her rouge and lipstick. Eva could not be bothered even though it had smudged with all her effort. She was a natural beauty while Charlotte needed a little more help from her makeup bag.

"Thank God, there were no major fluffs, Lottie," Eva said as her friend applied powder to her nose.

"It was as good as it gets. Come on."

They met Leonard by the bar laden with champagne for the guests and fruit juice and punch for the students. Eva held out her hand to him which he shook vigorously. He was taller than she expected with a gleam in his eye of admiration. When he smiled at her he reminded her of her father.

"So pleased to meet you. It was brilliant. You were both absolutely breath taking. I shall always remember it."

Leonard was genuinely enthusiastic. Charlotte noticed how happy he looked and how his admiration was not for her alone. His eyes flickered over to her while constantly paying attention to Eva. She felt mischievous. What a hoot it would be, to bring her two best friends together. Eva the virgin and Leonard practically so. After all, she had taught him everything he knew. She decided to leave them alone together while she circulated. Everyone there whom she came into contact with fell over themselves to give her the adoration she expected.

"How long have you been playing?"

"Since I was little. It's been a struggle but now I'm doing what I love most."

"I wish I could play an instrument. It must be wonderful. To hold an audience spellbound. The Lark Ascending was stunning."

"You enjoyed it. I'm so pleased. That's my favourite piece."

She accepted a glass of punch from Leonard and felt confused. He seemed so charming and friendly, not a bit like the person Charlotte described. She felt a mutual attraction between them instantly. The way the conversation flowed it was as if they had known each other for years.

"Are your parents here?"

"Oh yes. They always come. Even my grandparents are here. I must go and find them soon. I feel so sorry for Charlotte. Her parents hardly ever attend the concerts and now they're overseas."

"Me too." He finished his drink.

Charlotte joined them again and downed a glass of champagne followed by a glass of punch. "I'm thirsty," she defended herself when Leonard raised an eyebrow. The evening drew to a close. Eva went in search of her family and Charlotte threaded her arm through his. She led him away from the crowds and out toward the quadrangle garden. Once outside, she slid her hand down onto his buttocks and squeezed.

"Hey, are you drunk again? For God's sake, be sensible. Let's go and find Eva and say our goodbyes and head for home. We've got a long journey ahead of us."

"Look, no one will see us behind this giant palm tree, Lenny. I've waited so long. Haven't you missed me?"

She was slurring her words. The sight of her was beginning to disgust him. After spending just a few, precious minutes with Eva, her behaviour was intolerable. They found Eva in the entrance hall with her family. They were laughing together. Charlotte hugged her friend who introduced Leonard to her parents. Eva beamed, happy to be in his company again. When her middle aged father shook his hand, she could see the resemblance immediately. He had also been handsome once with a shock of wavy brown hair. Even though he was grey now, he was still tall and distinguished. Leonard congratulated her mother on having such a talented daughter. She had the same brown eyes as Eva and exuded a warm personality. As soon as a few pleasantries were exchanged, Charlotte led him away, staking her claim.

Outside, she felt demoralized to see an old, battered van awaiting her. Leonard had made it comfortable in the back with cushions and a blanket.

"Oh my. Thought you would ravish me on the way home, did you?" she hiccupped.

"You're tipsy. If I were you, I'd sleep it off in the back." For once, she did not argue with him. She was tired out after a long week of rehearsals, the performance and too much to drink on an empty stomach.

Leonard was relieved to hear her snoring all the way home. It took hours and he had a lot to think about on the journey. He couldn't wait to see Eva again. She was the loveliest girl he had ever met. Bright and beautiful. It was strange. Both he and Eva had befriended the wayward creature in the back. Somehow, he had to see her again without Charlotte getting in the way.

They arrived back in the early hours. Charlotte was still fast asleep so he carried her to the house and found the key under the plant pot in the porch. It was icy cold inside the house which caused her to wake up.

"Where's Mabel? She should have had all the fires lit for my return."

"Looks like she's been called away. An illness in her family." He handed her a sheet of paper with some childlike handwriting scribbled across it.

"Well, Betty had better have left some food for me. I'm ravenous."

"It's three in the morning. I'd better leave you to it. I'll come back later and help you light the fires. For now, you'd better get yourself to bed and keep warm under the covers."

"I thought you'd be doing that job."

"No, not tonight. I've still got so much to do at the yard before Christmas."

"You've changed your tune. Couldn't get enough before. Even when you had work to do. I saw how you looked at Eva, the little virgin." She sneered and snorted at the same time.

"Look, I'm not in the mood for arguing. I'm off."

"If you don't stay, I'll scream the house down and tell everyone how you forced yourself on me. Don't you know how much I've looked forward to this night?"

Leonard felt an overwhelming desire to slap her but resisted. He knew he would not be able to bargain with her.

"All right, but I shan't be sleeping with you. I'll light a fire while you get us something to eat and be on my way as soon as it's light."

Charlotte seemed satisfied for the moment and went to the kitchen in search of food. After the fire was lit and a plate of cold meat consumed, she seemed to have sobered up.

"Don't you love me anymore, Lenny?"

"I'll always love you as a friend." It seemed to him that the tables had turned and now she was the one in need.

"Come to bed then."

"I've already told you, not tonight. I'm whacked and so are you. I'll sleep here by the fire and when it burns itself out, I'll go."

"But you will come back and see me on Christmas day, won't you?"

"If you're a good girl." She could hear it in his voice that his resolve was weakening.

The room had warmed up and the fire was casting shadows around the walls. Leonard sat on a chair near to the fire while she squatted on the rug. She looked young and vulnerable with her knees tucked under her chin. If only she could be so innocent all the time, he might be able to love her again. He remembered how Eva had made him feel and knew he couldn't.

"Right, well I've warmed up. I'll be off to bed. Night. Night."

"Good night. Sleep well."

"Sure you won't change your mind?"

"Positive."

While he settled down in front of the blazing fire, Charlotte felt abandoned and tossed and turned. In the centre of her bed she curled up into a ball and cried herself to sleep. Before daylight, she woke up and remembered Leonard sleeping under her roof. She took off her nightdress and crept downstairs to find him still dozing. The fire had gone out but the room was still warm. Creeping over to the fireside chair, she knelt down in front of him and loosened his trousers as gently as she could. He stirred and half opened his eyes. He was putty in her hands.

"No... Char..." It was too late and he knew it. The sensation was too enjoyable to stop.

The next day he left her sleeping under a pile of clothes. It had to be the last time. He vowed he would never allow it to happen again.

Chapter 21

During the holiday between Christmas and the New Year, Charlotte had a visitor. Eva came to stay. They were delighted to be in each other's company again and felt very grown up alone in the rambling vicarage. Eva adored all its nooks and crannies and the huge gardens and orchards. On the morning of her arrival Charlotte was up bright and early to meet her at the station with Leonard. It was to be a surprise. Eva had not seen him since the concert and Charlotte was impatient to know how they would react to one another now. Leonard had willingly left the Miller lads in charge and was brimming over with excitement. It seemed ages since he had seen her.

Christmas day had been a dreary affair at the Blooms. Just himself and his mother for lunch and then he had made his escape to Charlotte's. He had hinted more than once to invite her for the day but his mother seemed oblivious. He sensed her dislike of Charlotte but came to the conclusion that she would be the same with any girl he brought home, unless she was Jewish.

The rest of Christmas day and Boxing Day had been the most debauched of all their couplings. They ate their way through a turkey, huge amounts of cheese and a Christmas cake, baked by Mabel, and consumed a crate of wine. When they were too tired to make love they slept in each other's arms in front of the fire which Leonard tirelessly fed. He had given in to her wanton behaviour but his New Year resolution was to break free of her. She would return to her studies and he to a more wholesome way of life.

When Eva stepped down from the train he was there to carry her suitcase. She had hoped, even dreamt of seeing him in the village at some point. Seeing him in the flesh, so soon, confirmed all her feelings. He was still as handsome as ever and the way he looked at her made her feel special. Charlotte couldn't take her eyes off them and offered to travel back to Shopley in the back of the van. As they chatted and became reacquainted she grew more and more jealous and dug her long talons into Leonard's seat. At the same time it amused her to see them so close and obviously infatuated with each other. She had used him time and again. He was hers and always would be. What harm would a bit of match making do?

"You must come into the shop and meet my mother and have an assortment on the house," he was saying.

"That would be lovely, wouldn't it, Lottie?" Eva noticed how quiet her friend had become. "But I couldn't possibly take anything without paying for it." He dropped them outside the vicarage and drove off.

After lunch of pheasant stew and left over Christmas pudding, the young women went for a long walk. Eva told her friend what a wonderful time she had had with her family. Being of an unorthodox persuasion they celebrated Christmas and exchanged gifts and had sing songs around the piano each evening. Charlotte was day dreaming about all the places where she and Leonard had had sex and pointed them out to Eva on their way back. Now it was no longer a figment of her imagination. What a shame, she thought, that Charlotte could not simply enjoy their time together, always setting out to shock her.

Eva loved Shopley village. It was so much quainter than King's Lynn where she had lived all her life. Agnes Ong was most courteous and made her laugh when she told her about Leonard as a boy.

"Old hag. I never liked her. She was putting on her posh voice to impress you."

"She seems quite a character. You mustn't be so harsh."

"Wait till you meet Leonard's mother. What a prig."

Eva remained silent until they reached the shop. Esther looked lovely as she weighed bags of sweets for her customers, mainly children. These days, she made bread as well and a new batch of freshly baked rolls made the shop smell heavenly. She welcomed Eva warmly.

"Do come inside and have a cup of tea. I'm just about to close up for the day."

Eva loved the sumptuousness of the small parlour with its chintz covers and antimacassars, ornaments and rows of photographs. She felt at home immediately. Her mother's sideboard was strewn with likenesses of similar looking relations. Charlotte felt bored and out of place. During tea she left them to it and was almost nodding off. They talked about new recipes for matzo meal balls, the lovely ingerblach, ginger sweets Esther had given her to sample and what was kosher. When it got to Jewish feast days and comparisons between what the Rosenthals ate and the Blooms, she yawned and reminded them that it was five o'clock and they should be leaving. She had only stayed this long in the hope of seeing Leonard and embarrassing him in front of his precious mother.

"So where is Leonard?"

"North Norfolk. I don't expect him back until very late." Eva noticed the colder edge to Esther's voice when she spoke these words to her friend. It was true. Charlotte was unpopular with almost everyone.

True to his word, Leonard was there to see her off. Business had taken him away from Shopley during her stay but Eva was grateful for any time with him. Although Charlotte hung onto his arm at the station, Eva sensed his indifference. His body language expressed an interest only in her. While Charlotte blew her a kiss from the platform, Leonard helped her onto the train with her luggage. Little did he know how much she wanted him to hold her but was afraid that Charlotte would notice if she gave any signs. Play acting did not come easily to Eva.

"Right, well, come and see us again soon," he said. "Sorry to have been so busy." He held onto her arm and settled her into a carriage, occupied by an elderly couple. Charlotte lit a cigarette and waited for him on the platform.

"I'll try. I really will." Eva held onto his hand and thanked him for everything. Leonard hated to see her go. The whistle blew. He had to get off. In a desperate attempt to tell her how he felt, he grabbed hold of her hand again and was half way to kissing her on the cheek, when he noticed Charlotte staring at them through the window.

"Right, better get off then. Take care of yourself and good luck with your exam results."

Eva sat down opposite the couple who averted their eyes. They could remember how awkward young love could be especially when saying goodbye in public. The train lunged forward and with a frantic wave in

Leonard's direction she settled back on her seat.

The next morning Leonard sat by his father's bedside. He felt numb. Joseph had suffered his final stroke. The doctor informed them that he was now living on borrowed time. It had been eight years since his first stroke. Leonard had grown used to him not being around and in charge. He could hardly remember Joseph as the strong man he used to be. Esther joined him. Together, they prayed for his merciful release but in her heart she still hoped for a miracle.

Until this happened, Leonard had begun to feel happier than ever before in his life. He had not had a chance to break the news to his mother. He was going to marry Eva Rosenthal. He had made his mind up. When or how he was ever to propose to her was still uncertain but he felt sure she would say yes. He decided to wait for a while, until this latest blow had time to sink in and then he would cheer her up. He knew she would be pleased. They had only met once but Esther had nothing but praise for the lovely young woman.

Both Eva and Charlotte graduated at the end of the spring term and were auditioning for private engagements. Charlotte had gone straight to the top of her profession but the London Symphony Orchestra had turned her down. They were looking for a more mature cellist. However, they were still interested in her talent and she was asked to reapply the next year.

Charlotte seemed to take this blow to her ego on the chin. Her parents were back from Africa. She seemed genuinely pleased to see them back and for that Leonard was grateful. She no longer depended on his company so much.

Then, he had received an invitation from Eva to attend a party at her house. It was to be a weekend affair. He was to stay over. She had even signed it with love and kisses. The evening he arrived it was pelting down with rain. When Eva opened the door, she could not believe it was Leonard, looking bedraggled and bashful.

"Leonard. How lovely to see you. Come in and get warm. I'll get Nora to make us some tea." She felt a little bewildered but kept the conversation flowing. Eva, like her mother, always knew the right things to say.

"You're so wet. You can dry off by the fire. Isn't it cold for this time of the year?"

"You're right there. I had a flat tyre. Got soaked changing it."

"You poor thing." She sat on the sofa and watched him strip off his wet shirt. She felt guilty. Nora placed a tray of tea and biscuits on the coffee table.

"Can I get you anything else, Miss?" the older woman tried hard not to seem judgmental. It came as a shock to find Eva with a young man, showing off his naked torso. She had never had any boyfriends as far as she could remember.

"A warm bath towel. By the way, this is Leonard Bloom, a friend of mine."

"Charmed, I'm sure." Eva knew what she was thinking and blushed. When the towel arrived, Leonard dabbed at his hair and chest and draped it around his shoulders. He took his tea off the tray and sipped at it.

"Lovely room." He couldn't help noticing how quiet the house seemed. Not at all ready for a party. "Would it be all right to bring my suitcase in now. I've got another shirt in there."

Feeling very confused, she placed another log on the fire and turned to face him. He had perched himself on the arm of a chair. His chest was brown and muscular. What was this all about? A spontaneous visit with a suitcase.

"Only Charlotte couldn't come with me. She's arriving on the five o'clock train."

"Oh?"

"When will your other guests be arriving?"

"Other guests?"

"Charlotte's told me a lot about your family. Your brothers seem a comical lot."

This was becoming more bizarre by the minute. What conniving game was Charlotte up to, this time? In her living room was the love of her life, stripped naked to the waist, believing he had been invited to a weekend party. Charlotte really was the limit. She knew, perfectly well, that this weekend her parents were away with her brothers. They had all gone sailing. She had set them up.

"Um...well...yes. I'll just go and fetch my case, then. Rain seems to have eased off." He felt a distinct atmosphere in the room.

"No, sit still. You'll get cold. I'll tell Nora to get it for you." She hardly knew how to break the news to him. It was so embarrassing and so she played along for a while. "You must be hungry after your journey. Can I get you anything more substantial?"

"Had a snack before I left home. I can wait until dinner."

Dinner. She had planned her evening meal already. Some cheese, biscuits and pickles. It was Nora's night off.

Thinking on her feet, she blurted out. "Do you like fish and chips? We could go for a stroll, down to the harbour and have some."

"That'll suit me, just fine." Nora delivered the suitcase and he quickly put on a thick jumper, to combat the weather. When they were ready they set out. She decided to tell him on a full stomach that their mutual friend had duped them both. She would telephone Charlotte, later that evening, when he was gone and give her a piece of her mind. For now, she was enjoying his company. She felt relaxed.

Down at the harbour, they laughed and joked and fed the persistent seagulls with bits of batter left over from their meal. Once or twice, she noticed how intent he was, gazing at her. Or was she just kidding herself? He belonged to Charlotte. Like it or not. That was the simple truth. They had had an inseparable bond since childhood. They strolled back to the house. One of the largest, Victorian mansions in the street.

"Leonard, I don't know how to tell you this but there isn't going to be a party, this weekend."

"But I've got the invitation, here, somewhere." He reached inside his jacket and brought it out.

"Yes, but I didn't send it. That's not my writing but I know whose it is."

"Let me guess. Charlotte."

"She's played a practical joke on us. I can't believe she would stoop so low. I'm so sorry."

"Don't be. I'm having the time of my life."

"But you've travelled all this way for nothing."

"Nothing! I wouldn't say time spent in the company of Miss Eva Rosenthal was nothing. In fact, I say Charlotte has done me a favour. I've wanted to talk to you alone... ever since I saw you, that night at the concert, I can't stop thinking about you..." He bent his neck, to kiss her but she pulled away.

"We can't...you shouldn't."

"You are right. I'm sorry. I'll collect my suitcase and be on my way." He felt awkward. Just because he had feelings for her, did not mean she reciprocated them. Eva felt confused. She wanted him more now than ever before but could not get the picture of him, with Charlotte, out of her mind. He had given into temptation with her, time and again, and she almost hated him for it.

"No, come in. Stay a while. It's just such a lot to take in."

For the rest of the day he behaved impeccably for which she was grateful. They talked into the early hours about their lives and family. Leonard loved feeding the fire with a stack of logs which came abruptly to an end. When it was bed time, Eva showed him to a room down the hall from her own. He kissed her on her cheek. Neither slept well that night. Leonard couldn't wait to be in her company again the next day.

Eva felt a mixture of emotions. It felt thrilling to know that he cared for her. Yet, whenever she imagined them together, Charlotte always reared her ugly head. As much as she tried to drive the sordid scenes out of her mind, she tossed and turned.

At breakfast she was quiet. If Leonard noticed, he did not allow her coyness to spoil their time together. As the weather was warmer, they sat out on the terrace. Leonard had a huge appetite and made all the conversation. After a while Eva relaxed and when the sun came out, they played croquet on the lawn. He could no longer contain how he felt.

"I love you, Eva. I always have from the first time we met and I know I want to marry you. If only you felt the same."

"I do Leonard. I really do but…"

"But what, my love?"

"What about Charlotte?"

"We're just friends."

"Is it really over, between you? Leonard, I'm sorry but she's told me everything, in the minutest of details and somehow…"

He looked ashamed.

"You seem to belong to her."

"Never. It's over. I never loved her, really. I thought I did, until I felt the real thing. When I met you."

"Leonard, would you do something for me?"

"Anything."

"Kiss me."

He reached across and kissed her. It felt warm and gentle and she loved him. She wanted him so much. That night, before he returned to Shopley they got engaged. When he saw her again, he would have the ring and speak to her father.

Chapter 22

"I am having his baby and that's all there is to it."

They were outside the gate of Blooms Timber Yard. Esther had spotted her snooping about. The sight of Charlotte put her nerves on edge. She was shouting at the top of her voice. Joseph would be disturbed and half of the village would hear her business.

"Come inside and we shall speak about this properly, over a cup of tea." Esther managed to control herself.

"Oh, all right. Have it your own way but it won't change anything."

Once inside, Charlotte heard Esther busying herself in the kitchen, little realizing how much the older woman was trembling with dread at what she was about to hear.

"I'm almost two months gone."

"How can the baby be Leonard's? He spends what little spare time he has with Eva. They are engaged to be married in October."

"Oh well...that won't be on the cards now."

"Why? What on earth do you mean?"

"She is my best friend. First person I told."

"Oh my God..."

"Well... she can't go marrying someone who belongs to someone else, now can she? A baby needs a father, after all."

Esther jumped up spilling most of her tea in her lap. It scalded her legs but she didn't seem to notice.

"I don't believe it. Not for one minute that the baby is Leonard's. You have the reputation of an alley cat. How dare you come here, with your sordid lies?"

"I thought I'd catch him at home. After all, it is our business and nothing to do with you. Haven't managed to tell my parents yet. As you know, they are doing God's work again in Africa."

And you are doing the devil's work here at home, Eva thought.

"You are a hypocrite. I would like you to leave. I shall speak to Leonard when he comes home this evening."

"I'll call back again tomorrow. The sooner he knows, the sooner he can make an honest woman of me."

"Just go!" Esther did not recognize herself as she shouted at the top of her voice. Charlotte clutched her stomach, dramatically.

"This is your grandchild I'm carrying, you know. You shouldn't upset me like that." Esther pushed her out of the room and out of her shop.

When Leonard finally came home, she was sitting in the dark waiting for him. Stoically, she told him of Charlotte's visit.

"I must phone Eva and explain."

"Surely there is nothing to explain, Leonard."

He looked harassed and guilty. He felt sure that what had happened a few months earlier had not resulted in a pregnancy. Charlotte had asked him to tea at the vicarage on a day that her mother was out doing her pastoral visits. Her father was immersed in sermon writing in his study. Over cups of tea and scones on the terrace they talked about his engagement to Eva. Charlotte seemed in a good mood and genuinely pleased for him. They chatted about old times and shared a couple of jokes. It was chilly for July and so they moved into the summer house at the bottom of the garden. The next thing he knew, her mood had changed. She grew impatient with him, picking on the way he dressed and what he did for a living. When he said he should go, she barred his way.

"I'm sorry, Lenny. I hope we can always be friends, even after you're married. I'll always have a soft spot for you, you know."

He had relented and sat back down. He felt sorry for her. She looked so lost and lonely. In that instant, he felt like the only person in the world whom she could depend upon. When she held her hand out, he took it and squeezed it. He had only meant to reassure her but she had taken it to mean much more. Soon she was sitting on his lap, kissing him passionately. He meant to be strong. He cursed himself. Then they were on the floor, writhing about. They had begun to make love but he had the presence of mind to stop. He felt certain she was lying but could not be a hundred percent sure.

"So, the child could be yours?"

"Yes...no...I don't know." He slumped down onto the settee and buried his face in his hands.

"Yours and a half a dozen other young men, I shouldn't wonder."

"Surely not. She's not as bad as they say..."

"Do not defend her to me. You had better make your phone call. It is a mess only you can clear up."

Eva was alone in the house. Her father was conducting business at the shipping office and her mother was out at her painting class. Her brothers had gone back to university. It felt good to be home, by herself. She had more time to dream about becoming Mrs. Leonard Bloom. He had come back to talk to her father. They had got on, famously, over brandy and cigars. He fitted in so well, she couldn't wait for him to be part of her family, as indeed, she would be part of his. She felt sorry that she would never get to know his father but his mother was adorable.

When the post came she rushed to collect it. They always had a lot of post. Most of it was for her father but there were two letters for her which she grew excited about. The first, hand written one, she recognized instantly. It was from Charlotte. She put that to one side because the second one looked more official. She had been waiting for two weeks for it to arrive.

"Please God, let it be a yes."

She opened it with some trepidation and could hardly believe that she had been offered the job. Her first success and a prestigious contract. Eva screamed with delight and danced about the room, singing at the top of her voice. She was to start touring with the Sussex Symphony Light Orchestra with dates in all the major cities in England and across Europe. Nora came running and Eva hugged her and told her to bring two glasses.

"I'm celebrating, Nora. Have a sherry with me."

"I'm not supposed to, while I'm working Miss Eva, but then, if you insist."

Eva explained how she had applied for many jobs as violinist and at last she had been accepted. Nora felt proud of the young woman whom she had known since a baby. They sat in the conservatory. After a refill, they were both a bit tipsy.

"I can't wait for Mum and Dad to know. Shall I tell them or Leonard first? He is such a love. Oh, I've just thought how much I shall miss him when I'm touring."

"Now don't you get maudlin', Miss. Parting makes the heart grow fonder. Well it did with me and my Arthur, in the war. This is peace time, so it'll be easy to meet up in between your engagements."

"Yes, you're quite right. I shall come home and he can come and see me."

Nora left her and got back to the kitchen and food preparation. Eva dozed, after so much sherry on an empty stomach. Life felt like it couldn't get any better. Then she remembered the other letter. Lottie. It probably contained news of her latest conquest, as was usually the case. They had not been so close since the engagement had been announced but she had sent her a card, wishing her well and to look after her Lenny Penny.

On first reading, the short, abrupt letter seemed to be about someone else. She switched the light on in the drawing room and read it for a second time. No, there it was, in black and white. Charlotte was pregnant. Leonard was going to stand by her. He still loved her. He was the father. Eva read and reread the letter. It was as if her brain was scrambled. She could not take it in. Leonard was no longer hers. He was to marry Charlotte. The letter slipped from her fingers. She felt too numb to be sick, even though her insides ached and went into spasm.

Seagulls carried on screeching overhead. The clock ticked and struck the hour. The sun continued to shine. Life carried on, heartlessly, around her. Then Nora came back and told her Leonard was on the telephone.

"Hallo Eva, it's me."

"Leonard, I know everything. Charlotte's written to me."

"I know darling. That's why I'm ringing you. She's lying."

"Leonard, listen to me. You and Charlotte have always been destined to be together. You know it and I know it. We were fooling ourselves."

"Don't say that. I love you, not Charlotte."

"But don't you see Leonard, she's always there between us. She'll never let you go and now you have to stand by her."

"But I don't even know if the baby is mine...for sure."

"Listen to yourself, Leonard. You've just told me that it might be which means you've been unfaithful to me."

"Oh God."

"It's over Leonard. Goodbye."

Inside Shopley vicarage time stood still. It was a week since Charlotte sent Eva the letter. She had received no reply. After informing Esther Bloom about her pregnancy, there was still no word from Leonard. She decided to leave it for another few days after which she would call round again. It surprised and annoyed her that he had not paid her a visit yet. It was out of character. Her appetite had increased vastly. While she gave herself up to gluttony she had no idea of the mayhem she had caused in the outside world.

Eva acted as if nothing had happened while her parents looked on, hoping and praying that she would not crack under the strain. They could see the pain in her eyes. She had broken off her engagement and was getting on with her life. There had been few tears. Several times they had broached the subject but she preferred to talk about her forthcoming tour.

Leonard could not bring himself to visit Charlotte. Hatred had taken the place of pity and he did not trust himself to be alone with her. Buried in his work he had not eaten or slept properly since Eva had broken up with him.

Charlotte read the latest letter from her mother, asking after her health and describing the missionary school she was helping to set up. They would be back within the month. She sneered at them and burped loudly, as she polished off a cheese and jam sandwich and half a fruit cake. Betty had gone home early. The cook sickened her these days, with her warnings about overindulging. She had cravings which had to be satisfied. Reverend Adamson who was taking services at St Mary's in her father's absence was certainly not a craving, she sniggered. Admittedly he was a lot younger than her father but had acne and a stutter and blushed whenever he saw her coming. In a way, it was a pity she was pregnant, she would have had such fun leading him on and embarrassing him, she thought. Morning sickness had put paid to that.

She rolled off her bed and wandered down to the kitchen where Mabel was taking a well earned break. Her feet shot off the edge of the table when she realized Charlotte was scrutinizing her.

"No time to be lounging about, Mabel. Mother wouldn't like to hear that you've been idle. Might have to dock your wages." She grimaced as Mabel scrambled about and left the kitchen in a hurry.

Alone in the pantry, she enjoyed the coolness of the brick walls. It was a freakishly hot day for September. Betty had left a plate full of angel cakes with butter cream beneath a fly net. She piled four onto a plate and grabbed an apple, orange and banana from the fruit bowl. Back upstairs, on her bed, she spat pips around the room and thought about her future.

Marriage and a family weighed heavily on her mind. Somehow, it meant more to her than joining an orchestra and playing music. That could wait. Right now, she needed a family of her own. This would be her chance. One thing was certain, the baby could have one of four fathers. Sam Miller and his brother were simpletons whom she had seduced in turn at the wood yard on days Leonard was away and Jonathon had proved to be brutish in his love making down at the lookout bridge on a sultry day in July. At last they had gone all the way and she had loved every minute of it. He swore it would never happen again. He was getting married to Amy Peart. Then the scrum down with Leonard in the summer house. She doubted very much that he could be the father but out of all of them she hoped he was.

When she thought about her parents, she wondered why they had not provided her with a sibling. Had they found parenting a chore? Well they could rot for all she cared out on the dark continent amongst the natives, clad in next to nothing, working themselves up into frenzies. Then carrying their women into the bushes to have carnal knowledge of them. Nothing more than savages and yet her father thought he could tame them with passages from the Bible. If it wasn't so hilarious it would be beyond contempt.

She noticed her two most treasured possessions. A photograph taken with Eva at the Henley Regatta with Eva's parents. The other was her battered, old teddy. She lunged forward, grabbed him by the ear and held him to her breast.

After a while she began to crave something else. Unable to make up her mind she ventured into her mother's bedroom and played with the silver hair brushes. A flannelette night gown lay folded on top of the bedspread. She wondered if they still did it. Out there in Africa with only thin canvass between them and the stars. As she took a final bite out of her angel cake a splodge of butter cream squirted down the front of her blouse. Eating was as good as sex at times like these, she thought and revisited the kitchen for something to quench her thirst.

After a glass of water she felt in need of something stronger. The study was the place where alcohol was kept. Over the years, she had helped herself to one or two drops of brandy, unbeknown to her father. Ernest Kemp enjoyed the occasional snifter. He had also taken to smoking cigars in the privacy of his study. A bottle of brandy and box of cigars were hidden inside his writing bureau. Charlotte forced the lock open with a letter opener. The fourth drawer down supplied her refreshments. With her teeth, she uncorked the bottle and took a swig. Its heat hit the back of her throat and took her breath away. It always did that to begin with but after a few swigs she felt warm inside. Next she lit a cigar. This was a new experience. It had always fascinated her how Eva's father cut the end of his cigar and then puffed on it until it was lit. This she proceeded to imitate. With a glass of brandy in one hand and the cigar in the other, she slid down into her father's leather armchair and rested her head.

"Heaven."

She had a go at blowing smoke rings. Henry had shown her how in the stables. This memory excited her so much she puffed on the cigar, only coming up for air to pour herself some more brandy. She dropped the stub into the nearest cut glass vase and stoppered the bottle. Flushed and inebriated, she pleasured herself. Afterwards, she felt satisfied in every way and dozed on and off for the next hour. When she woke up it was nearly dark. She flicked on the reading lamp and settled down to further amusement.

Now she decided to explore her father's bureau in more detail. The top drawer contained a Bible. Turning to the front page, she discovered that he had been awarded it, age eleven for winning a poetry competition. She wondered if this Bible had influenced him in his calling. She did not know that he possessed a gift for poetry. Come to think of it, she really did not know her parents very well at all. They never spoke to her about their lives or interests outside of the church.

Charlotte resented this. After shuffling through boring paper and envelopes, she arrived at a leather box, in the third drawer down. It contained more boring letters from parishioners, asking for intercessory prayers for them and their loved ones. Also, there were invitations to meetings and reminders about funerals that were methodically ticked off. Charlotte decided that her father led the dullest of lives that she could imagine. She yawned and opened the final drawer. On top of a book of household accounts was a metal box. It contained a float for Betty to dip into when the Kemps were away. Charlotte relieved it of two pound notes. A cunning explanation came to her should they notice the money missing. After all, Betty held the key to the bureau in her father's absence.

As she placed the metal box back inside the drawer, it landed with a thump on a catch at the side which she would otherwise have missed. Instantly, it clicked open revealing a false back to the drawer. Inside were some hidden contents. What fun she thought. Secrets. A leather bound file containing all manner of official looking documents. She removed them and turned them over in her hands, carefully, one by one. They were discoloured with age and smelled musty like old antiquities.

One was a birth certificate and another, a more detailed document with many signatures, scribbled on the bottom. She was finding it hard to focus, after so much brandy. She rubbed her eyes and the writing became clearer.

Baby girl, born 1st June, 1920. Shoreditch. London.   Father unknown, mother - Rose Drew.

"That's my birthday." she spoke the words, aloud, two or three times.

Charlotte Drew to be adopted by the Reverend and Rachel Kemp. An instantaneous headache forced her to close her eyes as her blood pressure rose above normal. The room swam around her when she opened them again. An overwhelming realization took her breath away.

"They're not my real parents." She slammed her fist down onto the writing bureau as another revelation gripped her.

"No wonder they have always despised me."

Charlotte saw a red mist during the next few seconds which was all the time it took to turn the study upside down. Every piece of furniture was kicked or overturned. The heavy cut glass vase which had been a wedding present was hurled onto the oak floor boards where it smashed into a myriad of splintery chards. Liars. They had lied to her. She had had every right to

196

know she was not theirs. Holier than thou, they had kept her right to know who she was from her. Kept secrets. They were no more than liars. She had never loved them and now she knew why.

"Just you wait....just you wait." she repeated over and over.

Her rage knew no bounds. She felt like head butting the walls but felt too unwell. A sharp pain was becoming more intense, deep in her groin and she spewed a rainbow mixture onto the floor. She knew if she was to survive this blow to her very core, she must get back to the sanctuary of her bedroom and try to sleep through it. Only in there could she feel safe and shut out the world.

Chapter 23

Earnest Kemp spoke the words somewhat reluctantly, facing the small number of guests attending his daughter's wedding.

"Should anyone here, know of any lawful impediment, why this marriage should not proceed, would they now speak or forever hold their peace."

Esther Bloom dug her finger nails into her friend's palm and prayed for God to strike the girl down. Then, as she prayed instantly for forgiveness, Mrs. Ong rubbed her friends back, to comfort her on what seemed the worst day of her life.

After they were pronounced man and wife, they faced the gathering and left the church. Charlotte looked unabashed while Leonard appeared withdrawn and deathly pale.

A month before, he had found her in a pool of blood having made up his mind to call round and put a stop to the mess she was making of his life. After banging on the front door and getting no reply he had peered through the letter box and heard her groaning in the distance. He had not been able to find the key in its usual place beneath the flower pot and so had forced the front door with all the brute force he could muster. She had miscarried at the top of the stairs. He phoned for an ambulance and held her in his arms until it arrived. She had looked so close to death that his anger with her dissipated.

Then he had visited her in hospital to find her sitting up with rosy cheeks, eating a three course evening meal. He had tried to reason with her that since there was no baby, he was free to marry Eva but she had other plans. She would tell the police she informed him that he had broken into the house and attacked her in the study. Yes, she would say that he had gone berserk and wrecked the place. He had been the cause of her miscarrying. If he did not agree to marry her, she would say all this and do more to discredit him. It would be in the paper and he would go to court and then prison. It would be the end of him and his cosy business. He would have to begin again, somewhere else, from scratch.

Leonard had instructed Mabel in her absence to clean and put the study back together and not to breathe a word to anybody. Charlotte refused to explain what had happened in there. Leonard no longer cared. All he knew was that he had to go on pretending or he would lose everything. Charlotte had returned all the documents to the secret drawer except for her birth certificate which she concealed beneath the mattress in her bedroom.

After the ceremony, Esther got back to Joseph, Agnes Ong to her shop. Betty had prepared some sandwiches back at the vicarage, for the vicar, Rachel, Charlotte and Leonard. Mabel agreed with her how disagreeable it all seemed. When someone married in their family, there was a grand do, with dozens of friends and neighbours present. They pitied Leonard. He had always seemed such a nice young man. The only good thing to come of it, they agreed, was her removal to Blooms shop where they were to live. Peace and harmony again at the vicarage. Just like when she was away at that fancy college of hers. For all her malicious and uppity ways, she had fared no better than they.

Leonard ate a sandwich, drank a cup of tea and then suggested that he and his wife should make their way to the Angel, to begin their wedding night. Leonard was sworn to secrecy about the baby. Mabel and Betty had been threatened with the sack if they breathed a word of what they had seen and heard. As far as the Kemps were concerned, on their arrival home they had found the two young lovers wanting to marry quickly and without any fuss. They were only too pleased to give their blessing.

The Angel was a sixteenth century inn which boasted several rooms above a bar, snug and smoke room. Heavily beamed, with beer straight from the barrel made it popular with locals and passing trade. A few regulars raised their tankards to the young couple, as they made their way up the stairs to the bridal room. One or two sneered. Amy Peart hung onto Jonathon Leggatt's arm and refused to drink their health. She fumed underneath. To think that the only desirable man for miles had succumbed to her lifelong enemy.

Leonard refused a bottle of red wine on the house which Charlotte happily accepted. She intended to get merry on her wedding night. As soon as she stepped out of the cream coloured two piece, borrowed from her mother, she ran a bath and busied herself. Leonard sank down into an old, battered armchair in a corner of the sloping room. They were up in the eaves. He felt detached from his surroundings and from the day itself. He had fulfilled his promise. Now he needed some rest and sleep.

He no longer hated her. He no longer felt very much at all. Tomorrow he would get back to work and keep out of her way. How she was going to fit into their lives at the shop, was beyond him. He could not believe she was acting as if nothing had happened. As if they were in love. Her voice rose and fell in between splashes of water from the bathroom. She was singing. He had never heard her sing before. It was torment as was everything else about her.

Then he could hear the suction of the water as it drained away and there she was wrapped in a towel and perched back on the bed.

"Well...well...well...Lenny. Here we are then on our wedding night. Cosy isn't it?"

He closed his eyes to block her out.

"Aren't you going to have a drink with me?"

She reached for the bottle and glass. "Oh, silly me. We need a corkscrew. I'll go and ask Ted for one while you rest."

Leonard opened his eyes and darted toward the door. "Stay where you are, I'll go." As if he could allow her to wander down to the bar dressed in next to nothing. She smiled and settled herself again. He snatched the bottle out of her hand and left the room. When he got back, he poured her a drink.

"Come on Lenny. Loosen up. Join me."

When he did not respond, she grimaced and poured herself another.

"I know you're angry with me now but it will pass, you know. You loved me once. Surely, you remember how that first time felt between us? I've always loved you. In fact," her voice trembled, "you're the only person, I ever felt loved me back." She had never told him this before but now he no longer cared.

After she had drank the bottle to herself, she fell asleep. At one time, the sight of her, so vulnerable on a bed would have aroused him but now he felt numb. He had been shocked and disgusted by her throughout all the years they had known each other. He supposed he had always been in her power and would never have known any other way had it not have been for Eva. He felt empty and impotent.

Laughter sounded far away, down in the bar. He envied them their freedom. He could not even join them for a drink to drown his sorrows. After all, what would a married man be doing with acquaintances in the Angel bar on his wedding night? He dozed on and off until dawn in the armchair. As soon as she woke up, they would return to his home and he could go back to work.

To begin with, Charlotte enjoyed the simplicity of working in a shop. She helped herself to as many sweets as she sold. The feeling of power over her young customers thrilled her. It reminded her of the time Leonard had stolen from the stock room for her. She even offered to knead the dough for the bread and rolls but Esther always refused. She did not want Charlotte's hands anywhere near her bread.

To make life bearable, the two women kept out of one another's way as much as possible. In the mornings, while Esther nursed Joseph and prepared the food, Charlotte served in the shop. Esther served after lunch while her daughter in law visited her parents. At the vicarage, conversation was polite, limited to the weather, their trips abroad and when she might start a family. Charlotte gave little away to do with her true feelings. For now, Leonard was all the family she needed. She would retreat to her old bedroom for the real purpose of her visit. To play her cello.

The most important distraction from the atmosphere in which the three of them lived was news each evening that came via the wireless. Talk of a war with Germany was on each and every bulletin. Leonard either took himself to the Angel or listened with keen interest to the prospect of being conscripted. He had to get away from the suffocating situation.

Charlotte seemed to respect his wish to keep his distance from her but after a while grew bored and frustrated with him. They had not consummated their marriage. Ironic she thought. To have had carnal knowledge of each other for so long as single people, when after two months of marriage they still lived like strangers. Well, she was willing to get to know him all over again, if only he would meet her half way. The trouble was, she had no one to confide in. She missed Eva terribly.

On the 9th September, Leonard would be twenty one and she planned a surprise birthday party for him, down at the Angel. She hoped to make him happy and invited everyone he knew. Leonard was popular. Everyone agreed to come. Reverend and Rachel Kemp, Mrs. Ong, the Miller brothers, Jonathon Leggatt, Amy Peart, Farmer George and others. It was to be a grand affair. Esther made him the biggest cake she could and set about altering her best dress, to bring it up to date. Charlotte could still get into her red, nylon concert dress and hoped to wet his appetite. Ted, the landlord, agreed to keep the lounge closed for trade. Tables were set back against the walls to make room for dancing. Charlotte practiced hard on the cello for the occasion. Leonard had mentioned a certain piece he had enjoyed at the Christmas concert two years before. She hoped to impress him with her skill and win his affection back.

The week before the party, as Esther altered her dress and Charlotte painted her fingernails, Leonard listened keenly to the bulletin that he had been waiting for. War was declared on Germany. Now he could get away and serve his country. Now he could be a man again and have a purpose. He vowed to himself that he would enlist as soon as he could. Both women seemed oblivious. They shook their heads and said how terrible but for the moment their minds were elsewhere.

On the day of his birthday, dressed in their finery, the women urged Leonard to get changed as soon as he came in from work. They were going to accompany him to the Angel and celebrate his important coming of age. For the first time, his mother and wife seemed to be making an effort to work together. For that he was grateful and had a quick wash and change of clothes.

Everyone had arrived before they got there and sang "For he's a jolly good fellow". Leonard smiled and felt very touched at seeing so many friendly faces. Jonathon Leggatt bought him his first pint of the night and slapped him on the back.

"What do you reckon about this 'ere war then, Len?"

"Inevitable really, after the Gerries invaded Poland."

"You'll be all right, anyway, with the timber yard. I bet you'll get away without any active service."

"Now then, you young men. Stop that talk - this is a celebration. Come and have some food to go with your drink." Even Betty had pulled out all the stops on the catering. After so many years of resenting the Blooms, she now had to admit that they were hardworking and brought no trouble. An asset really to the community.

Leonard who didn't drink very often consumed pint after pint, bought for him all night long. Charlotte noticed how much he drank. She planned on being sober when she coaxed him into her bed at the end of the night. No more sleeping in the spare room. Not after all this effort she had made. Once or twice she believed he had smiled at her across the room.

Before dancing commenced, it was her turn to perform and she was beginning to feel nervous. She had to excel. People stopped talking, as she took her place in the centre of the room. Bach's suite no 1 in G major, written for the solo cello, intoxicated both her and the room full of people. As she played, she thought about all the duets she had played with her dear friend, Eva. All the Beethoven, Mozart, Sibelius and others, which they had loved so much. Their favourite piece, together, had been the Handel Halvoresen Passacaglia, which had been very complex and they had conquered it together. Her eyes smarted, as she reached a crescendo. Then she opened them wide, at the wonderful sound of applause and shouts of encore, for which she played the piece Leonard had enjoyed at the concert. Ave Maria by Gounod. She played it slowly and deliberately, like a soothing balm for Leonard's senses. At the end they cheered and she felt spent. She could do no more.

Then it was the turn of the fiddlers and squeeze box players and dancing and jigging, until late with laughter and fun. She didn't mind that Leonard danced with everyone but her, or that he did not compliment her on her playing. He would be in her arms later. She sat next to her mother who was in deep conversation with Esther Bloom about Joseph.

"The nurse is with him, until I get back. Such a shame he had to miss this night. He would have been so proud."

Then Jonathon had her on her feet. She was being whirled around the floor, until she could hardly catch her breath. She felt, for the first time, a tiny sense of belonging. She stayed on her feet, until Amy Peart gave her a filthy look and sat back down again. Even that did not alter her high spirits. Then the barman was clanging the bell, not for last orders but for Leonard, who was standing up on a chair to attract everyone's attention. The music stopped and people stood gazing up at him, as if he were about to preach a sermon.

"I have an announcement to make. This morning, I went into town and enlisted for the army. I shall be going to defend my King and country at the end of the week. So come on lads. Let's be having you. Your country needs you."

Charlotte could not believe her ears. He had signed up and was leaving her. She had wasted her time and energy. It took her all the effort she could muster, to prevent herself from screaming the place down.

He stepped down from the chair and drunkenly placed a heavy arm around her shoulders.

"Thank you to my lovely wife for sending me off with such a splendid do and to everyone else who has made this night so memorable for me."

He winked at her, enough to say, "I'm getting good at pretending." The look did not go unnoticed by Esther Bloom. After this announcement, guests milled around him, buying him more drinks and telling him how brave he was. Esther got back to Joseph. She felt bereft already.

Chapter 24

A week after Leonard's departure for Dunkirk, Joseph Bloom died. Esther was consumed with grief, both for her husband and her son. Agnes Ong came to the rescue. Charlotte kept out of their way, at the vicarage, while funeral arrangements were made. The intensity and passion she had had to store up inside for months, she now poured into her lifelong companion. Music, which she had taken for granted seemed to be saving her life from the pit of obscurity into which she had fallen.

Esther was convinced that her son would never have volunteered to fight had it not been for his miserable relationship. She knew her son better than he knew himself. He would rather die honourably than live a lie. The war was his saviour.

It had not been easy for Esther to practice her faith since moving to East Anglia from London. The nearest Jewish community was in Ipswich but had long since disbanded with its synagogue demolished in the previous century. For years she had attended the congregational synagogue in Norwich whenever she could. When Leonard was small they had gone as a family. When he grew up and learned how to drive he had driven her there each week never stopping to worship himself. Always making work his excuse. His mother prayed for his faith to return.

On the day of Joseph's funeral, Earnest Kemp acted as chauffeur to the grieving widow while Rachel and Agnes, her oldest friend, sat in the back of the car holding her hand. Jonathon Leggatt stood in as funeral director, driving the body all the way to Norwich, in the timber yard's van. It was unorthodox but saved money which Joseph would have given his blessing to.

In every other respect, Esther adhered to tradition. She washed his broken body and prepared him for burial in his best, white linen. Due to the distance they had to travel, she acted on behalf of the Chevra Kadishah who should have been the one to oversee the purification of the body.

When the small party arrived, members of the congregation, some of whom had visited Joseph over the years, came to offer their condolences. Then it was time for the rabbi to read the Hesped which spoke kindly of Joseph. He had endured so much and was an example to them all.

"Let the living, take to heart, the lessons learned from the deceased and emulate their lives," he spoke in a warm, convincing voice which brought tears to their eyes.

Then it was time for the procession to the grave, where Esther tore her clothes over her heart as was the traditional Keriah. Agnes misunderstood and grabbed her hands until the rabbi ordered her to stand back. The mourners lined up and removed their shoes, while a memorial prayer was spoken. Most of the congregation had turned out to pay their respects to Joseph Bloom. Each stepped forward one by one to embrace Esther and her friends.

"May the Almighty comfort you, amongst all the other mourners of Zion and Jerusalem," was the last prayer spoken and then they were slipping their shoes back on, much to the relief of Rachel and Agnes Ong. Esther remained at the graveside, throwing hands full of soil onto the coffin with others following suit. Esther watched them automatically shovelling up the earth by the hand full and without ceremony discarding it into the hole. Leonard should have been amongst them. He should have been there to see his father off as chief mourner.

According to custom, a body had to be committed to the earth as soon as possible. With every hand full she prayed for his soul to find rest. She could have been praying for Leonard too.

That evening, on their return, Shiva began. Seven official days of mourning. Blooms sweetshop and bakery was closed and all mirrors covered. Esther sat in the same place on the horsehair couch while Agnes and Rachel tended to her every need. All except Charlotte visited, cooked or brought food for her, as was the custom. Charlotte had made her excuses for not attending the funeral. She was ill and distressed, caused by Leonard's sudden departure. In reality, she missed her power over him more than the man himself. It was only a matter of time, before, she too, would be leaving Shopley behind. She was busy making plans of her own.

Two months later the early morning train pulled into Ipswich Station, bound for London. Sam Miller handed back her suitcase which he had carried onto the windy platform. He had always been frightened of Charlotte and so had agreed not to breathe a word to anyone where she was going. She paid him with a pound note stolen from the till and three boxes of sweets. Sam stood back as the train pulled out of the station.

Sometimes, he wished he could run away and have an adventure but he had nowhere to go. Besides, he reminded himself, he had been left in charge of the timber yard and had use of Leonard's van for the foreseeable future. With these thoughts in mind, he pulled away cheerfully and headed back to Shopley.

Charlotte quickly found a seat in second class and stuffed her case into the overhead rack. She felt a mixture of fear and excitement. She was going to find her real family. The birth certificate was tucked away, safely, in a file with her music, at the bottom of her suitcase. She had decided to travel light. The cream suit she had worn at her wedding, a few skirts, jumpers and the red nylon dress, were all the clothes she had with her. The battered, one eared teddy her only possession.

She gazed out of the window, at the familiar landscape and hoped never to see it again. Unlike her parents, Charlotte was not religious but ever since finding the adoption papers, she had done nothing but pray. She prayed that she would find them and that they would welcome her with open arms. Although her pulse raced with anticipation, the determination she felt gave her courage. If she had no luck in finding them, she would find a job instead and begin a new life. She reminded herself that all the important orchestras were in London. She had practiced, obsessively, since marrying Leonard and was up to audition standard. Sam had promised to fetch her cello, as soon as she sent word. With these thoughts in mind, Charlotte arrived at Liverpool Street Station full of hope for the future.

It was a cold, wet day in late autumn. Charlotte found a lavatory and applied her lipstick. After a cup of coffee in a nearby cafe, she hailed a taxi instructing the driver to take her to the address she had memorized for so long. The taxi took her straight to Bow. On the way, she could see signs of London preparing for war. Sand bags piled high in front of official looking buildings. People in military uniforms strolling around. Notices about black out and possible air raids, all over the place. The taxi dropped her outside the adoption agency. She paid the fare and walked up the steps into an office with a reception. The grey haired woman on the other side of the window appeared friendly.

"I'm here to find my relatives. I've only just found out...you see... that I was adopted." The woman ushered her into a room and took all her details. She told her that she would have to do some exploratory work. She was to leave the document with her and come back later on that day. Usually, they were busy but most people were leaving London, not coming into it. Therefore, she could work on her case straightaway. Charlotte thanked her and left.

She decided to kill the time in a Lyons cafe. She ordered a pot of tea, some sandwiches and a cake. Her money was going down fast. As she sipped her tea, she caught sight of herself in a wall mirror and liked her reflection. She looked attractive. A woman of the world. Almost twenty, with a marriage behind her and a new life ahead. She had everything to gain. Out of the corner of her eye, she spotted a gentleman sitting alone. He was tapping the table and gazing out of the window as if waiting for someone. He was handsome, with dark brown hair and eyes. His clothes were immaculate and a beard covered his manly chin.

Just then, a messenger boy entered the establishment carrying a note. He handed it to the man and held out his hand for a tip. The man read it, tipped the boy and told him there would be no reply. The boy left and the man ordered. While he waited he glanced around the room. His eyes fell on Charlotte who pretended not to notice.

"Do you mind if I join you? That is, if you aren't waiting for someone? The thing is, I've been stood up and I hate eating alone."

He really was the most handsome man she had ever met. She smiled and allowed him to join her. They made polite conversation about the war and the weather and she lied about her visit to London.

"I'm meeting my husband for the weekend before he goes to Dunkirk."

"Well if you need anywhere to stay, I own the Salisbury Hotel, just round the corner. It's been delightful to make your acquaintance. I didn't catch your name?"

"Charlotte."

"Very nice too. I'm Alfred."

He smiled a knowing smile, shook her hand, very gently and left. Charlotte complimented herself, on not losing her touch and also left.

"Yes, we have managed to find your records, Miss Kemp."

The grey haired older woman motioned for her to sit in the chair opposite.

"You have quite a dramatic family background but you have to remember that what I am about to tell you, happened a long time ago and there is good, as well as, rather...well, for want of a better word...grotesque news."

"Well, I'll leave the good until last and get the bad out of the way," she braced herself with a growing dread. Since learning of her adoption she had dreamt of this moment. To find her real family was all she had been living for but now she was about to be told all manner of unsavoury details, she felt quite shaken. She had been hoping and praying for better.

Miss Stewart spoke evenly and quietly, reading from some papers, over her rimmed spectacles, "Jack and William Baldini, the uncles of Miss Rose Drew of Shoreditch, shall hang by the neck until dead, for the murder of George Hodgkiss,"

"I'm sorry, but I don't understand. Who are these people?"

"Rose was your mother."

"And her uncles murdered someone called Hodgkiss. Who was he?"

"A simple rag and bone man from the East End."

"Why did they murder him? Do you know?"

"Well now... this is where it becomes most macabre. It came out at their trial that he had interfered with their niece. Your mother."

"That is sickening. How old was she?"

"Our records show that she couldn't have been much more than a girl."

"So that's the bad news. Did she meet someone nice and have me? What...what happened to her?"

"I'm sorry to have to tell you, Miss Drew, that you were born of that rape. Hodgkiss was your father."

Charlotte felt cold and clammy, as if she might slip off her chair. She asked for some water. Miss Stewart felt justified in telling the absolute truth when people came looking for their true identities. Charlotte was no exception.

"Do you have a cigarette?"

"No. I'm afraid I don't smoke. Minnie, my assistant will make you a hot, sweet cup of tea."

"Yes...please."

The hot tea duly arrived and Charlotte gratefully sipped it. Miss Stewart gave her plenty of time for the news to sink in.

"So where is my mother, now?"

"The fact is, we're not sure. It was very sad. The documents say that she was placed in an asylum for the insane. I can only assume that it turned her mind."

"Oh yes. I read institutionalized on one of the documents I found with my birth certificate. I wondered what it meant. God I feel sick."

Miss Stewart quickly handed her a metal waste paper bin and a handkerchief. Charlotte heaved several times but then the nausea passed.

"So I have no one?"

Miss Stewart sensed how close to tears the young woman was and was pleased to be able to lighten the atmosphere.

"No, now for the good news. Your mother had five brothers and a twin sister called Ruth. You may have heard of her. Ruth Duthie. Here...I have a Vogue somewhere." She turned to the middle pages and pointed to a beautiful, auburn haired woman, singing at the Palladium. The article was about an East End girl made good. Charlotte felt a flicker of hope returning.

"Do you know where she lives?"

"I must confess to being an avid fan of your aunt's but articles do not run to addresses. However, I do have an early address for her. Ah yes, here it is. 92, Weymouth Terrace, Shoreditch. She may well have moved out of the East End by now but it's a good place to start. Old neighbours may know. I'm afraid that's all I have. Sip your tea and get your strength back. The number nine takes you all the way there. Bus stop is just over the road."

Charlotte drank her tea, blew her nose and shook hands with Miss

Stewart.

Half an hour later, the bus dropped her outside the Feathers Public House, at the top of Weymouth Terrace. Charlotte took a deep breath and powdered her nose. She had already applied more lipstick on the top deck. Hearing such horrible news about her family of origin added to her feeling of trepidation. She felt totally out of place as she looked about her. If Shopley had felt unfriendly, Shoreditch seemed positively hostile.

She passed the pub and could hear raucous laughter coming from inside and smell the beer soaked bar. It was as if she were the butt of their joke. A pawn shop came next with all kinds of possessions stacked up in the window. From a trumpet to a fur coat which had seen better days, to a baby's cot, piled high with cotton sheets and blankets. She wondered where the baby slept now. Did its parents have enough money to feed it. Charlotte had not had much time to appreciate that this was the environment into which she had been born.

Next she passed by Wormleighton's sweet shop. Mr. Wormleighton had long since died and now the shop was rented by his old housekeeper who had assisted him. The thin faced woman smiled through the window at Charlotte as she placed toffees into a dish for her customers to be tempted by. The shop brought back memories of Blooms and she hurried on. A hunch back in a rocking chair called after her outside a fish mongers.

"Pretty lady, can I tempt you to any of my fine wares." She smelled fish and pickled onions, and saw soused herrings and rollmops as well as mackerel and kippers placed haphazardly in dishes. A young lad cycled passed at the same moment and shouted a warning.

"You wanna watch him, missus. He'll have your drawers down as look at you."

"Go on. Get out of it. You little toe rag," the hunch back bellowed after him.

Charlotte quickened her pace past a butchers with carcasses suspended on meat hooks. The pavements had dried up from the rain earlier and the sun had come out. She felt her clothes sticking to her and could smell her own body odour.

A church bell struck five o'clock. Children playing in the road were noisy and aggressive with one another. They reminded her of the bullies she had had to contend with at Shopley Primary. One of their number, a small greasy haired boy, suddenly squatted down in the gutter and relieved himself. A woman beating a carpet against her front wall spotted him in the act and hollered at the top of her voice. "Go on you little bastard. Go and shit outside your own house. Dirty little bleeder." At which the boy stuck two fingers up and stumbled away with his trousers down around his ankles. Animals. No better than animals, she thought.

On the other side of the street, two soldiers smiled and saluted in her direction which cheered her up and gave her more confidence. She could smell food cooking which made her mouth water. Then she bumped into a coal man who was black from head to foot. The whites of his eyes stared at her menacingly. He tipped the contents of his sack down into the coal hole and counted the bags. As she dusted herself down and moved on, she heard him wolf whistle her. She felt repulsed and degraded.

The only thing which kept her striding down the terrace was the discovery of an aunt. A singer no less. Someone in her family, musical like herself. This confirmed that she had done the right thing to get away from Shopley. Over and over again she reminded herself that they had never loved her and that she was returning to the very bosom of her true family. She had not expected to find such a woman as Ruth Duthie and was not expecting to find her still here amongst such flea bitten ingrates. Surely she had escaped the East End because of her God given talent, just as she was escaping to a better life. Just as these thoughts were forming in her mind, she arrived at her destination. Number ninety two Weymouth Terrace.

Charlotte ran a comb through her hair and hoped her breath did not smell. A small woman with white hair and a shocking pink dressing gown opened the door to her. Her face was highly rouged and she wore bright pink lipstick.

"Hallo. Sorry to bother you but does my aunt still live here? Her name is Ruth Duthie."

The woman's eyes opened wide and she smiled.

"Come in...come in. You say Ruth's your aunt?"

"Yes, she is and I've come all the way from Suffolk to meet her."

"You must be Lottie."

"Yes well...Charlotte. No one calls me that anymore."

"I used to know her when we were young. She was always a lovely singer and now...well, I always knew she would be a star. Would you care for a cup of tea and a biscuit after travelling all this way? You must be famished."

She directed her guest into a parlour containing ugly walnut furniture, years out of date. The room was decorated with large floral wallpaper and had fitted carpets. It smelled of toast. Charlotte noticed a toasting fork in the hearth.

The woman left her and bustled down to the kitchen along a hallway. Left alone, Charlotte found her mind wandering. She wondered about Rose, the girl who had been her mother. Had she lived here before being sent away? She must have done. She began to imagine all sorts of horrible, morbid scenes, possibly in this very room. Just a young girl, Miss Stewart had said. The rape had turned her mind, she said, and what of Ruth her aunt. She too must have lived here with her twin sister. How on earth had she managed to survive such a terrible time?   Had she been a baby here herself?   Suddenly, she felt deeply oppressed and needed to leave the house but she had come for information as to her aunt's whereabouts. With deep breaths she managed to overcome her feeling of panic.

The woman came back carrying a tray with tea in china cups and chocolate biscuits. As they sipped their tea, she remembered the time when Lottie had been born and Rose had been the talk of the neighbourhood for getting in the family way.

"How do you know my aunt?"

"I used to live across the road until my mother died and then I moved in here with my husband who died a year later."

Charlotte did not want to be bogged down with another family history. She had heard enough for a life time.

"Do you know where she lives now by any chance?"

"Yes my dear. You are in luck. Your aunt is such a lovely person that she kept in touch with me all these years. Never missed my birthday or Christmas. I think she must have felt sorry for me. I have her address here."

She opened the top drawer of the walnut dresser and took out a small book. Slowly she jotted the address down on a piece of paper and handed it to Charlotte.

"If you walk up to the High Street, you'll be able to catch a taxi."

Charlotte thanked the sad looking woman and left. Sadie went back inside and got down her album full of cuttings of Ruth. As she turned the pages she hummed out of tune and wiped a tear from her eye.

Charlotte soon found a taxi which dropped her off outside a huge, Georgian house in Camden. She paid her fare and straightened her coat, applied more lipstick and took in the house. All the lights were on inside which gave it a warm and cosy feeling with an air of grandiosity which thrilled her. She rang the doorbell and reminded herself that she too was magnificent and talented. This is where she belonged with others of the same ilk.

"Hallo, can I help you?" A short, Scottish woman came to the door.

"Are you Ruth Duthie?"

"No, I'm Jane, her friend."

"Is she in?"

"Yes...but..."

"I'm Charlotte, her niece and I've come all the way from Suffolk to find her."

The woman leaned heavily on the door, as if in shock and then took hold of her hands and drew her in over the threshold. Behind her stood the lovely auburn haired woman from the magazine. She was clutching her bosom and seemed both shocked and on the verge of tears.

"Oh my God, Lottie, is it really you? After all these years."

CHARLOTTE, RUTH AND ROSE

1940 - 1946

Chapter 25

Rose placed two china cups on a tin tray. One for herself and the other for Queen Elizabeth. She loved to entertain her, more than the others. The Flora Dora had been going for a song at an old flea market but she always kept it for best, for her royal guest. Rose grinned, ironically. She had been conversing with her for as long as she could remember, putting her words into the Queen's mouth.

It had been time for a change. Lauren, Greta, and Marlene had become tiresome, old hat. Lauren was never able to converse, without bringing Bogey into it, which reminded her of one of her old habits. Greta was no company, with her one liner, "I vant to be alone." As for Marlene, her arched eyebrows and deep throated singing gave her the willies.

Before the Queen arrived, she still had to scrub fourteen steps and polish eight pairs of taps. Also, she had to make sure that no disturbing body odours lingered in the loos. She was proud to be a lavatory attendant in the heart of Piccadilly. On her monthly visits to see Doctor Munro she was always reassured that she was doing well. After four years of being an outpatient, Rose still could not believe she had managed to survive.

She began at the top of the stairs, as usual and worked her way down to the bottom. The rag floated on top of the scummy water and she wiped the last of the lather away.

"That's better. Good and clean, like when they were first put there," she said.

Rose hoisted the enormous weight off her knees and rested on a wicker chair, at the bottom of the steps.

"Lovely day for her to come out. Hope she's wearing the lilac dress and hat. Love to see her in that." She coughed a chesty cough. A stray pigeon landed half way down the steps. "Don't you dirty all my hard work, you

perisher," she chided. The pigeon spotted her at the last moment and
fluttered, timidly, back up to the top. After a minute or two, it flew back out
into the street. Rose watched it take off, following its flight, until it was no
more than a speck in the sky.

She heaved herself to her feet and emptied the slops down the drain.
Next, she hung the rag over the turn of the century radiator in her room,
marked Attendant. It was overheating as usual. Rose didn't mind a bit that it
was never fixed. She loved warmth. Always had.

She slipped off her ankle boots and gave her bunions a rub. Then, she
pulled them back on again and waddled from toilet to toilet, pulling all the
chains, systematically. One in particular smelled foul. Rose could never get
used to some peoples inconsiderate ways. There was no excuse for not
flushing away the mess you made. It angered her when people did not take
responsibility. Not when the good Lord had given everyone, at least one
hand to use the chain, designed for the job.

Back in her room, she lit the gas under the kettle and mashed a pot of tea.
Then, she flicked a duster round the room while it brewed. It contained a
pine table, chair and a dresser with shelves. She had enjoyed making it home
from home. In a corner stood a potted palm and on the walls, pictures in
frames of her favourites. She had added many more to her collection over the
years but the royals were her passion. King George V and Queen Mary and
now King George VI and Queen Elizabeth, with their lovely princesses,
Elizabeth and Margaret.

"You are my family. We are all in this, together", the Queen said, as
Rose poured out the tea. She had arrived and was sitting in the armchair, next
to Rose.

"I am so proud of our brave subjects. You Cockneys have such courage.
Did you know the palace had been hit?"

"No Ma'am."

"Yes Rose. Now I can look the East End in the eye."

Rose sipped her tea and studied her. It was the two piece she loved in all
the news reels. She noticed a droplet of tea about to fall onto Her Majesty's
lap and flicked it away with her duster. They smiled at each other.

"Thank you Rose, my dear friend. When this horrible war is over, you
must come and take tea with me, at the palace."

"I should love to, Your Highness - more tea?"

"No, that's enough, my dear. Keep up the good work. I shall have to be going."

Rose watched the elegant figure glide out on a cushion of air. She hated to see her go. Pulling herself together, she poured the last cup out of the pot and had a doze. It was short lived due to the rush hour across London. Women in uniforms, of which she liked the smart, navy blue best. She listened to all the talk of war while she busied herself in the background. Office workers, mothers with children who had not been evacuated yet, grannies and nannies, air raid workers and nurses sat side by side in her lavatories. She had not made many friends since Clara and Sophie at the asylum but all the women who used her loos, she considered to be her friends. Especially if they left her a tip or passed the time of day with her.

By the time the rush hour was over, it was getting dark and she pulled the steel gate across and padlocked it for the night. It felt like her very own air raid shelter. Since the war had taken a turn for the worst, she no longer felt safe, travelling to and from her digs. In her room, she had a quilted eiderdown that she tucked around her. When it got so cold that her teeth chattered, she put on a fur coat, bought from a pawn shop and her woollen hat. When the nightly bombardment became deafening she would put ear plugs in, pull her woolly hat down over her ears and hide beneath the table. No one knew she used the lavatories as her home. She thanked the Lord that everyone was too busy nowadays. As soon as the air raid siren wailed a warning, people doubled up as wardens or helped by driving ambulances. They weren't about to bother her. Whenever she got really terrified she would conjure up the kind face of Doctor Munro and truly believed that with him there to look after her, she would not perish in the raids.

When she needed a bath, she attended the slipper baths. Once in a while, she treated herself to jellied eels or was to be found sitting in a pie and mash shop. Apart from bloaters, pie and mash had always been her favourite. Regularly, once a month, her only real treat which she would not miss for love nor money, was the pictures. If she could still find one open she would sit in the front row and enjoy a bag of sweets. She looked forward to the interval and an ice cream cornet.

The only trouble was she was putting on so much weight. Even with rationing, she didn't seem to lose much. It had crept up on her so gradually. With the extra weight and her grey cropped hair, she looked much older than her years. Rose had no idea how to make the best of herself. Moisturizers and cleansers were an unknown quantity to her. She had never worn makeup. Her blood pressure was getting worse each year. For that, she had seen a doctor once who had prescribed a daily aspirin.

Rose understood from news reels that children had been evacuated out of London, to families in the countryside. She shuddered to think of those poor, little mites, leaving their parents behind. She did not remember much of her own childhood but London was her home and always would be. Rose loved films but the interspersed news reels, were becoming more and more distressing. She heard how atrocities were being carried out in camps across Europe. Poor Jewish people. Some of them made her cry. The footage reminded her of how she had been treated. Just like those on the screen, she had been herded with others, like cattle, into cold, dark, hostile rooms, just like a prison. No one knew or cared whether she lived or died, in much the same way as the images on the screen. That is, until Doctor Munro came along. At night, she prayed for them to be rescued too.

On one such visit to the cinema, while Rose dried her eyes and blew her nose, the news reel ended with a more, light hearted piece. The posh voice on the screen was speaking about someone who looked familiar.

"Ruth Duthie is wonderful. She has been entertaining us as well as the troops and bringing happiness to the sick and dying, throughout these war torn years."

The film was showing clips of her, at home with her family and then in a hospital ward, with children sitting in their beds. It mentioned how she had starred at the Hippodrome before the war in 'Hoofing It' but now with almost all of the West End theatres closed she was a glimpse of light shining out of such dark times, bringing hope to hundreds in and around London.

For some reason, Rose felt like slapping her head. Something she had not needed to do for years. Part of her felt like running out of the cinema, back to the safety of her bolt hole. Her curiosity, however, got the better of her and pinned her to her seat at the back of the cinema. A courting couple, next to her on the row, came up for air and whispered loudly,

"She's great. Love her."

Rose had not thought about her family for years apart from when she was in the containing environment of the doctor's office. Suddenly, she realized who it was up on the screen. Panic and confusion gave way to a wave of pride. Before she could stop herself, she raised her voice above the sound of the film.

"That's my sister."

"Eh, what you on about, love. You got a screw loose?"

"Shush. Quiet. Pipe down," came from along the row.

Rose felt hot and clammy. "That's my twin," she repeated to herself, over and over again. It wasn't until the lights came up that she remembered where she was.

"Rose and Ruth. Rose and Ruth. Like peas in a pod. Just like peas in a pod," she repeated under her breath. The lavatories gleamed, spotless, under her new regime. Ever since seeing Ruth on the newsreel she had returned to her old habits of cleaning obsessively. She could not keep still. When she stopped for a cup of tea, she would doze off immediately, worn out from over doing it.

Her dreams were always the same. Caged like an animal in the zoo or in a dark room with whispering all around her. In another nightmare she was being chased in amongst heavily, laden bushes. Rose woke up ringing wet after such dreams and spent the early hours mashing tea and trying to keep calm. This time she could not counsel herself. After two weeks of agitation, it was time for her outpatients' appointment.

"It's all about taking risks, Rose. Look how far you've come, because you dared to take risks that you never believed you could. It sounds wonderful to know where your sister is. It's all about your timing, Rose. When you feel strong enough, you may wish to pay her a visit. Come back and see me in a fortnight."

"If you're sure, Doctor...that I'd be all right...to meet her again."

"It may seem really scary Rose but she is your sister, your twin sister after all and it doesn't get much closer than that."

A week later, Rose made a decision based on what Doctor Munro had said. Although some of her confidence had returned, she was aware that what she was about to do felt dangerously outside her comfort zone. In the middle of a busy Saturday afternoon, she pulled the gate to the lavatories across and caught a taxi to the Hippodrome.

"OK, gel, you're here."

Rose got out and waddled up to the front of the theatre and mounted the steps towards the huge billboard displaying her sister's beautiful face. She ran her podgy fingers over it while the driver lit a cigarette scornfully watching her.

"Takes all sorts. Nothing to do with me."

Then he watched her rip away the notice which informed the world that the theatre was closed for the foreseeable future.

Rose took a step backwards, "My word, you've done yourself proud, Ruthie." Gradually it was beginning to sink in that this really was her sister. The newsreel had brought her to life but the torn and tattered photograph of Ruth on the poster was ghostlike. She walked round to the stage door which was shrouded in darkness and imagined her sister arriving for her performances.

Rose wiped away a tear and felt sad. If only she had known where to find her. Now she was gone and the war made it impossible for her ever to find her again.

Chapter 26

"So, ladies and gentlemen. Are you sitting, comfortably?"

A collective cheer from the audience ricocheted from wall to wall and echoed through the tunnels.

"Well then, we shall begin. Maestro, if you please."

The band leader took his place up on the makeshift staging. With a flick of his baton, he began the show. Charlotte sat astride her cello and looked forward to the concert. For the past year, she had taken part in underground performances, down in the tube stations used each night as communal shelters.

Beneath the fragile foundations of the city, these tiny townships stuck together. As much as air raids might destroy their homes and lives, nothing could destroy their cockney spirit. Humour and wit were rife which added to their defiant courage. Ruth jumped at the chance of entertaining her own. Every night, the faces smiling up at her, reminded her of performing in front of friends and neighbours, seated along the gutter, outside her home on Weymouth Terrace when she was a girl.

Charlotte, too, was doing her bit for the war effort. She could hardly believe that she was performing with her own flesh and blood. The other life she had come from seemed surreal and irrelevant now. The only down side to it was playing to the rabble, sheltering. Women in curlers and headscarves. Babies with snotty noses and coughs. Nearly all the men were old, as those able bodied and young were away fighting. The sickening smell of body odour, even more noticeable once they all bedded down for the night. She insisted on keeping close to her aunt, as the sound of muffled thudding went on overhead.

The German Luftwaffe blitzed the city night after night. Some wept out of fear or sadness. The air raids had already claimed members of their families. While others had lost loved ones fighting overseas. Sometimes, she thought about Leonard. Where he might be. Had he killed yet or been killed? The poor, stupid fool. It comforted Charlotte to know that Ruth was the closest person to her real mother. Ruth clung to her while Ivor cradled the boys. She was not about to lose her again.

The response she received from Ruth, from the very beginning, had been overwhelming. She had never known unconditional love before and was included in everything. Ralph and Ronnie, the twins and the love of Ruth's life, even made way for their long lost cousin. Their nursery was immediately, converted into a palatial bedroom for her. Ruth would not tolerate any objections from Jane or Ivor, as she moved mountains to make up for their lost years together.

Ivor sat with the twins and awaited his wife's entrance. It was wonderful to see her so happy. Now she had everything. She thanked him, repeatedly, for being so understanding. For taking Charlotte in. It had been no hardship. He had fond memories of her, as a baby years before, when Ruth had been no more than a girl and he had fallen in love with her.

He hadn't the heart to burst her bubble. To tell her that her beloved Charlotte was not all that she appeared to be. At first, he too, had been swept along on a tide of sentiment and nostalgia at the sudden appearance of a child who had been given up for lost. A young, beautiful woman with a family resemblance, who had never felt truly loved by her adoptive parents. She had fallen in love with a man who had really loved her best friend. It had broken her heart and now he was away fighting. When a telegram came to say he was missing in action, feared dead, she had had to get away. Then by accident, she had stumbled across the truth and it had given her courage to change her dreadful life. Such a tale was heart rending but after three months under their roof, she had tried to seduce him.

At first, Ivor shrugged it off when she flattered him or made suggestive remarks, putting her behaviour down to immaturity but one night, while Ruth and Jane entertained patients in one of many hospitals across London, he and Charlotte were alone in the house. The twins slept soundly after the blackout had been enforced by their father. He was in the study working on some fresh ideas for another volume of poetry and she was practicing her cello.

When the knock came on the door, he was deep in thought.

"Ivor, I'm going to help myself to a sherry. Would you like one?"

Without looking up from his work, he answered with some concern.

"No. I shall have a cup of tea soon, before I go to bed. Are you sure, you wouldn't prefer some hot milk, to help you sleep?" He had noticed how much she enjoyed alcohol. Whenever they had a celebration, she always ended up tipsy and flirtatious. On receiving no reply, he glanced over his shoulder to find her standing before him in a see through negligee. It was his wife's.

"What do you think you are doing? Take that off, at once."

She had been about to do so, in front of him, when he caught her by the elbow and marched her to the foot of the stairs.

"I meant, in the privacy of your bedroom. I don't know what your little game is, Charlotte, but I am not about to fall for it."

"Oh, come now, Uncle Ivor, you know you've been ogling me."

"I shall ignore that remark. It is so far from the truth. I love your aunt. Always have and always will. This fantasy you have is in your mind. Now go upstairs and change."

"Oh, all right then, but if you change your mind..." and she half stumbled up the stairs. He could smell sherry on her breath. She had already been drinking. Feeling confused and upset, he returned to his study.

"Thank you ladies and gentlemen. Well now, what we've all been waiting for. We all love her. She's been a great blessing throughout this awful time. An East Ender herself.   Give her your warmest welcome. Our own, yes, our very own, Ruth Duthie."

The audience erupted. How could he tell the beautiful woman, in the golden, glittering gown, that she had welcomed poison into their home. As she sang a melody of show stoppers and favourite war songs, Ivor reflected on Charlotte, in amongst the string section. After the incident, she had kept a low profile while he had kept it a secret. Then something else had occurred which confirmed his suspicions that she was a liar as well as a Jezebel.

The feeling Charlotte had for Ruth was the closest that she had ever come to loving someone. She was cosseted for the first time in her life and she appreciated being protected by her aunt. Every so often, the two would go on a shopping spree and bring back a fashionable dress for Charlotte to wear. Even in war time a girl had to look her best, Ruth said, handing over her clothing coupons that she had saved religiously for her niece. She loved doting on Charlotte who soon had a wardrobe to be envied, her own bank account and the run of the house with all the time in the world to practice her brand new cello.

Such adoration made some of her old ways redundant. For a while she did not have any desire to plan and scheme nor to make trouble but with so much time on her hands, she grew restless and needed some excitement. Men of her own age hardly ever appeared at Victoria House and Ruth insisted on chaperoning her everywhere.

While Ruth spent much of her time entertaining the sick and injured, during the day, Charlotte found herself alone. Ivor always had things to do and Jane managed her aunt's affairs as well as accompany her at the piano. For now she could tolerate Jane but secretly envied all the time she spent with Ruth. It was this boredom which had caused her to act outrageously with her uncle. Now she wished she had not been so impulsive. If ever it got back to Ruth she might be asked to leave. Besides Ivor was far too old. There was mention of uncles but three had emigrated to Australia and two were fighting in the war. Their cockney wives hardly ever came to visit for which she felt only relief.

More and more she fantasized about paying the handsome man a visit whom she had met on first arriving in London. He owned a hotel and she knew the address. Now established in the bosom of her family and even performing in the evenings with her aunt, it felt time to branch out. He had had a twinkle in his eye and looked fun. No one need ever know if she paid him a visit. She could be back by tea time and would say she had been visiting the war office for news of Leonard.

With these thoughts in mind she left the house in her latest finery. A taxi dropped her outside the Salisbury and she entered the foyer. A receptionist seemed impressed and friendly. Charlotte looked very glamorous in a black velvet suit with one of Ruth's pre-war fox furs resting nonchalantly over her shoulders. Her hair gathered in a thick roll at the back of her head, with a casual, flicked fringe, created just the right impression. Middle class girl about town.

"Is Alfred in?"

"Yes, but he's with someone at the moment. Would you care to sit and wait for him. I don't think he'll be long."

"Yes."

"Who shall I say is asking for him?"

"Charlotte."

"Can I get you a cup of tea or coffee while you wait?"

"A black coffee, please."

In truth, she detested coffee without milk and two sugars but impressions were of the utmost importance and she felt her order gave her an air of sophistication.

The receptionist rang through for a tray of coffee and wondered who the beautiful, young woman was. Alfred had kept this one quiet. Not like the others who were well known to her and everyone in the hotel. Alfred was a notorious womanizer. There was always more than one on the go.

Charlotte sipped her coffee and lit a cigarette. She felt a mixture of nerves and sheer mischievousness and would know at a glance if he recognized her and more importantly, if he desired her. Several magazines, two cups of coffee and three cigarettes later, Alfred appeared in reception. Still immaculately dressed, this time in a navy pinstripe suit and clean shaven, he seemed to recognize her instantly. He walked toward her with outstretched hands.

"So nice to see you again. Have you booked in with your husband?"

"No, I'm here all alone actually. His leave was cancelled at the last minute, so I find myself all alone in London without knowing a single soul."

"Well, I'm glad you remembered me, dear girl". Alfred liked nothing better than an adventurous woman.

"I hope you don't think I'm forward but as I have nowhere to stay, due to the cancellation, I..."

"You do now. I insist you be my guest." Charlotte couldn't believe her luck. He was making it all so easy for her.

"I'm just about to have lunch in the restaurant. Are you hungry?"

"Ravenous actually," she smiled and took the arm offered to her. After a sumptuous lunch including a bottle of merlot Alfred ordered coffee to be taken in his apartments on the top storey. It had originally been the honeymoon suite before he bought the hotel. Charlotte couldn't believe how grand it all was. The wine had gone to her head and she fell about laughing as she shared a cigar with him.

"How come you still have so much excellent food in your hotel when most Londoners would give a week's rations for a meal like that?"

"I have my ways and means, dear girl. Fingers in a few pies, here and there," he laughed along with her. He couldn't wait to get her into bed. He had never met anyone as young as Charlotte who was so uninhibited before. After being chaste for over two years, she made a meal of Alfred and enjoyed every morsel.

Afterwards, too exhausted to take the cigarette offered to her, she fell asleep in his arms. When they woke up it was time for black out.

"I have to be going."

"But I thought you were here for the weekend."

Charlotte loved the sound of him genuinely seeming to care about her.

"Stay and have dinner and then we can have more fun tomorrow."

It was too tempting. She lay back on her pillow and enjoyed the sensation of him fondling her breasts. To hell with it. Ruth would have to allow her a longer leash. He was irresistible. She kissed him all over including his shrapnel wound which had ended his service at the beginning of the war.

"Are you sure you won't be called back to active service?"

"My dear girl, don't worry your pretty little head. I'm out permanently and if ever they call me back I shall plead insanity."

The next day was a repeat of the previous. They spent most of it in bed. In fact, she had come into his life at just the right moment. There was a lull in his love life which was a strange phenomenon, unknown to him. Almost ten years her senior, she had never known a man like him. Although he laughed at all her silly jokes and her attempts to play the steamy seductress, she enjoyed how masterful and in control he was. The fact that he owned more property in town and was rich gave her an overwhelming feeling of satisfaction. She couldn't believe her luck.

Before she left in a taxi that evening he had just one question to ask her.

"There is one thing, dear girl, I've been meaning to ask you? How do you feel about cheating on your husband?"

"To be honest, he did nothing but cheat on me before the war. What's good for the goose, as they say." She tittered at her own gift for lying. Alfred seemed satisfied.

"Take her to Liverpool Street Station." As the taxi pulled away, Charlotte instructed the driver to take her to Camden. She couldn't wait to see him again.

Next, she had to think up an excuse for being out for almost two days. She would tell Ruth that she had been to the war office for news of Leonard. When there had been none, she had felt so upset that she had decided to visit her parents in Suffolk to reassure them of her whereabouts. It had been a very emotional visit. She hadn't realized how much they would miss her. She had tried ringing but the lines were down.

Ruth, who had been on the point of phoning the police, accepted the explanation willingly and suggested they open a bottle of champagne to celebrate her safe return. Ivor still had a few bottles left down in the cellar. While he uncorked it, he and Jane exchanged quizzical glances. Neither believed a word of what they had just heard.

Ivor hated having to sign every week at the police station. It was a degrading thing to have to do, after all the years he had lived and worked in England. However, while Great Britain was at war with Germany, he was classified as an alien and that was the law he had to abide by.

Apart from this chore, it felt good to be alive. It was a sunny day and the station was in walking distance from his home. After a brisk walk, he joined the back of the queue, lit a cigar and read his paper. Some days the queue went down quickly, others more slowly. Today he was in luck. It was moving steadily and he would soon be able to catch a taxi across town to the Salisbury hotel where he was meeting his publisher.

He tossed away his cigar butt and brushed his sleeves clean of ash. The sergeant on the desk smiled in acknowledgement and handed him a pen. Many manual workers, dockers, porters, restaurant skivvies and such folk passed through every week but this man was different. He had an air about him and was always well turned out. Ivor sensed his respect but also his pity at an unfair situation. It made him feel worse. He got out as quickly as possible and hailed a taxi.

When they reached Bow High Street, the traffic crawled to a standstill. Ivor had to walk the last block to the hotel and asked a stranger what had caused the diversion. A bomb, he was told had exploded a few streets away, only a couple of hours before and it was looking pretty bad. Inside the hotel, life seemed to be going on as normal. He waited in the foyer and smoked another cigar. At that moment, poetry seemed positively futile.

Suddenly, a whistle blew and a huge policeman, covered in dust and debris pushed through the revolving doors.

"Can I have your attention please ladies and gentlemen? The air raid last night has taken out two streets parallel to this one and a bomb exploded this morning just round the corner. The rescue team have just begun to bring victims out still alive. So I am requisitioning the Salisbury as a temporary hospital as we are unable to get them through to St. Andrews."

The receptionist phoned through to her boss. Ivor glanced at his watch and imagined his publisher caught up in tail backs. Soon people were being brought in on makeshift stretchers. Nurses and doctors were arriving looking worn out from being up all night. Ivor was roped in to administer pain killers and water, to mop a brow or to just hold a hand. He welcomed the opportunity to do something useful.

Cuts, bloody gashes to faces and limbs were being attended to as fast as was humanly possible. Some screamed while others hollered for help.

It was then that he saw her. Next to a tall, handsome man. She was draped in a fur coat, white faced and shocked. They were holding onto each other having just returned from a night club. Down in the bowels of the earth, inside the club that purported to be bomb proof, they had clung together on the dance floor while black musicians played their catalogue of jazz. For a few hours they had forgotten about the war and the dangers lurking outside. It was six o'clock in the morning when they left soaked with gin and perspiring. With no taxis around they had walked through deserted London streets and were now caught up in the mayhem.

Ivor made his way over to them. Charlotte blushed. He had never seen her look embarrassed before.

"Are you all right?" he asked her. She pretended to faint. Ivor and Alfred caught her between them and laid her on a leather couch.

"You know her?"

"Yes, she is my niece. Who are you, Sir?"

"I am the owner of this establishment and Charlotte's boyfriend."

"Do you know that she is married, Sir?"

"Yes I do but he sounds a bad lot, I must say. Poor girl left alone in London, not knowing a soul."

"On the contrary, she has a family here in London. It would seem that she has been deceiving us both."

Charlotte remained still with her eyes closed while the two men squared up to each other and then forgot about her. The burly policeman strode up to Alfred.

"I understand that you own the Salisbury, Sir?"

"Yes, indeed. Do you have everything you need?"

"For the moment, sir. This is a bad business. More dead than alive."

"Well, I am at your service, whatever we can do. Simply say the word."

Charlotte opened an eye. Alfred had joined Ivor and everyone else in looking after those in need. In the middle of the chaos she had been forgotten.

After a while Alfred came to see if she was all right and handed her a bowl of bloodied water to throw away. He told her to fetch more boiling water from the kitchen. She did as she was told. More people were being brought in and she rose to the challenge. Ivor noticed how remorseful she looked. He felt confused and wondered how long the affair had been going on. Had she met this man before or after she had tried to seduce him?

Later, Alfred dropped them off at Victoria House. Outside, Ivor warned Charlotte that he was not prepared to collude with her. It wasn't fair on Ruth or on him.

"That man is far too old for you and you should not be getting involved with him. Your husband, after all, might still be alive. You could have news any day."

Over dinner, Ivor described the awful scenes which he had witnessed at the Salisbury and how he had been able to assist where ever he could. Charlotte listened with frustration. She would have loved to impress her aunt with all her achievements but had to keep it a secret.

"So, what have you been up to today, Charlotte?"

"Oh...I've just been practicing."

"Excellent. We'll have to make haste. We have another show tonight in Bethnal Green."

Charlotte smiled weakly as Ruth and Jane bustled about getting everything ready. She felt shattered after such a traumatic day.

Chapter 27

Earnest Kemp sat in his study and pondered on his forthcoming sermon. He had been the rector of the church in Shopley village for more years than he cared to remember. These days, he was finding it more and more difficult to write something meaningful. A deep sadness had clung to him, ever since the death of Joseph Bloom and the disappearance of Charlotte. He could not shake off the feeling of failure. Not only had he failed Charlotte, he had also failed Joseph Bloom. A man who had lived in his parish for years. A Jewish man whom he had never made it his business to get to know. Only a handful of times had he even visited him over the years, leaving it mostly to Rachel. Neither of them had got to know the man. All they saw was a dribbling wreck, sitting in a wheelchair pushed by a weary widow.

He lay his pen down on the blank page and buried his head in his hands.

"God forgive me," he prayed out loud.

Joseph must have had hopes and dreams when he came to this place. A plan for his life with Esther and Leonard which had withered and died, inside his frail body, year by year. He felt a deep sense of shame. He now questioned the whole of his life's work, as if his relationship with Joseph had become symbolic of the way he had conducted his calling. He saw his ministry as shallow and superficial.

He had never desired to dig deep into the souls of his parishioners, his fellow man. When they acted unkindly toward Joseph and his family, newly arrived in Shopley, he had turned a blind eye but it had been his duty to guide the people to a better understanding of life. A Christian life. He was the greatest hypocrite of them all.

In just the same way, he had ignored his worst fears about Charlotte. He had allowed her to get away with unacceptable behaviour for years and now she had run away. He should have told her the truth about her background but he had buried his head in the sand. He had been terrified of the very outcome he now had to live with. He was weak. It had been easy to escape from his responsibilities at home and go on missionary work to Africa. There, the natives treated him like a god and he was all powerful. He felt like a fraud.

He decided to take a stroll in the garden, where he tried to pray for strength and guidance. The words would not come. He sat down on a stone seat and looked up at the sky. It was cool for May, even though the sun was shining. His son in law came into his mind. Leonard had been twice the man he was, even at his tender age. Away fighting and then taken prisoner. He had never known him either. Esther, now all alone, lived the life of a recluse. Only when she received a letter from her son, did she gain in strength to go on but then the final telegram had come, to tell her that Leonard was a prisoner of war. They all knew what that meant. Concentration camp. Her worst nightmare had come true.

He began to cry. He had kept his distance from Charlotte, not because she was wilful and spiteful but because she had been second best. He admitted to himself that he had never really accepted her as his own. He believed that she must have sensed this and despised him for it. He blamed himself, even though he guessed that Rachel had never really bonded with their daughter, either. They should have cared for her, instead of leaving her to her own devices.

He wiped his eyes and blew his nose as three children came running up the garden path toward him. They were competing for his attention. The first to speak was the middle of the three siblings. A ten year old boy with curly blonde hair and a cheeky grin.

"We saw a Gerry plane, over the village, Sir. We could even see the pilot." His sister, two years older, flopped down on the grass at his feet and their six year old brother sat alongside him, on the seat.

"He had blonde hair, just like yours," Ellen sneered at her brother, as if to say he was the enemy too. She had completely forgotten that they all had the same colouring. Roy looked up into the kind man's face and noticed a tear in his eye.

"No need to cry," he whispered, "He's gone now." Something in the way the small boy empathised with him, reassured him. He felt childlike himself.

Rachel struggled up the path, laden down with provisions for them all. The three evacuees from London were a huge responsibility but for the first time in her life, she had begun to feel maternal.

"Have they told you about the aeroplane? They're saying that he must have got separated from his squadron and got lost."

"It was a bit scary, till he smiled and waved at us," Ellen added.

"He didn't try to shoot us down or bomb us," John made a bloodcurdling sound, as his outstretched arms soared and dived and he crash landed onto the lawn.

"Right, well then... enough excitement for today. Who wants to go and make some lemonade?" Rachel glanced over her shoulder to look at her husband. He was still pining, she suspected, for Charlotte. She had done her best to block her feelings out. Then, when the three children turned up, she found she had more than enough to do to keep her mind occupied. He worried her these days. She feared he would never be able to snap out of it.

Roy sat closer to him and took him by the hand. Roy felt secure with his surrogate parents but deep down, he pined for his mum and dad in London.

The next evening Rachel climbed the hill toward her home and felt more weary than usual. There were more and more meetings to attend on behalf of her husband these days as well as looking after the evacuees and taking her turn in the fields. Thank goodness the parish council meeting had gone well. Its boring agenda nearly drove her to distraction with the two elderly farmers, Huffey and George battling out their hedge and ditch disputes year in year out.

At last they had made some progress about removing the huge chestnut tree along the main street and next year the school playground was to be gravelled. The forthcoming summer fete was the light at the end of a very bleak tunnel for her. She felt sure that the children in her care would warm to dressing up and entering the parade and this lightened her load.

She grew fearful at how detached Earnest was becoming from his parish and his responsibilities. He seemed depressed but refused to see the doctor.

How would she find him on her return, she wondered. He had been staring out at the children playing on the lawn earlier. It was the unpredictability she found so difficult. One minute he seemed genuinely pleased to join in with their fun but in a flash he would remove himself with no explanation and walk alone or hide in his study for hours.

Rachel felt guilty for welcoming the war. Without the children and extra work, she would have found life unbearable. For the past year, they had filled her days and given her a purpose. To begin with, she had prayed with Earnest and the congregation for her daughter's safe return but the day to day reality of the war had convinced her that she had gone for good. All she knew for certain was that she had made an unhappy marriage with Leonard and was lonely and that her need to get away was something to do with this. Where she had run away to or what had befallen her, she did not allow herself to dwell on but deep down she hoped that she had gone back to her family in London and was happy.

She lifted the latch on the heavy iron gate and closed it behind her. It was eight o'clock and the children would be in bed. They were good at keeping to rules and regulations, taking themselves off to their large bedrooms without argument. They were glad of the extra space which they had not known before. Rachel need not have feared that they would be rough and disrespectful, Cockney urchins. Although they were from the East End, they had been brought up to mind their manners and were from a hardworking family.

Raising her eyes to the bedroom which had been Charlotte's, she noticed Ellen sitting by the window. The girl had been waiting for her surrogate mother to return. When Rachel opened the front door, Ellen ran into her arms, crying hysterically.

"Oh Mummy Rachel, he's been...horrible to me."

"Who dear? Roy or John? Calm down dear and tell me what has happened." She led the child into the kitchen.

"Not my brothers. Him...daddy Kemp. He sent me to my room, ages ago. He shouted really loud at me. Told me to mind my own business when I asked him why he had made such a mess."

Her tear stained face seemed chubbier to Rachel than when she had first arrived with a healthier pallor.

"I thought he was going to slap me. He kept calling me Charlotte, over and over again. He hates me. I ain't done nothing wrong, honest."

"I believe you, Ellen. Now don't fret any longer. Sit there and I'll make you some nice, hot milk with sugar."

Rachel kept her voice even. Inside, she felt terrified. She put a pan of milk on the stove to boil.

"Where are Roy and John?"

"Still asleep. I could hear a racket going on downstairs. I'd written my letter to Mum and Dad and went to see if he was all right."

"Don't worry anymore. I'm home and everything is going to be fine. Just keep an eye on the milk, there's a brave girl and I'll be back in a minute."

Ellen applied herself to the task, grateful for a job to take her mind off things. She had seen tempers flare up between her mum and dad, between aunts and uncles. Neighbours were always falling out down her street, usually over cheeky kids. Many times she had witnessed a brawl outside the pub when the men had had too much to drink. She knew the nastier men went home and beat their wives but she had never seen a temper like the Reverend's before. It had come from nowhere. There had been no row, flare up and he never went to the pub.

Inside the study, Rachel found him on all fours, in the middle of papers and writing material. He noticed her and like a naughty child caught red handed, seemed surprised and embarrassed. All the drawers to his bureau had been turned out and much of its contents shredded or screwed up.

"Earnest, what is it dear? What are you looking for?"

"It's here somewhere. I know it is." He began to shuffle the papers in his hands again. Rachel knelt down next to him and held his hand. His eyes were sad and confused.

"I know where she is. The adoption certificate has gone."

"You mean Charlotte?"

"Of course I mean Charlotte. Who do you think I mean?" He spat out these last words with so much venom, Rachel reeled back in surprise. "Did you think I meant her upstairs?" he whispered sarcastically.

"Well, she doesn't fool me. Not for one minute. She's not Charlotte. She's just pretending to be."

"Oh Earnest, you're not well. We've been through this so many times. Yes, it has gone and she may well have gone to look for her natural family. If that is the case then we must allow her to do so. God may have guided her back to them but we do not know for certain, Earnest. Come and pray with me, dear, for her safety."

"How can I pray, Rachel? My soul is tormented day and night and my prayers are never answered. There is no rest for the tormented. I have preached that loud and clear over the years. You should be the first to know it."

"But Earnest, this obsession isn't doing you any good. Please come and sit in the armchair and I'll fetch you some soothing milk. It will help you to sleep."

He stopped his search abruptly and stood up, leaving her on her knees beside him.

"Rachel, I have booked a train ticket for London. I shall be leaving on the six o'clock train in the morning."

"But you can't, Earnest. It will be like looking for a needle in a hay stack. That is supposing she did go to London in the first place," she pleaded with him.

"She has found her birth certificate and gone back...back to her roots...but we are her parents. She belongs here, with us."

Rachel began to weep. "I'll come with you then. We travelled all the way to Africa together. I'm sure I can find someone to mind the children while we're gone. We mustn't be parted now."

"No. I have to go alone Rachel. I am the one who let her down. I shall bring her home."

He held out his hand and helped her to her feet. She dried her eyes. After thirty years of marriage, she felt completely alone for the first time.

Suddenly remembering Ellen, she hurried to the kitchen. Her head lay on her folded arms on the kitchen table. The milk had been drunk. The mug and saucepan washed, dried and hung back on the hooks.

"Come on Ellen. Everything's all right now." Half opening her eyes, the exhausted girl was led back to her room.

By the time she reached their bedroom, he was in bed. In a corner stood his suitcase, packed and ready. She took his overcoat from the wardrobe and

237

placed it on the back of the door, ready for him to wear in the morning. Rachel undressed, got into her nightdress and climbed in beside him. Neither slept.

The next morning, he arose at five o'clock, dressed and put on his overcoat. Rachel got out of bed and put on her dressing gown. It was very cold and when she spoke her teeth chattered.

"I'll make you some breakfast."

"Please, do not make a fuss Rachel." There was that aggressive edge to his voice again.

"Just be careful. That's all I ask."

"By the end of the week, we could have Charlotte back in her old room again."

He left the room and stumbled down the stairs. At the front door he looked back and surveyed the hall, glancing only for a second up at her. Then he was gone, crunching over the gravel to his car.

By the time Earnest Kemp stepped off the underground at Bow, a dark, misty day had descended on London. The air raid the evening before had been one of the worst but now all was silent again apart from people trying to get to work or go about their daily lives. He had an address in his pocket of the adoption agency and that he decided was his first port of call. As he walked along the streets crowds jostled him about and then an air raid siren began its shrill warning signal which meant a possible day light attack, when they all least expected it.

Then they were running toward communal shelters, dotted at frequent intervals. He was carried along to the nearest one. It all happened so quickly that the next bit seemed surreal. Just before entering, he hesitated for a few moments. Across the street, a young woman was walking arm in arm with a tall, handsome man. She was dressed like a film star with a tight fitting two piece and high heels. It looked like Charlotte. How wonderful. He had found her already. He tried to get out of the jostling crowd and cross the road to her but two heavily built service men grew angry and manhandled him inside.

"Sorry vicar," they apologized noticing his collar. "We don't want to get our heads blown off now, do we?"

The entrance was quickly sealed. Someone lit a hurricane lamp. A woman prayed out loud in the furthest corner while two young girls hummed their own nervous version of "Let's all go down the Strand". Earnest felt annoyed and confused. It might have been her but how could he possibly have such good fortune so quickly? What if it was though and she had slipped through his fingers. He tried to pray, as thoughts of devastation all around and what lay ahead also filled his mind. No, he felt sure he had seen her and thanked the Lord for his guidance.

A bearded man in a navy pinstripe suit sat next to him. He drummed his fingers on a leather briefcase and kept glancing at his watch as if he had to be somewhere in a hurry.

"Do you happen to know how far the Salisbury Hotel is from here?" he asked Earnest.

"No, I'm sorry. I've just arrived from Suffolk. A total stranger in this neck of the woods, I'm afraid."

"Bloody Germans are going to make me late for my appointment. I hate being late. Oh excuse my French, Father."

"You are entitled to swear. I've just seen my daughter who I have come to London to take home with me and ended up in here instead. This war is getting us all down."

"It's just that I've been given my first assignment today. Meeting Ivor Zalenski, the poet. He usually sees my boss but he was tied up with another client. I really do not want to be late."

"What time is your appointment?"

"Nine thirty at the Salisbury."

"My dear young man it is only eight thirty. You have another hour. This will all blow over and we'll be out of here before you know it." The siren wailed over their heads. "Anyway, if you are late, don't worry. He will understand the situation when you explain it to him. There is a war on." The young man looked reassured.

Overhead anti-aircraft were doing their utmost to stave off this daylight attack on the capital. Fortunately, they were winning the battle. Everyone inside the shelter suddenly stopped what they were doing and were completely silent. It was as if they held their breath they would be safe. A menacing sound way over their heads was gaining in significance. For a split second they were united. Some held hands. One of the soldiers shredded a woodbine with his fingers, shaking too much to hold the packet which slipped to the ground. The other soldier glanced at Earnest in need of some comforting words and noticed him tug at his collar. The young publisher held his brief case close to his breast as the girls screamed. It was getting louder. Half a prayer later a direct hit, half a mile away from where they shook and sweated, made a crater the size of a house. They breathed a sigh of relief and smiles broke out as gratitude spread amongst them. Some other poor buggers had copped it they knew for a fact but their number wasn't up that day. Then out of the blue an unexploded bomb which had landed six months before and was buried fifty yards away from them decided to detonate. Concrete pitched dozens of feet up into the sky and aggregate smashed out shop window frontages. The pavement where the communal shelter had stood imploded as if there had been an earth quake. Screaming and hollering and people lucky enough not to be sucked down into it ran for their lives. Carnage and chaos lasted for several minutes and then dust billowed around this part of London until the emergency services arrived tentatively, to sort it out.

Chapter 28

Eva still could not believe where she had ended up. A tiny, defiant part of herself could not accept her fate but it helped to keep her alive. Up on the dais, she played her violin every day. Her life depended on it. Some days, she felt too weak to play a note but could still think of some simple piece to please the guards. Emaciated, lice ridden and starved of anything human, the only thing which gave her life any meaning was the music she produced from her violin.

For a long while, after being taken prisoner, she had regretted visiting her uncle Maurice just before the war. The orchestra had returned to England and she had stayed behind. It was too tempting. They had played in Paris and she had promised to be back in two weeks when their next batch of engagements were due to begin. He lived near to the Sacre Coeur Basilica in Montmartre. She had found him easily enough. Such a lovely man she remembered from his visits throughout her childhood. He had been surprised and delighted to see her. Her mother's brother was also a violinist and a scholar. They ate splendid suppers and drank red wine. Eva bared her soul to him about Leonard. She enjoyed their time together so much that she sent a telegram to say that she would not be back for a while. Then as time went by, it got more and more difficult for her to return home as the Nazis invaded France. For a while she helped him in his music academy, teaching the children.

Then, there were no children as, one by one, parents withdrew them. They no longer required the teaching of a Jew and his Jewish assistant. What had been the most lovely of visits, turned into a nightmare. Bricks and stones shattered their sleep and the Star of David covered their windows, during the night. Nowhere was safe for a Jew. Eva could no longer deny it to herself. On the day of their arrest, she thought about Leonard and whether he too was caught up in the Nazi machine. She was no longer angry with him and had forgiven him for his weakness.

Then a long train journey ensued, to a camp in Poland where all manner of atrocities were being carried out. Thoughts of her mother, father and her brothers waiting for her back in England, helped her through the most hateful of conditions. Rancid air, no light, food or water for the whole journey and then separation from her uncle who had clung to her, a broken man. When they had been selected for work or the gas chamber, she had been lucky. Her violin had saved her. Unfortunately for her elderly uncle, he was not thought of as worthy of entertaining the new arrivals at the entrance to Auschwitz. The last time she had seen him, he had been pushed to the other side of the arrival platform by an uncouth guard and instantly marched away with hundreds of other men.

After a while, regret turned to gratitude. At least she had been with someone with whom she had much in common. She accepted that God had chosen her to help Maurice face his last days. For herself, she survived on extra pieces of bread and sometimes leftover cheese or meat from the commandants table. Sometimes they were called upon to play at meal times in the guards' quarters. Sadistically, scraps were left to tempt them. When backs were turned, they risked their lives. Anyone caught was taken away and shot.

Eva was determined to survive and did whatever it took. To begin with, her beauty was attractive to the guards. She was passed around, from one to the other. Soon the unbearable, searing pain became endurable. At least she had a normal meal afterwards and sometimes a carafe of wine. After a while, they left her alone, as fresh arrivals attracted their attention.

Up on the dais, she could no longer remember the coy, shy girl she used to be but she could still remember her first innocent kiss.

Leonard marched through the gates at Auschwitz a year later. An iron arch of words greeted him and hundreds daily; Arbeit Macht Frei. Everyone looked bedraggled after their tortuous journey, aboard trains, arriving from every major city across Europe. Nowhere to sit or stretch out, to curl up or sleep. It felt almost good to swing his arms and stretch his legs. The light was blinding when the guards released them from the wagons. Instead of the smell of faeces and urine, he gulped at the air, acrid with smoke. Many threw up or fell to their knees. Leonard noticed guards overhead on watch towers, rifles firmly fixed on them. A flashback to soldiers rounding up his division at El Alamein where most of his friends had been killed or wounded was almost too much for him to bear.

As soon as it was established that he was a Jew he had been beaten up and slung in a make shift solitary cell until he could be shipped to a camp. He had acquired a taste for killing Germans and a huge part of him wanted to break free from the mass of fellow prisoners and kill another. His eyes bulged in their sockets, his heart pounded in his chest and he sweated profusely as an inner voice attempted to calm him down and told him to ignore this overwhelming desire.

Music floated down from a dais and he pictured Eva playing for him. The young woman was pathetically thin. Her head was shaven and she wore a striped uniform with a star on her arm. Her red rimmed eyes were closed but he noticed a tear rolling down her cheek. He glanced at her momentarily, over his shoulder and vowed if he ever left this place alive, he would make it up to Eva.

Many had died en route and were thrown out onto the platform. An old man who had been thrown on board at one of the pickup points, had landed at Leonard's feet. He was a rabbi and he had comforted those around him with his prayers and courage. When he could no longer stand, Leonard had supported him. He had held onto the younger man like a child but had still found the strength to sing in Hebrew to them. His voice was soft but powerful and everyone in earshot, clung to his words, as a last symbol of hope. He had died in the night and on arrival had been slung on top of a heap of lesser mortals. His long grey beard hung down from his startled mouth. Leonard found the sight impossible to get out of his mind. Then they were divided into men and women. Wailing and screaming was shouted down by brutal orders, followed by gun shots. Every suitcase was taken away by other prisoners in stripes. Once inside a brick building he was allocated a bunk.

"You will get out of your clothes and put on your uniforms."

Too tired to resist, they did as they were told. Through barred windows, he noticed men being marched in their clothes to another block, with towels over their arms.

The next day, he was chosen to carry the bodies from the gas chambers to the incinerators. He worked in a pair with another young man, newly arrived. They dare not speak but carried out their work as quickly and efficiently as they could. The realization that he was involved with exterminating the very people he had fought to save numbed his brain. He no longer had any self respect and stopped sleeping. He loathed himself as much as the perpetrators. Each body he swung onto a cart represented his mother or father and he no longer wished to live.

After two weeks of such labour intensive work and very little rations, Leonard's manly physique shrunk to half the size. Then one night a fight broke out over a piece of stale, flea ridden bread. Leonard got the blame for stealing and concealing it and was taken to the standing cells. A prison within a prison, from which no one ever came back. He admitted to saving it for Henrik who needed to eat more than the others. Leonard felt protective of the sixteen year old from Poland. He reminded him of himself at that age and he wished to preserve the memory for as long as possible by feeding him any scrap that came his way. Henrik was grateful but not as devoted to Leonard. When the guard asked them who had perpetrated the theft, he was only too willing to turn his friend in.

During the final hours of his life, Leonard prayed to a God he had forgotten. He asked for forgiveness. He was sorry for leaving his mother behind and prayed that she would always love him and remember him kindly. He was sorry for being led along an unrighteous path but did not blame Charlotte. He now understood that she had been his temptation which he had given into.

A calmness entered the cell. He no longer wept. He would soon be with his father. A resignation came over him. He could not sit or crouch. Standing cell was exactly what it meant. You stood until death. This, he tried to do well. An inner warmth spread throughout his body, from his toes up through his torso, along his arms and seeped into his mind. He could see light and Eva within it.

She was smiling and kissing him sweetly on the lips. He remembered the kiss and how it had made him feel. Cleansed of any guilt, he held onto the memory and the light grew brighter, as his life ebbed away.

Chapter 29

"I think it's high time, we spoke about your real mother, Lottie. All the time you've been here, you've never asked about her." Ruth had been having a bad day, thinking about her sister. Throughout the war years she had never given up hope of finding her.

"I know all about her. The agency told me. She was raped and ended up in an asylum and is probably dead."

Ruth could not bear to hear Charlotte speak, in such a matter of fact way about Rose. As if she didn't care what had happened to her.

"That's why we have to have this conversation. Ivor has been doing some investigative work and any day now, I shall know where to find her. She is very much alive. I haven't seen her for over twenty years. I'm certain that if you came with me, together we..."

"Count me out, Ruth. You're all the mother I need." Once again, the hardness in Charlotte's voice made Ruth dislike her.

For nearly five years she had both nurtured and spoilt her. She hardly saw Jane anymore. Charlotte had persistently nagged her to accompany her at the piano on every engagement. She had indulged her every time. Jane had been more than understanding of the situation. Of course, she said, it was only natural that Ruth would want to include Charlotte, after all their years apart. She said how marvellous it was that they could share their love of music. She had her teaching and lots of other things to keep her busy. It was becoming clearer to Ruth how much her dear friend had felt pushed out.

Also, Ivor never complained but there was something in his manner, whenever Charlotte was around. An awkwardness which she quizzed him about on numerous occasions. Always, he came back with the same answer.

"Charlotte came in search of you. You need to spend time together. I don't like getting in the way of that."

Ruth studied her niece. She seemed preoccupied. She topped up their coffee cups and decided to drop the subject for the moment. To have such a traumatic history was extremely difficult for her. She was being selfish. Just because she was anxious to meet Rose again was not good enough reason to push Charlotte into a meeting with a mother she had never known. Once more she made allowances for Charlotte and put her own needs second.

"Anyway, Ruth, I have some news of my own. I've been seeing someone, on and off, for quite a while now."

"But what about Leonard. You don't know if he is dead or alive. He could come back at the end of the war and what then?"

"But he might not. Anyway, I don't have any feelings left for him. I love Alfred and he loves me."

"Why haven't you mentioned him before?"

"Because I thought you would judge me, as you are now."

Ruth tried to imagine just how hard it had been for Charlotte. First, adopted to a couple who sounded cold hearted, married to a man whose family did not care for her and then left alone to fend for herself. How might she feel, if Ivor had been called up and had been missing for almost five years? She could not judge her harshly.

"Where did you meet him?"

"In a tea room when I first came to London. He owns his own hotel. In fact he has several."

"I wish you could have told me before. When can we meet him?"

"He's asked me to go away with him. I would have told you but I could never pluck up the courage. I don't want you to think badly of me, Ruth. I couldn't bear it."

"It must have been horrible, having to keep secrets, darling. You've worked so hard with me, as well. When on earth, did you find the time to see him?"

"When you thought I was visiting my parents."

"Oh, Charlotte. Did you ever go back to see them?"

"No."

Ruth did not know how to advise her. She was certainly wilful.

"Well, I can't tell you what to do about all of that but they must have worried about you when you went missing; especially with a war on. Don't you ever feel guilty for running away?"

"Never. They left me all the time. I've already told you. When I found you, I knew this is where I belonged. I'd come home."

"It was a dream come true for me, too."

They sipped their coffee and the tension between them subsided.

"Ruth, when I come back from my holiday with Alfred, I'll come with you to meet Rose."

"When are you going?"

"Next week, to his hotel in Kent. He has to oversee the running and asked me if I'd like to go with him."

"So, in just a few weeks, I could be reunited with my dear sister and you with your mother. Oh Charlotte, it will be wonderful. I hope you won't change your mind."

"I promise, I'll go with you. I love you Ruth. I'd do anything for you."

For the next week, Charlotte felt happy and contented. Telling the truth about Alfred left her feeling unburdened. Even Ivor seemed less cold towards her. When Ruth told him about the new man in Charlotte's life, he felt relieved not to have to keep it a secret any longer. He could never trust her again but he felt grateful to her for coming out with the plain truth.

On their evenings off, Ruth and Charlotte joined Ivor in the parlour and listened to the wireless. The news was becoming more and more hopeful. Any day, the allies were expected to invade Europe and crush the Nazi regime, once and for all. A bulletin described exactly their next move.

"They will be forging ahead, to bring about the end of the war, by finding enemy launch pads and destroying them."

"What do they mean?"

"I think they are talking about the doodle bug launch pads. Those damn Gerries are so clever to have invented rockets like that," answered Ivor.

"Well, I for one don't admire them. Gives me the creeps."

Charlotte gave her opinion and shuddered. She had heard enough of them recently droning over London and then cutting out while they were sheltering on the underground. So many had lost their lives due to this latest invention.

"Yes, but it's good news that the allies are advancing. It must mean the war is coming to an end. Then we can all start afresh," Ruth reassured her niece and smiled an ironic smile at Ivor. Neither of them knew how things would work out for Charlotte after the war but it felt good to be talking to each other, honestly, at long last.

A week later, Charlotte and Alfred were on their way to Canterbury in Kent. It was a beautiful, sunny day and the hood was back on the convertible, allowing the wind to flirt with her long, blonde hair. Snuggled up to him, she felt a happiness unknown to her before. She knew, without a doubt, that she loved him and nothing could come between them. The war was nearly over and his endless love affairs a thing of the past. He had been faithful to her, he said, from the minute he had laid eyes on her, in the cafe.

She felt excited. The night before, he had proposed marriage to her. Once the war was over, he would sort everything out and she would be free to marry him. They would be together, always. They were going to make a day of it before he began work in the hotel. He had come to boost staff morale. First of all, they stopped at a village store and bought as much as they could for a picnic. Alfred had been saving a bottle of champagne for the right occasion and it was still nicely chilled.

"Oh look, darling, over there. It looks a lovely spot, with cherry trees and a pond and everything."

Alfred pulled over and held her hand. He loved her childlike quality and would do anything to make her happy. The lovers clambered over a stile and sat down on the tufted grass beneath an oak tree. Oast houses with their white, giant sized teats on top nestled in among the trees all around them. It was freakishly hot for April which made them grateful for its shade. A meat pie, cheese, bread and apples was one of the loveliest meals she had ever tasted. Good, honest, simple food. Even rationing could not spoil their precious time together. After drinking the champagne she began to wish her life had always felt as good as this. They made love and lay in one another's arms sharing a cigarette.

Charlotte wished the afternoon could go on forever and picked some daisies to make a chain. She wore it around her neck. Life could not get any better, she decided and sighed heavily.

"Anything wrong, darling?"

"Not anymore. I feel so safe with you Alfred. Like a different person."

She stared into his hazel eyes and saw affection and admiration gazing back at her. For a fleeting moment she remembered how others had looked at her. Disgust was always in Leonard's eyes, resentment in her mother's, disinterest in her fathers. Contempt, hostility, hatred. She had come up against them all. She reminded herself to be happy and not dwell on that. Impulsively, she began to tell Alfred how much she loved him and open up about her life.

He was a good listener and lay very still, blowing smoke rings. He had no idea that she had such a serious side to her personality.

"I've done some awful things in my life Alfred. I'm not the good, little girl you think I am."

"I know you're a sexy little minx, if that's what you mean," he said taking a lunge at her to try and lighten the atmosphere but she carried on. Before she began a new life with him, she needed to be absolved of her past.

"No, please listen. Leonard didn't love me. He loved my best friend, Eva. There… I've said it. I played a trick on them. Brought them together and then crushed them both. You see, I blackmailed him into marrying me."

Now she had his attention. "Steady on old girl. You do have a tendency to dramatize, you know."

"I was having a baby. I miscarried. I felt so wretched that I wanted him to take care of me. I threatened him that if he didn't marry me, I would say he had caused the miscarriage and he would be arrested and…"

"Calm down, dear girl. So you were having a baby before you were married. Quite right that he should marry you."

"The baby wasn't Leonard's. He was in love with Eva. They were engaged."

Alfred sat up and hugged his knees and whistled, deep in thought.

"So, who was the father?"

"Please don't ask me that."

"I think I have a right to know." He sounded indignant. She had never heard him sound angry with her before and it frightened her.

"The truth is...it could have been one of several."

"So, just how many have you slept with?" She detected disgust in his voice.

"A lot but...no more than you. You see, we're alike Alfred. It's a completely fresh start for both of us."

Somewhere, deep down in his psyche, Alfred knew this to be true but manly pride stood in the way. He got to his feet and put the rubbish into their bag with the empty bottle.

"Can you forgive me, Alfred?" The silence between them was deafening. She caught hold of his arm.

"What are you thinking?"

"To be frank, Lottie. I think you've been a bit of a slut. Come to think of it, you were a bit of a push over when we first met but I put that down to the war and having to sort of...you know...live for the moment."

"Not you too, Alfred. Please don't judge me like that. I need to wipe the slate clean with you. I thought I could trust you to understand."

He turned away from her and looked at nothing in particular. Like a stranger, he headed back to the car. Her head swam with emotion and she began to run in the opposite direction. Alfred, whose mild temper had blown itself out, turned in surprise to see her making her way round the edge of the field. He had expected her to follow him. He had called her names and felt sorry for it. He now wanted to make it up with her and allow her to talk about it again.

"Lottie, come back. You don't know where you're going."

That much is true, she thought. I've never known. Although, one thing she did know in that moment. She hated him. He had sneered at her and called her a slut, when she had been honest and truthful for the first time in her life. Well, it wasn't worth letting your guard down, she decided. She must be getting soft in her old age.

After walking for a long time, she noticed the heat of the day had vanished and a chilly wind was picking up. She cupped her hands over her eyes and squinted. A patchwork of fields which she had traipsed through lay behind. Her legs ached from so much effort and her feet were sore.

She sat down on a grassy mound and inspected them. Pulling off her sandals, she discovered a blister on each heel. He had gone too far, calling her names and had not tried in the slightest to understand. She doubted whether she could ever forgive him. He had made her feel small and inadequate. Overhead, she heard a skylark. It sounded lonely too. She would have liked to walk in her bare feet but there were thistles everywhere and so she slipped her sandals back on.

For now, she had to find the road and make her way to the hotel. More accusations, no doubt, would follow. Well she was ready for him now her temper was up. After traipsing through many fields she came to a sign, "Bull, keep out!" Retracing her steps she came to a wide ditch, brim full with water and slime which she managed to clear but came face to face with a herd of cattle. Not sure if they were friendly, she skirted round the edge of the field which led her into a wood. Distant memories from the past were triggered.

"Run for your life, Lenny. I'll save you."

Tears streamed down her face. One thing was certain. From now on, she would try to make amends to those in her life who had suffered because of her. She began to feel a bit better.

A cloud glided over the sun and she shivered. In the distance, she heard a sound that reminded her of swarming bees. The wood was no more than a thin copse of trees and she was soon through it and crossing a hop field. The first of many with long rows of the crop, freshly planted. They were growing well, ready for the harvest at the end of summer.

The droning was getting louder. Charlotte felt frightened and ran as fast as she could, praying that the sound was not what she thought it was but it was unmistakable. They had heard it time and again over London. She flung herself inside the hop bushes and crouched down on all fours. She prayed that the sinister, rasping wail of the flying bomb would not cut out.

"Oh my God," Alfred spotted the doodlebug way off in the distance and pulled over onto a grassy verge. It was on course to London, flying over doodlebug alley, where he remembered a few had landed, having been shot down or having fallen short of their target. A tractor towing a hay wagon, pulled up behind him. The farmer jumped down and stood watching next to him. They both held their breath. Then the engine cut out, as the rocket lost its power. For a few seconds they could hear songbird and the wind rustling the trees. Rooted to the spot, they both felt the vibration throughout their bodies as it exploded on impact, deafening everyone for miles around. Grey smoke and orange flames billowed up into the blue sky.

"Second one this month. I better get on over there. Looks like it landed in my hop fields this time."

Alfred shook from head to foot. "I'll take you. It'll be quicker...only my girlfriend went that way."

Chapter 30

At last, Ruth had proof of Rose's existence in her hand. A letter had come from Doctor Munro. In it, he explained that he would not normally breach confidentiality but in this case, he felt strongly that a reunion with her sister would be a risk worth taking. In their sessions, recently, Rose had talked about Ruth as if she desired it. She had been rehabilitated into the world successfully, for several years now. He felt confident that she would be able to cope with meeting her sister again. However, he felt that a fear of rejection might prevent Rose making contact. Therefore, he was taking the liberty of allowing Ruth to know where she was now employed as well as her address. Would she kindly write to Rose first before making an attempt to see her. This way Rose could get used to the idea of a meeting.

The letter felt bitter sweet. She had discovered a scribbled note from Charlotte, to say she would be gone for at least a month. She advised her to go ahead with meeting Rose and not wait for her. Ruth felt angry and let down. Charlotte had disappointed her once again. She was becoming unreliable and selfish.

"Well, so be it, Ruth. Charlotte can take care of herself, for now. You can do this without her."

Ruth could always count on Ivor's support. Although it gave her strength, she still felt nervous at seeing Rose again. She decided to write to her to cushion the situation for both of them.

' My dear sister Rose,

I hardly know how to write this letter. I hope it does not come as too much of a shock to you. For years, I have wanted to meet up with you again but I had no idea where you were and the asylum were not at liberty to tell me. However your doctor has given me permission to contact you as he thinks it will be good for you to see me again. I have never stopped thinking about you, what you might be doing, how life has treated you. Especially on our birthday which we used to share and at Christmas when family is so important.

Although more years, than I dare to think about have gone by, I have never stopped loving you, Rose, and hope with all my heart that you feel the same. Can we meet, and talk and get to know each other again? Please write back to me in the enclosed envelope. I look forward to hearing from you so much.

God Bless you,
Love Ruth

For weeks, she waited for a reply and when none came, she threw herself more than usual into her war work. At night she could not sleep. Had Rose moved on? Had she been killed in the bombing or had she simply withdrawn from her past altogether? Ivor noticed her poor appetite, her lack of interest in him and the children. He suggested they pay Rose a visit.

One afternoon, they hired a taxi which took them to Piccadilly Gardens, around which enormous, elegant, Georgian houses presided. They were looking for Love Lane where rows of terraced houses had been occupied by the staff of their wealthy employers, years before. Now, they were converted into flats or one room bedsits. Rose rented number eighteen. With trepidation, they climbed the stairs and knocked the door. Ruth was grateful to see that the area had not suffered from too much bomb damage. Ivor held onto her arm as she steeled herself to facing the unknown. Soon a grey haired, elderly man appeared breathless behind them.

"Are you looking for Rose?"

"Yes, we are."

"Cor blimey, you're Ruthie Drew. Well, well."

"She is an old friend of my wife's," Ivor had the presence of mind for which Ruth smiled weakly.

News of a long lost sister might spread like wildfire and make the papers. Neither she nor Rose were up to that sort of pressure.

"Truth is, she doesn't live here anymore. Well, that is to say she does but hardly ever comes home, especially with the war on and tubes not running as they should".

He seemed star struck and carried on a conversation until Ivor asked for the address. The man was not going to be got rid of so easily. He asked them to follow him into his bedsit. It stank of cat piss. Ruth and Ivor refused the cup of tea, offered to them, making a swift exit. At last, they had the address of the public lavatory. The taxi driver took them there and waited outside with Ivor. Ruth straightened her clothes and walked toward the steps.

Rose had been hobbling about on her plastered leg for weeks now. It had really annoyed her how it had happened. Some thoughtless bugger, she concluded, had left a tap running and she had slid the length of the toilets, on the flooded floor.

It must have been one of the prostitutes who were always frequenting her lavatories; making themselves up before hanging about outside the Rainbow Rooms. To begin with, she had thought they were a nice bunch of girls. They made a change from so many smart, uniformed women. She liked the way they looked in their bright coloured clothes and heavy makeup. Even the strong smell of their cheap perfume did not bother her but when she had overheard conversations about them, her opinion changed. They were not to be admired. She heard how they chatted the American soldiers up, doing anything for a pair of silk stockings or a bar of chocolate. Up against walls even. It disgusted her.

It had taken four to lift her and she had never felt so embarrassed in her life when a handsome, young man examined her at the hospital. He looked too young to be a doctor. Pain from the fall she could just about bear but being prodded and poked left her feeling vulnerable. After a week she was discharged with an outpatients' appointment to go back in a month, to have the cast removed. Her leg would be as good as new if she took it easy but Rose simply got back to her work.

The council had not replaced her for which she was grateful but the lavatories were in a sorry state and stank. French letters littered the floor and were stuck down the toilets. Many had missed their aim. She blamed the prostitutes.

Fortunately her room marked Attendant had been locked. Rose needed to get off her leg. She made a cup of tea and took two more painkillers. Someone had kindly left a bunch of sweet smelling lilies in water in a sink and she had lovingly displayed them as a centre piece on her table.

When Ruth descended the lavatory steps, she felt more tense and nervous than on opening nights in the theatre. Timidly, she entered Rose's arena. She could smell fresh cut flowers. Ruth glanced at herself in a mirror. Her auburn hair was smoothed back into a roll, with two mother of pearl slides each side of her head to control stray strands. It was uncanny how much she resembled her mother and she wondered if Rose did, too. The tan suit she had chosen to wear fitted well and she was three inches taller in the latest style shoes. Platforms lent themselves very well to her slight deformity and could be easily adapted without anyone noticing. Ruth hoped this style of shoe would never go out of fashion. Just a little make up was all she needed in the day. It was enjoyable to feel natural, after all the evenings she spent caked up in stage make up. Her nerves began to get the better of her and she blew warm breath onto her shivering cold hands.

An old woman came down the steps and used the first lavatory. She pulled the chain and walked past her. Ruth pretended to titivate her hair.

"Are you in there, Rosie," the woman enquired, sticking her head round the door marked Attendant.

"Yes dear. Ooh, hallo Betty." Ruth did not recognize the voice.

Betty disappeared inside the room and Ruth heard her make sympathetic noises. During the time which elapsed, she drew a snapshot of the life her sister had led. First, the asylum and now this wretched environment but at least she had survived. Thank God. Rose had found herself a niche and had a friend who cared about her. For a brief moment, she felt like an intruder and thought how easy it would be to make a quick exit. Rose need never know that she had found her in this degrading place. She felt convinced that they no longer had anything in common. The door flew back.

"Is it busy out there, Betty?"

"No love, just one. Anyway, take care and when you come back to the flats, call in for a nice meal."

"I will, don't you worry. Thank you for coming out of your way."

"No bother at all. What are friends for?"

"Tata dear. Oh Betty, was there anymore post for me?"

"No love. Just the letter I bought last time."

The old woman climbed the stairs and wondered why the lovely woman whose face looked familiar, was still hanging about. Ruth took a deep breath and knocked the door.

"I thought you'd gone, dear."

"No, it's me, Rose." Ruth pushed the door wide open, exposing a grey haired woman who seemed squashed into a wicker chair. She was overweight, with blotchy skin and was obviously suffering with her breathing. A huge pinafore covered her obese body and fell open, revealing a leg in plaster. This rested on another chair. She coughed violently and searched for something in one of her pockets. Rose found her spectacles and put them on, while at the same time trying to stand up. It was a great effort for her. The Rose of Ruth's childhood was transformed.

"No, don't get up. Did you receive my letter?"

Rose suddenly remembered the letter crumpled in her other pocket. The letter which she had read and reread until she could no longer cry over it. The letter which had taken her breath away and caused her sleepless nights. She struggled to her feet, sliding two crutches beneath her armpits. Ruth towered over her. The two women stood no more than a yard apart. Neither knew what to do or say. Ruth swallowed a lump in her throat and wiped away a tear.

"Well...here we are then. At last."

Rose stared at her sister with bulging eyes above black bags beneath.

"I hope I haven't shocked you."

Rose continued to stare. Ruth suddenly remembered her slapping her head years before and wondered if she still did.

"Shall I put the kettle on while you sit yourself back down? You look like you've been in the wars."

"We all have, ain't we?" Rose shot back.

Ruth saw the joke and smiled. The voice might sound deeper and gruffer but the old sense of humour was still intact. She struck a match under the kettle. Rose landed with a thud in her chair. The least activity made her sweat these days. She brought out a handkerchief and wiped her face clean. Ruth could see the pain in her eyes and helped, awkwardly, to lift her leg back onto the chair.

"Used to be you." Rose muttered under her breath.

"What?"

"How's your leg now?"

"Oh, I see what you mean. It's fine these days. I hardly think about it."

Ruth handed her a cup of tea and noticed how much she was trembling.

"Could you pass the sugar bowl. I still take two."

Ruth passed the sugar and pulled a stool nearer to her sister. She sat down. In her wildest dreams, she had never imagined a meeting like this. In a room, no bigger than a broom cupboard, with a woman who looked old enough to be her mother.

Rose, on the other hand, felt elated. Here, was not only her twin come to visit her but the singer, Ruth Duthie. Star of the West End whom she had recently seen at the pictures. She gulped her tea down, thirstily.

"Would you like some more?"

"No ta, Ruth."

"It's good to hear you say my name, Rose. Like music to my ears."

Rose grinned. She had pleased her and it encouraged her to ask questions.

"Do you like the royal family?" She nodded in the direction of her cuttings on the wall.

"Oh...yes, of course. I see you're a fan."

Rose chuckled covering her embarrassment while Ruth sipped her tea.

"I saw you the other day."

"You did? Where?"

"First at the pictures and then in front of the Hippodrome on a billboard."

"So you know what I do then?"

"Oh yes...yes. You sound lovely. I haven't heard such a lovely voice in years."

Ruth felt very touched by this remark. Rose had become a simple soul after all she had been through. What she said came out in an uncomplicated way. Her honesty was childlike. She could see just how pleased Rose was to have her there.

"I bet you're married. Is that your married name...Duthie?"

"No, it's my stage name. I have twin boys, Ronnie and Ralph. They're twins, like us."

"Well, fancy that. More boys in the family. Mum always wanted more girls."

"She did, didn't she?"

"Brought any photos?"

It was going so well that Ruth felt encouraged. "I'd like you to come back with me and meet them. I could take care of you until your leg heals properly."

Rose bit her bottom lip. It felt impossible. Doctor Munro was the only person who looked after her. Besides, she couldn't allow a star such as Ruth Duthie to take care of her. Rose felt confused.

"It's all right, Rose. My husband is a good, kind man. There's no need to be afraid."

For now, she decided not to tell her who he was. Instinctively, she felt Rose would link him to her miserable past which would not help the situation. Rose began to pinch her arms. Ruth changed the subject.

"I hear you sleep down here, even with the war on and now with your poorly leg."

"It's my home. I like it down here."

"Come home with me, Rosie."

"I ain't Rosie anymore. I'm Rose and I think you should go now." She was trying hard not to raise her voice.

"All right, I will go but Rose, now I've found you, I'll be back."

Ruth stood up and backed out of the room. She felt guilty leaving her sister in such appalling mental and physical health. It seemed so cruel, after all she had been through. Outside, she stumbled into Ivor's arms and sobbed. They had been doing so well but she had pushed things too far forgetting the doctor's warnings to take things slowly. On the way home, she did not utter a word.

Rose controlled her breathing by placing a paper bag over her nose and mouth. After several breaths she felt much calmer. She had been taught this simple technique which always worked. The panic attack subsided. She felt sorry that Ruth had left after such a short time and was scared that she might never come back. Part of her longed to be taken care of.

Ruth was famous now and rich. She probably owned a huge house up West and had posh grub, even though everyone else was rationed. What she would give for a comfortable bed and a hot roast dinner. It made her mouth water. She sighed and tore the paper bag to shreds.

Not just a figment of her imagination, like some of the other visitors to her lavatories. Ruth Duthie was real and her sister. After a while, she felt strong enough to make another cup of tea and shut up shop for the night. As she settled down for the evening, she wondered what the man was like whom Ruth had married. It gave her a hot flush to think about it. She said her prayers and dozed off.

A fortnight later, on returning from having the cast removed, she found a huge bouquet of pink roses outside her room. The card read, with much love from Ruth. Rose felt elated. As she prepared to put them in water an envelope slipped out, containing a ticket for a Saturday matinee for the new musical review written especially for her sister. With the end of the war in sight the West End was seeing most of its theatres reopening for business.

"The Joy of Freedom" was now showing at the newly refurbished Hippodrome and was receiving hit reviews every bit as complimentary as the Gaieties at the Winter Garden. She felt a mixture of excitement tinged with fear. How could she go to a theatre and walk in alone? She had never done it before. The cinema was different. Just a flea pit and always in the dark. The theatre was posh and she had no clothes to wear. What would she look like in her raincoat and ankle boots?

"Dear, oh dear, Ruthie. What you gone and done?" Rose felt a migraine coming on.

That day, all day, she scrubbed frantically and tried to forget the invitation.

"Two days to prepare yourself," she chanted over and over again. Later, when there was a lull in punters, she pulled the scissor gate across and walked to a second hand dress shop, not far away. She had used it a couple of times before when she felt an urge to impress the doctor. It usually worked. He always paid her a compliment, remarking on how much the pattern or colour suited her. Inside the shop, Rose searched along the racks of dresses, suits skirts and coats. They had all seen better days. Nothing was big enough.

"Can I 'elp?" the old woman asked from behind the counter. Rose remembered how strange she looked whenever she saw her, with orange permed hair and arched, penciled in eyebrows. She always appeared wearing a dress that looked more like a dressing gown as if she slept in between serving customers.

"No, just looking." Rose flushed and felt like leaving the shop.

"I've got a lovely dress and coat out the back. Just been brought in. Do you a treat. Hang on."

She slipped through the curtain behind her and came out with the said matching dress and coat. Rose was mesmerized and could hardly believe it. Did the Queen bring her old cast offs here, she wondered. They were mauve. Her favourite colour and yards big enough.

"Go on. Try them on, through there. If they fit, I'll throw in that purple hat in the window. Five bob the lot."

"I'll take the lot. Don't need to try them on. Have you any shoes to match?"

"Got just the pair. Hang on."

She disappeared behind the red velvet curtain again and like a magician produced the shoes.

"What size are you?"

"A four."

"Sorry, love, these are a six."

"I'll take them. My feet are always swollen anyway."

"Right you are. 'Ere, take a bit of tissue paper for the toes. It'll 'elp keep 'em on."

The woman neatly folded the garments and placed them, with the shoes, in a carrier bag. The hat, Rose carried in her other hand.

"Going anywhere nice?"

"Up West, to a show." Rose bit her lip but couldn't keep it to herself any longer. "My sister's the star. You might know her. Ruth Duthie."

"Very nice, too."

As she left the shop, the woman sneered under her breath. "Yes, my brother's Fred Astaire. Must be crackers."

That night, Rose slept like a baby. The day's shopping and visit to the hospital had worn her out.

Chapter 31

Rachel checked the post box every morning and afternoon for news about Earnest. To begin with, when he did not return, she convinced herself that he might be searching for Charlotte elsewhere. It had been more than two weeks. In his right mind, he would have written or phoned but she knew how mentally unstable he had been when he left.

When three weeks were up, she reported him missing at the local police station. They contacted the police in and around Bow and were able to tell her of a bomb that had gone off on the very day he arrived in the vicinity. It had killed dozens of people. He was now on the missing, presumed dead list.

Had it not been for the children in her care, she would have feared for her sanity but she managed to keep her mind focused on them. Also the camaraderie she had with her neighbours kept her strong. She enjoyed getting to know the women of Shopley by working alongside them in the fields. She felt like one of them instead of being set apart. From sowing the crops to harvesting, she took her turn and had even learned to drive the tractor.

After a year the new vicar and his wife moved into the vicarage. Agnes came to the rescue offering two rooms at the back of her shop. Rooms used for surplus stock had become redundant as the war progressed and so they were made into bedrooms. Rachel shared with Ellen while the boys were together in the other room. As she and the children settled in, she began to get to know Agnes Ong for the first time. Only brief snatches of conversation had ever passed between them at the end of church services and she remembered shouting directions at Agnes to act more fairylike in a Christmas pantomime now just a distant memory.

While the children were at school she helped in the shop and enjoyed weighing goods on ration and bagging them up. They were a sight better off than people in towns as fresh fruit, vegetables, milk, butter, cream and eggs were still more freely available in the countryside. Most people kept chickens. Homemade bread and cakes were enjoyed and the women of Shopley swapped recipes on how to make ingredients go even further. Carrots were used instead of sugar to sweeten them as well as honey from the hives. The evacuees including Ellen, Roy and John were receiving the first balanced meals they had had in their lives. Because most of the produce was grown locally Mrs. Ong could rely on producers to supply to her shop and so her shelves seldom seemed empty. After a hard day's work in the fields the women would come in for their provisions, ready for a good gossip.

Agnes had never had any interest in setting out her shop in an appealing way. Ordering, taking delivery and serving took up all of her time but now with an extra pair of hands the shop looked tidier and she left the feminine finishing touches to Rachel who seemed to thrive on it.

Before the mid afternoon rush when all the other daily chores had been done, the two would stop for a brew and have a chat. Rachel learned how Agnes had married into the business and how Arnold had been killed in the First World War. His parents had died and left it all to her.

"Do you know, Rachel. I never wanted this sort of life."

"That's funny because I can't imagine anyone else running the post office stores. It's as if you've always been here in the heart of the village."

"Oh yea. It's taken for granted that I belong here but I always wanted to be a school teacher. I could have taught arithmetic. Yes. I'd have made a good teacher. Never had any of my own...children that is. Arnold went away at nineteen. We didn't have a chance."

"That's very sad. Life's strange Agnes. I never wanted to be a vicar's wife but my parents thought Earnest was a good catch and encouraged me. Bless them, they both worked in factories from morning till night and thought it would be a step up for me. I would have loved working in a shop. I love it here."

"Well, that's good to hear. It's nice having you and the children around. Only took to one in this village before Ellen and her brothers came. The sort of son I'd have been proud of."

Rachel was thinking about how sad she had been when she had found out she could not have children of her own.

"Leonard Bloom. Scrawny little devil he was but turned out to be a genius. Terrible waste. Esther's heart's broken that's for sure. Never see her these days." She turned away to wipe her eyes and blow her nose.

"Since she closed the shop, no one does except Amy Peart who does all her cleaning."

Rachel felt she had nothing to lose. She had never confided to another living soul about the adoption. Suddenly, she felt she had nothing to hide.

"I never had a child of my own, Agnes."

"What about Charlotte?"

"Earnest and I adopted her before we moved here."

"Well, I never did..."

"So I know what that heartache feels like. Hoping for a child and one never comes."

"Hope you don't mind me talking candid to you Rachel but she was a bit of a hand full, wasn't she?"

"I know and of course, as her parents, we were partly to blame. I see that now. She would have perhaps been happier with a sibling but we decided to just adopt one child."

"She and Leonard were almost like brother and sister for a while back then."

"Yes, they had a strong bond."

"Perhaps they should have stayed that way instead of getting married."

The two women sat in silence for a while. Rachel broke it.

"Now they have both gone from Shopley and from our lives." Her voice broke and for the first time she shared her grief with another human being.

"Try not to upset yourself, Rachel. We all know where poor, dear Leonard ended up but you never know, Charlotte may come back some day. Was it another chap she ran off with?"

"Oh no, we never thought for one minute she had done that. You see, she found her adoption papers and as she was so lonely and unhappy after Leonard joined up, we believe she went in search of her real mother."

"Well I never... any idea who she was?"

"All we knew was that she was very ill and they took her to an asylum

266

for the mentally afflicted."

"Probably explains a lot...oh I'm sorry, I shouldn't have..."

"That's quite all right. I've often had my own suspicions. She may have inherited some traits...terrible business."

Once again, they sat in silence. It felt good to be able to talk to someone about this secret part of her life. Rachel knew she had found a friend in Agnes Ong and trusted her to keep it completely confidential.

Soon children were out of school and running errands for their mothers. Women were buying last minute things for supper after a hard day's toil in the fields.

The two women carried on as normal and the subject was never brought up again.

On the eighth of May, nineteen forty five, the end of the war was declared by Winston Churchill. Overnight, instead of working for the war effort, a different set of skills were being put to use. Street parties, processions and a multitude of celebrations were being organized. It felt like the whole world was free and out from under the claws of a manic monster. No one was going to waste any more precious time hidden behind masks. Gas masks which had been carried everywhere were soon discarded. Happy, smiling faces now appeared. Men, women and children waved flags victoriously at the side of endless parades. As men were demobbed and reunited with their families and sweethearts, the human race celebrated with an urgency, as if their freedom might, once again, be snatched away by a tyrannical practical joker.

Shopley celebrated, along with hundreds of other villages, the end of the war and the return of their men. Red, white and blue handmade bunting fluttered in the breeze, strung from cottage to cottage, house to house and along the main street from the vets to the Angel public house up to Ong's and all along the railings of the village school. On the common, trestle tables were set up and Rachel Kemp and her helpers put final touches to a wonderful spread of food. Everyone had found something to bring from their larder. Home baked bread and cakes, sandwiches and blancmange, plenty of fruit pies and biscuits. For miles around, every woman had baked, stewed, boiled, roasted, soaked or skewered their contribution. Such a miraculous feast would be remembered for years to come and be written about in the local press.

It felt truly good to be alive on such a momentous day. Rachel felt sad for her losses but would not allow even that to interfere with her joy. The war was over. It would be the final party she would have with Ellen, Roy and John. In a week's time, they would be returning to their parents. She intended to make the most of them. She prayed that they would take home some happy memories of their time with her in Suffolk.

"We'll come back and visit you. Perhaps in the school holidays." Ellen had promised but Rachel knew they wouldn't. In her heart, she believed that if she had been their mother, she would not let them out of her sight again until they were grown. To have been parted with them for five years in the first place was cruel enough.

Everyone began to arrive. Rachel sat between Agnes and Esther who had rallied ever since the two women had insisted on visiting her and not taking no for an answer. Now the three friends sat in the company of dozens of women and the men who had been too old or infirm to go to war. Farmer George played his fiddle, Sam Miller an old, battered mouth organ and Farmer Huffey the squeeze box. When music was a necessity the two farmers would always call a truce on their own personal war and enjoy themselves.

Sam had failed to get into the army due to being deaf in one ear. He envied Johnny and his brother all their adventures and could not wait to see them again. They were two lucky survivors and he looked forward to downing pints with them in the Angel as soon as they were demobbed. He felt sad that Leonard had perished in a concentration camp and wondered what would become of the timber yard.

Rachel, Agnes and Esther watched the young girls and boys dancing together to the lively music. Children who had grown up throughout the war years had become courting couples before their very eyes. Soon, their numbers would be depleted when the evacuees returned to their homes. Agnes raised her glass of elderberry wine and made a toast:

"To all our men folk, past, present and future. May most of them return to the love of their women and the warmth of their beds. And to those who will not be returning, God rest their souls. Here's to our brave boys."

Those who were within earshot drank the toast. Esther was instantly pulled to her feet to prevent her becoming melancholy again.

"Now, you two, up on your feet. This is supposed to be a party not a wake. Let's make merry while we can. We ain't passed it yet."

"Agnes, now I know you've had one too many of that wine of yours."

Esther reprimanded her friend. Rachel laughed and got to her feet.

"I'm game if you two are."

"No, it's not the wine. It's just that my sciatica is giving me some peace today and I have to make hay while the sun shines. Me and my Arnold loved to dance a jig and this is getting me going."

The three widows held hands and danced over to the bales, each light of foot. They suddenly felt younger and more carefree than they had in years and the children watched in disbelief. The vicar's wife, the shop keeper and the postmistress dancing and reeling. As their hair stuck to their foreheads and their clothes to their bodies they felt life returning where only decay had imposed itself for so long. Every sinew of their being knew beyond doubt that life was going to be different but as the sun went down on Shopley they knew they would journey on together through the remainder of their lives.

Chapter 32

Ellen, Roy and John loved the train ride back to London. The smell of the steam engine reminded them of boiled eggs and they loved the way it rattled along through the countryside, dipping into blackness every so often.

They ate their packed lunches, Rachel had prepared for them that morning and grew excited with every passing mile. They would soon be home. Rachel watched, as they chatted over this and that and made comments about the scenery. Little did they know that she would soon be a distant memory. She smiled at them. They had been her life for five years. She handed them their sweets, a gift from Esther, rooted out from of her old stock. Dolly mixtures, sherbet and gob stoppers. Their fingers were soon the colour of the rainbow.

The letter said that she could put them on the train. They would be met at Liverpool Street Station but she had preferred to take them door to door. They had become used to sleepy Suffolk and not the hustle and bustle of busy train stations. Besides, it would be an opportunity to meet their parents. She had arranged to be there at approximately midday. Their father always came home for his lunch and they would all eat together. Soon the journey was at an end. They now had to catch a tube to Shoreditch. It was an adventure for them all. Rachel had not been on the underground for years. When they came out of the station, the bombed out buildings took her breath away. How anyone could have come out of the Blitz alive was a miracle. Even the children sat in silence, gawping at the jagged remains of buildings that had made up their community. Houses, shops, museums, churches blown to smithereens. These children will be grownups before they see this carnage rebuilt, Rachel thought.

The tram dropped them outside the Feathers on Weymouth Terrace. Hardly any of the houses were left standing. The children ran on ahead. It was hard to catch up with them. At the top end, they stopped outside three houses that had for some reason withstood every nightly bombardment on the East End. The children waited for her outside.

"That's funny." Ellen said.

"What's funny?" Rachel asked

"That's the old house where a mad girl lived once. Number ninety two. My mum told us, she used to come round from her street, to try and see her through the window. She had a baby when she was younger than me. She went to the loony bin. She was the talk of the neighbourhood."

Ellen joined her brothers who had turned left into Eastbourne Road. Rachel looked at the house, now boarded up ready for the bull dozer. What a sad coincidence, she thought. Must have happened a lot in those days. It couldn't possibly be... She dismissed the thought from her mind and quickened her pace catching up with the children as they disappeared down an entry.

Not many miles away Ivor was feeling a mixture of emotions as he watched Alfred break down and cry. He had poured them both a brandy and listened to how, for the past six weeks Alfred had not been able to leave his hotel in Bow. He still felt numb from the shock. Ivor could see him visibly shaken, a shadow of his former self. It was hard to hear how she had been killed outright by the flying bomb, while he looked on powerless to help. Ivor was lost for words. What a cruel hand of fate for her to have been killed a month before the end of the war. Alfred apologized repeatedly for not contacting them before now but he felt unsafe to go out even after peace had been declared. There had been no funeral since there had been no body just her hand bag and a sandal found in a neighbouring field.

"I loved her, you know, I really loved her". It was as if he needed Ivor to believe him and to forgive him for leading her astray.

"I can hardly believe it." Ivor sipped his brandy and felt his heart beat rapidly in his chest. "What will you do now?"

"I'm going to sell the hotels and move away...perhaps go and live abroad somewhere." The two men sat in silence for a while sipping at the brandy every now and then. Then they stood at the front door, shook hands and Alfred left.

If only Charlotte had not come back into their lives. Ruth would not have to go through this ordeal of losing her again and this time for good. He felt angry. Then his thoughts turned to Rose. Finding her had been traumatic for Ruth and not the reunion she had hoped for. More heartache for her. They had been so happy even when the war came. They had stuck together with the boys but since Charlotte had come on the scene everything had changed. He had kept secrets to protect Ruth from the truth. Jane had made herself scarce and her close friendship with Ruth seemed more like a business arrangement these days. He felt guilty for not feeling genuinely upset about Charlotte's death. A huge part of him could not wait for things to get back to normal.

He remembered he had to get ready for the theatre. He had promised to be there early to watch out for Rose should she decide to show up. He had a seat in the dress circle next to her and would report back to Ruth how she had seemed. He cut himself shaving, his hand was trembling so much. He couldn't get Charlotte out of his mind. The way she had died was shocking.

When he was ready, he went to find his sons in the garden. They were playing war games. Ronnie was inside the den he had built for them. He was pretending to be a pilot flying over Germany and his brother was the enemy. Ivor hated them playing at war and spoke angrily.

"Come on you two. Can't you think of anything new to play. The war is over. We can all forget about it now." He gave them each a bear hug and left them wondering what was the matter. Perhaps Jane would explain what was wrong when she came to look after them later.

At the theatre, once installed in his seat, Ivor looked out for Rose. Minutes before the curtain was due to go up, she made her way to her seat. Ivor stood to attention allowing her to get past him. Rose felt like a toff in her new outfit and thought how gentlemanly he was. The shoes must have been a small fitting. She had not needed to stuff them with the tissue paper. As the orchestra struck up with hefty drum rolls and a clash of cymbals, Rose jumped. Then as the violins and violas joined in she calmed down and felt more peaceful. She had never heard such a beautiful sound in her life.

Then the dancers dazzled her with a myriad of sequins catching the mixture of lights. Lights which changed colour and mood. Every now and then she popped an aniseed ball into her mouth and wondered if it was her imagination that the man next to her was watching her every move. Perhaps she should not eat sweets in the theatre and it was irritating him. Then she remembered the words of Doctor Munro. "It is normal to feel self conscious in strange situations." Well, this felt strange but magical all at the same time.

Rose thumbed her way through the programme and discovered that Ruth would be making her entrance soon. She wondered if she had butterflies in her stomach backstage just as she had now. The first routine came to an end and the curtains swished together. In a flash, they swished back to reveal Ruth in all her glory. She was dressed from head to toe in a cream, lace dress with a matching parasol. Her chestnut hair piled high on her head was glinting and glittering under the lights. Rose felt highly emotional and got her handkerchief out. Ruth began to sing. Her voice sounded much crisper than the clips she had heard on the newsreel. It was heavenly. Ruth was a full blown artiste. An angel. A posh angel who trilled and reached all the top notes.

Rose felt so proud and clapped spontaneously. No one else seemed to bother. She wondered what was the matter with them. Then the spotlight shone down upon the set which resembled Trafalgar Square. Fountains shot water into the air. Rose couldn't believe it and sucked even harder on her aniseed balls. Ruth was being led around the stage by a very handsome man. She wondered if her leading man might be her husband. Shivers went up and down her spine when the two harmonized but she preferred it when Ruth sang alone. Her voice seemed to fill the entire theatre. Three songs later and they still hadn't clapped. Rose fidgeted in her seat. Things seemed to be reaching a crescendo. Everyone on the stage moved toward the front. One last high note from Ruth and after a moment's silence, applause thundered around her. She eagerly joined in and was the last to stop.

The scenery changed again without her noticing and so had Ruth. This time she was wearing a pink satin ball gown and looked more beautiful to Rose than all the royalty and film stars put together. She was being pushed on a swing while others were waltzing round a grand ballroom. Rose soaked up all of the music and songs as they blurred one into the next. How her sister remembered all the words and what to do baffled her. Then the lights came up and people were leaving their seats. She decided to stay put. The man next to her also remained seated. He smiled at her and Rose attempted a smile back. His face seemed vaguely familiar. She wondered if he was a film star.

"Are you enjoying the show?" Ivor asked.

"It's...it's...wonderful," she stuttered.

"What do you think to Ruth Duthie?"

"Sings like an angel. Always did."

"You've heard her before?"

"Oh yes. When we were kids."

Ivor smiled at her and felt very touched. Rose offered him a sweet and he accepted. Throughout the second half she shared her bag of aniseed balls with him. The orchestra notched up another gear as they approached the finale. Rose held her breath when Ruth held the last note of the show, a little longer than usual. The stage blacked out. It was all over and everyone was on their feet around her giving a standing ovation. Rose watched her sister accept a bouquet of flowers from her leading man and as the cast took several curtain calls she applauded until her hands were stinging.

Then it was time to file out into the foyer where the man was waiting for her. He asked if she would like to go back stage and meet the cast.

"Oh no. I couldn't do that...could I?"

"Ruth's sent me to take you to her dressing room."

"Really? You're a friend of hers then?"

"Yes, indeed and she would love to see you."

Every instinct in Rose was to leave the theatre, catch a taxi and get back to her place of comfort and safety but a big part of her jumped at the chance.

"Oh all right then. Just for a minute. After all, she is my sister."

The next day, Rose woke up with one of her worst migraines, but felt a light heartedness she could not remember feeling ever before. She had been to the theatre she reminded herself, seen Ruth in her dressing room after the show and drank champagne for the first time with her weary legs up on a chaise longue. She had been allowed to wear one of the many wigs her sister had on display in the dressing room and everyone said how much it suited her. They had hugged and not once had she experienced palpitations. The only time she had pinched herself was to see if it was real not to relieve any anxiety. Ruth had laughed and seemed so happy to see her and they had arranged to meet again soon. The nice gentleman had escorted her to an awaiting taxi which had taken her back to the lavatories. It had been a double celebration. The end of the war and being back with her sister in her dressing room. It had certainly been worth the wait.

Rose felt disappointed not to have been invited to stay with Ruth, but felt sure that she would be asked to do so very soon. Years had divided them but they were still sisters and got on famously. Eventually, her headache wore off and she imagined herself cleaning for Ruth inside her dressing room. What a lovely job that would be; to take care of her sister and clean the huge mirrors with the bright light bulbs around them. To lay all her lovely gowns out for her each day and put them safely away for her each night. To pour out her champagne. Suddenly she felt jealous of the person who did this job now. She had never experienced an ambition of such magnitude before. Her life had been underground in Piccadilly and she had been content.

As the days passed she found herself yearning to be back with Ruth but after a week she still had not heard from her. She had hoped, no expected another lovely bouquet to cheer her room up and make the toilets smell nice but none came. She was beginning to feel depressed and was relieved when her appointment with the doctor came round again.

"You see, we were getting on so well. She said it was just like old times. Not that I can remember many of those but she said it, so I believed her."

"It sounds good Rose that you believe your sister and that you had such a wonderful time at the show and afterwards. How long has it been since you heard from her?"

"Three weeks and three days. Sweet Fanny Adam."

He could hardly believe that Rose was making an attachment to her sister, after so few meetings. In one way, it was wonderful but if Ruth was going to let her down, then it would be terribly painful and he had to be prepared. Rose might need to be admitted again.

"It sounds like you're disappointed, Rose."

"I am. You see, I'd like to go and work for her."

"Well, maybe you should go to the theatre and tell her so."

Once again, he could hardly believe how confident she sounded. She knew her own mind and after all she had been through still had some ambition left.

"Do you think so?"

"I know so. You are the most thorough cleaner I have ever had the pleasure of knowing and she would be lucky to have you."

Rose blushed and thanked him.

"Right, well doctor, I shall give it another week and then if I hear nothing I shall go to the theatre."

"A very good plan Rose. You can tell me all about it in a fortnight."

Chapter 33

Ivor crept by Ruth's bedside and drew back the curtains a fraction to let in some daylight.

"Who's that? Oh, it's you. Please pull them back. I need to sleep."

"Can I get you anything, darling?"

"Just the usual."

"Are you sure you won't come down and have some lunch with us? Jane's here and the boys are asking about you."

"Just porridge and tea. Now let me sleep," she snapped.

It had been a month since Ivor had broken the news to her about Charlotte. He had chosen his moment, two days after she had had such a wonderful time with Rose at the theatre. He knew she would be shocked by the sudden traumatic news but he hoped and prayed that she would find the strength to go on, now Rose was back in her life. He was wrong. Ruth had collapsed and taken to her bed. The doctor prescribed tablets for depression. She was told to rest as much as possible. Ivor worried about how dependent she was becoming on her medication. She needed to get up and back to her life in the theatre. Jane was the one to broach the subject of bringing Rose to stay.

"Do you think she might, only she is fiercely independent?"

"Ivor, go and see. You can but try. Like you, she doesn't seem to want to open up to me."

Rose cleaned the lavatories as never before. Her hyperactivity kept her from feeling anxious about not seeing or hearing from her twin. Her daily chats with the Queen had completely stopped. Reality had kicked in and she craved more of the same. In just two days' time, she was going to pay her sister a visit and, more importantly, ask her for a job. She stopped to make herself a cup of tea and realized that her room did not give her so much satisfaction as it used to. Even her cuttings of the royal family and film stars went unnoticed most of the time. Betty came with her post.

"Hallo, Lovie. You're looking a lot better than last week."

"Am I? It's a wonder."

"Still ain't heard from your sister, then?"

"Not a sausage."

"Anything there from her?"

"Just my appointment with the doctor."

"Never mind, Ducks."

An unfamiliar voice sounded at the top of the stairs.

"Hallo there, Rose. I can't come down there so can you please come up here?"

She recognized the foreign voice from the theatre and perked up.

"Here, Betty, hold my overall." She whipped it off over her head and handed it to her friend. Wiping the sweat from her forehead onto her handkerchief she climbed all the way to the top of the stairs, stopping halfway to get her breath back.

Betty watched as she exchanged a few words with a handsome man in a pinstripe suit and bowler hat. Rose descended the steps and walked past her friend leaving her in complete suspense. She then took out her suitcase from under the dresser and began to pack. In less than five minutes she had everything packed of any importance. On her way out she gave Betty a hug and told her she would be in touch but for the foreseeable future she would be looking after Ruth Duthie, her sister. Rose never looked back. Had she done so, she would have seen Betty staring open mouthed after her for quite some time.

To begin with Ruth did not improve. Every day she seemed to wallow in her own misery, sitting on a chintz sofa, gazing at nothing in particular. Try as Rose might to interest her sister in life going on around her, things ground to a halt. Rose, always a firm believer in good, old fashioned food, tried to encourage Ruth to eat more. She cooked bloaters in vinegar and peppercorns with onion, unaware that her skill had been memorized from childhood.

When they were refused she tried butter mash with pie and mushy peas to no avail. Even tripe and liver with a nice thick gravy poured all over was rejected. How she survived on porridge and toast was a mystery. Ruth did not seem to care that the war had been won and they were on the winning side. Rarely did she leave her bedroom, only going in to kiss the boys goodnight and tuck them in. Ivor was at his wits end.

All she could do was sit with her and listen to whatever she had to say. Sometimes, she would talk about her life and many times Rose found her crying over photographs of a young, blonde woman whom she did not know. They talked about their childhood. Ruth helped Rose to piece it together. Rose joined in when Ruth chuckled about the exploits of her brothers around Shoreditch pretending to remember. She would do anything to cheer her sister up.

"I never did get those ruddy piano lessons." Rose said one day in one of her more lucid moments. She looked down at her chapped hands that had been made to play piano but had only ever known hot water and soap. Sometimes it was easier for her to talk about sad things than it was for Ruth.

"When did Mum die then, Ruth?"

"Just before we all went our separate ways."

"One minute there and the next…gone and I never saw her again. She had another baby, didn't she? I remember she had no time for me when it was born."

Ruth was inconsolable at these times, hardly believing that Rose was talking about her own child. She had completely blocked out the birth and therefore, felt no grief. Rose would turn the topic of conversation to lighter subjects, feeling somehow that she had said something wrong.

"Ronnie and Ralph are lovely. I think they're getting used to their fat, old aunt bit by bit."

"That's good."

"But they need you, you know." Such pearls of wisdom fell from her lips so naturally that Ruth would begin to cry all over again.

"Ivor turned out to be a good dad, didn't he? I still love the smell of his pipe tobacco. Fancy me not recognizing him. He worries about you, you know."

"I know. I know."

"And you know what else? I bet they miss you at that lovely theatre. All your fans having to make do with understudies all the time. T'aint right, Ruth. It's you they want. It's your name in lights above the door."

Somehow, when Rose spoke the words, Ruth would reflect more and think about working again. Ivor and Jane had given up trying to persuade her and left it to her twin. After a few months Rose dared to broach the subject closest to her heart.

"Anyway, it wasn't just to look after you that I came back with Ivor that day."

"Oh? I thought you were happy here."

"Oh yes, don't get me wrong. I am. Happier than in many a year but I had something I wanted for myself as well."

There was that honest, childlike quality again which Ruth loved to hear. It grabbed her attention.

"What was that then, dear?"

"I've finished down in Piccadilly as you know. It was when I saw all those wonderful costumes. I knew I wanted to come and work for you in the theatre."

Up to this point Ruth had felt numb. Suddenly she felt a pang of guilt. Rose had led such a miserable life and had never asked for a single favour. Now she was wasting even more of her precious time, sitting around moping when it was within her power to help her sister achieve an ambition. Over the next few days she mulled this over in her mind and then made a phone call to the theatre manager who agreed to a month's trial. When Rose heard the news, she immediately declined the offer.

"No Ruth. I only want to work when you're better and we can be together. I can't work with strangers."

"Yes you can, Rose. You've done it before and you can do it again."

"Do you really think so? Well it would be good to keep an eye on all your lovely things until you go back to work, I suppose but only on one condition. That you hurry up and get back to what you were born to do. I ain't heard you sing since I came here."

"I promise Rose. I will try."

The next week Rose attended her outpatients' appointment and was reassured by Doctor Munro that she was ready to take on another challenge.

"By the way. How is your sister now? Any better?"

"A bit. She gets dressed and eats a bit more but she's always so sad. Yet, she has everything she could wish for. A lovely husband and children and a lovely job. I just don't get it."

Frederick Munro had thought for months how fascinating it would be to treat Ruth. He felt sure he could help her and it would also help him to fill in the missing pieces of Rose's life. He said as much. Rose's jaw dropped. How marvellous for Ruth to meet the man who had saved her life.

"You would have to come to the house. She never goes out."

"For you, Rose, I would be prepared to make an exception."

Life felt like it could not get any better. The war was over, she was reunited with her sister and was going to work for her. Now, Ruth was definitely going to get better.

Over many sessions the doctor learned how Rose had been raped and had grown mentally ill. How she had given birth to a baby and how Ruth had bonded with it instead. Both women had suffered severely over a child who should never have been conceived in the first place. Poor Charlotte. He felt sorry for her too. She had played such a massive part in both their lives and now she was gone. Miraculously, the sisters had survived the war and were together again. Theirs was one of the most heart breaking stories he had come across.

At times, Rose felt jealous when she was asked to leave them in private. She was tempted to listen at the door but soon, as her sister's therapy progressed, she began her new working life at the Hippodrome. On a daily basis she found herself in amongst the theatres magical paraphernalia which had never entered her wildest dreams and loved every second of it. Fabulous gowns, handmade for the productions. Fur stoles, feather boas, plumed head dresses, sequin costumes with bodices of velvet and lace. Coronets, tiaras, crowns, snoods and various other headgear and hats. Shoes that had been tailor made for her sister's feet brought a tear to her eye.

Her days consisted of sewing on missing buttons or piping that had gone astray, stitching on extra sequins, bobbles, pompoms, tassels, beads, clasps and studs. Hemming as well as ironing costumes and sending others to be steam cleaned. At times, she was called on to alter costumes to accommodate the wearer, thrilled to be using seamstress skills which had laid dormant all her life. Every job she carried out with enthusiasm and paid a great deal of attention to detail. Her hands made to play piano had found their niche for intricacy and precision at last.

As well as having endless things to do, she turned the cleaner away from Ruth's dressing room and made it look spick and span herself. After cleaning and polishing the mirrors and furniture, she turned her attention to the costume jewellery and accessories. Pendants, rings, necklaces, chokers, bangles, armlets and earrings. Whatever it took to be the finest dresser she could be, Rose had the energy for each new task.

The month's trial passed and then two more months. The theatre manager was impressed with all her hard work and she was engaged permanently. After a while Rose began to feel younger and took more pride in her own appearance, gaining respect from members of the cast and crew. However, she had no time for making friends, hardly sparing a moment to talk to the understudies who came and went. Her sole purpose in life was to have everything in order for the day when her sister made her comeback.

Ruth's return to the stage coincided with a Royal Variety Performance to be staged at the London Palladium. Rose was more excited than her sister when the invitation came for her to perform in the show. Backstage they sat. Rose and Ruth. Soon it would be Ruth's turn to entertain all the toffs in the front stalls and the ordinary folk up in the gods. Rose had everything ready for her return to the stage and had ironed Ruth's costume twice, just in case. Her champagne was on ice just as she liked it. Ruth being so far up on the bill commandeered a dressing room of her own. She was a bag of nerves but agreed that for now singing just two songs was a good way to make her comeback rather than carrying a whole show. The continuity boy knocked on her door.

"Five minutes, Miss Duthie."

"Well Rose...wish me luck."

"You don't need luck with the talent you've got." Rose helped her into her dress. "God given talent."

"Can I have a hug anyway Rosie. You are my lucky charm you know."

"Course you can." Rose flung her arms wide and they embraced. She had grown used to cuddles and hugs since living with her sister and enjoyed them again. They walked to the door and Rose followed her sister to the wings holding aloft the long train to her dress. Flanagan and Alan were just finishing their comedy routine. The audience was in uproar. Then an introduction was being made by the compere and out she stepped into the spotlight. Camera bulbs flashed and the audience rose to its feet. They were welcoming her back. Rose held her handkerchief to her nose to stifle her tears. Then all went silent as the band played the introduction to the first song Ruth had rehearsed for the show.

Rose watched her brothers Johnny and Jack, survivors of the war on the front row with their wives. She was looking forward to getting to know them again. Next came Doctor Munro, Ivor, Ronnie and Ralph with Jane last in the row clutching a tissue.

Up in the royal box she could just make out the shape of King George and beside him Queen Elizabeth. The Queen leaned forward and Rose could see that she was wearing a beautiful silk gown with a diamond encrusted tiara for the occasion. Ruth sounded wonderful as if she had never been away. Rose felt relieved. She had made a successful comeback.

The King and Queen were applauding and Ruth first curtsied to the audience and then to the royal box. Everyone was cheering. Soon all the cast would line up to be presented to their majesties back stage after the show. As Ruth led the singing of the national anthem the Queen glanced past the cast assembled on the stage to where Rose was standing in the wings. She caught her eye. With a serenity all her own, she waved her gloved hand and smiled at her. Rose curtsied and smiled back.

Seeds Of Doubt

Cover design by Megan Wilson

Printed in Great Britain
by Amazon